TRAPPED BY SCANDAL

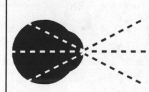

This Large Print Book carries the
Seal of Approval of N.A.V.H.

TRAPPED BY SCANDAL

JANE FEATHER

THORNDIKE PRESS

A part of Gale, Cengage Learning

GALE
CENGAGE Learning®

Farmington Hills, Mich • San Francisco • New York • Waterville, Maine
Meriden, Conn • Mason, Ohio • Chicago

GALE
CENGAGE Learning·

Thorndike Press® Large Print Basic.
The text of this Large Print edition is unabridged.
Other aspects of the book may vary from the original edition.
Set in 16 pt. Plantin.

LIBRARY OF CONGRESS CATALOGING-IN-PUBLICATION DATA

Feather, Jane.
   Trapped by scandal / Jane Feather. — Large print edition.
     pages cm. — (Thorndike Press large print basic)
     ISBN 978-1-4104-8603-5 (hardback) — ISBN 1-4104-8603-6 (hardcover)
   1. France—History—Reign of Terror, 1793-1794—Fiction. 2. Large type books. I. Title.
PS3556.E22T734 2014
813'.54—dc23   2015034944

Published in 2016 by arrangement with Pocket Books, an imprint of Simon & Schuster, Inc.

Printed in Mexico
1 2 3 4 5 6 7 19 18 17 16

TRAPPED BY SCANDAL

ONE

London, October 1795

Lady Hermione Fanshawe drummed her long fingers on the gaming table in one of the private gambling rooms leading off the Rotunda at Ranelagh Gardens. Her vivid green eyes held exasperation as she watched Sir Anthony Cardew toss the dice onto the baize-topped table.

"Perish it," he grumbled as once more he lost his bet. His took a long swallow from his glass of burgundy, and his gaze, narrowed and bloodshot, flicked across to Lady Hermione. "Come, Hero, sweetheart, let me have that pretty bracelet . . . I swear I'll win it back next throw." He reached across to take her narrow wrist encircled with the dainty diamond-and-pearl bracelet.

She snatched her hand away. "No, Tony. You're too drunk to see straight, let alone make a decent wager. You may write your own IOUs." Pushing back her chair, she stood up amidst a chorus of protests from the men around the table, all convinced her presence was bringing them luck. With a brief gesture of farewell, she picked up her silver eye mask, which she had discarded earlier, and turned from the table, her domino of lustrous emerald-green silk swirling around her as she walked away, ignoring the protests. She paused in the doorway to the central area of the Rotunda to tie the mask once more before venturing out of the private room. This masquerade was a public one, and the brilliantly illuminated gardens beyond the Rotunda were filled with rowdy crowds enjoying the license of anonymity in their masks and dominoes. Not without cause were the public masquerades at Ranelagh and Vauxhall known for their licentiousness.

Hero glanced around the throng gathered for the concert in the Rotunda as she deftly tied the strings of the strip of silver silk behind her head. And her fingers abruptly stilled. She stared through the slits in her mask, her heart banging against her ribs.

It wasn't possible. Not here.

She stood unmoving, her gaze riveted to the tall, slender figure in the black domino and black velvet mask. She knew every line of that lithe body, and when he moved across the Rotunda, she recognized with a jolt to the pit of her stomach the almost leonine stride, powerful yet soundless, seemingly indolent yet pulsing with energy. His dark chestnut hair was cropped short in the fashionable style, but the single unruly lock she remembered so well still fell across his broad forehead.

She felt suddenly suffocated, grateful for her mask and domino, as she edged through the concertgoers to the fresh night air of the gardens. Why was he here? Frivolous enjoyment was not something one associated with William Ducasse, Viscount St. Aubery. He could be congenial company, with his ready sense of humor and dry wit, but no one in his company ever failed to realize that he was driven by some much stronger motivation than simple pleasure.

Her heart was still beating uncomfortably fast, and the last words he had spoken to her rang in her ears. In the last twelve months, she had forced herself to forget or at least not to think about him or how they had parted, but all resolution fled the moment she laid eyes on him again.

He hadn't seen her, and he wouldn't have recognized her if he had, not dressed as she was. Her step quickened on the gravel path as if she were fleeing some pursuer, but there was no way he would be following her.

However, someone was. The old sixth sense prickled, lifting the fine hairs on her nape. She had been so wrapped up in her thoughts she hadn't realized how far she had drifted from the illuminated walks and lawns, and somehow she had wandered down one of the many dark, shrub-lined walks that were favorite spots for illicit assignations and any kind of knavery.

A voice called from behind her. "Hey, sweetheart, you could do with some company, I'll warrant." The voice was slurred with drink, and a second voice, equally slurred, chimed in, "Stop, sweetheart. 'Tis a chill night. Stay for a kiss to warm you."

Her heart stopped its frantic beating, and a cool stillness entered her. She had faced worse than two drunken sots on a darkened path at Ranelagh. She called over her shoulder as she took a quick step sideways onto a narrower walk, "I thank you, sirs, but I have no need of company."

She heard them laugh, close behind her now. And it was not pleasant laughter. Hero stopped on the path and turned to face them. Of course, she presented an inviting target. No lady of breeding would be caught wandering alone in the shadows of Ranelagh. They probably took her for a harlot trolling for custom off the beaten track.

They lurched up to her, laughing, one of them holding an open bottle of champagne. They had discarded their masks and wore their dominoes open to show the fine silk of their knee britches and embroidered coats. A pair of overprivileged sots, Hero decided contemptuously, who thought they could do exactly as they pleased with anyone they deemed fair game, any member of the underclasses.

She had only herself to blame for such a misinterpretation, however. Hero stood facing them on the narrow path. The shrubs on either side were tall and thick enough to prevent either of them from outflanking her.

"Oh, I believe we have a fighter on our hands, Carlton," the one with the bottle said, hiccuping. He swung the bottle in a sudden vicious swipe towards Hero's face. She ducked and swiftly brought up her knee as he advanced unsteadily. He doubled over, gasping, but his streaming eyes were filled with malicious intent as he looked up at her. "Get her, Carlton. She needs a lesson from her betters."

The other hesitated for a moment, and in that moment, the butt of a pistol came down on the back of his head, knocking him

11

senseless to the path. His fellow assailant, slowly straightening from his crouch of pain, was dropped similarly.

"Good evening, Hero. Up to your usual tricks, I see." William Ducasse slid his silver-mounted pistol into his coat pocket beneath his domino. His tawny gold eyes regarded Hero with a gleam of amusement not unmixed with exasperation. "Why would you invite such discourtesy?"

"I didn't," she said shortly, wondering why she hadn't heard him come up, but then one never heard the Viscount when he didn't wish it. "I hadn't realized how far from the Rotunda I'd walked, and those two . . ." Her lip curled as she regarded the senseless bodies on the path at her feet. "They were too drunk to reason with."

"I'll grant you that." He held out his hand across the bodies. "Step over them."

She put her silk-gloved hand into his and stepped across to stand beside him. "What are you doing here, William?"

"I *was* minding my own business," he stated with emphasis. "Until you, my dear girl, made yourself my business." He looked around the shadowed shrubbery. "Where is your escort . . . you *do* have an escort, I take it, despite evidence to the contrary?" That golden cat's gaze was turned once more upon her in an uncomfortable scrutiny.

"I did," she said crossly. "Right now, he's losing the family fortune at dice with a brain too addled with drink to comprehend anything."

"I see." He bowed gravely, but his mouth curved in the oh-so-familiar smile that made her pulses race again. "Then allow me to escort you to your carriage, Lady Hero." He offered his arm, but she hesitated, unwilling to show meek obedience to the man who had always commanded it. There had been a time when no one in their right mind would have questioned his right to command it and to receive it, but that was then, and this was now, in London, on her own home ground, where she was quite capable of managing her own affairs.

"How did you recognize me?" she asked, not moving.

He gave a soft chuckle. "Oh, my dear, I could never fail to know if you were in the same room. I saw you standing in the Rotunda as you were tying your mask. I followed you because, well . . ." He shrugged. "Because I had the not unfamiliar feeling you were going to walk into trouble. Come, now." He took her hand and drew her up beside him as he turned to walk back towards the lights and the music and the raucous merriment of the crowd.

She made no attempt to disengage her hand now. It would be a futile and undignified effort. "I came with Tony Cardew, and I can't just take his carriage; he'll need it."

"Nonsense. I think Cardew, in all chivalry, should expect to see you home one way or another, and I intend to inform him of that fact." He added, "I have no idea why you, of all people, would trouble yourself with such a brainless fop."

"I daresay you don't," Hero muttered as they approached the long line of private carriages awaiting their owners' pleasure. "But Tony can be pleasant company when he's sober."

"Can he, indeed?" was the sardonic rejoinder. "I never seem to see him sober."

So how did William know Tony Cardew? she wondered. How long had he been in London? She had always understood that his visits to London were infrequent and didn't involve much in the way of social mingling. Yet here he was in the thick of Society. What was his business this time?

It was an interesting, if unsettling, question but not one she could dwell on at present. It was always necessary to be on one's toes around William, and she couldn't allow herself to be distracted from giving as good as she was getting in this exchange. Later she would have the chance to think clearly enough to look at what might be implied by his presence.

William raised a hand and waved at the carriage bearing the Cardew arms, and the coachman moved out of the line, turning his horses on the wide drive to bring the vehicle up beside them. The footman jumped down to open the door.

"Grosvenor Square," William instructed the driver as he handed Hero into the carriage. "Sir Anthony will not be leaving for a while yet."

She sat on the richly cushioned bench and regarded William as he stood in the doorway, one foot resting negligently on the footstep. "You're not going to make sure I go straight home, then?" she inquired with a provocative smile.

For a moment, he returned her gaze steadily. Then he laughed, shaking his head. "Don't tempt me, my dear. You may be careless of your reputation, but as you know full well, I am not. Go home, and be good." He stepped back and closed the door, watching as the coach moved away down the drive.

William had known he would probably

run across Hero while he was in town —
his present business meant that he would
be moving in the Society circles she would
naturally frequent — but he had thought he
would be able to treat their inevitable meeting as a casual renewal of a chance acquain-
tanceship.

And what a foolish hope that was.

She was as lovely as ever, her hair that
same rich mélange of burnt caramel shot
through with streaks of gold. Her eyes were
as brilliantly vivid as they had ever been.
He had glimpsed her about town in the last
weeks, and he was now used to seeing her
in the delicate gowns and the glitter of gems
that were her birthright, but she herself, that
indomitable, reckless, spirited girl whose
courage never failed her, seemed un-
changed. She was still taking risks, still
walking the edge of scandal. And dear God,
he could not pretend to forget what they
had been to each other. He had managed
once to let her go, to force her away from
him, for her sake as much as his own, but
the sight of her, the sound of her voice, the
touch of her hand, brought back the whole
flood of sensation he could not afford to
indulge . . . not if he was to stay focused on
the only reality that mattered.

He turned back to the Rotunda. Sir Anthony Cardew at least would get the rough edge of his tongue. The man needed to understand he couldn't bring a lady of Hermione's standing to a public masquerade and then abandon her. But then, he reminded himself caustically, knowing Hero, Tony Cardew probably hadn't had much say in the matter. He gave a fleeting thought to the two young lordlings unconscious in the shrubbery and dismissed them. They'd received their just deserts. For a moment, he wondered how Hero would have dealt with them if he hadn't appeared when he had.

He didn't give much for their chances. The reflection brought a reluctant, reminiscent smile to his lips.

Two

The carriage drew up outside the Marquis of Bruton's imposing double-fronted mansion on Grosvenor Square, and the footman jumped down from the box to let down the step and open the door for Lady Hermione.

"My lady." He offered a hand to help her alight.

"My thanks, Derek." She gave him a friendly smile as she stepped down into the quiet square. It was long past two o'clock in the morning, but her brother's house was still brilliantly lit in every window. She would have expected some illumination — even if the majordomo had already retired, the doorman would be waiting to let her in — but the house looked as if a ball were in full swing, which, considering that the Marquis and his lady had been intending to dine quietly, seemed somewhat unlikely.

The front doors opened as she set her foot on the first of the shallow steps leading up from the street, and the Marquis's major-domo stood bowing in the doorway, the lamplit hall behind him. "Lady Hermione . . . I trust you passed a pleasant evening, my lady."

"Pleasant enough, thank you, Jackson." She moved past him with a smile, then paused in the marble-floored hall, conscious of a strange feeling in the house, a certain expectant tension in the air. "Is his lordship still up?"

"In the upstairs parlor, my lady. I believe he's waiting for you." Nothing in the man's expression gave a hint of anything unusual, but then, Jackson was renowned for his inscrutability.

Hero drew off her gloves; she had untied her mask in the carriage. "I will go up to him, then. Good night, Jackson." She ascended the curving horseshoe staircase, twirling her mask on one finger, the silken folds of her domino swishing around her sandaled feet.

The upstairs parlor was a small, intimate family sitting room overlooking the garden at the rear, behind the grand formal salon, which ran the length of the front of the house, looking down into the square. The equally intimate morning room, where the family dined when they were alone, was opposite the parlor. The parlor door was slightly ajar, and Hero pushed it open.

There was a chill in the October night air, and a fire burned in the grate, the candelabra all illuminated so that the room seemed a blaze of light. The Marquis of Bruton was sitting in a chair beside the fire, nursing a brandy goblet. He did not look in the least restful and jumped to his feet the instant his twin sister stepped through the doorway.

"Oh, Hero, thank goodness you're back. I've been waiting for you."

"Is something amiss, Alec?" She looked in some alarm at her brother. He was usually very careful of his appearance, but tonight his reddish fair hair was tousled and his collar unbuttoned.

"Yes . . . no, no, I don't think so, at least I hope not." He pushed a hand through his tumbled hair. "Marie Claire's pains have begun, and I don't know what to do."

Hero unbuttoned her domino and tossed it over the back of a sofa. "Dearest, have you called Dr. Barrett yet?"

"Oh, yes, of course. He's with her now. And Nan's there, of course. But she's hurting, and I don't know how to help."

Hero offered a reassuring smile. "I don't know a great deal about these matters myself, Alec, but I think hurting is inevitable. And if she has Barrett and Nan in attendance, she could not be in better hands." She moved to the sideboard to pour herself a glass of brandy and took it to the fire. Her apple-green gown was of the most diaphanous silk, as was de rigueur, the décolletage pronounced and the little puff sleeves offering no protection from drafts or the evening chill. "When did it start?"

"Just after dinner. We dined quietly — you know how Marie Claire tires so easily these days — and we were sitting to a game of piquet when the first pain came." He looked distraught. "Oh, Hero, I wish I could suffer it for her."

"I know you do, love." She kissed his cheek. "But nature didn't plan it that way. Where's Aunt Emily?"

"Fast asleep. You know the last trump wouldn't wake her once she's taken her nightcap. She decided to have dinner in her own quarters, a quinsy developing, apparently." Despite his anxiety, Alec grinned. Great-aunt Emily was always developing something or other. "Anyway, she has no idea the house is in an uproar."

"Hardly an uproar," Hero said with a responding grin. "Jackson would never permit it, baby or not. I'll go up and see Marie Claire. Will you come?"

He shook his head miserably. "Nan told me to stay away. She said I was agitating Marie Claire."

Hero couldn't help a chuckle. Nan had been their nursemaid and the person most responsible for bringing them up. Their parents had had little or no interest in their offspring, once the heir was assured, much preferring the giddy whirl of London Society life, with frequent travels to Paris and Italy, over any form of domesticity. The twins had scrambled into adulthood under Nan's direction and the rather ineffective schooling of a series of governesses, who did not last very long in the twins' schoolroom, and rather more effective tutors, who remained for as long as they could hold their pupils' interest in their subjects. Since both Hero and Alec had decidedly lively minds and much preferred to direct their own lines of educational inquiry, the tutors who did succeed in teaching them were those who were prepared to follow their lead. As a result, they were very accomplished in some subjects and woefully ignorant in others.

"Well, I'll run up and see what's going on. I'll report back." She hastened from the parlor and up the narrower staircase to the bedroom floor. She heard voices and soft moaning from behind the double doors to Lady Bruton's bedchamber and opened it quietly, slipping into the room, where a fire blazed in the hearth and candles illuminated the large canopied bed. It was insufferably hot in the room, the windows closed tight against drafts and blocked by the long damask curtains.

An elderly woman turned from the foot of the bed at the sound of the door. "Ah, 'tis you, Lady Hero. Now, don't you get in the way."

"I wasn't going to, Nan." Hero stepped quickly to the bed. "How are you, darling?" She smiled down at the white face on the white pillows.

Marie Claire struggled to find a responding smile. "Well enough until the pain comes." She put out a hand, and Hero took it in a firm clasp. "Is Alec all right?"

"No, he's tearing his hair out, poor love," Hero said. "He looks half demented. You know how he can't bear not to be able to control things."

Marie Claire smiled feebly. "Just like you, Hero."

"True enough," she said, then stopped as the other woman's grip on her hand intensified and her face contorted with pain. Hero didn't wince, although her hand felt as if it

23

was going to break, but then Marie Claire's grip weakened and she fell back against the pillows with a little sigh.

"Leave her be, now, Lady Hero," Nan instructed. "There's things we need to do."

"I'll come back later," Hero said, bending to kiss her sister-in-law's damp brow. She moved away from the bed, and the doctor followed her to the door.

" 'Tis likely to be a long night, my lady," he informed her with appropriate gravity, his somber black suit and the pince-nez swinging from a chain around his neck giving him a reassuringly professional air. "But everything is going as it should. Try to reassure his lordship."

"I'll try." Hero moved aside as a maid came in with a pile of linen, followed by another carrying two jugs of steaming water. The landing was cold after the heat of the bedchamber, and she turned aside to her own room to fetch a wrap before returning to her brother.

Alec was standing in front of the fire when she entered the parlor. "How is she? Is it over?"

She shook her head. "No, love, it's likely to be quite a few hours, according to Barrett, but she's managing wonderfully. Better than I would, anyway." *Would or will?* She

24

dismissed the unbidden reflection instantly. It was irrelevant. She had no intention at this stage in her life of bearing children.

"I saw William at Ranelagh," she said abruptly, almost as if her reflection had given birth to the statement.

"Ah." Alec refreshed his glass from the decanter, his back to her.

Hero looked at him, her eyes narrowed. "You don't sound surprised."

He shrugged, still with his face averted. "I'm not, particularly. It was inevitable at some point."

Hero perched on the arm of the sofa. "You knew he was in London." It wasn't a question.

"He's been here for several weeks." Finally, he turned back to the room, lifting the decanter in invitation.

She shook her head. "No, thank you, I've had my fill for tonight. Why didn't you say anything?"

Her brother sat down with a sigh. "I was . . . am . . . sworn to secrecy, Hero."

She frowned. "He's on business, then?"

Alec merely looked at her, and she took his silence for an affirmative.

"And I'm not to know of it, is that right?"

"I'm sorry, love. I cannot break a confidence."

"No, of course you can't. But why? Does he think I can't be trusted . . . after everything?" She couldn't disguise her hurt and anger.

"I can no more speak for William than you can," Alec responded. "He didn't tell me as such that I shouldn't confide in you, but, as I say, he swore me to secrecy with no specific exemptions."

"He can't be on the same business as before," Hero mused, pressing her brother no further. "The Terror is over; Paris is quiet again . . . or at least, no longer rioting. The Directory is in charge after that Brigadier Napoleon finally defeated the mob with his 'whiff of grapeshot,' and now he's commanding the army with a host of victories behind him. So I wonder who William is working for." Alec said nothing, and after a moment, his sister asked, "Are you joined with him in this work, whatever it is?"

Alec sighed. It was impossible to keep secrets from Hero; he knew her technique all too well. She would duck and dodge around a subject until she somehow trapped him into giving something away. "Only very peripherally. Can we not talk of it anymore, please?"

"Well, it would take your mind off what's going on upstairs," she stated. "I won't ask questions, but I'll speculate and watch your face."

"Hero, don't do this . . . please," he begged, half laughing despite himself.

She merely smiled. In truth, she *was* more interested in keeping his mind from his wife's labor than anything else. It was going to be a long night, and Alec already looked worn to a frazzle. "So, is he spying *for* the French government or *against* them? He is spying, isn't he?"

Alec stared into the fire, struggling to keep his expression neutral.

"Of course he is," Hero continued briskly. "It's the obvious answer, after what he was doing before. So, is it his French or his English half that commands his loyalty at this point, I wonder?" She regarded her brother quizzically, her head tilted to one side, her eyes bright. "Or is he still an independent, managing his own operation? That would be most likely. He'll be following his own true north, as usual, throwing himself behind whatever issue on either side catches his sense of fairness . . . ah!" She gave a little crow of triumph. "I saw your eyebrows move. I'm right, aren't I?"

Alec shook his head in resignation. "So what if you are? Hero, you know him better than I do."

"In some ways," she agreed tartly. "But obviously not in others." She stood up restlessly. "I won't pester you any further. Would you like to play piquet?"

"I don't think I could concentrate."

"All the better for me, then." She picked up the deck of cards that Alec and Marie Claire had discarded earlier and shuffled them. "Come, it'll distract you a little, love."

He nodded and took the seat opposite her at the table as she dealt swiftly. "Are you not fatigued? You must have had quite a night at Ranelagh."

"Oh, I did. Tony was so besotted with drink he lost everything at dice and then tried to get me to stake my bracelet, and then two ruffians pursued me down one of the pathways. Oh, and of course, I met up with William," she recited blithely, picking up her cards.

"I do wish you wouldn't go to these public masques and ridottos, Hero." He frowned at his hand as he sorted the cards. "You know it's indecorous. Tom wouldn't have permitted it."

Her expression darkened, shadows dimming the luster of her eyes for a moment. "Tom would never dictate to me, Alec, you know that."

"Maybe not, but he still had some influence on you. You were never so wild and reckless when he was alive."

Hero called carte blanche on her hand. She had no answer to her brother's statement. It was undeniable, but before Tom was killed, she had a sense of purpose, a sense of the future. Once he had gone, all that went, too. She only felt properly alive these days when she was walking some kind of tightrope. And at twenty-three, it was high time she stopped. But that dangerous, exhilarating time with William and his dedicated group had given her everything she needed, a purpose, a challenge . . . and, of course, the passion.

A sudden unearthly scream shattered the moment of silence in the parlor. Alec jumped up, his face ashen. "Dear God, it's Marie Claire." He started for the door, but his sister came after him, laying a hand on his arm.

"No, Alec, don't go upstairs. You'll get in the way, my dear." Her own face was as pale as her brother's, but her voice was resolute. "Let those who know how to help get on with their business. You can't do anything for Marie Claire, and if she sees how distressed you are, it will only make things worse for her. You know how she frets over you."

Alec resisted his sister's restraining hand for a moment and then let his own hand fall from the doorknob. "I suppose you're right. But I can't bear it, Hero, to hear her in such agony."

"I know." She looked at him with compassion. It was always harder to bear someone else's pain than one's own. "I'll go up and see if the doctor has any further news." She left her brother and hurried back upstairs. Another scream assailed her ears as she reached the landing, and she shivered, telling herself that it was all perfectly natural, that women had suffered like this since the world began and would continue to do so until it ended. But the pragmatic acceptance of reality didn't help much as she softly opened the door to the Marquess's bedchamber and slipped inside.

Nan turned from the bed at the sound of the door. She came over to Hero. "I daresay Lord Alec is in a right state," she commented. "Everything is normal. She's a strong lady, for all that she's such a delicate mite. It'll all be over afore dawn. You go down and tell his lordship that."

Hero glanced anxiously over to the bed. "What does Dr. Barrett say?"

Nan sniffed. "What does he know? Birthing is women's business. And I tell you,

Lady Hero, the baby'll be born before the night is out. You can trust me for that."

Hero smiled. She would trust Nan for anything. She certainly knew who she'd want at her bedside. She nodded and let herself out of the chamber, going back downstairs to report to her brother.

It was a long night, but just as the sky began to lighten and the first sounds of the dawn chorus came from the square, the door to the parlor opened to admit Dr. Barrett, looking as impeccable and unruffled as if he had not been up at his patient's bedside throughout the night. "My lord, I am happy to announce that you are the proud father of a baby girl," he pronounced with appropriate solemnity. "If you would care to go up, her ladyship and the child are ready to receive you."

Alec sprang from his chair like a jack-in-a-box and sprinted from the room, leaving the doctor standing expectantly in the doorway.

"You must be in need of refreshment, Dr. Barrett." Hero stepped into the breach, controlling her own impatience to worship at her new niece's crib. "Her ladyship is really doing well?" She poured him a large glass of cognac.

"A little tired but very well otherwise. My

thanks, Lady Hero." He took the glass with an appreciative nod.

Hero poured a small measure for herself to join him in a toast to the new arrival and then escorted the doctor to the front door and saw him out into the cool early morning. Jackson appeared in the hall as she stepped back inside.

"I understand his lordship is to be congratulated, my lady."

"Yes, and her ladyship," Hero reminded him, wondering why it was always the man who was congratulated on the birth of a child, as if the poor woman who had labored to provide his offspring had had nothing to do with it. "A baby girl," she added. "I am going up to see them now."

She hurried upstairs to the bedchamber, where Nan still reigned supreme at the bedside. Marie Claire lay propped on pillows, her baby daughter wrapped tightly in a lacy shawl, lying on her breast. Alec sat on the bed beside them, gazing in misty-eyed wonder at his wife and child.

"Just a few minutes, now, Lady Hero," Nan instructed, straightening the coverlet. "Mother and baby need to rest. And so do you, Lord Alec. Worn to a frazzle, you are."

"What are you going to call her?" Hero asked, lightly touching her niece's tiny dimpled fist. "She's so delicate and new, like a rosebud."

"Actually, she's to be called Fleur," Alec said proudly. "Fleur Elizabeth Louise . . . after Marie Claire's mother."

"How perfect." Hero leaned over to kiss her sister-in-law and then hugged her brother fiercely. "May I hold the Lady Fleur Fanshawe for a moment?"

Marie Claire lifted the bundle from her breast, and Hero took the baby, gazing with wonder at the infant's perfection. She had no experience of babies or children; her own parents had had no siblings, so there were no cousins in the family. In fact, when she thought about it, she and Alec had basically grown up with only each other for company. It was a wonder they weren't more eccentric than they were, she reflected with a slightly cynical smile. And no wonder they were both drawn to people and worlds that were far beyond the run-of-the-mill company and experiences of their peers.

Dangerous men like William Ducasse, Viscount St. Aubery, and the equally dangerous world they occupied.

THREE

La Force Prison, Paris, 1794, thirteen months earlier

"Merde." The expletive emerged from a grimy bundle of clothes tossed onto the filthy, straw-covered floor of the prison cell. A large gray rat scuttled in alarm out of the straw as the barred gate clanged shut. The figure lay stunned for a few seconds before uncurling itself and jumping to its feet, turning to hurl a stream of vigorous street insults into the shadowy corridor beyond the bars.

The cell's other occupant stood, arms folded, leaning against the corner of the far wall, his casual stance belied by the alert set of his shoulders as he regarded the new arrival from a pair of shrewdly inquiring tawny eyes, eyebrows quirked as he listened to the fluent stream of invective. When the new arrival paused for breath, he observed into the moment's quiet, "I shouldn't draw too much attention to yourself, if I were you.

You're lucky they didn't realize what you are; otherwise, you'd be on your back in the yard with a stream of guards half a mile long waiting their turn."

Slowly, the figure turned from the bars to regard the speaker warily. "How can you tell?"

"You should bind your breasts," he said, looking at her more closely. As far as he could tell, beneath the grime streaking her face and the obligatory red cap pulled low over her forehead, she seemed quite young, although unmistakably feminine. The swell of her breasts beneath her filthy shirt was obvious to his eye; he couldn't imagine how it had escaped the guards. But they'd probably been too drunk to notice, at least for the moment.

"I did bind them," the girl declared, vivid green eyes glaring at him in the gloom. She plucked at her coarse linen shirt with a grimace of disgust. "But the mob's on a rampage, and I needed something to bind the wounds of a man they'd left bleeding in an alley."

He nodded his comprehension. "It's madness out there, I grant you. However, I doubt you'll find it more peaceful in here."

She gave an involuntary shudder as a scream pierced the rustling silence. "Who

35

are you?"

He stepped slightly away from the wall. "Guillaume at your service, mademoiselle." He swept her an elaborate bow. "But I do also answer to William," he added in English.

A little frown creased her brow. "Is it that obvious?" she asked in the same language.

"Only to a trained ear. My compliments, mademoiselle, on your mastery of the language." He bowed again. A lock of dark chestnut hair flopped onto his forehead, and he brushed it aside with the back of his hand.

Despite the dire circumstances of her present predicament, the girl laughed. The bow was such a ludicrous gesture from a man in the rough garments of a French laborer. His red cap and his homespun ankle-length britches, like her own, identified him as a sansculottes, a peasant who couldn't afford the silk knee britches of the gentry. He could be any one of the revolutionary peasants rampaging through the streets beyond the prison, mad for blood, someone's blood, anyone's blood. But clearly, all was not as it seemed with Monsieur Guillaume, who answered to William.

She returned his greeting with a mock bow of her own. "My thanks, sir. It's a pleasure to make your acquaintance."

"Now, mademoiselle, you have the advantage of me," he stated, his dark eyebrows lifting higher. "With whom do I have the honor of sharing my humble accommodations?"

"Hermione," she said flatly.

He laughed outright. "Hermione? I have to say, that's not a name that fits a ragged street urchin with a tongue to shame a sailor."

She grimaced. "No, it isn't, is it? I'm usually just called Hero."

"Less of a mouthful," he agreed, thinking to himself that it was probably an appropriate enough name for a girl who ran around the streets of terror-ridden Paris bandaging up mob victims. "So, Hero," he continued, "let us turn our attention to leaving our present accommodations."

"How are we to do that?" She looked doubtfully over her shoulder at the barred gate behind her. She knew that the corridor beyond opened out into the prison's main courtyard, but little enough light reached through the bars of the cell.

He glanced up at the tiny window, little more than a skylight, at the top of the high wall. A glimmer of sunlight showed. "Judging by the sun's position, I'm guessing it's close to mid-afternoon. At four o'clock, they begin the cull for Madame Guillotine's evening meal. There is always a fracas, a lot of noise and confusion as they herd people into the tumbrels. We will take advantage of the rampage to slip away. Just make damned sure you don't get forced into a cart. There'll be no saving you then."

"Forgive me for being obtuse, but how the hell do we get out of this cell?"

"That's where you come in. I can't do it alone, which is why I'm still here," he said with a sardonic smile. "You will stand at the bars and create mayhem, scream, rattle the bars, hurl every insult and provocation you can think of. The guardroom is just at the end of the corridor; they'll hear you soon enough. And they will certainly react. If you provoke them sufficiently, they'll open the gate to drag you out. At which point, I will step in."

"What if there's more than one of them?" Hero asked somewhat skeptically. It seemed to her she would be taking all the risk in this scenario.

"Oh, there will be," he stated firmly. "But no more than two or three, and I can handle that number easily."

"What with?" she exclaimed.

"I happened upon a lucky find in my

explorations." He reached into the corner behind him and produced a heavy wooden stave. "This was under the straw in the corner . . . quite amazing how neglectful those illiterate ruffians are. They're drunk and senseless on wine and brandy when they're not drunk on blood and power." His voice was laced with acid loathing. "And if this is not enough, then . . ." He bent down to reach into his boot, withdrawing a wickedly sharp blade.

Hero took in the small arsenal. "I have this." She reached up her sleeve and pulled out a very small knife. "It's quite sharp, although I've never used it as a weapon, more as a useful tool, good for cutting bandages and things like that."

He nodded. "Indeed. But I'm sure you could inflict some modicum of damage if necessary."

"I daresay I could," she responded with a degree of enthusiasm that in other circumstances would have made her companion smile. "So what happens after they get here?"

"You have to make them open the gate," he repeated. "Leave the rest to me, and as soon as you see your way clear, run as if all the devils in hell are after you. The tumult around the tumbrels in the yard should be in full swing, and the gates will be standing open. Get through them and into the street, and then lose yourself in the crowd."

"Will you be behind me?" Hero felt a sudden twitch of alarm that this oddly reassuring stranger might disappear.

"If I can. But don't think about me, think only about yourself. Get clear, and if you don't see me, make your way to Rue St. André des Arts. Number seven. Tell them Guillaume sent you."

She nodded slowly. She knew the street, on the left bank of the Seine quite close to the Conciergerie. It would be helpful to have a safe haven for her own mission. Since she'd arrived in Paris two days earlier, she'd been finding shelter in insalubrious hostelries, where the presence of a ruffian lad with a few sous for a bed would not draw attention. Of course, given that she knew nothing about her cell mate, this safe haven could well be a den of thieves, but in present circumstances, that seemed immaterial. It wouldn't be a prison cell, and she had nothing on her worth stealing anyway.

She approached the gate and took hold of the bars with both hands. "So when do I start?"

Guillaume moved into the shadows behind her, holding the stave loosely in one hand, his knife in the other. "Now," he instructed softly.

Hero rattled the bars as she shouted, pouring forth a stream of abuse, interspersed with shrieks and yells that wouldn't have been out of place in Bedlam. Results were almost instantaneous. Two guards came pounding down the corridor, yelling their own abuse, cudgels raised.

"Cretins!" she yelled, shaking the bars again. *"Cochons!"* A cudgel came down, aiming for her fingers, and she whipped her hands off the bars just in time and spat at them. *"Salopards!"* They yelled and whacked the bars with the cudgels, but they didn't unlock the gate.

Why weren't they unlocking the gate? There was one way to make sure they did. Hero tore at the buttons on her shirt, ripping it open to reveal her bare breasts. She stood there, challenging them, laughing at them. She heard Guillaume draw a quick breath behind her, and then they were unlocking the gate, salivating as they came into the cell, reaching for her. She grabbed the hand of one of them and bit hard. He screamed, aimed a fist at her, then fell to his knees as the stave smashed into his skull. The second guard was momentarily stunned, and the moment was sufficient for

41

Guillaume to bring down the stave again. Even as the guard crumpled, Hero was out and running for the yard.

The scene that met her eye as she emerged blinking into the sunshine of late afternoon was pure mayhem. Four tumbrels stood in front of the open gates, horses pawing the cobbles, restive in the midst of so much noise and movement. Men were shouting, herding groups of prisoners, hands bound behind them with rough rope, men and women alike with bared necks, hair tied back or in some cases shorn. They were prodded into the tumbrels with cudgels and pikes, some stumbling up the step into the cart. Helpless, they were hauled up by the guards, and beyond the gates the mob bayed for the blood of the aristos.

Hero could not spare a thought for today's victims of the Terror. She ducked and weaved through the throng, her head down but her eyes fixed upon the open gate. She plunged beneath a horse's head and dived headlong into the triumphant mob beyond the gate. And no one seemed to notice her. In the midst of the crowd, she was safe. She looked like one of them; she knew how to behave like one of them. She paused and for the first time dared to look behind her, to see if her cell companion had reached safety.

"This way. Don't dawdle." An arm came out and swept her almost off her feet, propelling her through the odiferous, exultant crowd and into the relative calm of a narrow alley. "You did well," Guillaume commented as he finally released his hold, and they stood panting, listening to the rabble's screams coming from the street beyond.

"It's amazing what fear for one's life can do," Hero observed, wiping the sweat from her brow with her sleeve.

"Amazing," he agreed. "Stand still for a minute." Deftly, he rebuttoned her shirt. "That was a risky move but courageous. However, you don't need to advertise your sex to the entire city." Hero felt herself blush as his fingers brushed, presumably accidentally, across the swell of her breast. "Here. Wrap this around you." He pulled off his sleeveless woolen jerkin, holding it out to her. "It'll drown you, but it'll cover a multitude of sins."

She took the garment, thrusting her arms into the armholes. It came almost to her knees, but ill-fitting clothes on a ragged youth would draw no remark in this city. She pulled the sides together across her breasts and laced and tied the two strings that held it closed. The jerkin still held his body's warmth and gave off a slightly musky masculine scent that made her feel strange but at the same time gave her a welcome feeling of anonymity.

"So where to now?" Her voice sounded normal enough, she decided.

"Rue St. André des Arts." He took her hand in a gesture that felt perfectly natural in this most unnatural of worlds. "But first, I think, a drop of something to revive us both. Come." He drew her along beside him, weaving his way through the narrow cobbled alleyways, where children played in the kennels and slatternly women lounged in doorways idly watching the passing scene, until they emerged into a small square with a broken fountain in the middle. Noise and laughter spilled from the open door of a tavern on one side of the square. A pair of mangy mongrels rolled and snapped in the gutter. Wine barrels formed rudimentary tables on the cobblestones in front of the hostelry, where men lounged, tankards in hand, throwing dice with raucous shouts of triumph or irritation.

Guillaume shouldered his way through a knot of drinkers in the doorway. "Hey, Guillaume, where've you been these last two days?" one of them demanded. "You owe me three sous."

Guillaume reached into his pocket and withdrew a handful of small coins. "Here, François." He tossed the coins onto the top of a wine barrel. "Next time you roll the dice, I'll make sure they're not loaded."

The other man grinned and pocketed the money. "You had a run of ill luck, that's all. What can I get you and this lad? Looks like he could do with some hair on his chest."

Guillaume laughed. "Brandy . . . and not that ghastly gut rot you pass off on poor innocents."

"Oh, aye, only the best for you, *citoyen*." François touched his forelock in mock humility and disappeared into the crush of people within the tavern.

"Stay close," Guillaume murmured to Hero, who had no intention of doing anything else. Despite the jerkin, she now felt conspicuous amidst the rough crowd, but she was also comfortingly aware of her companion's height and the strength in his lithe, slim frame. In just his shirt-sleeves, he seemed taller and somehow more powerful than most of the men around them, and he exuded a confidence that was immensely reassuring.

François came back with two tankards.

45

"Best cognac for my friend and his little companion," he declared, slamming the tankards onto the top of the wine barrel. "That'll be five sous." He caught the coins as Guillaume tossed them to him. "So where've you been hiding?"

"In La Force," Guillaume said tersely.

The men around them whistled softly. "What did they pick you up for?" the innkeeper inquired.

Guillaume drained his tankard in one long swallow. "Wrong place, wrong time," he said. "Same with my friend here." He slapped Hero's shoulder amiably. "We gave them the slip when they were taking the last lot of aristos to Madame Guillotine."

Someone spat in disgust, and there was a low rumble from the group of men that made the fine hairs on Hero's neck prickle. There was something terrifyingly unpredictable about the mood of these Parisian streets, a volatility that could swing from raucous good humor to horrifying violence in the blink of an eye. She sipped cautiously at the brandy in her tankard. It burned as she swallowed but heartened nevertheless.

"Did they take the Latours yet?" Guillaume inquired casually. "Or have they gone to ground already?"

"Aye, bastard aristos gave us the slip," one

46

of the drinkers declared. "God knows how they knew we were coming for them, the maggots. We knew they were hiding in the attic, living like rats up there, but when we went for them, they were gone." There was more spitting amidst a chorus of disgruntled disgust, and Hero kept her eyes fixed upon the dark liquid in her tankard. The one thing she had learned in her days on the streets was to avoid eye contact with anyone.

Guillaume set down his tankard. "There's plenty more where they came from, right, *mes amis?*"

"Aye, and we'll send them all to the guillotine soon enough," the landlord declared.

Guillaume nodded and adjusted his red cap. *"À bientôt, citoyens."*

He scooped Hero ahead of him, followed by a chorus of farewells. "Just what in the devil's name is a young English girl doing roaming these streets?" he demanded abruptly as they entered a wider street.

Hero looked up at him, surprised by the note of irritation in his voice. It seemed to have come from nowhere. "I might ask *you* what an English gentleman, and you are most clearly both of those things, is doing here," she retorted.

"You might ask," he agreed, "but you would not necessarily get an answer."

"And I might say the same to you," she retorted, half running to keep up with him as he lengthened his stride.

He frowned down at her. "I'd venture to suggest that I am more able to look after myself in this murderous city than a young, untried girl." As she opened her mouth to respond, he shrugged and said curtly, "Well, it's no safe topic for the open street, so we'll have it out when we get somewhere private."

They had reached Place de la Révolution, where the guillotine stood in the center. The vast square was packed with spectators as the tumbrels rolled across the cobbles. Across the river, on Île de la Cité, the great, grim bulk of the prison of the Conciergerie dominated the skyline. Hero forgot her annoyance with her companion's high-handed tone and averted her gaze from the spectacle in the midst of the square, clinging closer to Guillaume's shadow as they threaded their way to the first narrow bridge across the Seine. The thud of the guillotine's bloody blade and the roar of the crowd were repeated endlessly and could still be heard even when they had crossed the second bridge from the island to reach the left bank of the river. Only when they had turned into one of the lanes leading away from the river did the sound fade.

Rue St. André des Arts climbed steeply from a square just out of sight of the river. Number 7 was tall and narrow like its neighbors. Hero's companion knocked in a swift rhythm against the wooden shutters beside the front door. He repeated the sequence after a moment, and the door opened just wide enough to admit a man. Guillaume propelled Hero ahead of him through the gap and stepped in smartly behind her. The door closed, and she heard the heavy bar drop into place.

She found herself in a dark, narrow hallway. The only light flickered from a tallow candle held by the man who had opened the door for them. He was dressed like her companion in the rough clothes of a sansculottes and stared at her in unabashed curiosity.

"Who's this, then, William?" he asked in English.

"A question I'm hoping to have answered myself, Marcus," William replied in the same language. He hung his cap on a hook by the door and with a neat flick removed Hero's and hung it beside his own. Her hair, drawn into a tight knot on top of her head, was the color of burnt caramel, rich, dark, and honey-streaked. He had a sudden urge to see it loose. An urge he instantly quelled.

"We got the Latours out, then, I gather."

"Aye," Marcus replied, still regarding Hero with interest. "They got 'em out before the city gates closed last night. Our folk should be back before curfew tonight . . . if the gods smile," he added.

"If the gods smile," William agreed somberly. He nudged Hero forward towards an open door at the rear of the hallway. "In here, Hero."

She stepped into a small empty room, where a single lamp burned on a table and a small fire flickered in the grate.

William filled two pewter cups from a flagon on the table and offered her one of them. He brushed aside the recalcitrant lock of dark chestnut hair falling across his broad forehead before taking a sip from his own cup. "A pleasant enough Canary," he observed. "So, Mademoiselle Hero, who exactly are you, and what the devil are you doing roaming the streets of Paris in the midst of a revolution?"

FOUR

Hero examined the contents of her pewter cup intently, as if it contained the answer to his question, before saying, "Hermione Fanshawe. My brother is the Marquis of Bruton."

William was rarely dumbfounded, but he found himself so now. "Lady Hermione Fanshawe," he murmured. "Sweet heaven, what are you *doing* here?" The earlier note of irritation was in his voice.

"Looking for my brother, if it's any business of yours," she said tartly. Hero was unaccustomed to being questioned about her activities or her motives. It had been several years since anyone had presumed to have the authority to do so, and while she was prepared to acknowledge that this gentleman had earned her gratitude and maybe the right to a few questions, he certainly hadn't earned the right to pass judgment, and from his tone, it sounded

51

very much as if he was.

His mobile brows quirked, and his expression was quite unreadable. "I think, my lady, you'll find that it is very much my business." He reached for the flagon. "More Canary?"

She shook her head. "No . . . thank you."

He was infuriating. How could he possibly say something like that? He didn't know anything about her. When at a disadvantage, Hero had long ago decided, attack was the best way forward. "So, sir, you know who I am. Will you return the favor?" Her tone was curt almost to the point of rudeness, but it seemed merited.

He responded promptly with a courtly bow. "William Ducasse, Vicomte de St. Aubery, at your service, my lady."

"I thought you were English," she said, puzzled.

"My father was French, my mother English. The title is my father's. And if the mob had their way, I would have lost my head by now because of it," he added with a short laugh that contained no humor.

Hero felt a shiver prickle her spine, hearing in her head the baying of the mob in Place de la Révolution as the guillotine rose and fell. "Can you not leave the city?"

"Oh, I could, but I have work to do here," he replied.

Slowly, the shards of the conversations she had heard between William and the men at the tavern and between William and the man Marcus began to make sense. There were men, she knew — everyone in London Society knew — who risked their heads helping French aristo families escape the bloodbath that was Paris. It would seem the Viscount was one of them, and the Latour family was one of the lucky ones.

"My brother . . ." she said hesitantly. "Alec, he came over to look for his fiancée. She and her family came to Paris months ago hoping to save what they could of their assets before they were stolen. There's been no word from them since, so Alec came to find them. Do you perhaps . . . ?" It seemed too good to be true that she had stumbled upon someone who knew where her brother was, and superstition kept her from asking the question directly.

"Perhaps," he responded. At this point, William had no idea whether Alec Fanshawe was alive or dead. If he was alive, he would be trying to get back into the city before curfew with the rest of the group who had extricated the Latour family from their besieged attic. But it was just as likely that the young man would not return safely.

Hero turned away, her gaze resting on the

flickering fire. She thought she understood his hesitancy. "You have seen him, though?"

"I have seen him."

She nodded. "When?"

"I saw him last three days ago, before I found myself in La Force."

She nodded again. "Well, that is something. At least now I know he was alive three days ago, and maybe you can tell me where to look for him."

"Maybe." It was as oblique a response as before, but again, Hero understood what he was not saying. She sipped her wine, trying not to allow optimism to blind her to reality.

William looked at her, almost absently noticing the delicate curve of her bent neck as she gazed into the fire. The flicker of flame caught the rich mass of colors in the stray locks of hair that had escaped the tight knot once her cap was gone. She was quite tall for a woman, but her willowy slenderness was belied by the hint of curve to her hips and the sideways swell of her breast as she half turned towards him. She would not get away with her boyish disguise for long, he reflected. Not if she stood still long enough for a sharp-eyed watcher to get a good look.

He said briskly, "Well, I, for one, am

famished. Are you not, after our adventurous afternoon?"

Hero turned fully to face him, suddenly aware of the gnawing hunger that had been her companion for days. For the first time since she'd got off the fishing boat at Calais, she felt safe enough to eat without looking over her shoulder, ready to run at the first sign of trouble. "Ravenous. I don't even remember what I last ate or when."

He went to the door, opening it to call out, "Marcus, is there any food in the house?"

Marcus appeared instantly. "Our *bonne femme* left something meaty in a cauldron over the range. God only knows what's in it, pigs' ears and tails and trotters, tripes and brains and hearts, for all I know, but it smells good enough. There's bread and cheese if you don't fancy the stew." He stepped further into the room and nodded towards Hero. "So, whom do we have here?"

"The Lady Hermione Fanshawe," William said. "She's in search of her brother. Hero, may I introduce Sir Marcus Gosford?"

"Sir." Hero nodded acknowledgment since her present guise didn't permit the regulation curtsy.

Marcus looked astounded, casting an interrogative glance at William, even as he

55

murmured, "Delighted, Lady Hermione."

Amazing how ingrained habits somehow survived the most unlikely circumstances, Hero thought, her lips quivering a little at this studied formality. "May I help with the food?" she offered.

"No . . . no, of course not, ma'am. I'll bring it in, won't take a moment."

"No need, we'll eat in the kitchen." William moved to the door. "If you need the outhouse, Hero, it's this way, behind the kitchen." He gestured ahead of him down the corridor.

"Thank you," Hero said. Taking care of her personal needs had been rather hit-and-miss in the last week. Hedges and ditches and public outhouses in unpleasant city hostelries were not easy to negotiate as a woman in general, let alone in disguise.

The kitchen was hot and steamy and filled with the most delicious aromas emanating from a great iron cauldron hanging over the fire in the vast range. Marcus was lifting the massive pot from the stove with both hands, and William moved swiftly to make space on the stained pine table in the middle of the room. Hero ducked out of the back door and into the small kitchen yard, disturbing a couple of black crows pecking at something unrecognizable in the dirt. Their indignant caws followed her into the outhouse, which, as expected, was primitive and noisome, but at least she was certain she wouldn't be disturbed.

When she returned to the kitchen, it was clear to her that she had interrupted a conversation. Neither man appeared disconcerted as she walked in, but there was something in the air that told her they had been talking about her. For the moment, she was content to let it rest, but anything they knew about her brother she would know before she laid her head on her pillow that night. If, indeed, the luxury of a pillow was afforded her.

"Sit down." William gestured with his head to the bench on the far side of the table as he ladled stew into bowls. Marcus set two crusty loaves on the table and filled pewter cups with dark red wine.

"So how did you get to Paris, Lady Hermione?" Marcus inquired, swinging a leg over the bench as he sat down.

"Please, I answer to Hero," she said, flashing him a smile as she inhaled the rich scents from her bowl. "A fishing boat from Dover. It landed at Calais, and I made my way from there."

"Hero, then." Marcus gave her a quick smile in return, asking through a mouthful

57

of stew, "How many passengers were on the boat with you?"

"Just one other . . . a man. We did not introduce ourselves," she added with an ironic smile, breaking bread to dip a crust into her bowl.

"What did he look like?" William regarded her over his wine cup.

Hero frowned. "It was dark and very windy, hard to see properly. Besides, he was swathed in a boat cloak, and I wasn't anxious to draw attention to myself."

"So you can't give us a description?"

"I didn't say that." She ate the sopping crust of bread with relish. "I could draw him if we had pen and ink, paper . . ."

"But you can't find the words?" William was looking at her quizzically.

She shook her head. "No, but I can fashion the image from my head onto paper. It's just something I can do," she added, sounding almost apologetic.

The two men once more exchanged looks. "I can probably scrounge some paper and ink from the old man upstairs," Marcus said. "In return for a bowl of stew and a crust of bread." He got to his feet and fetched a bowl from the dresser.

"Are you certain he's safe?" William asked with a frown, once again flicking aside the

58

persistent lock of hair.

Marcus shrugged. "As safe as anyone these days. It's all a risk." He ladled stew into the bowl.

William nodded. "True enough." He handed Marcus a thick chunk of bread to accompany the stew. Marcus nodded and, still chewing on his own mouthful, disappeared into the kitchen yard.

"Who else lives in this house?" Hero asked, washing down a mouthful of stew with a deep draught of wine.

"There are no fixed inhabitants," William replied. "Except for an old man in the garret who's always lived here. He keeps himself to himself, and we do the same." He refilled her cup from the flagon. "The garret can only be accessed by the outside stairs."

"Can he be trusted?" Hero glanced anxiously over her shoulder at the door to the yard, repeating William's question to Marcus.

William shook his head. "We don't take chances. We keep him sweet, and we keep out of his way. When the owner of the house ran at the start of the trouble, the old man took advantage of his absence and set himself up as landlord. We pay the rent, supply him with wine, and he seems content enough. I suspect he's no more interested in drawing attention to himself than we are. The Committee of Public Safety could as easily turn on someone they suspected of making money out of the revolution as on an aristo. They're not choosy when it comes to naming enemies of the state."

Hero nodded, glancing over her shoulder again as the door opened and Marcus came back into the kitchen. He set an inkpot, a quill pen, and a single ragged sheet of coarse paper on the table. A smear of blood decorated a corner of the paper. "Sorry about that. I gather something from the butcher was wrapped in it."

Hero wrinkled her nose, but at least the blood was dry. The quill was blunt, and the ink in the pot was little more than a clogged film at the bottom, but she did what she could, watched by the two men. "Do you think you'll recognize the man I traveled with?" she asked, sketching swiftly, as if capturing something before it could leave her. "Why would you?"

"Anyone traveling secretly from England to France these days is either with us or an enemy," William said. "It's not a journey anyone makes for pleasure anymore."

Which made sense, Hero reflected, shading the image with a few deft strokes.

"There. That's the best I can do with the tools I have." She frowned at her handiwork before pushing the paper across to William. "One of his eyebrows was oddly shaped, like a question mark. Do you see?" She pointed with the tip of the pen.

William stared at it. "Yes, I see." He passed the paper to Marcus. "What do you think . . . the Lizard?"

"Could be, with that eyebrow," Marcus agreed, holding the sheet closer to the candlelight. "Did he speak at all, Hero?"

"Not to me, but he said something to the fishermen. Not much, but he was French . . . or at least, that's what I assumed. Who's the Lizard?"

"An agent of the Committee of Public Safety," William replied. "A dangerous man. We've been watching him for quite a while. He's a hunter."

Hero absorbed this in silence for a moment before saying, "A hunter of men . . . men like you, who are helping families get out of Paris."

"Precisely."

"Is that what Alec is doing at the moment?" Finally, she asked the question directly.

"Yes, he was helping to get the Latour family out of Paris and to the coast. If all

61

went well, he and the others will be back here sometime tonight."

Hero nodded. It merely confirmed what she'd thought. "Do you know what happened to the St. Julien family? Alec was here to look —" She stopped in mid-sentence at the sound of a brisk rap at the kitchen door behind her.

Marcus was already on his feet as the door opened and a man slipped into the kitchen, closing the door quietly behind him. He, too, was dressed as a sansculottes, his red bonnet pulled low over his forehead.

"Stephen. Is all well?" William greeted the new arrival by filling a pewter cup with wine.

"Aye, we all made it through the gates before curfew," the man said. "We split up as usual through the city . . . the rest'll be here in their own time." He took the cup with a nod of thanks and sprawled with a sigh of exhaustion onto the bench at the table. He frowned at Hero. "Who do we have here?"

"Alec's sister," Marcus supplied. "The Lady Hermione Fanshawe."

"Good God," Stephen said simply, and drank deeply from his cup.

William chuckled. "That was rather my reaction. Food?"

"If there is any." Stephen regarded Hermione with frank astonishment. "Alec said nothing about a sister."

"He didn't know I was coming," Hero told him, bristling a little at the sense of being discussed as if she were some exhibit in a museum.

Marcus set a bowl of stew on the table in front of Stephen. "Hero, let me introduce Stephen Baynard, one of our little band of brothers."

"Hero . . . welcome." Stephen nodded matter-of-factly as he took a spoon to his stew. "A woman might be useful to us, William."

"Certainly," William agreed.

"What's Alec going to say to that?" Marcus asked, refilling tankards from the flagon. "I doubt —"

"Just a minute." Hero interrupted him sharply. "Alec has nothing to do with what I choose to do or how I choose to do it."

William smiled. Hero's reaction didn't surprise him in the least. "Which of you is the elder?"

"Alec, by two minutes," Hero replied.

"I thought there was rather more than an ordinary family resemblance between you," William observed.

Another alerting rap at the door brought

another figure slipping stealthily into the kitchen, and the introductions began again. Despite her irritation at being discussed sometimes as if she weren't there, Hero was pleasantly surprised to find that none of the men actually seemed shocked at her presence or her disguise. Their London selves would have been horrified at the very idea of Lady Hermione in such a place and in such dress, but then, she reflected, in their present incarnations, they were hardly recognizable themselves. And they'd seen and experienced more than enough horrors to find nothing shocking. She settled quietly on a corner of the bench, listening to the account of the rescue of the Latour family as men continued to slip in from the dark beyond the kitchen door.

It was close to midnight when the door finally opened to admit the Marquis of Bruton. He closed the door behind him and stood for a moment leaning wearily against it as his eyes ran across the gathering, counting his fellow conspirators. "Good, we all made it," he said with a sigh, his shoulders relaxing as he pushed himself off the door. Then his green gaze fell upon the figure at the end of the bench.

"*Hero.* What the *hell* are you doing here?"

The intensity of relief at the sight of her

64

brother had stunned Hero into immobility at first, but now she jumped up from the bench and ran to him, flinging her arms around him. "Thank God you're safe, Alec. I've been looking everywhere for you. I went to the St. Juliens' *hôtel* on Rue St. Honoré, but it had been ransacked. The mob were burning and looting in the courtyard. I was so afraid you had been caught up in it." She leaned back in his arms, looking at him as if she would devour him whole. "How could you leave me all these weeks without a word? Didn't you know how frantic I'd be?"

"There was no way to get word to you," her brother said, his hands on her shoulders, gripping tightly. "It never occurred to me you'd come into this pit of hell after me." He gave her a little shake.

"Perhaps it should have done," William remarked. "From what little I've seen of your sister, Alec, I would have expected nothing less."

Alec took his eyes from his sister at last and blinked rapidly, as if to dispel a dream. "How . . . how did you find her? Or, I mean, how did you get here, Hero?"

"It's a long story. Why don't you sit down? You're dead on your feet." Hero pushed him towards the table, once again in charge of the situation. Her brother made no demur.

Since early childhood, he had relied on his sister's strength as she had relied upon his. Quarreling was something quite foreign to them both.

He sat down and drank deeply from the wine cup someone passed him. "Tell me this story."

FIVE

William sat at his ease, one hand curled around his wine cup on the table, one leg crossed casually over the other, watching the twins as Hero told her brother the story of her journey and the last few days in Paris. He noted almost absently that while the family resemblance was powerful, Hero's hair, escaping now from its pins as she talked animatedly, was of a much richer and more complex hue than her brother's, and her eyes seemed larger, wider apart, and a more vivid green.

William had spent little time in the land of his mother's birth and was not well versed in the intricacies of the aristocratic families that made up England's elite Society. He knew almost nothing about the Bruton family, except that the Marquis possessed vast estates in Hampshire and vast wealth as a result. He himself had a more modest estate in Norfolk, inherited from his mother, and he kept lodgings in Half Moon Street in London for his occasional visits to the city, but his heart lay in France. He had grown up on his father's country estate in Bordeaux and spent most of his young adulthood in Paris in the grand mansion of the St. Aubery family on Rue Varennes, from where he had entered the closed circles of the French court. When the first rumblings of trouble among the people of France had been heard and they had demanded that the King call the Estates General for the first time in generations, William's sympathy had been with the people and their grievances. He had joined with two other aristocrats, members of the First Estate, the Comte de Mirabeau and the Duc d'Orleans, in voting with the people's Third Estate when it declared itself the National Assembly.

But how quickly that early promise of rational, legal redressing of ancient inequalities had degenerated into the terror that now ruled the country. Disgusted by the violence, the indiscriminate brutality that followed the orderly beginnings of the revolution, William had devoted himself to getting his threatened compatriots to safety. And now he found himself questioning his French self. This country could never feel like his home again, and he had learned over the last months to appreciate the selfless bravery of these English gentlemen who fought by his side.

And not just gentlemen, he thought with an inner smile, listening to Hero tell her story. She was a lively narrator, her hands moving rapidly in illustration of her experiences. She didn't dwell on the fear she must have felt so often, the threat of danger that must have accompanied her every step, but her audience had no difficulty imagining it. Occasionally, she brushed strands of falling hair from her cheeks and once or twice muttered a curse as she tried to refasten the pins in what was rapidly becoming an unruly tumble of rich color. It aroused in William an urge to run his fingers through it, tangling them deep amidst the thick, loosely curling locks.

"And so here I am," Hero finished, spreading her hands wide. "And thank God I've found you safe, brother."

"Aye," Alec said, frowning grimly. "How could you have risked your life on such a quest, Hero? We have to get you out of here with the next group." He glanced interrogatively at William.

"Why?" Hero demanded before William

could say anything. "No one knows I'm here."

"Well, where does Aunt Emily think you are?" Alec demanded. Their father's distant elderly dowager cousin had lived with them as nominal chaperone for the unmarried Hero since the death of their parents.

"As far as Aunt Emily is concerned, I'm in the wilds of Inverness staying with relatives of the Camerons. No one knows I'm here," Hero repeated with emphasis.

"I wouldn't be so sure about that," William said thoughtfully. "You came over on a clandestine fishing boat, most likely in the company of the Lizard. He's going to be wondering who you are and what brought you to France. Even if you exchanged no words with him, he's still going to be curious. That's his business, and," he added, "it's one he's very good at."

Hero frowned. "But he couldn't possibly know where I am now. It took me over a week to get from Calais to Paris, but I saw him get into a hired coach at the quay. He didn't give me a second glance, I'm sure of it."

"I doubt you would have known what to look for," William stated. "However, you're here now, and we might have a use for you."

"I don't want Hero involved in anything,"

70

Alec declared. "It's too dangerous."

"Nonsense," Hero stated. "It's no more dangerous for me than it is for you, and if William thinks I can be useful, then of course, I'm staying. I'll leave when we've found Marie Claire and her family. And I daresay," she added, "Marie Claire will want you to accompany her, Alec, so we'll go home together."

Alec didn't attempt an argument that he knew he would lose anyway. Hero had always been her own person, with her own very strong opinions, and since the death of her fiancé, she had become even more so. The natural reckless streak in her personality had become stronger and she seemed sometimes deliberately heedless of consequences. It troubled her brother deeply, but he didn't know how to intervene. He knew she was still struggling with her grief at Tom's loss, at the loss of a future she had been so certain of, and Alec didn't know how to help her through it, except to support her need to find a renewed purpose in her life. He accepted her statement with a mental shrug, saying instead, "We have to find them first."

His mouth twisted as he thought of his delicate fiancée somewhere in the bloody madhouse of the city, probably rotting in

71

some filthy prison. Marie Claire had none of Hero's strength. How should she have, sheltered and cosseted as she had been all her life? His eyes seemed to glaze, and he shook his head like a drunken man, before hauling himself up and falling in a sprawl of limbs into a rocking chair by the range. "I'll just shut my eyes for a few minutes."

"Me, too," Stephen announced abruptly, yawning deeply as he swung himself off the bench. There was a chorus of agreement, and the men around the table rose wearily to their feet, moving to the door that opened into the interior of the house.

Hero glanced at her brother. He was sleeping like the dead. "Is there a quilt, anything I can cover him with?"

"In the top drawer of the dresser over there. You should find something." William gestured to the dresser.

Hero found a rather grubby blanket. She draped it over her sleeping brother and then swallowed a yawn of her own. The wine and the food were taking their toll after the exigencies of the day.

"It's time we were all in bed," William observed, taking up a candle. "Come."

"I can sleep on the bench," Hero said as he moved to the door. "It's warm enough with the fire."

"But hard and narrow," he pointed out, turning back to her, beckoning imperatively. "Come."

Hero had little strength to resist, as the idea of lying full-length somewhere and allowing herself to sleep properly for the first time in days offered a siren's call. She followed him out of the kitchen and up the narrow flight of stairs that led to the dark hallway beyond. Several doors opened off the square landing, and faint snuffles and snores came from behind them.

William led the way up a second, even narrower stairway, shielding the candle flame with one hand, and opened a door at the top. It led into a small eaved chamber with a low, unshuttered window. The air was chill, although the early September day had been quite warm, but the bed, which took up most of the floor space, appeared to be well supplied with covers, and Hero looked longingly at it.

William set the candle on the shelf above the empty grate, then bent and pulled out a truckle bed from beneath the bigger bed. "You should find this comfortable enough. It's too short for me." He threw several quilts from the bed onto the smaller one and sat down to pull off his wooden sabots.

Hero perched on the low windowsill to

kick off her own rough clogs. Her companion snuffed the candle and climbed into the bed, pulling a cover over him. The room was dimly lit by the moon shining in the unglazed window, and Hero could make out enough to get herself onto the truckle bed without stubbing a toe. She hesitated a moment, then resolutely untied the strip of cloth at her waist that kept up her grimy britches and shook them off her feet with a sigh of relief. She'd been sleeping in her clothes for days. She tugged her coarse linen shirt down her hips, deciding it made a decent enough covering while she was in bed, and gingerly settled onto the straw mattress of the truckle bed. A coarse sheet covered the mattress, and there was a flat pillow of sorts. The quilts were thick, and her limbs slowly relaxed into the growing warmth. She could hear her companion's deep, rhythmic breathing above her, and a feeling of security washed over her. Her eyes closed.

She awoke bewildered in full daylight and lay for a moment with her eyes still closed, trying to remember where she was. She was snug and warm in her nest, her limbs feeling deliciously leaden, and she could hear sounds like water splashing, the scuffle of bare feet on wooden floorboards. Memory returned in full flood, and she opened her eyes slowly. A naked man stood shaving with his back to her in front of a washstand against the wall. He dipped the cutthroat razor into a basin and tilted his head back, drawing the sharp blade up under his chin.

Hero gazed sleepily at the long, muscled back, the tight buttocks, the length of his thighs and powerfully muscled calves. His short chestnut hair was wet as if he'd just washed it, and drops of water glistened on his shoulders.

"I thought you still asleep." William spoke into the silence. "Forgive me if I've shocked your maidenly modesty, my lady."

Hero propped herself on an elbow and heard herself say, "I haven't had any to shock for two years." Why on earth was she confiding such an intimate detail to this naked man?

"Ah," he responded, wiping his face with a towel. He wrapped a second towel around his loins as he turned to face her. "You have a paramour?"

"I had a fiancé," she returned. It didn't seem either possible or pointful to stop sharing her intimate past at this point. "He was killed last year at sea." She tried to keep her eyes from following the line of dark hair that

75

curled down his belly, disappearing into the skimpy towel.

"I'm sorry." He leaned back against the washstand, rubbing his wet head with the hand towel. "You anticipated the marital bed?"

Hero smiled in reminiscence. "Many times."

William chuckled. "I can't say it surprises me. I gather you found it pleasurable."

"Oh, yes," she responded with a grin. "Very." Then her smile dimmed as the old sorrow flooded her again. She had almost mastered her grief after all these months, but at times, the thought of Tom's life cut so short, of the life they had planned together now merely a dream, threatened to overwhelm her anew.

"How was he killed?" William asked. He could almost see the black shadow of her sadness hovering around her and was prepared for her to rebuff his questions if she felt them intrusive.

"He was a lieutenant in the navy. His ship had a skirmish with pirates off the coast of Spain, or at least that was what I was told. He was wounded, and the wound festered." She blinked back tears. "It was such a waste. Tom was so young, so vital. We were to be married when that tour ended. He would have made captain on his next voyage, and I would have gone with him." It was almost a relief to speak of it to this man, who to all intents and purposes was a complete stranger . . . except that they had shared a prison cell and he was standing there naked but for a skimpy towel as casually as if they were in full dress in a London salon. He didn't feel in the least like a stranger.

William made no further comment. He went to a chest and began to rummage through its contents, pulling out various garments. "Turn your back," he instructed.

Obediently, Hero rolled onto her other side.

After a few minutes, he said, "If you want clean clothes, you can see what's in there. You'll have to roll the britches up, and the shirt will swamp you, but at least they're clean."

She sat up. He was fully dressed now, fastening the buckle of his belt. "Is there any fresh water?"

"I'll send your brother up with a jug." He picked up the basin he'd been using and tipped its contents out of the window with an alerting shout of *"Gardez l'eau,"* in case any unwary pedestrian was passing below. "There'll be coffee in the kitchen."

The door closed behind him, and Hero

got out of bed, stretching. She felt amazingly refreshed, although she could smell her own sweat and feel the dirt ingrained in her skin. Soap and hot water and clean garments would be wonderful. She was examining the contents of the chest when Alec came in on a brisk alerting knock. He carried a steaming jug.

"How did you sleep?"

"Remarkably well. I dare swear better than you in that chair," she replied, straightening from the chest. She saw that her brother was surveying the small chamber with a questioning eye.

"You slept on the truckle?"

"Yes, my dear. And William slept like a monk in the bed. You didn't really imagine he would ravish me, did you?"

Alec shook his head with a rueful grin. "No, he's too honorable . . . not so sure about you, though, sister dear." He set the jug on the washstand. "I'll see you in the kitchen."

Hero stripped to her skin, wondering whether William was so honorable that he would refuse a little love play if it were offered him. It was a shocking reflection, she thought, surprising even herself with its lack of modesty. But then, nothing about her present circumstances could be anything but shocking. She probed the idea as delicately as if it were a nagging tooth. Perhaps just telling him about Tom had released in her some kind of pent-up need, because she certainly found the idea exciting. The thought of such love play sent little prickles of arousal across her skin and caused a familiar sinking jolt in the base of her belly. And why not? she thought defiantly, although whom she was defying she didn't know. The one thing she did know was that Tom would not mind. He had had far too generous a soul to condemn her to a life of chastity.

The hot water and harsh lye soap felt wonderful as she scrubbed her body vigorously with a scrap of toweling until her skin glowed red. She rubbed herself dry as best she could with the only dry corner of a towel she could find and then returned to the chest. She found a clean shirt of coarse linen. It swamped her as expected, but it smelled fresh. The trousers were more of a problem; the waist was too big, and they slid to her hips while the legs flapped off her feet.

The door opened on a brisk knock while she was contemplating her swamped lower limbs somewhat plaintively. William burst into laughter as he came in. "Even worse than I thought," he said, setting down the mug of coffee he held. "Let's see what we can do to improve matters."

"I was using a strip of cloth before." Hero indicated the strip she'd discarded with her old clothes. She couldn't move to get it herself without tripping over her feet or letting go of the waist of the britches.

"I think we can do better than that." William looked through the chest. "Here." He took out a narrow belt and wrapped it around Hero's waist, pulling it tight. "I'll put a new hole in it . . . about here, I think." Marking the place with his finger, he drew his knife from the sheath at his waist and punctured the leather. "Now try it." He buckled the belt and stood back.

Hero sighed with relief. "Thank you. But what do I do about this?" She flapped a leg in illustration.

"Sit on the bed, and I'll roll them up. I don't want to cut them, because you're not going to be wearing them for very long."

Hero assumed he meant that she would have her own washed soon enough. She sat on the bed while he knelt and rolled the britches up to her mid-calves. This easy intimacy was making her feel rather strange. When his fingers brushed over her bare legs as he worked, she had to control a little

80

jump of wholly pleasurable sensation. She recognized the feeling and knew it for what it was: a pure, simple jolt of lust. With a surge of embarrassment, she hoped that William couldn't sense it. But he looked up at her suddenly, and his tawny gold eyes held a look of startled recognition.

Then he smiled slowly, sitting back on his heels, looking at her with a quizzical gleam, his hands encircling her bare ankles. "I suspect that my lady is something of an adventuress," he said, running his hands up her calves.

"Perhaps," Hero replied, holding herself very still, fighting the urge to brush that errant lock of hair from his forehead. "We live in adventurous times."

"Hazardous, certainly," he agreed, releasing his hold and standing up in one easy movement. He leaned over her and tilted her chin with his finger, bringing his mouth to hers. It was a light touch, a promise of a kiss, but it sent her blood thrilling through her body like a bolt of lightning. He straightened. "We'll continue this later."

Hero remained sitting on the bed after the door had closed softly behind him, wondering what exactly had just happened. It was one thing to harbor a secret impulsive attraction for the Viscount St. Aubery, quite

another so shamelessly to reveal that powerful attraction to its object. But it seemed
that it was not unreciprocated.

After a while, she slid off the bed and
thrust her feet into her wooden clogs. The
coffee he had brought her was cold. She
poured it out of the window with the dirty
water in the basin, shouting the customary
warning cry, then slowly made her way
down to the kitchen.

Six

William and Marcus were the only men in the kitchen when Hero entered. They were sitting at the table deep in conversation but broke off as she came in. "Good morning, Marcus." She greeted him with a smile.

"Good morning, Hero. Coffee?"

"Thank you." A copper jug of coffee stood on the table beside the remnants of a loaf and a jar of apricot jam with a knife stuck in it. She filled her coffee mug and broke off a piece of bread, spreading it with jam before sitting down. "Did I interrupt something?"

"It concerned you," William said. "We were trying to decide what exactly we're going to do about the situation."

Hero bristled. "I don't think I'm a *situation,* and I don't particularly care for being discussed like some external problem. I will decide for myself what I shall do next."

"We are accustomed to making decisions

as a group," William told her sharply. "We're all dependent for our safety on one another. There's no room for unilateral decisions or actions."

"Should I just leave?" she inquired sweetly, reflecting rather less sweetly that the moment in the upstairs chamber was clearly not at the forefront of his mind.

"I'm afraid that's not an option," William stated. "You know too much, my dear girl. We value this house, and while I'm sure you would have no intention of giving it away . . ." He shrugged. "The agents of the Committee of Public Safety are everywhere, and intolerable pressure can be brought to bear, however resolute one might be." His eyes were flinty as he held her gaze. "I trust you take my meaning."

Hero did. And she had no illusions that she would be any stronger than anyone else when it came to resisting such pressure. Those cold eyes, gold as a cat's, were also making it very clear to her that Viscount St. Aubery would make a formidable opponent should such an unpleasant confrontation arise. She inclined her head in rueful acknowledgment, saying simply, "I came to Paris to find Alec and to help him, if possible, to find Marie Claire and her family. I still intend to do that."

"We are all agreed that finding the St. Julien family will be our next priority," William said, his tone no longer sharp. "We work on priorities. Those families at immediate risk of arrest are always our first focus. We had nothing to go on with the St. Juliens, and the Latour family were in the most urgent danger. Alec understood that. But we'll concentrate on them now."

"It'll be the devil's own job," Marcus put in somberly. "Families not yet arrested give us a better chance of getting them out of the country. And we don't even know where the St. Juliens are."

Hero sipped her coffee, wrinkling her nose at its bitterness. "It seems hopeless."

"Not quite. We have a contact in the Committee of Public Safety who has access to lists of the people condemned to execution," William explained. "They aren't always complete, of course, but so far, no St. Julien has appeared on any list we've seen, so we're assuming they're in one of the prisons awaiting trial."

Hero's spine prickled at the memory of her brief incarceration, the tumbrels, and the terrifying mob. Marie Claire was a fragile flower, sweet-natured and very pretty; it was hard to imagine how she would survive the filthy rat-ridden straw of a

Parisian prison, let alone the brutality of the guards. "How do we go about finding out which prison?"

"We have sources," Marcus explained. "A few guards in both La Force and the Conciergerie can be bribed, but it takes time. We've been waiting for something from them for several weeks."

"And there are other smaller prisons around the city," William said grimly. "It's impossible to get information on them all."

Hero pushed aside her coffee mug, leaving the last swallow, and dipped her finger into the apricot jam pot, licking off the sweetness to relieve the coffee's bitter aftertaste. "So did you come to any conclusions about the *situation*?" She couldn't help the slightly sardonic emphasis.

William chose to ignore it. "It's time you put on women's clothes," he informed her. "Alec has gone to procure some."

"Why?" She looked indignant. "I feel safer in this disguise on the streets."

"Believe me, you'll fool no one for long," he stated.

"I'll bind my breasts again."

He shook his head. "It won't do, Hero. I'll spare Marcus the embarrassment of a detailed description of your womanly assets, but trust me, my dear, they cannot be hidden from any interested eyes. And none of us can afford to attract attention. Besides," he added with a sudden wicked chuckle, "if you continued with your disguise, it would be necessary to cut your hair, and that would be positively criminal."

Hero wasn't sure how to take the last comment in present circumstances. She decided that in Marcus's company, it was safer to ignore it. She was forced to admit, however, that while her disguise could probably pass muster in a crowded street, anything out of the ordinary would draw attention to her — a scuffle, a fall, an altercation with an unruly cart horse, all perfectly normal occurrances in the life of the streets — but if her disguise slipped in any way, it would be disastrous.

"Well, I can't see myself being much use as a woman," she pointed out.

"That remains to be seen." William stood up. "For the moment, you need to stay safely in here. Marcus and I have somewhere to go." He pulled his red cap over his head as he spoke.

"What am I supposed to do here?" Hero demanded as the two men went to the kitchen door. "Twiddle my thumbs?"

"Well, if you have a turn for kitchen duty, there's plenty to do." William gestured to the pile of dirty crockery on the dresser. His eyes held a gleam of teasing amusement. He could well guess how Lady Hero would greet such a suggestion.

"I thought there was a *bonne femme* for such work." Hero eyed him with a degree of malevolence.

"Sometimes she comes, and sometimes she doesn't," he responded blithely. "Stay off the streets." He went out, followed by Marcus.

Hero fumed for a moment or two and then got up to deal with the dirty dishes. After that, she would wash the clothes she'd been wearing earlier and hang them in the kitchen yard to dry. Whatever opinion William held about her disguise, she would still prefer to have it at hand. Such domesticity was an anodyne activity and left her mind free to wander along whatever paths it chose. Despite the grim purpose that had brought her to this house on Rue St. André des Arts, the physical excitement she felt in William's presence was too powerful to be ignored. Just the thought of him now, as she plunged dirty mugs into a bowl of scummy, tepid water, sent shivers of anticipation along her spine and a liquid weakness to the base of her belly. She had felt like this with Tom and had desperately missed this glorious sensation of arousal. The now familiar recklessness infused her, a feeling that she had nothing to lose by indulging this lust, and that was what it was, pure and simple. Here in this dreadful place of death and horror, what could societal convention matter?

She set the clean mugs on a shelf on the dresser and wiped her hands on her britches. It wasn't as if she had a reputation to lose. No one apart from Alec knew where she was anyway. As she had said last night, Great-aunt Emily, her companion and ostensible chaperone, thought she was visiting friends in the wilds of the Scottish Highlands. The old lady wouldn't worry for a moment about not hearing from her; indeed, knowing her great-aunt, Hero thought she would be too occupied with some new and as yet undiagnosed ailment to add to the compendium of her physical infirmities.

Hero smiled affectionately. Aunt Emily was a valetudinarian but a lovable one, and Hero was fond of her. She wouldn't cause her a moment's anxiety if she could help it, and her present journey had been meticulously planned to ensure that her aunt slept peacefully in her bed at night.

A half hour later, she was hanging her

freshly washed britches and shirt on a makeshift washing line in the kitchen yard when the gate from the alley creaked open. Her heart raced for a moment, her hands stilling on the wet garments pinned to the line as she looked to the gate. Alec came into the yard, a bundle in his arms. He looked curiously at his sister. "Washerwoman, Hero? That's a strange occupation for you. Are you all alone?"

"It appears I'm considered a liability on the streets," she said tartly, turning away from the washing line. "Or so William seems to think."

"He's probably right," her brother said with a careless shrug. "He usually is. See what I've found." He went into the kitchen and set his bundle on the table.

Hero approached cautiously, wondering what her brother had obtained in the way of suitable female wear. He himself was dressed, as they all were, in the uniform of the sansculottes, his red cap tilted at an angle. She fingered the pile of coarse homespun. "Where did you find this?"

"Bought it all off a woman in the market in the Marais. I think it will all fit you well enough, but you don't want to look too smart." He laughed as he shook out a striped kirtle and holland apron. "They're

90

not new, of course, but clean and well darned in places."

Hero examined the petticoat and laced bodice, which would go over her own chemise. There were no stockings, but then, most of the peasant women went barelegged, and her wooden sabots would be fine, as would her red bonnet. "I'd better go and put them on." She gathered up the garments and hurried upstairs to the little bedchamber. When she came down the stairs again, she could hear voices from the kitchen. It sounded as if most of the men were back, judging by the level of noise. She pushed open the door, feeling suddenly shy.

"Ah, there you are." William turned from the dresser with a foaming ale tankard. He took in her appearance with an assessing frown before pronouncing, "That should do well enough . . . much more suitable."

"It feels strange after all this time in britches," she observed, smoothing down the apron. "Rather restrictive."

"You'll become accustomed soon enough." He tipped his head back and drained his tankard. Hero found her eyes riveted to his sun-browned throat, the steady movement of his Adam's apple as he drank. Everything about the man set her skin on fire. And it was beginning to be

91

inconvenient, she decided. It was getting in the way of clear thinking.

"Let's go and test the new Hero on the street." William set down his empty tankard. "Fetch your bonnet, and we'll go to market."

"Market?" she exclaimed. It seemed such a mundane activity in the circumstances.

"We have to eat," he said matter-of-factly. "Let's see how you fare as a Parisian *femme de ménage.*" He unhooked a shopping basket from behind the door and, with an exaggerated bow, offered his arm. *"Citoyenne, allons-y."*

There seemed no help for it. The man appeared to sweep all before him. Hero shook her head, laughing, and put her hand on his arm. "My thanks for your escort, sir."

They went out into the street, walking briskly to the food market in the square at the bottom of the steep street. The farmers and peasants had driven their laden carts into the city from the countryside at dawn and would leave before the city gates closed at curfew, but for now, the stalls, although depleted, still had produce, and Hero found to her surprise that she was enjoying herself. The sense of threat she had lived with for so many days was no longer with her. Was it because she was not in such an extreme disguise and so had little to hide? Or was it just the reassuring presence of her companion? She was aware that he was on guard; she could feel it in the tension of his supple frame as he walked close beside her. He had his hand resting casually on the hilt of the knife in his belt, and his eyes were everywhere.

"Meat?" he suggested, pausing in front of a butcher's stall.

"Does anyone know how to cook it?" she asked, looking in bemusement at the bloody piles of flesh. "I don't even know what any of it is. I could recognize a chicken, but what's the rest of it?"

"Then it had best be chicken." He steered her in the direction of a poultry stall, where chickens clucked mournfully from baskets piled high.

"But we have to kill them." Hero was aghast. She hadn't the faintest idea how to kill a chicken, let alone pluck it. In her experience, chickens came to the table carved and lapped with some delicate sauce.

"If the poulterer won't do it for us, I can wring a chicken's neck," William said firmly. "We can roast it on a spit over the fire."

Tentatively, Hero asked the poulterer for three chickens. The man looked astounded and then suspicious, and she realized belatedly that peasant women did not buy chickens in bulk. One bird would have to go a long way to feed a large family. "It's a celebration feast," she offered hastily, reaching into the pocket of her apron for a handful of sous. "A new baby in the family."

The man said nothing, but he still looked suspicious. "You want 'em alive?"

She shook her head hastily, and with swift efficiency, he wrung the necks of three scrawny birds, dropping the still-pulsating carcasses into her basket. To her relief, William took the basket from her as she paid the poulterer.

Hero turned away. "What now?"

"Bread, cheese, vegetables," her companion said in an undertone. "Try to remember the revolution started in the first place because people were starving and there was no flour for bread, let alone meat for the asking."

"I know," she said in the same undertone, flushing a little, shocked at how easy it was to make a mistake. "But I've only ever shopped for hats and dress material before."

"Just keep your wits about you."

Hero watched her fellow housewives and copied them, poking and prodding vegetables, sniffing at cheeses, selecting carefully but frugally. Nevertheless, the old, familiar

94

feeling of menace was back with her despite William's presence. There were so many pitfalls just trying to pass unnoticed through the crowds, even though her peasant dress was indistinguishable.

She was moving away from the back of a cart from which a woman with thick forearms and reddened hands was selling loaves of day-old bread when she felt it. Her scalp crawled as if an army of lice were nesting, and the hairs on her nape lifted.

William was a few paces behind her as her step faltered and her eyes slid sideways. Her breath caught in her throat. William moved up beside her, not looking at her as he said under his breath, "What?"

"Over there, in the doorway of that cobbler. The eyebrow."

William glanced once and said swiftly, "Take this." He gave her the basket. "Now, walk through the market and take one of the side streets, any one. If you think you're being followed, do *not* go back to the house. Lose him if you can; otherwise, just come back here."

"And do what?" Her heart was battering against her ribcage.

"Just wait. Do you understand?"

Mutely, Hero nodded and continued to stroll through the stalls, her eyes on a steep and narrow lane, more an alley than a street, that led out of the square and ran parallel with Rue St. André des Arts. Every inch of her skin seemed sensitized, but she didn't dare stop to look behind her to see if she was being followed. On impulse, she moved sideways back into the melee of stalls and carts, pausing casually to examine a mound of cabbages. She glanced quickly behind her. The man with the eyebrow was nowhere to be seen.

"Fine cabbage, *citoyenne.*" The seller held out a head for her inspection.

She shook her head with an assumption of regret. *"Non, merci, citoyen."*

He shrugged with resignation, and Hero moved on, glancing once more behind her. She couldn't see the man with the eyebrow and moved with more resolution to the steep side street. It was quieter there, and if she was being followed, she'd have a better chance of seeing her pursuer. She toiled up the hill, changing the heavy basket from hand to hand. It gave her the perfect excuse to pause now and again, glance casually behind her, and listen closely for steps, a change in step, a pause, anything that would indicate a pursuer. But she could detect nothing.

Halfway up, she took a side alley that

96

would connect with Rue St. André des Arts. It was dark and narrow, overshadowed on both sides by shabby houses. Her heart was pounding again, her breath coming fast as she strained to hear, to sense if anyone was behind her. She knew she could not betray the house, however inadvertently. But she could detect nothing as she emerged onto her own street.

She set her basket down, pressed her hands into the small of her back, and stretched as if weary of the steep climb. No one paused to give her a second glance; no one appeared from the side street, which remained silent and shadowed. Dare she risk it?

Hero picked up her basket and crossed the street. She could access the back of the house by the passageway between two of the houses. It was little more than a corridor, stinking of ordure from the kennel that ran through it, and she had to pick her way over the slimy cobbles. But here she could be confident that no one was behind her. The gate leading into the backyard of number 7 stood slightly ajar, its hinges loose, the latch broken, just like its fellows. She walked to the end of the passage, then turned and walked back. There was no one in sight, and she had no sense of eyes upon her. She listened and could hear no foot-steps, just the sound of iron wheels on the cobbled street at the end of the alley, the sharp yelp of a dog from somewhere, a child crying. Nothing out of the ordinary at all. She was alone.

Swiftly, she pushed open the gate, catching her breath as the hinges squeaked. She paused again, listening, peering over her shoulder. Nothing. She slipped sideways through the gate into the bedraggled kitchen yard, glancing up at the very top floor of the house, wondering if the old man in his garret was watching the gate. The wooden shutters were open, and she thought she caught a shadow of movement across the window. But William had said the old man was safe enough, so what did it matter if he had seen her?

She tried to walk slowly to the kitchen door, to look as if she was just an ordinary housewife with a heavy shopping basket. She lifted the latch on the door and pushed it open, stepping into the kitchen with a warm rush of relief at the familiar room and the circle of faces turned as one towards her.

SEVEN

Sometime after Hero let herself into the yard of number 7 Rue St. André des Arts, Viscount St. Aubery strolled, hands in the deep pockets of his loose britches, down Rue du Bac. He stopped outside a wine shop, glanced casually up and down the street, and then pushed through the door into the dark, noisy interior, where customers crowded the shelf that served as a bar while the owner filled leather flagons from the wine barrels piled against the wall behind him.

"Bernard." William nodded at the man, elbowing his way to the front.

"*Citoyen.*" The owner set a tankard in front of his new customer with a nod of acknowledgment. William raised it in a toast and drank, smiled his appreciation as he turned with his back to the counter, and surveyed the men and women gathered around the small space. After a moment, he pushed himself away from the counter and threaded through the crowd of drinkers to a shadowy corner, where a man sat alone at an up-turned wine barrel, hunched over a tankard of rich ruby-red wine.

William gestured with his head to the empty stool on the other side of the wine barrel and, receiving a wordless nod in exchange, straddled the stool, setting his own tankard on the barrel. His companion at the barrel was dressed in serviceable leather britches and jerkin, a pair of fine leather boots on his feet and a sword at his waist. He was clearly a more substantial citizen than his fellows in the wine shop, who all wore the standard uniform of the sansculottes.

"So, Armand?" William inquired softly.

"So, Guillaume . . . the St. Juliens," the other responded in the same undertone. "The parents went to the guillotine this morning."

William drank from his tankard, only his narrowed eyes showing he had heard his companion. "The daughter?"

"Marked for execution with tomorrow afternoon's cull in Place de la Révolution. She's held in the Conciergerie."

William nodded, drained his tankard, and stood up. "My thanks, Armand." His hand rested for a moment on the makeshift tabletop, then lifted. Armand's hand slid swiftly across and then disappeared into his lap. William turned and walked out of the wine shop, his expression somber even as his mind worked swiftly, selecting and discarding possible plans for effecting the escape of Alec's fiancée from the very steps of the guillotine.

"Where's William?" Marcus asked, looking over Hero's shoulder as she stepped into the kitchen.

"I don't know, exactly." Hero closed the door behind her and set her basket on the table with a sigh of relief. "We were in the market in the Place St. André, and I think I saw the eyebrow . . . the Lizard. William told me to come back, making sure I wasn't followed, and —"

"And you weren't?" Stephen interrupted sharply.

Hero shook her head. "I'm as sure as I can be that no one saw me come here. I don't know where William went."

The men in the kitchen exchanged grim looks. "If the Lizard's onto us, we'll have to close down and move on," Marcus said after a moment.

"But how could he be?" someone asked,

then added, "Unless he's been following Hero."

Hero began to feel uncomfortable, as if she were somehow being held responsible. "He can't have followed me from Calais," she protested. "I've only been in Paris for three days."

"When you were arrested, did they question you?"

"No. I was at the St. Juliens' house in Rue St. Honoré. The mob was tearing it apart. A fight simply exploded around me, and I got caught up in it somehow, and the mob just carried me along with it until soldiers — or whatever they were, guards of some kind — appeared at the end of a street, and there was a skirmish, and everyone disappeared. I was trying to help a man who'd been injured, and the guards grabbed me, and the next thing I knew, they were throwing me through the door to the cell in La Force where I met William." She looked around the circle of eyes fixed upon her. "They didn't even ask who I was."

"The Lizard has his tentacles reaching into every prison, guard post, and gatehouse in the city," Alec said. "It could as easily have been any one of us who caught his attention. Even William."

"True enough," Marcus agreed. He stood

102

up to examine the contents of Hero's shopping basket. "Who's good at plucking chickens? We may as well get on with dinner while we're waiting for William to get back."

The awkwardness passed, and Hero relaxed again, discarding her shawl and bonnet. She finished unpacking the basket while Stephen took the birds into the yard to pluck and dress them. They were roasting on the spit over the fire when William finally came in.

"Something smells good." He sniffed hungrily.

"Where have you been?" Hero asked.

"Following our friend," he responded. "You're sure no one followed you?"

"As sure as I can be."

He nodded. "Fair enough. I kept the Lizard in sight for a good while after you'd left, so it was only a question of whether he had any cohorts." He poured himself a goblet of wine from the flagon on the dresser. "We're safe for the moment, I think, but the dogs are getting too close for comfort. We'll need to make a move soon."

"But what of Marie Claire and her family?" Alec asked, unable to conceal his anxiety.

"I had a meeting with Armand just now." William glanced at Hero, explaining. "Armand is one of our paid informants in the Committee of Public Safety. We have a rendezvous point if he has any information for us. He was there this afternoon." He turned back to Alec, regarding him with a degree of compassion. "The Marquis and his wife went to the guillotine this morning . . . I'm sorry, Alec."

Alec had paled, but his expression remained resolute. "And Marie Claire?" There was not a tremor in his voice.

"Marked for execution at Révolution tomorrow afternoon, which gives us little enough time, but we're lucky to have any." William gave him a reassuring smile. "Gather round, children, and I will tell you my plan." He swung a leg over the bench at the table and cut himself a hunk of cheese.

The noise was the worst of it. The girl barely noticed the chafing of the rough rope at her wrists, the stench of the crowds, the blur of faces filled with hatred and menace surrounding her, but the noise was unendurable. It seemed a million voices were raised in a baying cacophony emerging from the sea of open mouths clamoring at the sides of the wooden cart, where she stood desperately trying to keep her feet as it swayed over the cobbles, swung wildly from side to side as the crowd leapt against the tumbrel, hanging on to the railing, hurling abuse, fists and staves raised in a wild fury.

Marie Claire St. Julien closed her eyes as if blindness would offer her some protection from the violence around her, but she could not block out the noise. And then something, some sound, seemed to separate itself from the pandemonium surrounding her.

"Marie Claire . . . Marie Claire."

The sound was insistent, low and yet penetrating. The girl opened her eyes, looked around, trying to see past the ugly, vicious faces, and she caught the vivid green stare fixed upon her as if it could bore into her skull. She knew the face, knew those eyes, the heart-shaped face. But her brain would not accept what her eyes were seeing.

"Maire Claire." Again, that insistent voice, demanding her attention.

"Marie Claire, it's me. Hero. Listen to me." A hand came out, reaching for Marie Claire's arm as she swayed close to the edge of the cart when it bounced over the cobbles. "Get near the back so that you'll be the last off. Now." And then the face disappeared as a woman waving a cudgel pushed Hero aside and she lost her grip on

105

the rail, half jumping, half falling back into the crowd, only just managing to keep her feet.

Marie Claire looked wildly around, returning finally to her senses, feeling herself alive again in the midst of this horror. Hero jumped up against the cart again, waving her hand. "Move to the back."

It was hard to move in the violently swaying cart, her hands bound behind her, but somehow she managed to inch through her fellow victims, squeezing her way to the rear of the tumbrel as they lurched from side to side. Now she could hear the screaming of the crowd from Place de la Révolution, and the smell of blood was strong in the air. She thought she would be sick, but then Hero's face appeared at the rear of the cart, just for a moment, but it was long enough to keep Marie Claire conscious of her surroundings.

The cart halted suddenly, sending its occupants tumbling backwards against one another. The vehicle was one of a line stretching across the Place to the stark silhouette of the guillotine against the reddening sky of late afternoon. For a moment, Marie Claire's eyes were mesmerized by the blade as it fell, seemingly so very slowly, from the sky amidst the roar of the crowd. Then the cart lurched forward once again as it moved up to take the place of the one in front. For an excruciating ten minutes, the cart moved forward as the ones in front disgorged their victims at the steps of the guillotine. And Hero kept pace, her face popping up whenever Marie Claire thought she must have dreamt her.

And then came the moment when the gate at the rear of the tumbrel in front was lowered and the victims were hauled out to the square, instantly surrounded by men with pikes, who pushed back the crowd seething forward to hiss and spit as the condemned were prodded towards the blade, which had never paused in its relentless rise and fall.

Marie Claire pressed back against the rear of the tumbrel as it lurched forward to the place immediately in front of the steps. The gate was lowered. She saw Hero's face once more, at the opened rear of the tumbrel, as she stumbled forward in the midst of her fellow passengers, unable to halt her progress, pushed and pulled as she was by filthy hands. She half fell out of the cart and, even as she seemed to lose her footing, felt hands grab her, push her down under the waving arms of the crowd. She was being pulled along, so fast she could hardly keep her feet on the ground, desperately trying to keep her balance with her bound hands, her eyes fixed on the cobbles beneath her feet, confusion and terror engulfing her, making her faint with dizziness. But the hands that held her were strong, and amazingly, she could hear the thud of the blade and the roar of the crowd receding. Her head seemed to spin, and the world around her faded into blackness.

"Marie Claire, sweetheart . . . sweetheart, it's all right. You're safe now. I'm here." A remembered voice penetrated the dark, and she swam upwards to awareness again.

Alec was kneeling on the ground, holding her up against his shoulder. Someone else was cutting through the rope that bound her wrists. Marie Claire leaned sideways suddenly and vomited into the kennel. Alec thrust his kerchief into her hand, and she lay back helplessly against his shoulder, wiping her mouth, her gaze slowly taking in the faces looking down at her.

"Hero?" she managed to say. "I saw Hero."

"Yes, you did," a man said briskly. He was standing over her, a tall figure exuding a power and strength that seemed to enfold her. He was dressed in rough peasant garb, a red cap on his dark head, but he spoke English, and while his tone was almost brusque, there was compassion in his tawny

108

gold eyes. "And you'll see her again. But for the moment, we have to get off the street. Can you walk?"

Marie Claire nodded, turning her own blue eyes up to Alec, who still leaned over her, supporting her. "I can walk," she said, with more strength now, seeing the instant relief in Alec's intense gaze. He half lifted her to her feet, and she swayed for just a moment, then straightened. "I can walk," she repeated, shaking the numbness out of her freed hands.

The man who had cut through the rope gave her a reassuring smile as he slipped his knife into the sheath at his belt. "I'll leave you here, then," he said. "The fewer we are, the less conspicous." He raised a hand in farewell and loped off back in the direction of Révolution.

"Come, then." William gestured down the narrow alley in which they stood. "We'll cut back and then cross the river on the Pont Neuf." He set off ahead of Alec and Marie Claire.

"Who is he, Alec?" Marie Claire whispered, still dazed and yet conscious of a miraculous sense of safety.

"Just call him William, or Guillaume if we are in French company," Alec said. "I'll explain everything once we're off the street."

■ ■ ■ ■

Hero was still in the Place, surrounded by the screaming horde. She closed her mind to the scene and focused. She had never felt so completely alone before. Marie Claire was safely away with William, Marcus, and Alec. She had to make her own way back to the house. It was what they had agreed upon. The fewer they were, the less likely they would draw attention to themselves. And even though she had agreed to it, she still felt vulnerable and very lonely, despite the mass of humanity pressing around her.

She moved casually away from the guillotine, slithering through the throng all gazing upwards at the rise and fall of the blade. It seemed unbelievable, but William had been right. In the chaos, amidst the stumbling prisoners, their pike-thrusting guards, and the screaming, vengeful crowd, it *had* been possible to extract Marie Claire as she half fell from the cart with her fellow victims. Her rescuers had been waiting at the cart's tail when the gate was opened, and Alec had caught his fiancée at the moment she took a step forward. The three men had bundled her against them, drawing her beneath the outflung arms of the crowd and away from the cart, and for the moment, at least, it seemed that no one had actually noticed one of the prisoners was missing.

Would they bother to count the heads in the piled baskets at the end of the day's murders? Would they notice the absence of one young woman's head? The St. Juliens were an old and wealthy aristocratic family, but they had never been active in political life or even particularly prominent frequenters of the court at Versailles. Marie Claire would not be well known to the crowd. She would just have been one of the many heads that fell that afternoon — young, pretty, and worthy of death simply because of her name.

Hero reached the riverbank and stopped, breathless, as the fear-fueled energy that had brought her out of Place de la Révolution ebbed, leaving her feeling weak and shaky. She leaned against the low parapet, looking down at the river below, where the great shadow of the Conciergerie on the opposite bank rippled and wavered in the swift current. William had told her not to cross directly into Place St. Michel as she would normally have done but to make her way along the river and cross the ancient rickety wooden bridge at the great cathedral of Notre Dame. And, as always, to be abso-

111

lutely certain she was not followed.

After a moment, she turned and stood with her back against the parapet, looking around her with what she hoped was a convincing air of indifference. There were people around, vendors pushing wheeled barrows reeking of fish leftover from the markets and the rotting leaves of vegetables too old to find customers. Voices spilled into the lanes from the open doors of wine shops. Soon enough, they would be packed to the rafters with the crowd from Place de la Révolution, their thirst for blood slaked, their throats hoarse from screaming, and their thirst for wine piqued by the afternoon's spectacle. She needed to get well away from the area before they started streaming out of the square.

She could see no one watching her; indeed, no one seemed to be aware of her as she stood there. She was an unremarkable figure. Feeling stronger and more confident, Hero turned to walk left along the riverbank under the lime trees.

A tall, thin man, his red cap pulled low over his forehead, stood leaning idly in a doorway, watching the woman move away down the river. There was something about her that didn't seem quite right, something that set her apart from the other women in

112

similar garb scurrying around the streets. He had been trained to look for the different, the not quite right, and he set off after the woman, his stride lengthening as she quickened her pace. Her back was too straight, her head held too high. She moved with all the pride and confidence of an aristocrat.

Eight

Marie Claire was flagging as her escorts supported her stumbling steps through the narrow streets. She seemed to be moving through thick sludge, each footstep a gigantic effort despite the strong arms on either side. She found it hard to breathe after the weeks of incarceration in the filthy dungeons of the Conciergerie, where the air had been damp and pestilential and the moans and groans of her despairing fellow prisoners were never silent.

With a muttered curse, Alec bent and lifted her in his arms. She was incredibly light, even for someone who had always been small and fragile — in appearance, at least. But now she seemed almost weightless, and it frightened him. He started at a half run down the street, heedless now of drawing attention to themselves, his one thought to get his beloved into the warmth and safety of the house.

William frowned but followed, quickening his own pace even as his eyes darted from side to side, looking always for a watcher. "Go around the back," he instructed as they approached the house. "I'll make sure all's clear here."

Alec turned into the narrow passage alongside the house, carrying Marie Claire easily. He edged the gate open with his elbow and stepped into the yard, pushing the gate shut with the heel of his boot. The sun had gone down, and a chill was creeping into the evening air as the evening star rose bright against the darkening sky. Marie Claire shivered in his arms, and he cursed again, hugging her tightly against his chest. "Just a few minutes, and you'll be in the warm, sweetheart." Lamplight showed through the unshuttered window alongside the door. He kicked at the latter, and it was opened almost instantly, a circle of anxious faces turned towards him as he stepped inside with his burden.

William waited on the street until he was certain no one was paying him or the house any attention before rapping on the shutter in the familiar pattern. The door opened, and he stepped quickly inside, demanding over his shoulder as he strode to the kitchen, "Is Marcus back yet?"

"Not yet," Stephen replied. "All went well?"

"Aye. We have the girl safe, at least." He walked into the kitchen, where Marie Claire slumped in the rocker in front of the range, Alec kneeling at her feet, chafing her icy hands.

William poured brandy into a glass and brought it over to the girl. "Drink this slowly. It will warm you . . . Alec, she needs food."

Marie Claire shook her head. "No . . . no . . . please, I couldn't eat, it will make me sick again." She took a wary sip of the brandy and leaned her head back against the chair, her cheeks deathly white, her fair hair hanging in lank strands around her small face.

William merely nodded his acceptance and went to pour brandy for himself and Alec. He had just set down the flask when the kitchen door opened to admit Marcus. "All well?" William asked tersely.

"No one followed me." Marcus helped himself to brandy and turned to look more closely at their rescued prisoner. "Poor girl," he murmured to William. "She looks half dead."

"Hardly surprising." William glanced at the unshuttered window. It was almost full

116

dark. "Where the hell is Hero? She should be back by now."

"Maybe it took her a while to get out of the crowd," Marcus suggested. "It was packed pretty tight."

"Mmm." William didn't sound convinced. He glanced at Alec, still kneeling beside his fiancée, chafing her hands, urging her to drink the brandy. After a moment, he left the kitchen and opened the door to the street. He looked down the hill, where the darkness seemed to be climbing upwards from the river below. There was no one around, no clop of wooden clogs on the cobbles, although the sounds from the wine shops and taverns in the square at the foot of the hill were clear enough on the still air.

He frowned, tapping his fingers impatiently against his thigh. He should not have left her to make her own way. He had had his doubts, but Hero had sounded so confident, and from everything he'd seen of her, she had an instinct for looking after herself. There was nothing of the naïve ingenue about Lady Hermione Fanshawe. She had made her own way from Dover to Paris, for God's sake. Of course, she could get herself from Place de la Révolution to the Rue St. André des Arts without mishap.

So where was she?

117

She'd been careless enough once to get herself thrown into the prison of La Force. But then, so had he, he reminded himself. The streets were hazardous at the best of times and to anyone on them. He took a step down the hill and then stopped. There was no point going to look for her; she could be approaching from any one of a number of directions, and he could easily miss her. With a muttered oath, he turned back to the house, glancing once more up and down the quiet, darkened street before going inside.

The great square in front of Notre Dame was usually a crowded public space, but it was quiet when Hero crossed beneath the shadow of the building, heading for the narrow wooden bridge across the river. The clergy were no longer an active presence in the city, or indeed in most of the country, vilified almost as much as the loathed aristocrats, and religious edifices were shuttered if they had not already been ransacked. In the daytime, a thriving market occupied the square, but now, with most of the citizens watching the afternoon executions at the various sites around the city, it was almost deserted. She made her way towards the narrow bridge. It had once been the only pedestrian way across the Seine, but since the erection of the Pont Neuf, it had fallen into disrepair, and the wooden footboards were rotting in places.

As she stepped onto the bridge, a prickle of alarm ran along her spine. Her footstep hesitated for a second, but then she strode out more confidently, the fine hairs on her nape pricking but her mind clear. If she was being followed, she must not show any sign of awareness or alarm. Halfway across the bridge, she paused, leaning idly against the splintering wooden rail, looking up the river towards the Conciergerie as casually as if she were simply taking an evening stroll, except that every muscle in her body was as taut and rigid as steel.

"Bon soir, citoyenne."

The voice from behind her made her heart race, but she folded her arms on the railing and turned her head, offering the speaker a polite nod. *"Citoyen."* Her heart was like an out-of-control racehorse, but she remained steadily where she was, and after a moment, the man walked on across the bridge to the Quai de la Tournelle on the far bank, his tall, thin figure disappearing into the shadows.

Was he following her? Waiting for her . . . waiting to pounce over there in the shadows?

Every inch of her skin warned of danger; she felt like a doe, hearing the hunters' trumpets, the baying of the dogs. And her mind told her, cold and clear, to trust her instincts. The man meant her harm, whether he was an agent of the Committee of Public Safety or simply a man seeing a lone woman as prey. Either way, she was not crossing the bridge now.

Behind her lay the cathedral and beyond that the bustling lanes and houses of the Île St. Louis. She could lose herself there and find some other way back to Rue St. André des Arts. Without a second thought, Hero swung on her heel and walked fast back across the bridge, prepared now to lose herself in the blood-satiated crowds pouring from Place de la Révolution into the square in front of the cathedral. She didn't look behind her to see if he was coming back across the bridge again but plunged into the nearest crowd of people, dodging and twisting her way to the maze of crooked streets running behind the cathedral, avoiding the darker ones, keeping to those lit by lamps from house windows. She had no idea of the time, intent only on keeping herself surrounded by people, blending with them as she threaded her way through the maze, finally ducking down a shallow flight of stone steps to the riverbank, where a wherry bobbed against the quay, its owner sucking on a pipe, staring at the black waters of the Seine.

"Ten sous to take me across to the steps at St. Michel?" she asked, pulling her red cap down over her forehead with one hand as she dug into the pocket of her grimy apron with the other.

The wherry man spat into the river, took the handful of coins she held on her flat palm, and untied the little craft while Hero stepped into it, sitting down hastily as it dipped and swayed with her movements.

The river was quite narrow at this point, but Hero had specified the steps at St. Michel, so the wherry man had to pull strongly upriver against the evening tide. Hero's gaze remained riveted to the far bank as they went beneath the Notre Dame bridge, lit fitfully now by sconced torches flaring in the evening breeze. Was he still waiting? But he couldn't be. She had no idea how long she'd been dodging the lanes and crowds, but too long, surely, for anyone to be waiting for her to reappear. And she was positive no one was on her trail now.

At the steps, the oarsman offered no help as she clambered out of the rickety boat, merely whistling through his teeth as he gazed trancelike at the dark river. Hero dived once more into the rowdy crowds packing the narrow medieval alleys of St. Michel. It was a short walk to Place St. André des Arts, through a fetid lane, and from the square, she began the steep climb up the hill. Hero was as sure as she could be that no one was on her heels as she left the noise and drunken revelry behind her. But when she reached the door of number 7, she walked past it, crossed the street, ducked into an alley, and waited, listening. Nothing. No warning sixth sense, no eyes on her back, no loitering presence on the street.

Confident at last, she walked back to the door of number 7 and rapped the rhythm on the shutters.

The door was opened almost instantly, and she found herself facing a wall of fury. "Where the devil have you been? Everyone else has been back for hours." Even as he spoke, William's hands were on her, yanking her into the house so fast her feet seemed to lose touch with the ground. He was propelling her upstairs, his hand at the small of her back, driving her upwards even as his angry words poured over her. His voice was low but nonetheless ferocious as he pushed her into the small bedchamber on the top floor. "Do you have any idea what we've been going through, worrying about you? Your brother's beside himself . . ."

His hands were on her upper arms now, his grip tight as he shook her, the guilt, anger, and fear of the last several hours finally unpenned.

"For God's sake, girl, it's hell out there."

"Do you think I don't know that?" Hero cried in an undertone as fierce as his. "I've been dodging and ducking those savage beasts for hours. Just stop it . . . let me go." She twisted desperately in his hold, and then abruptly, her angry protests were lost as his arms came around her, encircling her, holding her tight against the taut, muscular power of his body, and his mouth hard on hers silenced her.

The maelstrom of anger, passion, confusion, and relief coalesced into a single need. She fell back onto the bed as he came down with her, his hands pushing up her skirts, pulling apart her bodice, as she fumbled with his britches, tugged at his shirt. They came together in a glorious surge of sensation, in the violent aftermath of anger, of relief after the hideous tensions of the afternoon's events. Hero's back arched as the tight coil of rough passion seemed to tear her apart. William's hips pressed into hers before he wrenched himself sideways with a low cry, grasping her to him so that she felt his seed pulsing hot against her belly, and her body felt as if it were melting, simply a formless mass, her limbs sprawled where they fell.

But finally, reality intruded, the contours of the small room took shape once more, and the feel of the mattress beneath her became solid. Hero lay still and silent for a moment, wondering why she had responded to the violence of his lovemaking. He hadn't hurt her, and she had responded with the same flaring passion, but it had been like nothing she had ever experienced or could have imagined.

He lay heavily still half upon her, crushing her into the bed, and she asked softly, "What was that? Why such ferocity?"

William rolled away onto his back, his chest heaving, sweat still glistening in the hollow of his throat. He reached out a hand to rest on her bared belly. "I don't know, exactly. Suddenly, all the fear, the tension, the anxiety, the need . . . responsibility . . . to get these innocents out of the hands of the Committee, to save them . . . sometimes it's a spring too tightly wound, and it gives way. Worrying about you was somehow the last straw. I knew that if anything had happened to you, it would be my fault, and when I saw you, knew you were safe, something just broke inside me."

He turned sideways, resting on an elbow, a finger tracing her collarbone, trailing down into the damp cleft of her breasts, his eyes warm but also apologetic.

"I didn't hurt you?"

She shook her head, smiling a little as she reached up to brush the stray lock of hair from his forehead.

"Did I frighten you?"

Again, she shook her head. "Surprised me, perhaps, but I had the same need, I think. I wanted what you wanted." She gave a little laugh. "Except, of course, that I didn't know it." The feeling of safety, for all its impermanence, was for this moment almost overwhelming. Marie Claire was safe downstairs in the kitchen, and in this small, separate space under the eaves, the hideous noise and riot of the city were held at bay. For now, this purely human passion could be indulged without guilt or fear.

"So what happened?" William asked. "Where have you been all this time?"

"I did what you told me to do. I felt danger, someone watching me. A man accosted me on the Notre Dame bridge, so I

125

worked my way through the lanes to Île St. Louis and then crossed the river by boat at the end of the island. I came straight back once I was sure it was safe." She turned her head to look at him, her gaze both questioning and a little defensive. "Did I do anything wrong?"

William flung his hands above his head, staring ruefully up at the cracked plaster ceiling. "Forgive me, Hero. I was so anxious for you . . . I felt such guilt, I suppose. You're so untried at this business, but then, in other ways, you're not untried. I told myself you could and should be able to do this, because we needed you. I was thinking only of the mission." A grim smile touched his mouth.

Hero leaned over and ran a finger over his lips, smoothing away the grimness. "You have to understand, William, that I didn't ask or want you to consider me except as necessary to the business of rescuing Marie Claire. I know I must seem young and untried; after all, I'm a sheltered, privileged brat, product of the English aristocracy." Her laugh had a touch of acid to it. "But I'm probably stronger than you think."

He sat up, swinging his legs to the floor. "That, my dear, is a lesson I learned well this afternoon." He reached down and pulled her to her feet. "Can you make yourself respectable enough to appear downstairs? Your brother has been out of his mind with worry, and Marie Claire needs the attentions that only a member of her own sex can give her."

Hero found this return to business oddly reassuring. She felt not a smidgen of guilt for those moments of passionate need. She had no reason to feel guilt. She was betraying no one. And then she heard herself ask abruptly, "Is there a woman waiting for you somewhere, William?" Her gaze went to his face, watching his response with an almost painful intensity.

An unmistakable shadow crossed his eyes, but he shook his head. "No, Hero. I don't live the kind of life that would make that possible."

"So you love where and when you please?" she asked lightly.

"Where and when it's practicable," he corrected. He came over to her, taking her chin between finger and thumb. "I cannot make promises, Hero. I enjoy your company. I enjoyed our lovemaking and will enjoy it again if you wish it also, but I have nothing more . . . more —"

"More permanent to offer," she interrupted with a quick shake of her head. "I no more wish for that than you do, William."

His fingers tightened for a moment on her chin. "What do you wish for, then?"

She shrugged. "I haven't discovered yet. But for the present, I'll take what I'm offered."

"We understand each other, then."

She smiled. "It would seem so. You go ahead of me. There's some water in the jug; I would freshen myself a little."

William looked closely at her for a moment and then nodded and left the chamber. Hero moved to the jug and basin on the washstand, shrugging out of her unlaced bodice, stripping off her skirt and petticoat. As she washed the day's grime and the remnants of that ferocious passion from her skin, she wondered if she would ever discover exactly what she wanted . . . now that all her assumptions about her future life had been drowned with Tom in the deep blue sea.

NINE

Hero entered the kitchen feeling much refreshed. She had no idea what any of the kitchen's occupants thought about her absence with William, but no one referred to it, although Alec gave her a quick searching look. She smiled her reassurance and instantly turned her attention to Marie Claire, who seemed only half conscious in the rocker.

"What can we do for her, Hero?" Alec's voice had a note of desperation in it. "I can't seem to rouse her. None of us knows what to do to help her."

Hero had no nursing experience, but she knew exactly what she would need in Marie Claire's place and said with conviction, "Hot water, lots of it, and a screen in front of the fire so we'll have some privacy, and then something for her to wear. Those clothes are probably crawling with vermin; we'll have to burn them. One of your shirts

129

would do, Alec, and a mantle of some kind. Your traveling cloak will do for the moment."

Her demands were met in short order. "And now we need fresh milk, brandy and sugar, cloves, cinnamon, any spices you can find," Hero said finally. "A sack posset will give her some strength, and then perhaps she'll sleep properly."

William stood up. "I'll get the provisions. Everyone else, make yourselves scarce, give the ladies some privacy. Alec, there's nothing you can do here for the moment."

Within minutes, Hero was alone with Marie Claire. The girl tried to help as Hero undressed her, but she was so weak that every movement was a supreme effort. However, she was finally naked, and her filthy prison garments were burning in the fire, the lice popping merrily as the flames swallowed them. Hero managed to wash the girl's hair with harsh lye soap that would kill anything that came in contact with it, and Marie Claire managed to stand, holding on to the chair, so that she could wash her body.

"Hero, thank you," Marie Claire murmured as Hero maneuvered her arms into Alec's shirt of soft linen, lace edging the sleeves and collar. She had a diminutive

130

figure, and Alec was tall and broad, and the garment swamped her, falling to her knees.

"That's repectable enough," Hero said cheerfully, "but wrap up in the cloak, too; it'll keep you warm." She rubbed Marie Claire's damp hair, combing out the long, silvery, fair strands with her fingers. "I don't have a brush or comb," she said apologetically. "I had a small cloak bag when I left home, but I didn't have it with me when I landed in jail, and of course, there's been no opportunity to go back for it."

"You were in jail, Hero?" Marie Claire seemed to be regaining her strength. She stared at Hero in astonishment. "I . . . I don't understand anything. What are you doing here? I couldn't believe it was you at the tumbrel . . . it was like a dream." She shook her head with a shudder of remembered horror. "I thought I had already died, that it was all over at last and seeing you was a death dream." She crossed her hands over her breasts with another convulsive shiver.

Hero could think of nothing to say; the stark horror of Marie Claire's experience overwhelmed her for a moment. Finally, she said, "Try not to dwell on it now. You need to get your strength back, because we'll be leaving here soon, and I don't think it will

131

be a particularly smooth journey." She offered a wry smile. "I'm getting accustomed to thinking of it all as an adventure. Not all pleasant, I admit, but nothing to what you've been through, my dear. But that is over now," she added with a conviction that she didn't entirely feel. "You're among friends, and I doubt Alec will allow you out of his sight."

She moved the screen aside and settled Marie Claire back in the rocker, wrapped in Alec's velvet-lined cloak. Then she went to the door and called, "Alec, can you help?"

He had been waiting on the stairs for the summons and was there instantly. "How is she?" He rushed past his sister to see for himself without waiting for her response. "Oh, you look better, my dearest." He bent to kiss her pale face, and Marie Claire managed the semblance of a smile.

"She'll be better still when I can make a posset," Hero declared. "Could you get rid of that dirty water and put the screen away?"

Alec accepted the tasks with ready good humor and was just folding the screen when William came in through the yard. He set the provisions on the table. "I think that's everything you asked for, Hero, but I also found some fresh eggs." He placed four brown eggs carefully on the table.

"Where did you find them?" Hero asked, picking one up admiringly. Fresh eggs were hard to come by in the city.

"Ask me no questions, and I'll tell you no lies," he said with a teasing grin.

"You stole them?"

He merely shrugged. "They were just asking to be collected . . . I found cinnamon in the wine shop and some cloves. He set a twist of paper beside the eggs. "Brandy we have in plentiful supply."

"Then I'll get on with it." Hero took a small pan from the dresser and poured in the milk, adding the cinnamon stick, sugar, and cloves and curdling the mixture with brandy as it heated. She had a sudden longing to drink it herself as the heady fragrance rose from the pan, and she realized that she'd eaten nothing since that morning. As far as she knew, none of them had. She poured the posset into a pewter tankard and handed it to Alec, cautioning, "Go slowly with it; it's quite strong, and it's hot."

She turned back to the room with an involuntary sigh and saw William's eyes fixed upon her. "You're dead on your feet," he said. "Come and sit down here." He indicated the bench beside him. "You need to eat."

"I own I'm starving," she said. "Did you eat?"

"While we were waiting for you to come in out of the cold," he said, a trifle drily. "However, the eggs are for you. Sit there, drink this, and don't move." He poured wine for her, set it in front of her, and went to the range.

"Can you cook, too?" she asked with mock surprise. "It seems there's no end to your accomplishments, sir."

"You don't know the half of them," he responded, breaking the eggs into a bowl.

"Then I can't wait to discover the rest," she murmured with a suggestive smile, for the moment forgetting that they were not alone. The fierceness of William's silencing scowl reminded her with a sharp shock, and she felt herself blush, burying her nose in her wineglass even as she thought with a touch of defiance that it could hardly matter if their companions knew of their intimacy. It was no one's business but their own. Alec might be entitled to an opinion, but he certainly wouldn't judge his twin or challenge William to a duel to defend his sister's honor. She suppressed her laughter at the latter thought, reflecting that in present circumstances, the still-scowling William would certainly consider it unseemly levity.

It was strange that he should have this prudish streak, she thought. He seemed such an adventurer, a man prepared to take life on its own terms even as he steered for his own true north. A deep yawn suddenly overtook her, and her eyelids drooped as a wave of sleepiness swept over her.

"Here, eat this, and then you can sleep." William set a plate before her. She glanced up at him with a tentative smile and was relieved when he returned it, saying lightly, "I trust my omelet meets with your approval, madame."

"It looks perfect." She took up her fork and pierced the golden brown exterior. It tasted as good as it looked, delicately flavored with herbs.

"You and Marie Claire will share the bedchamber on the top floor," William continued. "I'll take the first watch. Marcus, you can take over in four hours."

Marcus nodded. "Do you expect trouble?"

"I don't know." William spoke thoughtfully. "But I have a feeling that they're close, and we can't afford to be taken unaware. I want to assume that whoever was following Hero did indeed lose her, but I'm not prepared to take any risks, so we leave at first light."

"All together?" Stephen asked.

"No, in twos. We'll rendezvous at Châtelet and go down together to take the underground route out of the city."

Marcus grimaced. "I suppose we must, but it's a loathsome route."

"We haven't had time to make preparations for a more conventional exit," William pointed out.

"Marie Claire needs clothes." Hero scraped up the last of her omelet.

"Yes . . . she'll have to wear the britches and shirt you were wearing. You'll stay dressed as you are."

"At least they're washed," Hero observed.

"Believe me, dear girl, in these circumstances, it would almost be better if they weren't," William stated.

"No, indeed," Marcus agreed with a grim smile.

Hero looked puzzled, but before she could ask for enlightenment, Alec stood up with Marie Claire in his arms. "She's asleep. I'll carry her upstairs. Come with me, Hero. I won't leave her alone."

"No, of course not." Hero got up from the table instantly. She glanced a little ruefully at William. There was nothing to be done, of course, but she had hoped they would be spending the night together. His eyebrows flicked upwards in amused comprehension, and she felt a touch of resentment that he should treat her obvious disappointment so lightly.

With a cool good-night, she followed Alec out of the kitchen and upstairs. He laid his burden gently on the tumbled bed, and Hero moved swiftly to rearrange the coverlets over the sleeping girl.

Alec smoothed Marie Claire's hair before straightening. "I'm guessing your plans for the night have been disrupted." He regarded his sister with narrowed eyes. "Are you sure it's wise? William Ducasse is no Tom."

"If he were, I wouldn't find him attractive," Hero responded, her voice, like his, barely above a whisper. "Any man who could be in any way compared to Tom would . . . would be anathema. I couldn't abide the possibility of making comparisons, Alec. William is so different, and, well . . ." She shrugged. "He suits my present mood. I find him exciting, invigorating. Life seems worth living again."

"Then I have no more to say on the subject." Alec smiled at her, although his green eyes still contained the touch of concern they had held since the news of Tom's loss. He looked back at the sleeping girl and gave a deep, worried sigh. "Dear God, I don't know how Marie Claire will hold up on the journey. She's so weak."

"I think you'll find her stronger than you believe," Hero said softly. "She has survived all these months in hell. A good sleep and some decent food will do wonders."

"I hope you're right." He bent and kissed his sister's cheek. "Don't leave her, will you? I couldn't bear her to wake and not know where she is."

"Don't worry, love, I won't let that happen. Now, go and get some rest yourself. I have a feeling that tomorrow's not going to be an easy day."

Alec shook his head. "That's for sure. But call me at once if Marie Claire needs me."

"I will do." She shooed him out of the chamber and sank onto the bed to take off her shoes, swamped once more with invincible weariness as she undressed. She was about to slip naked into bed beside Marie Claire when the door opened softly and William stepped in, closing it softly behind him.

His gaze ran over Hero's naked form, poised with one knee on the bed as she prepared to get in. "Oh, dear," he said softly. "That really isn't fair, you know."

"What isn't?" Her fatigue seemed to diminish as she read the lascivious look in his eyes.

"You know quite well. For the love of God, get under the covers."

Hero chuckled softly but obliged. It was not fair for either of them to continue a game they could not possibly conclude.

"I came up for my jerkin." He went to the chest for the garment and then walked to the window, looking down on the street far below. "I wish I knew where they were."

"You don't really think I led them here, do you?" She sat up in bed, hugging her drawn-up knees.

"It doesn't matter if you did. It was going to happen sooner or later," he responded with a dismissive gesture. "We've already overstayed in this house for safety's sake. Usually, we move every couple of weeks, but we've been busier than usual just recently. They seem to have stepped up the rate of executions, and it's as much as we can do to get one family out a week. And now . . ."

He didn't finish his sentence, and after a moment, she prompted, "And now?"

"And now we have to get out of the country for a while. I am convinced we have the Lizard's attention, and once he sets his mind to a certain quarry, he doesn't rest until he has it in the net. I'm not so altruistic that I'm prepared to stay in the dragon's den and offer my head on a platter."

Hero shivered and drew the cover up tighter beneath her chin. "No. So you'll come to England with us?"

"For a while." He turned back from the window. "Which means that we leave a host of people with no hope of rescue." His expression was dark, his eyes unreadable.

"You cannot take responsibility for every one of them, William," she said softly. "No one could expect you to feel that you must."

"Maybe not." He shook his head briskly. "But I do, nevertheless." He snuffed the single candle, but bright moonlight lit the room through the unshuttered window. "Someone will wake you before dawn. Can you help Marie Claire get dressed?"

"Of course."

"Good . . . then we will leave at first light. You, me, Alec, and Marie Claire."

"But isn't that too many of us together? You said we would go in pairs."

"Alec cannot manage Marie Claire alone." He put his hand on the door latch.

"Then you accompany them, and I will make my own way."

"Oh, no, that you won't . . . not after this afternoon," he said firmly. "We'll all go together, and you, my dear Hero, will play

140

your part exactly as I direct. Understood?" His eyes held hers with unmistakable determination.

"If you insist, sir," she said with feigned meekness, fluttering her eyelashes at him.

His eyes narrowed. "Tread lightly, my dear. You're on perilous ground."

Hero merely chuckled. "I bid you good night, sir." She slid down beneath the covers as William opened the door, his own good-night hanging for a moment in the air before the door closed behind him.

TEN

They were like rats, just like the huge sewer rats scurrying through the evil darkness. Hero suppressed a shudder of revulsion as she splashed barefoot through the foul-smelling water of the underground stream, careful to keep her hands from touching the slimy walls on either side. No one spoke, all unwilling to open their mouths to take in the filthy air any more than they had to. She breathed only when she had no choice. Alec was just in front of her, supporting Marie Claire, who struggled to keep her footing and gamely tried to keep herself from leaning too much weight upon Alec, who was having his own difficulties keeping his balance.

William came behind Hero, holding aloft a pitch torch that sent the eerie shadows of the little procession climbing the concave walls of the tunnel. It illuminated the rats but also served to send them scurrying into the shadows ahead.

It was hard to believe that above them lay the city, with its shrieking mobs and yelling vendors, the broad, dark waters of the Seine and the great buildings and wide spaces, the thronged crooked alleyways and narrow medieval streets. They were in the under-belly of one of the greatest cities in the world, the place where the glittering gran-deur of palaces and grand *hôtels* of the aristocracy excreted their waste into the underground streams that crisscrossed the metropolis.

They had been walking through the reek-ing stream for so long that Hero had lost track of the time. She knew they had five miles of these waterways to traverse before they would emerge beyond the city walls at the river, and until then, there was nothing to be done but to put one foot in front of the other and try not to think of what she was walking through.

Marcus led the little procession, holding his own pitch torch high. He disappeared around a corner, and when Hero turned it herself, she saw that the group had stopped on what looked like a makeshift beach at the side of the sewer stream. She stepped out of the water onto relatively dry ground with a sigh of relief. Alec held Marie Claire close to him, supporting her weight.

William stepped up beside Hero. "Is the skiff here, Marcus?" His voice sounded unnaturally loud after the silence of the last hour.

"Aye, we're in luck." Marcus stepped gingerly around the huddled group and came over to William. "It's tied to a stake just a few yards ahead. I reckon it'll just hold Alec and the girl."

"Good . . . she can't go any farther under her own steam." He spoke softly to Alec. "You and Marie Claire will take the skiff. There's a paddle of sorts. Just follow the stream, and it will take you to the grating at the end. Leave it unlatched for us."

"Hero should go with her in the skiff, not me," Alec declared.

"No," Hero stated firmly. "You'll be better paddling the boat than I will be. I'm perfectly all right as I am."

"I don't want the women going alone, and Hero's perfectly strong enough to keep walking." William's decisive tone settled the matter.

"Yes, tough as old boots, I am," Hero said with an attempt at jocularity. "What's a little sewage between friends when all's said and done?" She felt William's quick glance of approval, and it warmed her. He expected nothing else of her, and that gave her renewed strength.

Alec still seemed to hesitate, but then Marie Claire moaned softly and bit her lip hard to keep the sound from escaping again. "Let's go, then. The air down here is probably plague-ridden. She doesn't have the strength to combat it."

"Come." William lifted Marie Claire easily and carried her to the tiny skiff, little more than a raft with low sides and a single thwart. He set her down on the bottom of the boat, and Alec stepped gingerly in to sit on the thwart, taking up the paddle. "We'll see you in the fresh air, then."

"Just follow the stream." William stepped back, and Alec dipped the paddle into the scum, propelling the small craft down the dark tunnel.

"Let's go, people." William waved a hand forward, and the group set off again, splashing doggedly through the stream.

Hero let time slip away, concentrating only on breathing as little as possible and keeping her eyes on the torch Marcus still held at the front of the line. He and William had replenished their lights at the beach, and they flared more strongly now. After what seemed an eternity, Hero caught a sense of something against her cheek, the merest sensation of moving air. She snapped back to full awareness, seeing Marcus's torch flare and gutter as a draft caught the flame. Ahead was the faintest glimmer of light, real light, daylight.

William's hand had been on her back for hours now, a warm, encouraging pressure, propelling her forward. "Light at the end of the tunnel," he murmured into her ear. "A few more yards."

She increased her pace as those in front of her surged ahead. The skiff was tied to a post at the end of the tunnel, with no sign of Alec or Marie Claire. Closing off the end of the tunnel was a grating. Marcus pushed against it, and it swung open. He wriggled sideways through the gap, jumping down from the ledge onto a narrow sandy strip at the edge of the river. The sewer stream debouched into the river at this point, and above him rose the riverbank.

Hero followed the others into the air, jumping onto the sandy strip. Instantly, without a second thought, she paddled into the river shallows, cleansing her feet in the water with a sigh of relief.

"There's no time for lingering," William said briskly. "Get up onto the bank."

Reluctantly, Hero left the cleansing water and began to scramble up the steep bank to the flat ground above. William's hand was under her backside, pushing her upwards as she felt for toeholds in the unstable soil, and a hand came down from above to haul her up the last foot. She stood, breathing deeply of the fresh air, wondering if she would ever feel truly clean again, ever get rid of the stench in her nostrils. Alec was kneeling on the bank beside Marie Claire, who lay full-length, her eyes closed, her breast fluttering unevenly with each shallow breath.

William hoisted himself onto the bank behind Hero. He went to kneel beside the supine figure, lifting her wrist to feel her pulse. He shrugged off the knapsack he was carrying on his back and set it on the grass. "Brandy," he instructed, taking out a flask, which he held to her lips, forcing a few drops into her mouth. She choked and coughed, and her eyes opened.

"Forgive me," she said. "I don't mean to be so feeble."

"You're not," he said gently. "You're a trooper, my dear. Once we put a few miles behind us, we will stop, and you may rest for as long as possible. But we cannot stop here." He stood up, taking a swallow of brandy himself as he did so. "We'll carry you until we can commandeer a boat. Hero, you need a swallow of this, but not too much. You've still got a fair way to go." He gave her the flask.

Hero took a deep draught. It made her head spin but seemed to clear some of the noxious fumes of the sewer from her throat and chest. She passed it to Alec and then sat down abruptly on the grass. She felt suddenly as weak as a kitten, but there was no way this enterprise could carry two invalid ladies. And Marie Claire had a lot more right to protective treatment than she did. She pulled the knapsack towards her and rummaged for her shoes, which William had carried with his own.

William shot her a quick assessing glance. She was very pale, but he could not afford to be overtly considerate. From what he had seen of Lady Hero in the last few days, he had the feeling that she would gain more strength from the assumption that she would manage because it was expected of her than from sympathy.

"I'll be back in a minute," he said, and went over to where the other men were gathered on the riverbank.

Hero remained where she was, watching the conclave, wondering only idly what they were discussing. It didn't seem to matter too much in her present enervated state.

She wasn't particularly surprised when, with brief handshakes, they went off in pairs. She knew now that they never traveled together in the open.

William came back to where the three of them were sitting. "Come now," he said briskly, giving Hero his hand to pull her to her feet. "We can't hang around here; we're still too close to the city, and there are spies everywhere."

Hero nodded and resolutely looked around at their surroundings. The walls of the city were only about half a mile away, and she could just glimpse through the trees lining the riverbank the narrow roadway leading to the city gate. She could hear voices and rolling cart wheels. They were certainly too close to city traffic for comfort.

"Which way do we go?"

William gestured along the bank. "That way. We'll steer clear of the road for as long as possible." He bent to pick up the knapsack. "Do you think you can carry this, Hero? Alec and I will have to carry Marie Claire."

She nodded, and without saying anything further, William held out the straps so that she could sling it onto her back. It was heavier than she expected, but gamely she settled it into the small of her back, supporting it with her hands behind her.

William hesitated for only a second, then turned aside briskly. "Alec, we'll cross hands and make a chair for Marie Claire."

They made slow progress, but the sense of the city's proximity eventually faded, and the countryside opened up around them. They had skirted several hamlets, and open fields stretched in front of them, when William set Marie Claire on her feet and shook the tingling out of his hands. "Let's look for a boat somewhere along the river. There were fishing nets in the gardens in that last village, and fisherfolk tend to have boats."

"But we can't steal it," Hero exclaimed, shocked. "It's someone's livelihood."

"And *our* lives," he pointed out grimly. "However, we'll leave payment enough to salve your conscience, *citoyenne.* Stay here and rest a bit." He moved away along the river, his eyes searching the bank. When he disappeared from view around a bend in the river, Hero felt very vulnerable. She glanced at Alec, who was sitting beside Marie Claire, chafing her hands. He obviously had no thought for anything or anyone but his fiancée. And she could hardly blame him. The girl looked utterly exhausted, her face and lips bloodless.

Hero shrugged gratefully out of the straps

150

of the knapsack and set it down, rolling her aching shoulders and stretching her neck. The knapsack held basic provisions as well as the brandy flask and a flagon of wine. It was no wonder it was heavy, but she was now so ravenous she would have carried anything twice as heavy if it promised food at the end of the journey.

William returned in ten minutes that seemed like hours to the trio on the bank. Hero watched his approach, thinking he moved, ever watchful, with all the grace and stealth of a panther, his shadow falling long on the grass ahead of him. "There's a boat hidden in the rushes about a quarter of a mile away. There's a copse just back from the bank, and we can rest up in the shade through the afternoon and take the boat just after dark, when we can be sure no one will be around."

"Don't fish bite best in the evening?" Hero inquired, remembering words of wisdom from the keeper who managed the trout streams on the Bruton estates in Hampshire.

A fleeting smile touched William's lips. "They do, Milady Fisher, which is why we will wait until dark, when they'll all have returned from the evening's fishing."

Hero grinned and scrambled to her feet, shaking down her skirt and apron. The muck from the sewer stream had dried hard and crusty around the hem, but at least the noxious damp no longer clung to her bare legs. She hoisted the knapsack onto her back again, reflecting that a quarter of a mile was no distance. The men formed the hand chair again, and they set off for the small copse along the bank.

It was cool in the trees, the dappling sun filtering through the leaves on the mossy ground beneath their feet. It was pleasantly springy underfoot, and Hero paused for a moment, listening. She could hear the faint sound of trickling water somewhere up ahead. It was a peaceful sound after the fearful mayhem of the city so wonderfully far behind them. The quiet of the copse was disturbed only by the rustling of tiny forest creatures in the undergrowth and the call of a bird.

"I could stay here forever," Hero announced.

"You can certainly stay for the afternoon," William responded prosaically. "There's a glade up yonder, with a little stream. We'll stop there."

Marie Claire gave a little sigh of relief when she was set down on the mossy turf with her back against a broad oak tree. Her eyes closed.

"Let her sleep," William instructed, helping Hero off with the knapsack. "I'll fetch water from the stream. You see what you can put together for a meal, Hero." He glided away across the glade.

Alec covered his fiancée with his cloak, making a pillow for her with his jerkin, then gently eased her flat to the ground. She made a little sound, curled into a fetal position, and within seconds was deeply asleep.

Hero rummaged in the knapsack. She found bread and cheese, a thick garlic sausage, apples, and a paper twist of coffee. "How do we make coffee without a fire?"

"We don't." William, returning as soundlessly as ever, knelt beside her, setting down his flagon of water. "It's too risky to light one this close to the city. Maybe later tonight, when we've moved downstream. Later this afternoon, I'll see if I can tickle a trout or two."

"Oh, I'm quite good at that," Hero said. "Better even than Alec. We used to do it all the time when we were children. Of course, the river keeper considered it unsportsman-like and was most unpleasant if he ever caught us at it. D'you remember, Alec?"

"Mmm," he murmured, still too occupied with the sleeping Marie Claire to pay serious attention to his sister.

153

Hero shrugged. "We'll try together this afternoon." She took out her small knife from the pocket of her apron and began to slice the sausage. "I am famished."

William chuckled. Society ladies in general did not admit to the grosser needs of the flesh; in fact, if they were to be believed, they lived on air. But then, of course, Hermione Fanshawe was no ordinary Society lady. And the reflection brought a deep frown between his brows. What possible life could she lead when she so clearly didn't fit into the one she'd been born to? He knew to his cost what happened to those who stepped beyond the boundaries of acceptability, and the thought of Hero, with her indomitable, reckless spirit suffering that fate was something he could not countenance. But, for the moment, there was nothing to be done about anything except getting themselves to safety, and that was his responsibility.

"What's the matter? Why are you frowning?" Hero felt a little chill. His sudden displeasure was almost palpable. It had happened several times before, and it always seemed to come from nowhere. It was directed at her, but she couldn't for the life of her imagine what caused it.

"Something we're going to have to discuss

at some future time," he said, spearing a piece of sausage on the point of his knife. "But the issue is moot at present." He tipped up the flagon of crystal clear water and sent a stream down his throat before passing it to Hero.

Alec left the sleeping Marie Claire and came over to them, helping himself to bread and cheese and sausage. He looked drawn and worried, much as he had looked in the months spent waiting for news from her family.

"She'll be all right, love. Once she's had some rest and fresh air and decent food." Hero laid a hand on his arm, offering what reassurance she could. "Perhaps we could find some fresh milk?" She glanced interrogatively at William.

"I've never milked a cow," he said, "but there's always a first time for everything."

"I'm sure we could buy a cup from a farm somewhere," Hero pointed out in a tone of reproof. He didn't seem to be taking the matter seriously enough. And then she reflected that he rarely seemed to make heavy weather of anything — except when his sense of responsibility overwhelmed him, she reminded herself, remembering that fury-borne passion of lovemaking. But however relaxed he seemed, most of the time whatever needed doing always got done, however impossible it appeared.

"Later," he promised. "For now, I intend to have a nap, and I suggest you do the same." He rose to his feet in a leisurely stretch and wandered away into the bushes, presumably to answer a call of nature.

Hero glanced around for a secluded spot for herself as she stood up. A group of shrubs close to the river looked suitable, and she took herself off into their seclusion. She was preparing to leave her private spot when she froze in the process of shaking down her skirts. Voices rose from the river below. They sounded very close, and her heart beat faster. The last thing they needed was inquiring strangers.

She crept as quietly as she could out of the shrubs and back to where Alec was now lying beside Marie Claire, one arm protectively around her sleeping figure. William was repacking the knapsack. He looked up, instantly alert, as she approached softly over the grass. "Men," she whispered. "On the river just a few yards away."

He nodded. "Stay here, and keep quiet." It was a whispered command but nonetheless imperative. Then he strolled casually back the way she had come. Hero hesitated and then followed him, her heart in her throat. Crouching behind a tall stand of reeds, she could see the two men standing on a sandy spit at the side of the river. They didn't look like villagers; they carried muskets slung across their chests, and they wore the cocked hats of members of one of the local militias who patrolled the countryside, sniffing out any antirevolutionary sentiment, accusing and arresting at will those who fell foul of them for any reason, personal or otherwise. They were universally loathed, uneducated and brutish.

She held her breath, watching as William approached them, raising a hand in greeting. They turned and surveyed him as he came onto the spit. He walked casually towards them, his red cap tilted to one side, and Hero saw that his hand was on the slim knife sheathed at his belt. It was a rapier blade, she knew. As lethal as all such weapons were intended to be.

William gestured to the river running by the tip of the spit, and they both followed his hand with their eyes. He was talking with animation. Hero could not hear a word, but she saw as they moved that he was encouraging them to go to the end where it jutted into the river, which flowed fast at that point, a swirling eddy around the sandy tip. They had their backs to him, shading their eyes as they looked across the river to the far bank, following William's gesturing hand.

What happened next was so fast Hero barely caught it. She saw a silver flash, heard a short cry, and one of the men fell forward, his head in the river. The other swung around in surprise, and the knife caught him, so that it looked almost as if he fell upon it. He toppled backwards as William withdrew the knife.

Hero stared in momentary incomprehension. Then it became clear as day. There were two dead men at the end of the spit, and William was now manhandling the bodies into the river, where, with the speed of the current, they would be whisked downstream. Without further thought, she scrambled through the reeds and ran along the spit, bending to help him as he heaved and maneuvered the second body into the whirling eddy of the river. She stood watching blankly as the dead man turned, spun around, and then, caught by the current, disappeared beneath the water, reappearing a few yards farther down, visible for only a moment as the body was swept out of sight around a bend in the river.

She looked at William. "You just killed two men."

"Yes," he agreed, his voice harsh, as he bent to wash the blade of his knife in the water. "Before they took us. If you can't stand the heat, child, you need to stay away from the fire." His voice was cold, a tone she had not heard before, and his expression was dark as the grave. He straightened and turned to her, taking her by the upper arms. "Now, listen to me. When I tell you to stay put, you stay put. Will you understand that?" His fingers were hard on her arms but not painful. They didn't need to be. His point was unmistakable.

She nodded, thinking of Marie Claire, so vulnerable in the glade behind them. They could not have run from the militia with an invalid, and if the militia had taken them, they would all have died. She said tentatively, "You were glad of my help to get rid of them, though, weren't you?"

"Don't try to cozen me," he responded. "I could have managed well enough without you, as you well know. But if you disobey me again on this journey, I won't answer for the consequences. Is that understood, Hero?"

"Yes, up to a point. But supposing a situation arises that you hadn't anticipated, and I can do something about it but it would go against your dictates? What am I supposed to do then?"

She looked genuinely anxious for his answer, and after a moment of disbelief, he said, "I give in. In such a situation, you will follow your own instincts, as always, But believe me, if they lead you astray and cause more trouble, then beware my wrath."

The harshness had left his voice, and there was glinting amusement now in the tawny gold eyes, but Hero understood that some kind of bargain had been made. He was willing to trust her in extremis, but she must be prepared to accept the consequences if her instincts played her false.

"So be it," she said.

"Now that we understand each other, I suggest we take that nap before we try to tickle some trout."

ELEVEN

Hero awoke from her comfortable spot in the indentation between tree roots after a blissful period of unconsciousness. She hitched herself onto an elbow and glanced across to where her brother and Marie Claire lay. Alec was sitting up, his arm around his fiancée as he helped her drink from the water flask. He glanced at his sister as she pulled herself into wakefulness.

"You slept well?"

"Yes, thank you. How is she?"

"Stronger, I think." He set aside the flask and rearranged Marie Claire against his shoulder.

Hero edged over to them, taking the other woman's hand. "How do you feel, love?"

"Better." Marie Claire managed a feeble smile. "I think I just need to sleep."

"Could you eat anything?"

She shook her head. "No, not yet. Just sleep." She slid down again into the mossy space that had held her before. Alec helped her to position herself and covered her again with his cloak. She was instantly asleep.

"It is the best medicine, they say," Hero said with a tentative smile, laying a hand on her twin's arm. "I do think she will make it, Alec. We will all make it out of here."

He nodded slowly. "I don't want to leave her alone."

"No, of course, you mustn't." Hero knelt up, looking around the glade. There was no sign of William. After a moment, she said, "William killed two men just a short while ago."

Alec looked at her, his gaze sharp. "Who were they?"

"Militia. I heard them by the river." Her attempt at a casual shrug was unconvincing. "I told William, and he just killed them . . . with his knife. And pushed them into the river."

Alec looked closely at his sister. "Them or us," he said quietly.

She took a deep breath. "Yes, I know that. My brain knows it, at least."

"But you can't quite accept it?" he said.

"Not quite," she agreed. "And I know it's stupid. I know the danger. I spent a week in that blood-filled city, fighting for my life. And yet there was something so cold, so calculating . . . I don't know, Alec. Maybe I'm a weak and feeble woman after all, when all's said and done."

"When all's said and done, it's hard to have strong feelings for an assassin," her brother stated with brutal clarity. "But you do; it's as simple as that. And William does what he has to do to fulfill a higher purpose. He knew we could never have escaped with Marie Claire the way she is, so he simply did what he always does. What needed to be done."

Hero leaned back against the tree trunk. Nothing Alec had said was surprising. And this most powerful attraction she felt for William Ducasse included that aspect of his character. He asked for no quarter, and he took no prisoners. It was for her a most potent attraction . . . and what that said about her she didn't know.

After a few moments, she stood up, stretching, feeling absurdly well for the circumstances. William would be at the river tickling trout. She set off, careful not to make a noise crackling through the underbrush, and emerged on the riverbank a few minutes later. William lay on his belly a few feet ahead of her, his hand in the water. She stopped to watch him, his utter silence and concentration, and the stillness seeped into her as she took a deep breath. She knew what it felt like, that quiet, perfect moment when it was just you and your intention, a battle of wits and will with the fish under the stone.

She trod soundlessly to the bank and slipped onto her belly, looking into the brown shallows of the river under the bank, where the swift current didn't reach. And she saw the speckled brown trout he was after, lying still and flat under a stone amidst the rushes. If William was aware of her presence, he gave no sign, and she made no move to disturb his concentration.

His fingers moved delicately through the water, taunting the trout, challenging it, and then his hand moved, swift as an eel, and caught the fish above the gills, lifting it thrashing out of the water. Hero reached for the heavy stick she had seen lying ready beside William, and with a swift, neat movement, she gaffed the wriggling trout. It was over in a moment, the fish falling still on the bank, William pushing back onto his knees, smiling down at her.

"Well, you are quite the fisherman, my lady. My thanks for a speedy save."

"You were ready for him," she said, rolling onto her back on the bank, her eyes smiling. "Did you rest at all?"

"I did." He knelt above her, wiping his wet hands on his jerkin. "You seemed to be sleeping peacefully."

She stretched, lifting her arms to him. "I did, but I seem very wide awake now." She linked her hands behind his neck, drawing his head down to hers. For a moment, he hung above her, his tawny gold eyes filled with light, his mouth firm, his body braced on his elbows, and then he brought his mouth to hers, and this was a soft, gentle, exploratory kiss, so unlike the rough, needy passion of their previous connection. His tongue moved within her mouth, stroking the sides of her cheeks, teasing her own tongue with little darting movements, sliding over her lips, and Hero responded, tasting his mouth, her tongue dancing with the suppleness of his, relishing the soft sweetness of his inner cheeks.

He lifted his mouth from hers for a moment, rearing back on his heels, moving a hand over her face, tracing its lines and contours, a finger painting the curve of her lips. Then he unlaced her bodice, slowly, carefully, parting the sides to reveal her breasts. His lips caressed her nipples as they rose erect beneath the touch of his tongue. His hands spanned her ribcage as he opened the bodice even further, so that she felt the air cool on her belly. His lips painted a liquid caress through the cleft of her breasts and down to her navel, dipping into the sweet indentation, before flicking sideways to brush a moist kiss across her hip bones as his hands pushed her loosened skirt down over her hips.

She lifted her hips, and he pushed the skirt and petticoat down to her knees, his flat palm stroking her belly. A finger slid between her thighs, exploring, feeling the heated core of her sex rise hard beneath his touch. Hero gasped as his fingers slid inside her, teasing, stroking, flooding her with sensations more intense than any she had experienced. Her hips bucked, her hands tightened around his neck, and she gave herself up to the exquisite moment of fulfillment as the last rays of the dying sun warmed her closed eyelids.

Even as her body still pulsed from that delicious moment of pure pleasure, he unfastened his britches, rising above her for a moment, his eyes holding hers, before he entered her in a slow glide, his penis sheathing itself within her moist and welcoming body. She tightened her internal muscles around him as he pushed against the very edge of her womb, and he gave a little cry of surprised pleasure, then withdrew to the edge of her body, watching her face, her smile as the tip of her tongue touched her lips in a moment of pure sensual delight, and then he plunged deep within her to become a part of her, his sex throbbing deep into her core, and Hero heard herself cry out, her hips lifting, her buttocks tightening, as the shafts of sensation shot through her body with such intensity she was no longer sure whether it was pain or pleasure she felt.

And then it was over. She felt herself sinking into the earth beneath her, her hips falling heavily, her legs sprawled, and William fell alongside her, his penis still pulsing against her thigh, one arm flung across her body.

No anger had fueled that explosion. Passion, pure and simple, Hero thought, her hand resting on his chest, feeling the rapidly beating heart. And it was wonderful. For a wistful moment, she thought how lovely it would be to fall asleep now in a deep shared bed, with nothing to worry about. Instead, there were two dead men surging on the tide downriver, a weak and ailing young woman, and many miles as well as the Channel to cross before the possibility of a bed, shared or otherwise, could be considered as anything more than a dream.

William stirred first. He rolled sideways and stood up, fastening his britches. He looked down at Hero, still inert on the bank. "It's almost dark, and you have to move, sweetheart. We need to take the boat and get downstream, where we can make a fire and cook the fish." He bent to take her hands, pulling her to her feet.

Hero shook down her skirts, refastened her bodice, and flexed her shoulders. "How do we take the boat?"

He tilted her chin on his forefinger. "Such an indomitable Hero you are. Alec and I will take it, while you help Marie Claire to her feet. She will need certain things," he added delicately.

Hero interpreted that correctly as meaning that the other woman would need to relieve herself before they set off again. "Will you gut the trout?"

"When we get where we can cook it." He picked up the fish and tore loose some reeds from the bank, wrapping them around the glistening trout. "You take care of Marie Claire. Alec and I will see to the rest." He gestured ahead of him back to the glade.

Alec was sitting up beside Marie Claire, hugging his knees, as they reappeared. His eyes met his sister's for barely an instant in the gathering dusk, but it was enough to tell

168

him what they had been doing in their prolonged absence. "Did you catch anything?" he asked lightly.

"A big brown trout," Hero told him with a suggestive flicker of a smile. She knelt beside Marie Claire, who was sleepily awake. "It's almost full dark, love. We need to leave."

The girl nodded. "Yes, I know. I feel much stronger, in fact," she added in a tone of some wonder. "I appear to be hungry."

Hero laughed and helped her to her feet. "Let's see if you can make it to the river."

The open fishing boat was secured to a pole deep within the rushes a few yards down the bank. It was barely big enough for the four of them, but it would have to do, William reflected from his hiding place in the rushes. Anything was better than walking. Alec was beside him, watching the bank for any sign of movement. The evening star was bright in the night sky, and a crescent moon was rising slowly over the water. It would make them visible to anyone who happened to be out and about instead of tucked away where they should be beside their own firesides. But it was a risk they had to take. There was no way of knowing where or when the bodies of the two militia men would wash up, but if they got snagged in the reeds too close to where they'd gone in, there would be an instant hue and cry, and any stranger would be suspect. They needed to put as much river behind them as they could before dawn.

William crept towards the boat, seeming barely to part the reeds in his stealthy approach. He untied the painter and pulled the boat along for a few yards to a spot on the bank clear of reeds. Hero slithered down the bank while Alec helped Marie Claire down and into the craft and took up the oars. Hero hoisted the knapsack into the boat and climbed in herself. William pushed the boat out into the river and hauled himself in, sitting in the stern, his bare feet squarely planted, his britches rolled to his knees. Alec pulled strongly into midstream, where the current would help them on their way.

Marie Claire sipped water and nibbled on a piece of bread, gazing around her, fully aware of her surroundings for the first time since her escape. The night quiet was broken only by the hoot of an owl, the plash of the oars breaking the moonlit water, a pair of stately paddling swans. They passed small groups of cottages along the bank, but they were all in darkness. Hero sat with her back against William's bracing legs in the stern and felt his fingers idly trawling through her hair, which had long since escaped its tight knot on top of her head and fell in unruly tangles to below her shoulders. After an hour, William took the oars from Alec and pulled steadily until sometime in the early hours of the morning, when he took the boat into a narrow inlet in the river, where the bank sloped down to a small beach, sheltered by tall reeds.

Hero awoke as the boat ran onto the beach. Alec had jumped out to secure the painter to the trunk of a slender sapling. She uncurled herself from the bottom of the boat, her muscles protesting at their cramped position, and jumped down onto the beach. It was very quiet, and the moonlight was dimmed, filtering through the low branches of the trees along the overhanging bank.

William issued crisp orders, sending Hero to find wood for a fire, Alec to bring water, while he himself made short work of gutting the fish in the shallow water. Within the half hour, a fire crackled on the little beach, and the fish was cooking on a flat stone over the heat. Above it hung a makeshift trivet with a pan of water boiling for coffee.

William, squatting on his haunches before the fire, looked up from tending the fish as

171

Hero approached with an armload of twigs and small pieces of wood. She let them fall from her arms to the sand and sniffed hungrily. "I'm famished."

"We all are," he said with a swift smile, his gaze lingering on her for a second. He found her irresistibly attractive, with her grubby skirt hitched up to her knees, her bare feet firmly planted on the sand, her hair a honey-colored tangle around her unmistakably dirty face. "You are a complete urchin," he said, somehow making of the words a most intimate caress that sent that little jolt of desire through her belly.

"I feel filthy," she said, smiling despite herself. "When we've eaten, I'm going to bathe in the river."

"I'll join you," he responded, turning the fish over on the stone with the edge of his knife. "Is there any bread left?"

"Half a loaf." She withdrew it from the knapsack. "And some cheese and a few apples. A positive feast. And the coffee smells wonderful."

Alec and Marie Claire joined them at the fire as William took the fish from the heat. He sliced down the backbone with his knife, then pulled a piece off with his fingers and popped it into his mouth. "Eat up, children." He broke a piece of bread and put another piece of fish on it.

It was a big trout, but it didn't last long among the four of them. Hero wiped her sticky fingers on a tuft of grass poking out of the bank and took a long sip of coffee from the single beaker they had brought with them, before passing it to Marie Claire, who had more color with each mouthful and each sip. "Can we keep the fire going until I've had my bath?"

William nodded. "Alec, why don't you take Marie Claire up onto the bank and find a place to sleep for an hour? I'll stay here and keep watch. We'll go on until dawn. Then we'll pull out and rest for the day."

Alec and Marie Claire disappeared, and William leaned back on his elbows, regarding Hero with a slightly wicked smile. "Go on, then, take your bath. I'd like one myself, but we can't both be in the water at the same time."

It was a disappointing truth, Hero reflected, kicking off her skirt and petticoat. The thought of their naked bodies in the water together was almost enough to send her into a spontaneous climax of passion, but someone had to keep watch. She shrugged off her bodice and chemise and walked to the water, dipping her toes in a little wavelet that broke on the beach. It was

173

colder than she expected, and she glanced over her shoulder. William was watching, with desire clear in his golden eyes and in every line of his alert frame.

"Get in," he instructed softly. "My will-power is proving much more feeble than I thought."

She laughed with pure exhilaration, twirled once on the sand in a teasing little dance, then turned and plunged into the cold waters of the Seine. It took her breath away but felt wonderful, washing the filth of the day's grim journey from her skin. She had no soap, but there was no point reaching for the stars. She lay back, letting the water stream over her hair as she scrubbed her scalp with her fingers. It was probably the closest thing to heaven she would ever experience, she decided.

"Come out now." William was standing at the edge of the river. The fire, freshly fed, glowed and crackled behind him.

Reluctantly, Hero obeyed, splashing her way to shore, squeezing the water from her hair. William pushed off his britches and flung aside his shirt before taking two steps into the river, then diving beneath the water. She stood on the sand, wringing out her hair, watching his powerful arms cleaving the water as he swam. Then, still naked, she walked to the fire and stood turning herself slowly in its heat, like a chicken on a spit, until her skin was dry. She didn't dress, instead wrapped herself in William's discarded jerkin and sat on the sand to watch him as he swam back to shore, rising dripping from the river like some male Venus. No, it would have to be an Adonis, she corrected, watching him with the same lascivious gaze that he had had watching her.

"Oh, you *are* hungry," he said softly, coming to stand above her, water glistening on his skin. "I can see it in your eyes."

"Are you not?" she whispered, her tongue touching her lips.

"Stand up." He reached down for her hands and pulled her up, the jerkin falling from her shoulders. He glanced once around, then murmured, "Oh, to hell with it," and pulled her beside him back into the river. He walked until the water lapped around her thighs, then turned her into his arms. "Hold on to me." She put her arms around his neck as he lifted her against him, and she wrapped her legs around his waist, her body opening with an aching need for the delicious feel of him sliding within her beneath the water. She clung to him as he moved, just little movements that sent needles of arousal across her skin, filled her loins with urgent desire. She kissed him, her mouth hard on his, and his tongue pushed within her mouth as his sex pushed into hers, and she felt herself climbing slowly up and up, hanging for a long and glorious moment at the very peak of pleasure before she seemed to explode with joyous sensation and felt the tears of joy streaming down her cheeks as she clung helplessly around his neck, unable to move until the glory began to fade.

TWELVE

For nearly a week, they kept to the river, traveling only by night. William and Alec made short forays into the towns they passed to buy provisions, and to both Hero's and Marie Claire's joy, on the third day, they returned with new clothes. Secondhand but clean, together with a bar of that most precious commodity: soap. The two women spent a blissful hour alone in the river, bathing, washing their hair, before dressing in clean clothes. Marie Claire was ecstatic at being able to discard the britches and jerkin for a peasant's petticoats, kirtle, and laced bodice, but they still wore the necessary red bonnets.

It felt to Hero rather as if she was living through a dream during those long warm days of Indian summer. Everyday life and concerns seemed to be quite irrelevant. True, there was the ever-present fear of discovery, of making some fatal slip that would endanger them all, but even so, the hazy, trancelike nature of their journey was something she knew she would never forget. And the exquisite sensuality of her relationship with William was a daily entrancement. There were opportunities aplenty for lovemaking during the day, when they rested in readiness for the night's journey, and they took full advantage of every one.

Alec was content as always to leave his twin to manage her own life as she thought best and was too busy himself bringing his beloved fiancée back to full health. Indeed, Marie Claire blossomed under the sun and fresh air, plentiful rest and food. Her grief for her parents was now a part of her, but she no longer lived in fear, and that freedom was evident in the way she moved, the way she would sing softly to herself when doing some chore or other, and Alec lost the worry from his eyes and the tension from his mouth.

Just before dawn on the seventh day, they drew close to the town of Honfleur on the southern bank of the estuary of the Seine. William shipped his oars and rested, leaning his elbows on his thighs, looking across the estuary to the port of Le Havre.

"So we made it this far," Hero said softly, following his gaze. "Will we find a packet boat to take us across to England, or should we look only for a fishing boat? It's a lot farther across the Channel from here than it is from Calais, and it would be horridly uncomfortable." She reached across to brush the errant lock of hair from his forehead.

"Yes, we'll certainly need something more substantial than an open dinghy," he agreed, looking somewhat ruefully at his callused palms. "We can pay for passage; it's just a question of not drawing too much attention to ourselves. The ports are actively watched by the agents of the Committee of Public Safety."

"I wonder if we could commandeer a small sailboat," Alec suggested. "Hero and I are competent sailors. We grew up with boats. Our family home is on the Beaulieu River."

"Oh, yes, we've sailed the waters of the Solent many times," Hero said with enthusiasm. "If we could . . ." She hesitated for a moment. "If we could *borrow* a sailboat from someone, I'm sure we'd manage to sail it across the Channel."

William chuckled. "I don't doubt your abilities. As it happens, I'm not exactly inexperienced with sails myself, so, yes, I'm sure we could manage under our own steam. It'll probably take several days, depending on the wind, so we need a craft with some kind of cabin."

He would, of course, be a competent sailor, Hero reflected with an inner smile, wondering if there was anything at all at which William Ducasse, Viscount St. Aubery, was not an expert.

William took up the oars again and turned the little boat back the way they had come. "I noticed an inlet just a little way upriver. We'll tie up there out of sight and take a look around."

"Why don't Marie Claire and I go into Honfleur and look for a suitable vessel?" Hero suggested as they entered the narrow inlet, protected on both sides by tall reeds. "Two women with shopping baskets are less likely to draw attention than either of you. And I know perfectly well what to look for."

William inclined his head in acknowledgment. "True enough. But don't do anything, and don't speak to anyone about a boat, is that clear?" He fixed her with a steady stare and held her gaze until she nodded.

"As crystal."

"In that case, you may go." He shipped his oars as Alec stepped out of the boat with the painter. His feet sank into swampy mud, and he swore vigorously, splashing through the reeds until he found what passed for a bank, pulling the craft behind him.

"I'll be glad to be done with this river business," Alec muttered, securing the painter. "Give me the open sea any day."

Hero hitched her skirt and petticoat above her knees and, carrying her shoes, stepped into the water and up onto the bank. Marie Claire, with a little more reluctance, followed suit. She was not quite as unconcerned as Hero about exposing her legs thigh-high.

"Bring back fresh bread and fruit." William handed them a basket that Marie Claire had woven from reeds one idle afternoon. "And anything else to make a satisfactory breakfast. And Hero, I repeat, do not mention boats to anyone. Use your eyes, but keep your tongue still."

"Yes, milord." She gave him a mock curtsy, and he shook his head in warning, but there was a glint of amusement in his eyes.

"Just be careful. This is not a good time for games."

"Spoilsport," she threw at him, hitching the basket on her arm. "Come, Marie Claire, let us go to market like any other *femme de ménage.*"

Marie Claire followed her along the nar-

181

row bank towards the little town. She was accustomed now to the banter between William and Hero, but she couldn't imagine herself and Alec indulging in anything that was quite so sharply provocative, and the sparkling, keen-edged sexuality it revealed intrigued her even as it slightly shocked her.

Hero strolled along the quay, her eyes on the craft bobbing at anchor in the bay and tied up at the long piers. They would want one docked at a pier. It would be easier to take than one at anchor farther out. And it needed to be an undistinguished working boat, one that would draw no attention if they passed other shipping in the Channel.

"What do you think of that one?" she murmured to her companion, gesturing casually to a fishing boat, about twenty feet long, with a small cabin, shabby, peeling paintwork on the decking, but from what she could see, the hull appeared sound, and the presence of lobster pots and fishing nets indicated that it was sufficiently seaworthy for regular use.

Marie Claire swallowed, watching it toss in the wake of a larger fishing craft passing in the harbor behind it. "I'm sure it'll do us well."

Hero shot her a quick concerned glance. She seemed suddenly rather pale. "What is it? Aren't you happy to think that soon we'll have kicked the dust of France from our shoes?"

"Yes . . . yes, of course." Marie Claire didn't sound too convinced. Then she confessed, "I feel so silly, but I get most dreadfully seasick, Hero."

"Oh, you poor love." Hero was instantly sympathetic, but there really wasn't anything to be done about such an affliction except hope for a calm sea. "The weather's been so nice, we might just be lucky and have a pleasant breeze and no swell," she offered.

"Just don't tell Alec or William, please?" Marie Claire begged.

"Not a word. Now, let's find the market."

It was just before midnight when the four of them crept through the dark streets of Honfleur towards the quay. "This one," Hero murmured, stopping at her choice. The sky was overcast, and there was little natural light. From a tavern in one of the narrow lanes leading up from the quay came the sounds of raucous laughter and the strains of an accordion. But the quay itself was deserted.

"Get aboard," William instructed. "Marie Claire, after Hero, and get down into the cabin out of sight. You, too, Hero."

"I thought I was sailing this tub," she protested.

"Alec and I will take her out of the harbor. Now, do as you're told before anyone appears."

Hero swallowed her indignation; the need for speed and silence was too great to quarrel with William's high-handedness at the moment. Later, on the open waters of the Channel, she would tell him how little she appreciated it.

Somehow they managed to slip away from the dock without drawing any attention and tacked slowly across the harbor under a foresail beneath a gentle breeze until they reached the harbor's sheltering headland and open water. The wind stiffened, and Hero, who had been crouching on the top step of the gangway to the cabin, stepped up onto the deck and came to stand against the railing. They were running before the wind, and William had the tiller, his eyes on the edge of the sail, correcting course when it fluttered.

"I think we can risk the mainsail," he said. "Can you and Alec get it hoisted?"

Hero shot him a withering look, which made him laugh aloud, and called for her brother.

The wind stayed fair, and the sea air seemed finally to blow away the last shreds of the terror of Paris, the last reek of blood and dirt. The Needle rocks and lighthouse appeared on the horizon early in the morning of their second day. Hero was at the tiller, lost in the motion of the little boat as it rose and dipped in the waves. Marie Claire was, as usual, curled in the far corner of the deck. She did much better in the fresh air and bravely kept her misery as much to herself as she could. Alec hovered, but there was little he could do except offer brandy and water, which seemed to ease the nausea somewhat.

William emerged from the cabin with a hunk of bread and cheese and a cup of wine, coming to stand beside Hero at the tiller. "Shall we stop for a night and a day on the island?" he asked casually. "We can round the Needles and dock at Yarmouth. We could even manage proper beds in a hostelry and a decent dinner, if that would appeal."

"Would it?" she exclaimed, her eyes shining. "What an absolutely wondrous idea. A real bath, maybe. Perhaps some proper clothes. And meat, and wine, and even sheets . . . oh, can you imagine anything more delicious?"

"Not easily," he agreed, grinning at her enthusiasm. "But I can think of one other delight that might enhance the experience."

Her eyes seemed to melt with seductive languor, just as he had known they would. "Take over," she demanded, pushing the tiller towards him. "I'm going to tell Alec and Marie Claire that in a few hours we'll be on dry English soil." She skipped away, and he watched her, wondering anew how it was that she could fill him with such pure pleasure just with her natural high spirits and optimism. Just a fleeting glimpse of her body made him ache with desire.

And all too soon it must come to an end. They would enjoy their idyll on the Isle of Wight for a day or so, and then he would tell her what had to be. He would make his own way across to the mainland. Any one of the little fishing boats plying the Solent would be more than happy to take a paying passenger across to the little town of Lymington, and from there he could make his way by road to London. He would buy a horse, and a two-day ride would bring him to the capital. Alec and the two women could take their "borrowed" boat across the Solent, along the coast a short way and up the Beaulieu River to the Bruton family estate. It was the perfect solution. They would be safe at home, as if they had never left it, well beyond the reach of the Lizard and his agents without once traveling on English roads, and he would be free to concentrate on the business that awaited him in London, until he could return to his work in Paris.

But they had a short time yet before that difficult conversation became necessary.

It was early evening when they docked in the little fishing town of Yarmouth. Clear across the narrow strip of water, they could see Hurst spit, with its grim castle guarding the entrance to the narrow waters of the Solent. It was a familiar sight for the Fanshawe twins, who had sailed these waters since they were children, and for a moment, as they stood at the railing of the fishing boat, their hands touched in recognition that they were home.

Marie Claire came to stand beside them, still a little shaky after her Channel ordeal but smiling. She had little knowledge of the English countryside and had never visited the Bruton country estate. She and Alec had met in London when her parents had brought her over for her first Season. French aristocracy mingled easily with the English in both London and Versailles, and they had fallen in love the first time they met.

Hero was already engaged to the Honorable Thomas Lancaster, first lieutenant in the Royal Navy, and her brother's happiness merely augmented her own. Until both their hopes had vanished into the blood-soaked streets of Paris and a patch of the Mediterranean Sea. But Alec had his love back — grieving, certainly, but safe.

Hero was dry-eyed as she looked across to the familiar piece of land that represented home. She had ceased the deep, soul-wrenching mourning for Tom now and discovered with William that it was possible to love again, with as much intensity, indeed, to experience physical love again with even more intensity. And now she felt no guilt for that comparison, either. She drew a deep breath, and it felt almost as if it were the first truly deep breath she had drawn since the news of Tom's death had reached her. She exhaled slowly, and her vision seemed to clear, to give her, finally, an unobstructed view of her future. She and William would work together at whatever mattered to him; they would love, they would live life to its fullest, as they had been doing. And for a moment, her happiness was exquisite. Everyone she loved was safe. And her past love was now a part of her, never to be lost but no longer an ever-present anguish.

THIRTEEN

London, October 1795, thirteen months later
Hero gently placed her baby niece in Marie Claire's arms and kissed her brother, who still seemed stunned as he sat on the edge of the bed, regarding his wife and child with amazement. "Everything is well, love," she whispered against his cheek. "I'm going to bed now."

"Yes . . . yes, of course." He reached up to hug her. "Thank you for staying up with me, dearest."

"As if I had a choice," she said in the teasing, rallying tone they both understood. "Marie Claire and Fleur will need to sleep soon, so you should, too."

"Aye," Nan declared brusquely. "You all need your beds. Run along, Lady Hero, and you, my lord, can sleep in your own bedchamber. Her ladyship needs time and privacy to recover. Don't you worry about little Lady Fleur; she'll sleep in her cradle next to her mother." She shooed the twins away, and Alec, after a last kiss on his wife's forehead, obeyed the only maternal voice that had ever meant anything to him.

Hero reached her own bedchamber. She had sent her maid to bed long since, but the flimsy silk evening gown was easy enough to cast off. She pushed the delicate material away with her foot, a vivid memory of the filthy peasant clothes she had worn during that long journey from Paris to safety suddenly overwhelming her. William was there in her mind's eye. His hand on her back supporting her through the filthy underground stream, killing the two militia men on the riverbank, gutting a trout.

And most of all, joining with her in the waters of the Seine, in the reeds, on the sandy riverside, in sun-dappled glades. And at the end, in the deep feather softness of the bed in the Eagle and Childe on Yarmouth quay.

She lay gazing up at the embroidered tester above her as early daylight filled the long windows of her bedchamber. The embroidered scene depicted an Elizabethan knot garden, with a young girl and a peacock, its brilliant turquoise tail at full fan. But she didn't really notice any of the beauty. She was too tired to sleep, her legs moving restlessly beneath the covers, which were suddenly too heavy and hot. And once again, the memory rose, clear and vivid, of waking on that other lovely morning full of promise that had brought an end to it all.

The Eagle and Childe on Yarmouth quay was a pretty little inn with a lively taproom generally filled with local fishermen and farmers. Hero and William occupied a charming bedchamber overlooking the water, a room dominated by a big feather bed, which they had rarely left in the two days since they'd arrived. They saw little of their traveling companions, taking most of their meals in their own chamber. Hero had awoken on the third morning when the sun was high, filled with energy, which was surprising given how little sleep she had had the night before. There had been something urgent about the long hours of lovemaking, an edge to William's passion, to which, as always, she had responded with her own insistent fervor. Now she lay in the feather softness of the bed, feeling the sun warm on her face. She was alone, which did not surprise her; her bedfellow was always up betimes. Sleep seemed a commodity of which William had enviably little need. She had just swung her legs out of bed and was indulging in a long, luxurious stretch when William returned. He was dressed and carried a mug of coffee, which he set down on the dresser.

"I thought you might appreciate coffee."

"Thank you. I need it." She smiled at him, waiting for his good-morning kiss, but he remained where he was, standing with his back to the window, regarding her gravely. And the first inkling of a premonition came to her. "Is something wrong, William?" She could hear the tentative note in her voice, the little tremor of unease.

"It's time for this to end, Hero." He spoke almost without expression, as if he was merely delivering a message that had nothing to do with him. "We have run our course together."

She stared at him. "I don't understand . . . what are you saying?"

He sighed and passed a hand over his face in a weary gesture. "I am saying, my dear, that we have enjoyed each other a great deal in the last weeks, but now it is time to bring our liaison to a close. From the first, I made it clear that this could never be permanent, that we would enjoy each other while we could, but it would have to end."

"Why must it? I know you have work to do, and I know how vital that work is to you, but I would not stand in your way, hold you up in any way. I haven't so far, have I?" A note of challenge entered her voice as she felt her fighting spirit come to the fore. Whatever he thought, he was wrong.

"No, you have not. But my work then concerned you, getting you to safety. I will not involve you in anything that will not benefit you. And believe me, my dear Hero, nothing about me from this time on will benefit you. You must now —" He held up a hand as she opened her mouth in protest. "No, be silent, and let me finish. It is time for you now to start living the life you were born to. You cannot go racketing around Europe, or anywhere else, for that matter. Your reputation is still intact, but it won't be for long if you persist in your reckless disregard for your world's rules and obligations."

"I don't give a fig for them," she said furiously. "I don't give a tinker's dam for my reputation. Why should I?"

"Don't be a fool," he responded harshly. "You're not in the least foolish, so don't pretend to be. I will not be responsible for ruining you by tarnishing your reputation."

"My reputation is not *your* responsibility," she responded as fiercely as before. "It is *mine* and mine alone."

"No, there you are quite wrong. You are simply too young and inexperienced to understand the consequences of your impulses and your reckless insistence in following your own urges and wishes. You *must* put a bridle on your unschooled self-will, and if you won't, then someone else has to do it. I will not play any part in your social ruin. You have no idea what it would be like to live as a social outcast."

"But where has all this come from?" She was bewildered at the suddenness, the harsh finality of his demeanor. "Why now?"

"Because you are safe now. You're within a few miles of home, and you can get there with no one knowing even that you've been away. Spending time in the country at this time of year is perfectly acceptable; most of Society spends the summer in the country. The London Season will soon begin, and when people start trickling back, you will, too. Marie Claire's wedding must be arranged, and you'll be deeply involved, as she has no family of her own. By the time all that is settled, you will once more be established, and there'll be no danger of your hotheaded, foolhardy escapade of the last weeks becoming public."

Hero had become accustomed to William's assumption of authority, his habit of giving orders, and on the whole, she had accepted it as a necessary responsibility of leadership, and their escape had required one clear leader. No one had questioned his authority, but this was different. They were safe in

England, she was on her own home ground, and once more, she was her own person, responsible for herself and her actions. He had no right to assume any authority in their relationship now.

She shook her head emphatically. "No, who I am and what I do are no longer your responsibility. When it was possible that my actions might endanger others, then I was perfectly happy to accept your edicts, but not now, not here. As it happens, I do not choose to return to London for this Season or any other. Society bores me, even more so after the last few weeks. How could I possibly settle for the interminable round of balls and rout parties and the endless chatter of debutantes and the foolish vanity of men with not a sensible thought between their ears after the time *we* have spent together?"

His expression hardened, his tawny eyes narrowing, and he spoke with a deadly quiet ferocity, articulating every word. "I can give you nothing, Hero. I have nothing to give. You will simply be in the way of what I have to do. I cannot love you. I *do not* love you. What we have had was a delightful interlude, but there was never a promise of permanence. You understood that. You must return to your place in the world, and you must learn to live within its rules. You will find happiness with some other man if you accept your life and understand that a careless liaison will ruin you."

And as she stood, numbed by his words, he left her. No farewell kiss, no softening of the hard finality of his statement, just the firm click of the closing door.

She took a deep, shuddering breath, going to the window to look down onto the quay, to see if he emerged from the inn. All her optimism, her exhilaration at the promise of the future she had imagined they would have, was as dead as the one she had lost when Tom was killed.

And when he came out of the inn and strode without a backwards glance up towards the bedchamber window where she stood, Hero remembered those disturbing moments in the past when he had seemed to disapprove of something she was doing. She had puzzled then about the strange puritanical streak that had led him to upbraid her for some careless attitude or action, and now, in that dreadful scene, she heard the culmination of that puzzling anger. But she still didn't understand it or where it had come from.

Hero rolled onto her side, trying to find a cool patch on the crisp white pillow. She tried to think of Fleur, tried to think of the life that lay ahead for the baby, a life of

197

privilege and joy and love. But the grim memory of that last morning in Yarmouth would not leave her in peace. She had finally managed to dress and make her way down to the taproom of the inn to find Alec, hoping that he might be able to throw some light on William's cruel departure. But her twin had little to offer. He had told her that William had decreed that he, Hero, and Marie Claire would take their purloined little sailing boat across the Solent and up the Beaulieu River to home. As far as Alec knew, William was heading for London, but what business took him there Alec didn't know. William Ducasse always played his cards close to his chest.

And that had been the end of a surreal idyll that had combined horror and passion in almost exact proportions.

Until tonight . . . or, rather last night, at Ranelagh.

For twelve months, she had endured her anger, confusion, incomprehension in silence. She refused to invite pity from her brother or Marie Claire, refused to feel a victim, to feel rejected, and by immersing herself in all the numerous details of planning Marie Claire's speedy wedding to her brother, she had found herself back in Society life as if she had never left it. The wedding had been quiet, as Marie Claire was still officially in mourning for her parents, but the love the two of them so clearly held for each other banished any reminders of grief. The bride, well recovered from her ghastly ordeal, was radiant in a gown of dove-gray embroidered damask, and the groom's joy was so overwhelming it brought smiles to everyone he came into contact with.

They had honeymooned quietly in the country, and Hero, anxious to leave them alone despite her stated dislike of the rituals, had plunged back into Society life in the mansion in Grosvenor Square, where Great-aunt Emily took up her position once more as chaperone with her usual vague benevolence.

Hero had thrown herself into the social round with a vengeance, heedless of raised eyebrows or the whispers of gossips as she did exactly what she felt like doing, most of it quite unsuitable for a young lady on the marriage mart. And deep down, she knew that she was defying William, proving to him that whatever he said and did to keep her from shocking the world, her reputation was her own to keep or lose as she chose. It was childish to take pleasure in thinking of his disapproval, but it offered some balm for her hurt.

And at last, once the first edge of that hurt and loss had blunted, it had occurred to her that his cruelty might have been to protect himself from his own emotions. Perhaps there had been something deep within him that had forced him to push her away. And there were moments when she felt with absolute conviction that he *had* loved her. And at those moments, the pointlessness of her behavior seemed puerile, and she began to modify her recklessness a little, slowly coming to terms with the inevitability of living a life that did not include William Ducasse, Viscount St. Aubery.

Then, of course, he had to cross her path just as she was reaching equilibrium, and the attraction had been as powerful as ever. Now Hero felt only a determination that what they had had was not over. She was not going to permit it to be over. Either he was going to convince her with a rational and honest explanation why they could not be together in some way — she didn't demand marriage or any formal kind of commitment — or they were going to resume their relationship as and when and where they could.

She would settle for occasional visits to London, for snatched moments anywhere, anytime, but she would not accept the end when it was so clearly unnecessary.

On which determination her finally heavy eyelids drooped and closed, and sleep claimed her.

William rode along the tan in Hyde Park as the sun was coming up. It was a time of day he had always loved, when the city was still mostly asleep, the air was fresh and clean before the many rancid odors of daytime activities thickened it, and the grass was still damp with dew. There were few other riders in the park and no obligation to offer more than a nodding bow of acknowledgment as they passed on the tan. Despite his apparent ease, he was as watchful as ever, aware of everyone he passed, constantly aware of who was behind him. The agents set to watch him were often dilatory, particularly early in the morning, which aroused his scorn. Once the political situation in France had stabilized after Napoleon's swift military action to break the power of the mob in Paris and the Directory was now in charge, the authorities seemed to have decided he was a "sleeper," not a sufficient threat for a more extensive and arduous surveillance.

More fools they.

But what was he to do about Hero? She would reiterate, of course, that she was none of his business, and she'd be right . . . up to a point. It seemed obvious from her escapade at Ranelagh the previous night that she had not taken his words to heart over safeguarding her reputation. He had hoped that she would be engaged, if not married, to someone suitable by now, and yet he could not deny the surge of happiness he had felt when he had learned on first arriving in London that she was as free of attachments as she had been in Paris.

But his own situation had not changed in the last year. If anything, he was even more unsuited for any kind of long-term commitment than he had been. His life was too dangerous and would make anyone close to him unacceptably vulnerable. The agents of the Directory were as unscrupulous as their predecessors of the Committee of Public Safety and would not hesitate to use any tool that came to hand to attack him if they decided it was worth the effort. Keeping Marguerite safe was enough of a worry without adding a reckless and unpredictable Hero to the mix. But dear God, how he had missed her. Just catching a glimpse of her in the last few weeks had caused a torment of longing. And last night, the touch of her hand, the laugh in her eyes, the sharpness of her tongue, had reduced him to a lovelorn swain from a medieval tapestry. All he needed was a lute to pluck plaintively as he gazed adoringly at the object of his love.

He shook his head in disgust at such a ridiculously inappropriate image, and his muscles tightened. His horse, feeling a nudge against its sides, broke into a canter and then lengthened its stride into a gallop, and William gave the horse its head. Galloping on the tan in Hyde Park was frowned upon, at least where female riders were concerned, but at this hour of the morning, there were few enough folk around to comment. It would also tell him if he was being followed. Anyone on his tail would have to gallop, too, which would break his cover. He wondered fleetingly how often Hero indulged herself in this forbidden activity. He was as sure that she galloped at will around Hyde Park, probably for all to see at the fashionable hour of five o'clock in the afternoon, as he was sure that he was galloping now. The reflection made him smile even as it exasperated him. She was utterly impossible to bridle, and he had never refused a challenge. But Hermione Fanshawe was not a challenge he dared take on. She was dangerous for him in every way.

Just as he was dangerous for her. He had made one catastrophic mistake in his life, and he would not make another.

Certain he had no one on his tail, he rode out of the Stanhope Gate and turned up Piccadilly, heading away from Mayfair and towards the less fashionable village of Knightsbridge. It was a quiet area, with tree-lined streets and shady squares, an area popular with well-to-do bankers, lawyers, business owners, and genteel widows with their spinster companions, usually poor relations grateful for the charity and willing to be at the beck and call of their demanding and frequently querulous employers.

He soon left the more fashionable and populous parts of Knightsbridge behind and found himself in a lane on the outskirts of the comfortable residential area, a part that was closer to a country hamlet than well-to-do Knightsbridge itself. The cottages were small and inhabited for the most part by farm workers and their families.

William drew rein at the gate of a pretty whitewashed cottage at the farthest extremity of the hamlet. Fields stretched to the horizon in one direction, the jumbled and smoke-hazed lines of the city in the other. He dismounted, looking along the narrow lane with customary caution. He was certain he had not been followed from the park, but as always, he took nothing for granted. A yoked milkmaid came down the lane carrying full pails from one of the nearby farms, stopping at the various cottage doors as their occupants came out with their jugs to be filled. William waited for her to reach him and opened the gate for her.

"Why, thank you, sir." She managed a bobbed curtsy despite her burden and went up the path ahead of him. The door opened as she reached it, and a small girl stood there holding up a jug with an air of importance. A woman appeared behind the child and helped her lift the jug for the milkmaid to fill, for the moment unaware of the man standing a little to one side of the path, watching the little scene.

"Oh, my goodness," the woman exclaimed as she saw William. "You're here, Guillaume. Why didn't you send word?"

William stepped forward and swiftly took the full jug from the child as it dipped dangerously from the little hand. "I wanted to surprise you, Jeanne. Don't frown at me so." He bent to kiss the child's cheek. "Good morning, Marguerite."

She regarded him solemnly. "Good morning, Uncle Guillaume. You haven't been to see me for a long time, weeks and weeks and weeks."

He laughed and handed the jug to Jeanne. "Has it been that long? How shocking." He picked up the child, swinging her onto his shoulders. "Come, you shall tell me everything that has been happening in all those weeks and weeks and weeks." He carried her into the cottage, ducking low beneath the lintel and following the woman into the kitchen at the rear of the cottage.

"You'll be wanting your breakfast, I daresay," Jeanne declared, setting her jug on the pine table. "Marguerite needs hers, too. I've veal cutlets and coddled eggs."

"Sounds wonderful." He set the little girl on her feet.

"I shall have porridge and an egg," the child announced solemnly, clambering onto the long bench at the table. "Sit here, Uncle Guillaume." She patted the bench beside her imperatively.

"At your service, mademoiselle." He straddled the bench.

"What have you brought me?" she inquired, reaching out for his pocket.

"Marguerite, child, you do not ask for presents," Jeanne scolded, setting a bowl of steaming porridge in front of the little girl. "It's very rude. Maybe your uncle has brought you nothing."

"Oh, but he has, of course he has," Marguerite protested. "He always brings me something." She slipped her hand into the deep pocket and withdrew it with a triumphant squeak. "See . . . this is for me. It has a red ribbon around it. It is for me, *mon oncle,* isn't it?"

"I don't know how you guessed," William teased. "But yes, it is for you."

"And is there anything in the other pocket?" she demanded, setting the package beside her plate.

"You must wait and see. You may open that one, then eat your porridge. After that, you may see what you can find . . . Oh, my thanks, Jeanne." Gratefully, he raised the tankard of ale she had put before him and drank deeply.

The child tore open the wrapping with impatient fingers and revealed a squat wooden doll figure, the features on its round face brightly painted. She examined it in some puzzlement. Its clothes were painted on, and shiny black boots formed its base. "What does it do?"

"Twist her head," William said, smiling over his tankard.

Marguerite struggled for a moment with the head, a deep frown of concentration drawing her delicate fair eyebrows together.

She was so like her mother, William thought, with her creamy complexion, the rosebud mouth, and her long pale hair.

"Ah," she exclaimed as the doll's head finally came loose. "Oh, look, there's another one inside."

"She's called a *matryoshka,*" he told her. "They make them in Russia. Inside each doll is another smaller one."

The child needed no further instruction, revealing each delicately painted doll until finally the very smallest stood on the table in line with the others. "Oh, it's lovely," she said. "I shall put them all together again."

"Eat your porridge before it goes cold," Jeanne directed, although she was smiling at the little girl's fascination with the intricate present. She set a plate of veal cutlets and coddled eggs in front of William and refilled his ale.

William ate heartily; the early-morning ride had given him an appetite. When he'd finished, he said to Marguerite, "Aunt Jeanne and I have to talk for a little while in the parlor. Play with your doll, and when we come back, you shall have your second present."

The child merely nodded, all her concentration once again on lining up the family of dolls. Jeanne wiped her hands on her apron and went ahead of William into the parlor.

"You've seen no one?" he said, closing the door softly behind them.

"No, no one untoward," the woman responded. "I let her play with the village children sometimes . . . she can't be kept alone with only me for company; it's not good for a child."

"No," he agreed. "But it still worries me. Perhaps it would be safer if you moved out of London."

"You can't move her again, Guillaume. The child needs some continuity. This is the third place she has lived in, and she's barely four. She needs to play with other children, to feel some sense of permanence in her life."

William sighed. Jeanne was right, and yet the risk was ever present, however watchful they were. He had made too many enemies in the last six years ever to drop his guard. He reached inside his coat and drew out a bank draft. "This should suffice for another six months. If you need more, just send word."

Jeanne took the draft and put it on the mantel shelf. "Our needs are small, but Marguerite's feet are growing apace. She needs new shoes."

"And what of you, Jeanne? This is no life for a woman. Are you not lonely?" He spoke with difficulty, aware as always of the great debt he owed this woman, Marguerite's mother's sister.

"No lonelier than I would have been had I taken the veil," Jeanne replied with a smile, placing a hand on his arm. "Indeed, I find caring for Isabelle's child a more worthwhile use of my life than one of silent contemplation in a convent. Maybe when Marguerite no longer needs me, then I will seek that life again, but for now, I am content."

William kissed her cheek. "I have no words to express my gratitude, my dear."

"Nonsense. This is my calling, and I find it a deeply satisfying one. Let us go back to the kitchen. Marguerite will be growing impatient for that second present."

William left an hour later, feeling the imprint of the child's kisses still on his cheeks and the warmth of her little arms hugging his neck. She was more precious to him than anything in the world, and that terrified him because it weakened him.

FOURTEEN

The three men sat around a fire in an upstairs chamber of the Gull, a small inn just up from the busy quay at Dover harbor. They were drinking hot spiced wine, and two of them looked cold and pale, still huddled in their boat cloaks after a particularly rough crossing from Calais. The third, Everard Dubois, his swarthy, angular face distinguished by a strangely shaped eyebrow like a question mark, was clearly more at his ease, lounging in an armchair, his cloak cast aside on a settle beneath the window, as he read through a sheaf of documents.

"So finally, Barras wants us to take him," he murmured. "And thank God for it. But what's changed? Ducasse has only been in London a couple of weeks. God knows where he was before that. We've been keeping an eye on him, of course, but he's not been doing anything out of the ordinary. Just idling around amusing himself, as far as I can tell."

One of the others sneezed violently and cursed, burying his nose in the steam from his tankard. "Doesn't sound much like Ducasse," he mumbled. "Maybe you've been out of Paris too long, Everard. Barras says he was sighted in Austria, and we have information that connects him with the Duc d'Enghien and the émigré Army of Condé. There are sympathizers aplenty among the émigrés in London, and it's thought he's organizing support for another Royalist plot."

"Yes, and all those émigrés are under watch." Everard Dubois sounded impatient. "Ducasse has not made contact with any of them."

"Maybe you've missed something or someone," one of his companions suggested with a snide smile. It was rare to catch the Lizard in any kind of carelessness.

Dubois did not dignify the comment with a response. He returned to his perusal of the documents they had brought him. Paul Barras was the generally acknowledged leader of the Directory that had controlled France since the fall of Robespierre. He was a wily politician, an expert manipulator, and for the moment, at least, his orders were set in stone.

Everard Dubois knew which side his bread was buttered, but these orders also satisfied a long-held need of his own. An impersonal, politically justified reason to exact vengeance against William Ducasse. The man had thumbed his nose at the Committee of Public Safety and slipped again and again through all the traps Everard had set for him. Now in these orders lay his opportunity to see his old enemy's head roll at the guillotine.

How he had longed in the last couple of weeks to slip the assassin's blade between Ducasse's ribs, but he had restrained himself, knowing full well that without direct orders from Paris, he would fall foul of the powers that be. Guillaume Ducasse, Viscount St. Aubery, was a powerful enemy of the state and at his most dangerous when he was seemingly quiescent. Everard was well aware of that and had been convinced that he was plotting something. There would be a network operating with him even if they weren't immediately visible, and a premature strike might remove the Hydra's head, but others would sprout quickly enough in its place. They had to spread the net wide enough to catch them all. Now it seemed Barras himself had decided it was time to behead the beast.

"Were you told whether we are to break him here or take him straight back to France?" he inquired. There had been no instructions in the papers he held.

"Both, if possible. But if he's too tough a nut to crack, then he goes back to the experts. He's to be taken and returned alive, that much is definite."

"Mmm." Everard nodded, quietly resolved that once he had his hands on his old enemy, he would wring every last truth out of him and enjoy every moment of doing so, before he returned him to his masters in Paris.

"So what now?" one of the men demanded with another vigorous sneeze.

"Well, I, for one, am for my bed and a warming pan," his fellow sufferer declared. "I'm frozen to the bone, haven't felt my feet for hours."

"You haven't supped as yet," Everard pointed out mildly. "The ordinary here does a decent enough supper."

"I've been puking my guts out for the last six hours; the last thing I want is food. You coming, Gerard?" He headed for the door.

"*D'accord,* Luc." Gerard hauled himself from his chair by the fire and followed his friend, with a brusque nod of farewell to Everard Dubois.

Everard stretched his feet to the andirons and sipped his spiced wine. He had few men in London, so these two would be welcome additions as he started this new operation. Ducasse knew, of course, that his old nemesis was in the city. Everard had made no attempt to conceal his presence. The émigrés he was keeping under surveillance were all to be found in the same five square miles that also contained Ducasse, and he could not watch each and every one of them from some remote corner of London, so he moved around on the outskirts of fashionable Society, not a full participant but a familiar and unremarkable figure who drew little attention to himself. It was inevitable that Ducasse would be aware of his presence. So the element of surprise was lost to him.

There had to be some other way to snare the bird. He leaned forward for the jug on the hearth and refilled his goblet. Ducasse was not a man who could be snatched from the street or ambushed in some dark alley. He was too formidable a swordsman and marksman for such an attack to be certain of success, and Everard knew there would only ever be one chance. So he had to take a more roundabout approach.

Unless . . . A slow smile curved his thin

lips. There was a full frontal approach that *could* surprise his quarry. If Everard were suddenly to be seen in Society, at Almack's, riding in Hyde Park, at Tattersalls, innocently attending the more public social events, no longer on the fringes of Society but a visible and active participant, Ducasse would certainly be taken aback. A cultivated French émigré would draw no remark in fashionable London. Indeed, the Chevalier Everard Dubois would probably be welcomed as a refreshing addition to the usual social circle. And such a position would afford him much greater access to Guillaume Ducasse. There would be some soft point in the man's armor that could be exploited. Everyone had something.

No, brute force was not the answer; subtle pressure might well be.

He drained his goblet and went downstairs to the noisy ordinary for his supper.

It was almost noon when William reached his lodgings on Half Moon Street after his visit to Knightsbridge. He was oddly restless, and he didn't have to look far for the reason. Hero. Last night's encounter had thrown all his carefully assembled detachment to the four winds. He wanted to see her . . . no, he *had* to see her. She had

216

become a compulsion he could not resist.

But what did it matter now? Once they had met again, the dam was breached. Besides, he needed to talk with Alec, who was so much in his twin sister's company that it was inevitable they would come face-to-face. Better to control those meetings himself and thus ensure that Hero's impetuosity was kept on a tight rein. Even as he told himself this, William knew he was desperately rationalizing his submission to that irresistible compulsion.

He changed from his riding britches into dark silk knee britches and coat, a plain black stock at his throat. The days of sans-culottes and the red bonnet were long gone. He walked from Half Moon Street to Grosvenor Square and crossed the square garden, where the leaves, already reddish brown, were beginning to fall and crunch beneath his feet. He bent to pick up a shiny conker from beneath a horse chestnut tree. It was large and luscious and reminded him of his childhood so vividly he could smell the roasting chestnuts on the braziers around the gardens of the Tuilleries Palace, where he had often played as a small boy, and hear the satisfying smack as his conker struck true against his rival's. His mother had taught him the game. It was one beloved of English children, and his own boyhood friends had taken to it with his own eagerness. He dropped his prize into his pocket and looked for another. Next time he saw Marguerite, he would teach her how to play.

A clear, light voice behind him said, "I'll challenge you to a game, sir."

He spun around. Hero came towards him along the narrow gravel path, a bright shiny conker in her hand. "Alec and I still play for hours." She regarded him with her head slightly tilted, a questioning gleam in her green eyes, a quizzical little smile on her lips. "Although I daresay he'll be too busy for some weeks for such frivolity."

"Oh? How so?" He held himself back from her with supreme difficulty.

Her smile widened. "I think you should let him tell you himself. Were you coming to see him?" Carefully, she had not included herself in the question, although the unspoken words hung between them.

"I thought to do so," he replied. "I had a question for him."

"Then come and ask it, but don't be at all surprised if you find him less than coherent." She took his arm in the most natural gesture in the world, and he could not for the world find an objection. "Is it not the most beautiful day?"

William couldn't help smiling at her bubbling pleasure in the crisp, sunny autumn day. She was bursting with some secret, her step more of a dance than a sedate walk as they crossed the road and mounted the short flight of steps to the front door. Hero rang the bell, and it was opened immediately by a bowing footman.

"My lady . . . Viscount St. Aubery." He bowed them into the hall.

So William had been here before, Hero thought, and wondered when. She certainly hadn't seen him. Alec seemed to be getting rather proficient at keeping things from her. "Come above to the small parlor. Alec will most probably be there."

William followed her up the wide sweep of the horseshoe staircase, aware of the atmosphere of excitement in the air. The maids they passed all seemed to be smiling, and even Jackson, who appeared on the landing as they reached it, bore an expression that could almost be called a smile.

"His lordship is in the small parlor, my lady," the majordomo said, moving to open the door for them.

"Oh, has Nan chased him away again?" Hero said with a chuckle. "Alec, dearest, you have a visitor."

Alec, who had been standing dreamily

219

gazing into the fire, whirled around, then beamed as he saw William. "Come in, come in. Sherry or burgundy?"

"Sherry, please." William perched without ceremony on the arm of the sofa. "So, children, tell me what is going on."

"Marie Claire had her baby last night, a little girl," Alec informed him in a rush of pride.

"Congratulations, dear boy." William shook his hand heartily. "And they are both well?"

"Oh, splendid. Yes, indeed, doing splendidly, and Marie Claire was such a trooper, you wouldn't believe." He handed William a glass.

"Yes, I would," William corrected. "She always was."

"Yes, of course. For a moment, I was forgetting." Alec's expression dimmed a little but then brightened. "But that's all in the past. Her name is Fleur."

"Very pretty." William approved, and his mind went for a moment to Marguerite, another delicate flower in the world.

Hero felt a strange shift in time. It was once again the three of them, in that easy fellowship they had developed during the terror and beauty of their escape.

But of course, it wasn't. "I'll go up and

220

see them. William had a question for you, Alec, and I don't think I'm included."

Alec looked uncomfortable, but William's unperturbed expression didn't change. "Yes, thank you, Hero," he said.

She left them, managing not to flounce as she did so.

"Can you not take her into your confidence, William?" Alec asked as the door closed behind his sister. "You know she would never betray you. Has she not earned your confidence?"

William sipped his sherry reflectively. "Yes, of course she has. But I don't want her involved, Alec, and neither should you. She needs to put such adventuring behind her and start living the life she was born to."

"I wonder if that's your decision to make for her," Alec said, looking straight at him. "You have no claim on her; you have always made sure of that."

"True enough. But I know, as Hero doesn't, as I suspect you don't, what happens to a woman when she becomes a social outcast. I cannot bear the thought of that happening to Hero."

"But —"

Whatever Alec was about to say was cut

off as the door opened and a voice trilled, "Such an exquisite baby, such a dear little thing, Alec, my dear boy. I have just been worshipping at the cradle, oh, and dear, sweet Marie Claire, how well she looks after such a dreadful ordeal . . . Oh, my goodness, why didn't someone tell me we had a visitor? Goodness me, sir, forgive my inattention."

The speech emerged from a small round figure trailing shawls and scarves and surrounded by the unmistakable aroma of sal volatile and lavender water. She flapped a fan in her obvious consternation as she bobbed a curtsy in William's general direction.

"Aunt Emily, may I present the Viscount St. Aubery," Alec said, stepping forward hastily. "William, the Lady Emily Harrington, my sister's companion."

"I am honored, ma'am." William swept her a courtly bow. "I was just congratulating Alec on the wonderful news. Lady Bruton is doing well, I trust?"

"Oh, yes, indeed, sir, splendidly." Emily plied her fan vigorously. "I cannot imagine the torments she must have endured, and I heard not a sound." Then she blushed as if realizing that the subject of childbirth was not one generally discussed in male company.

"A glass of sherry, Aunt Emily?" Alec offered opportunely.

"Just a small one, just to give me a little strength. I did find myself rather weak this morning." The lady sank onto a daybed in a silk and cashmere sea of shawls. "A little sal volatile, I think . . . I must have it somewhere . . . oh, where could it be?" Distressed, she fluttered her mittened hands among the scarves until she found a small reticule. "Oh, dear me, how silly of me. I'm always forgetting things." She lay back on the daybed, dabbed the bottle beneath her nose, and took the glass of sherry Alec brought her. "I do trust I'm not interrupting any business," she asked after a moment, looking at the two men, her faded blue eyes suddenly wary. "I would not intrude for the world."

"Indeed, you're not, ma'am," Alec said swiftly. "But we were about to adjourn to the library as you came in. May I send for Harper?"

"Oh, yes, you may. Thank you, dear boy. I shall ask her to rub my temples with a little lavender water. I feel the headache coming on . . . all this excitement, you know."

"I will fetch her at once." Alec pulled the bell rope and went to the door, and when a footman arrived in answer to the summons, he gave instructions to fetch Lady Emily's maid. "William, shall we go down to the library?"

"With pleasure. Your servant, Lady Emily." William offered another sweeping bow to the lady and followed Alec into the hall. "That lady, estimable in every way, I am sure, considers it her duty to *chaperone* Hero?" He sounded astounded.

Alec laughed. "Yes, absurd, isn't it? But Hero is very fond of her, as am I, and it suits Hero very well not to be chaperoned in any conventional way."

"Quite," William said drily. "Which takes us back to our earlier conversation." He followed Alec downstairs to the hall and along a corridor behind the stairs which led to the library at the rear of the house.

"I think that is a conversation you had best have with my sister," Alec stated. "I am not her keeper or her guardian. And if you want to set yourself up as either, I wish you luck."

William shrugged. He'd come to much the same conclusion himself. "Well, I would ask that you keep my confidence in this matter for the moment, Alec."

"Of course. So what do you need me to do?"

William walked to the fireplace, putting one booted foot on the fender as he looked into the flames. "The Lizard is in town."

Alec whistled softly. "He cannot threaten you here, surely?"

William gave a short laugh. "Of course he can. Not in the same way, certainly, and for the last couple of weeks, he hasn't been particularly attentive. But I need someone to watch our contacts, to let me know if the Lizard or, indeed, any Frenchman unfamiliar to them approaches them in any way. I cannot have eyes everywhere. I know Barras has to have other agents operating in the city, and I'm trying to identify them all, while gathering what information I can on those with the resources to aid the Duc d'Enghien and his Army of Condé."

"What of Marcus?"

"He has his hands full, as I do. We need more help, Alec."

"Of course," Alec agreed readily. "I will do what I can, gladly, but . . . well, with the baby and Marie Claire, I am not expecting to be much in company in the next few months." He regarded William anxiously, unwilling to refuse his help but at the same time certain of his priorities.

William looked at him with a half smile. "No, of course you're not, and neither should you. Marie Claire has been through enough on her own without sacrificing time with you at this juncture."

"Hero will do it."

William groaned. "Does neither of you understand anything I've said?"

"Yes, of course we do. But I don't agree with you when it comes to wrapping my sister in cotton wool, quite apart from the fact that you won't be able to do it anyway. Why not accept her for who she is and let her help? She'll be every bit as good as I would be, in fact probably better. She knows more people and makes friends as and where she chooses. If you ask her to become acquainted with some of the émigré families who don't frequent the usual circles, and there are plenty of them who can't afford to put on the necessary show to participate, she will do so easily. She has a talent for making friends."

William frowned. Once again, he felt he was choosing between his need for Hero's help and his responsibility to keep her safe. A self-imposed responsibility and one he knew Hero would fight tooth and nail. And once again, he knew which way he would eventually choose, and he would have to live with stress and unease as a result. But there

226

was an inevitability about it.

An inevitability about Hero herself.

FIFTEEN

Hero stood at her chamber window, looking down onto the street, watching for William's departure. She was ready to go out, wearing a dark green ermine-trimmed cape over her muslin gown and half boots of soft green leather. Her eyes held a mischievous gleam as she gazed intently into the street, and the moment the front door opened and William emerged onto the top step, she was moving swiftly to the chamber door.

William stood for a moment, as always glancing around, assessing his surroundings. He could see nothing out of the ordinary, a footman carrying parcels and hatboxes into one of the houses along the street, a lady's maid walking a small, fat pug dog, a groom holding the heads of a fine pair of grays in the traces of a phaeton outside a house around the square. A perfectly peaceful scene on an autumn day in one of London's most fashionable squares. He trod lightly down the steps to the street and crossed over into the square garden.

He heard the front door of the Bruton mansion open as he stepped onto the gravel path that led beneath the horse chestnut trees to the far side of the garden. He paused, glancing over his shoulder, his senses instantly alert. Hero came running across the street, waving merrily.

"I said I would challenge you," she called, holding out her tightly fisted gloved hands towards him. "Which do you choose?"

He stood, hands on his hips, watching her approach. She came up to him, her cheeks delicately flushed, her vivid green eyes shining, her hair coiled in two fat caramel- and honey-colored plaits around her bare head. And as so often in the past, he had the greatest urge to loosen them and run his fingers through the shining multicolored cascade.

"Oh, you look just like some stuffy, disapproving old uncle," she declared, missing the quick needle of lust that had come and gone in his eyes. "The garden is for playing."

Opportunely, a pair of small boys emerged onto the path ahead of them, flourishing wooden swords and engaged in a mock fight, which seemed to involve a great deal of shouting and fierce war whoops.

"Come on, William, which hand?"

"You're incorrigible," he stated. "Why aren't you wearing a hat?" He tapped her extended right hand with an air of resignation.

"You can't play conkers wearing a hat," she scoffed, opening the chosen hand to reveal a shiny chestnut on the end of a string. "They've both been soaked in vinegar, so they're equally hard." She opened her left fist and swung her own conker in a purposeful arc. "To the death?"

"To the death," he agreed, and with a swift twist of his hand sent his conker flying on the end of its string to make contact with Hero's.

She laughed, but even through her laughter and the sparkle of her eyes, he could see her determined purpose. He should have remembered that Lady Hermione Fanshawe was a deadly serious competitive fighter, whatever her weapon.

And suddenly, he found himself playing in earnest, as determined as she that his would be the winning chestnut, unbroken and still attached to its string.

Hero danced around him, and he matched her speed but realized early on that she had a more practiced wrist action than he did, her conker snapping and jumping against his own. And at the end, when his smashed into pieces, falling from the string to the ground, he was laughingly surprised to find that their little battle had drawn quite a crowd of small children and their nurse-maids.

"You win, you outrageous creature," he said, sweeping her a deep bow of concession. "How on earth did I allow you to engage me in such preposterous childishness? Now, take my arm as if you were a respectable lady, and we'll stroll decorously around the garden in the hopes that we'll cease to be a spectacle more suited to a zoo."

Hero, still laughing, first curtsied to their audience, then obeyed, tucking her arm into his. He led her away from the little crowd and down a narrow gravel pathway between laurel hedges.

"Are you living in Half Moon Street again?" she asked, her tone now serious, the laughter fading from her eyes.

"Yes." His voice was wary.

"Can we go there now?"

"No."

Hero glanced sideways at his set profile and said nothing for a few minutes. Then she slipped her hand from his arm and asked, "Why do you attach so much importance to my reputation, William? I care nothing for it, so why should you?"

"You care nothing for it because you don't know what it means to lose it," he responded curtly.

She stopped on the pathway, standing slightly in front of him, blocking his way. "And you do? It makes no sense to me that someone who lives the life you live should give a fig for convention and reputation and all the societal silliness that means. I don't understand it." She spoke fiercely, struggling to convey to him the vital importance of her question. She had to learn why he had felt it necessary to bring their love affair to such a cruelly abrupt ending on the Isle of Wight, when in her heart, she knew he felt, or *had* felt, as deeply attached to her as she was to him.

"I have seen what happens to people when they lose their place in their world," William stated, his expression darkening. "And you have not. I have lost one person whom I loved more than I can say because of it, and I will not stand aside and let the same thing happen to you."

"Who was it? Will you tell me about it?"

"No," he said flatly, his tawny gold eyes shadowed. "That is not something I will share with anyone. It is not all mine to share."

Slowly, Hero nodded. She had a horror of intruding on anyone's privacy, just as she had a horror of anyone intruding on her own. She wanted most desperately to know what had happened, because it held the key to any resumption of their own loving liaison, but she knew she had gone as far as she dared for now.

William looked at her bent head, the frown on her usually smooth forehead, and he could feel her hurt. He reached out a finger and lifted her chin, obliging her to meet his eyes. "That subject is closed, Hero. But all is not lost. You may invite me for dinner tomorrow evening." A smile quirked the corners of his mouth, and the shadows left his eyes.

The old familiar William had returned, and Hero forced down the flicker of resentment that he thought he could so easily move beyond something that still mattered so deeply to her. She had no choice at this point and in this public space but to accept what he would give her. She executed a perfect curtsy, saying sweetly, "Pray, sir, would you do us the honor of dining with my brother and myself tomorrow evening? I fear Lady Bruton will be obliged to excuse herself, but my companion, Lady Emily, will, I'm sure, be more than happy to receive you."

He bowed solemnly. "Indeed, madam, the honor will be all mine."

"At seven o'clock, then." She turned to retrace her steps.

"Allow me to escort you to your door, ma'am." He took her arm firmly in his again.

"Thank you. I'm sure my reputation would suffer dreadfully from my walking alone in Grosvenor Square in front of my own house," she murmured.

"Put the claws away, sweetheart. They don't suit you," he said, laughing at her. "Cry peace."

"Truce," she amended.

"As you wish." He escorted her to her door and waited until she had been admitted before walking away, heading for St. James's Street and White's Club.

The Lizard was sitting beside the fire in the main salon of White's Club. He was alone, a glass of claret at hand, a copy of the *London Gazette* open in front of him. But he was not reading the latest pieces of Society gossip or the latest political news, despite the paper's preoccupation with affairs in Europe and most particularly in Paris. His gaze slipped sideways to survey the salon's occupants, the arrivals and departures. He was not a well-known member. Indeed, his membership had been finagled through discreet diplomatic channels by Chauvelin, the French ambassador to the Court of St. James before the execution of the French king ended diplomatic relations between the two countries. From the point of view of the members of the exclusive club, Chevalier Everard Dubois was simply an unfortunate émigré from the chaos that had destroyed French Society.

He was aware of William Ducasse's presence almost before the Viscount walked into the salon. There was something about the man that commanded instant attention — unless, of course, he had no wish to be noticed, Dubois reflected grimly, his eyes studiously fixed on the newspaper in his hands. When Ducasse had a mind to be invisible, somehow he achieved it. But clearly, this afternoon was not such an occasion. He strolled through the salon, greeting acquaintances, pausing at a card table to watch a game of whist, laughingly offering a word of advice to a pair playing chess in the bay window looking onto St. James's Street. If he was aware of his nemesis, he gave no sign, until, with a glass of claret in his hand, he crossed the salon to the fireplace and stood with his back to the fire, idly surveying the room before turning his seemingly languid gaze on Everard Dubois.

The Lizard lowered his paper, and for a moment, the two men looked at each other in silence, a look of acknowledgment, of rapiers drawn. Then Ducasse nodded once and strolled away towards double doors at the end of the room, which led into a further card room.

"Ducasse, come and take my place. I've lost enough for one day." Sir Marcus Gosford hailed him from a card table where they were playing faro.

"Gladly, Marcus." William walked over to the table. "Are the cards not running for you today?"

"The devil's in 'em," Marcus declared in disgust, pushing back his chair. "See if you can do any better."

"A word with you first." William walked a little to one side, exchanging his empty glass for a full one from the tray of a passing footman.

Marcus followed, his eyes now watchful. He had worked long enough with William in the bloody furnace of revolutionary Paris to know when caution was necessary. He took a glass from the footman and glanced nonchalantly around the card room. It looked the same to him now as it had done when he'd entered an hour earlier.

"The Lizard is in the next room," William observed casually, his tone evenly modulated, as if he was imparting a perfectly ordinary piece of gossip.

"Why?" Marcus's tone was equally bland, although his eyes had sharpened like the tips of daggers.

"Your guess is as good as mine. But it bodes nothing good, you can be sure." He sipped his claret. "He's been around town for a few weeks but never made his presence as obvious as it is now. So just a word to the wise." He nodded as casually as before and went to take his friend's place at the faro table.

Marcus walked away and took a side door from the card room, which took him out to the hall without having to cross the main salon. He retrieved his cloak, hat, and cane from the porter and went out into the crisp air. There was a game afoot once again, and he felt a little of the old thrill from the Paris days, as well as an almost palpable sharpening of his wits.

Everard Dubois remained in the main salon, his eyes seeing nothing of the printed page in front of him. He had made the first move in the game, and while Ducasse had shown no chink in his impassive demeanor, the Lizard knew that his openly thrown gauntlet would have caught the other man by surprise. They were both so accustomed to working in the shadows that bringing the game into the open was bound to catch the enemy wrong-footed. Of course, Ducasse would be even more watchful now, but Dubois was confident that unless his quarry went completely to ground, which would be out of a character for a man who had never resisted a challenge, something or someone in his life would offer an opening for the poisoned tip of the sword.

Carefully, he folded his newspaper along the fold and laid it aside as he rose to his feet and sauntered out of the club, well satisfied with his afternoon's work.

As far as his card-playing companions were concerned, William Ducasse, Viscount St. Aubery, was his usual genial, if slightly reserved, self. He played as astutely as he always did, although the game was essentially one of chance, and after half an hour, he gathered up his modest winnings and made his farewells to the table.

He left the club, nothing in his bland

demeanor offering a clue to the swift calculations his mind was making as he walked to Half Moon Street. The Lizard had come into the open, a move that changed the rules of the game by which they had always played. William could congratulate his old enemy on such a sideways maneuver, but it made it imperative that he find out what lay behind it. What was Everard Dubois planning? If he wasn't working in the shadows anymore, what did he hope to achieve by moving into the open?

As he strolled casually down Piccadilly, William, as always, looked for followers, but he had the feeling that was an old technique, one the Lizard had abandoned. His quarry was to be free to walk the streets and go about his business without a close follower. It was intriguing, and it also made him unusually anxious. He hated the idea that he didn't know what was in the Lizard's mind.

He arrived at his leased house in Half Moon Street, a tall, narrow residence with a front door that opened directly onto the narrow pavement. A curricle swept past him in the street as he inserted his key in the lock, so close he could feel the breeze of its passing against his coattails. As soon as he stepped into the hall, he sensed something was out of place. He looked around the narrow hallway. Everything was in its usual place.

"André?" He called for his servant as he hung his beaver hat on the hook by the door.

The man appeared from the baize door behind the stairs, looking a little agitated. "Forgive me, my lord, but you have a visitor, and . . ."

"That's all right, André, you need not explain my presence to his lordship."

William stared with growing anger at the figure who had appeared in the doorway of the small sitting room to the right of the hall.

"You must not blame André, William," Hero said swiftly. "But —"

"Oh, believe me, I do not," William interrupted emphatically. He seized her shoulder, spun her around, and pushed her back into the sitting room, closing the door with a click behind them.

"Just what do you think you're playing at?"

Hero shrugged lightly. "If the mountain won't come to Mohammed . . ."

Sixteen

"I swear to you, I wasn't followed. You know you can trust me for that." She pushed back the hood of her dark cloak, which effectively concealed both face and form.

"Where's your maid?"

She gave him a look that conveyed how idiotic she considered the question. "No one saw me, no one followed me, no one knows I'm here." She articulated every word, her green-eyed gaze fixed upon him with a resolution that stated clearly that she was not going to back down. And she said nothing more, merely waited for him to speak, outwardly calm although her heart was fluttering against her ribs. Fury glittered in his eyes, and his lips had thinned, a pulse jumping in his cheek.

"You make me so angry," he stated slowly. "I try very hard never to lose control of my anger, but you, Hero, make that all but impossible."

With great difficulty Hero stood her ground, although she flinched inwardly. But he made no move towards her, despite the clear threat in his voice and expression. "No one followed me, no one knows I'm here," she repeated doggedly. "We are quite private, unless you cannot trust your servant?"

William didn't dignify that with a response. He turned and opened the door. "André." He barely raised his voice.

"My lord." The man appeared instantly.

"You will escort the lady immediately to Grosvenor Square."

"*Oui,* my lord."

"No," Hero said. "I am not leaving here, not until we have talked properly. I will not be brushed aside any longer, William. You owe me an explanation for behaving as you did in Yarmouth, and I want it. I don't accept this vague fuss about reputation. My reputation is not yours to guard. You have not earned that right." She stood defiantly, her feet unconsciously braced as if she were about to do battle with a wolf.

William jerked his head at André, who, with clear relief, stepped back again into the hall and closed the salon door.

"So," William said, "I have not earned the right to be concerned for you. Well, let me tell you this, Hermione, I am responsible for any harm coming to you through any act of mine. That is a fact, and one you would do well to accept quickly. I will not relinquish that responsibility, and if you fight me over it, you will lose. I can safely promise you that."

She looked at him in disbelieving astonishment. "Who on earth do you think you are? You did not oblige me to fall in love with you. I was a more than willing partner in our relationship, if that's what it was. It was a love affair, one that you brought to a wretched finish without a word of explanation. You left me high and dry, not knowing what I'd done wrong. For that, William Ducasse, you are certainly responsible, and I demand an explanation." One booted foot stamped in vigorous punctuation.

Golden fire flashed across his eyes, and he spoke with icy control. "You, madam, are a termagant."

"And you, sir, are a bully," she fired back, no longer afraid of his anger. "You think your opinion is the only right one, you think that everyone must obey your slightest dictate, you think you only need to give orders without explanation and everyone must jump. Well, I, for one, am not going to." The other boot made emphatic contact with the floor.

"Are you going to compel me to put you out?" His voice was now dangerously low.

"Oh, do so if you wish, but I can assure you it will make the biggest scandal Half Moon Street has ever seen. I will ensure that, and I will sit outside your door until you *have* to let me in again."

"You are the most unschooled, ill-disciplined, self-willed, spoiled brat it has ever been my misfortune to know," he exclaimed.

"And you are a prudish hypocrite who thinks he can ride roughshod over anyone in his path." Hero reached out blindly, and her hand closed over the first object it met, which turned out to be a jug of late September roses. She hurled it at him and then stood, her hand over her mouth, staring at the damage she had wrought. William stood dripping, a rose caught in the unruly lock of hair on his forehead, several more adorning his shoulders. The earthenware jug, miraculously unbroken, lay on the carpet at his feet.

"You . . ." He took a step towards her, grabbing her by the shoulders. "For two pins, I would . . ." His words faded as he saw the sudden laughter flare in her green eyes as she looked at him.

"I . . . I'm sorry." She gasped through a

bubble of laughter.

"No, you're not," he denied savagely. "You're a wicked, lawless woman, and may God help me, I cannot resist you."

He caught her against him, his lips crushing her laughing mouth as his arms encircled her in a grip so tight it was almost punitive, but Hero reveled in the strength of him once more, the power of his body against hers, so familiar and so long missed. She reached up a hand to pluck a rose from his hair and brushed the wet lock off his forehead, even as her mouth remained riveted to his, her head bent back beneath the pressure of his kiss. His arm moved to her waist, supporting her as his body bent over hers, before his other arm slipped beneath her knees and he lifted her against him.

"Obviously, I have to find another way to make my point," he declared, lifting his mouth from hers. "It seems there's only one thing you understand."

He carried her out of the sitting room and marched with her upstairs, kicking open the door of a large firelit bedchamber on the first landing. He tossed her unceremoniously onto the big four-poster bed.

"Get your clothes off, *now.*"

Hero's skin tingled with excitement as she

sat up and reached down to unlace her boots, watching as William threw off his clothes, dropping them carelessly where they landed.

Naked, he turned and hauled her to her feet as she pushed off her stockings with her feet. "You're too slow," he said, deftly unfastening the little looped buttons that ran down the back of her gown. He pushed it off her shoulders and dropped it over a chair. "Take off your chemise." His voice had suddenly dropped a note, and the urgency of passion was a deep throb.

Slowly now, with great deliberation, Hero peeled off the flimsy silk chemise, sliding it down her hips, stepping out of it as it puddled at her feet. She stood facing him, her bare skin gleaming opalescent in the fire's glow.

He put a hand on her shoulder and gave her a light push so that she fell back onto the bed, feeling the slight roughness of the embroidered coverlet against her back. He leaned over her, sliding a hand under her bottom and shifting her slightly so that she lay at full length on the bed. He moved to kneel at the end, holding her feet lightly in both hands. He moved her feet apart, spreading them wider on the coverlet, opening her thighs. His flat hands moved up the insides of her legs, parting her thighs even wider. Hero felt her skin grow hot with anticipation, her sex growing moist and swollen with longing. When he touched the core of her body with the faintest brush of a fingertip, her hips bucked with the jolt of lust.

William smiled, a very slow smile, as he moved his hand from her body. "Don't move an inch. Stay just as you are." He stood up from the bed and moved away out of her sight for a moment. When he came back, he held something concealed in his hand. He looked down at her, his eyes narrowed and darkened as he gazed at her spread-eagled body, caught the flicker of uncertainty in her eyes warring with the sensual longing in their green depths.

Putting one knee on the bed beside her, he leaned over, opening his hand to reveal a small brush, one she knew well. She had watched him shave often enough. It was of the softest badger hair, and as she realized what he was going to do, her heart seemed to leap into her throat, a flush suffusing her skin. "Please," she whispered, not knowing if it was a protest or a plea. She had only the faintest inkling of what it would feel like.

The faintest inkling bore no relation to the reality. The brush lightly flicked against the insides of her thighs, stroked upwards one tantalizing millimeter at a time. She held her breath, waiting, waiting for what took an eternity to come. When the soft brush touched her moist and heated sex, she heard herself gasp, a little moan escape her. Her hips jerked against the coverlet, and he laid a restraining hand on her lower belly. "Be still. I'm not finished yet."

It was unbearable, and yet it was the most exquisite torment Hero could ever have imagined. She writhed beneath the soft, flicking caresses, wanting it to stop, wanting it never to stop, and William, a smile playing over his lips, continued with the silken strokes until she could contain herself no longer. A cry broke from her lips, and her hips lifted as the muscles of her backside and belly clenched tight and the storm of delight ripped through her, finally casting her ashore to lie flat on the bed, her limbs in an abandoned sprawl, her eyes closed as tears of ungovernable pleasure oozed beneath her lids.

William knelt astride her, slipping his hands beneath her bottom to lift her on his palms, holding her open as he slid inside her. Instantly, her inner muscles tightened around him, and he moved his hands to grip her hips, holding her steady as he moved with a swift, urgent rhythm that Hero picked up without a breath, concentrating now on giving back something of what he had given her. And so hard was she concentrating on giving pleasure that her own crept up upon her, catching her by surprise just as his pleasure peaked, and he cried out the instant he withdrew from her body, falling on top of her, his penis throbbing hotly against her belly.

When finally he managed to roll off her, he lay beside her, his hand on her belly, a faint laugh escaping him. "Let that be a lesson to you, Madam Termagant."

Hero grinned weakly, her fingers trawling through his hair. She found a stray rose tangled in the chestnut crop and held it up. "You're quite a flower garden. Perhaps I should make a habit of throwing things at you."

"I seriously don't advise it," he said.

Hero decided that on second thought, she would heed his advice. William, for all his iron self-control, had his limits. Besides, she was not in the habit of exhibiting childish bouts of temper herself. She drifted into a trancelike half sleep and was only vaguely aware when he moved sideways and slipped from the bed. She heard him moving around and finally rolled sideways to prop herself on one elbow.

"So what now, William?"

"Well, now you're here, I see no reason to hurry you away," he said, fastening the tie of a dressing gown at his narrow waist. "Unless you have some other engagement this evening."

Hero thought rapidly. She was engaged to go to the theatre with a party of friends, but the prospect seemed no longer in the least inviting. "No," she said firmly. "But could André take a note to Alec? To say I won't be home for dinner?" Alec would also make sure that her previous engagement was canceled appropriately, but that she kept to herself. There was no knowing what would offend William's overly cautious sense of social propriety. Better he thought she had nothing else to do than that she was deliberately canceling a previous engagement at short notice to indulge in an evening of unbridled licentiousness. She couldn't quite manage to swallow the mischievous little chuckle of anticipation at the thought.

"You'll find pen and paper on the secretaire." William gestured to the desk beneath the window. "I'll bring up some wine." He left the chamber, and Hero slowly got off the bed. There was a jug of water on the washstand, and she cleansed her body of the residue of that passionate interlude, then put her chemise back on, before writing her note to Alec.

"Oh, I had it in mind that you should remain naked for my delectation this evening," William said, coming back into the chamber, a hint of sensual amusement in his voice. "Let's take that off. I'll keep the fire hot, I promise."

The idea sent prickles over her skin as Hero slipped out of the chemise. In truth, there was something wonderfully liberating about being naked. And it reminded her of the many occasions on their journey through France when they had enjoyed the freshness of the river air on their naked bodies. Somehow it sensitized the skin, made one more wholly aware of one's surroundings and the sensual opportunities they embodied.

"What of you?" she asked.

He inclined his head. "It would please me greatly if tonight we played a little game. You stay as you are, I stay as I am."

A host of scenarios flooded her already overactive imagination, each one more compelling than the last. "If you wish it, sir," she murmured, regarding him through lowered eyelashes.

He gave a soft laugh. "Oh, yes, I wish it."

William bent and threw more logs on the fire. "Do you have your note written for André to take?"

"On the secretaire." Hero hitched a velvet-covered ottoman closer to her with her foot and sat down facing the fire. She took the glass of pale gold wine he gave her and sipped, watching the spurt of flame as the fresh logs caught.

William took the folded sheet from the secretaire and dropped wax on the fold, pressing his signet ring into the hot seal. "I'll give this to André. What would you like for dinner?" He looked down at her bent head, smiling at the gorgeous richness of its multicolors caught by the fire's light, remembering how many times he had longed to run his fingers through the massed tumble of curls and how many times he had had to refrain from the indulgence. For the next few hours, he could do as he wished.

"Dinner?" Hero turned her head lazily to look up at him. A smile touched her mouth as she read the lascivious gleam in his eye. "I have no particular wishes. Am I to stay the whole night?"

"I will take you back to Grosvenor Square at dawn," he returned. "Probably no later than any other night you spend gallivanting about town at masquerades and ridottos."

"Calumny," she accused, taking another sip of her wine. "In general, I seek my bed before midnight."

"Truth twister," he responded, leaving the chamber with a soft laugh.

If she had troubled to think about it, Hero would have been surprised at how easy and relaxed she felt, sitting naked in a strange bedchamber awaiting the return of her lover. It was almost as if she were existing outside herself. And yet, on another plane, she was inhabiting her own body in the fullest sense. Her skin still tingled, her loins still felt spent, used by pleasure, and there was a slight soreness between her thighs. She had been used and devastated by sheer physical joy, and it was the most wondrous feeling imaginable.

But she still had no answer to the question, the demand that had begun this evening's wild ride of lust. She still felt as if her natural desires, her passion, her love for this man, a love she could not as yet properly admit, were trapped by some unknown and untellable secret, which only William held.

The fire's warmth lulled her as she sipped the golden wine, and her eyelids drooped, but she came to with a jolt as the door opened and a cold draft flickered against her bared back.

"Forgive me. It's much cooler on the landing." William closed the door smartly behind him. He set down the tray he was carrrying on a side table beside Hero's ottoman. "I thought we might start with some oysters."

Hero examined the large oval platter of opened oysters, their succulent pale gray offering resting against the pearly glimmer of their shells.

"André has taken your letter, so I shucked them myself." William turned up his palms ruefully. "They are the very devil, I had forgotten how difficult. But madam, nothing is too much trouble for you." He knelt beside her ottoman and lifted one of the largest shells, holding it to her lips.

Hero sucked the gleaming flesh from the shell with a practiced movement of her tongue and swallowed the fishy liquid as he tipped it against her mouth. Her eyes closed involuntarily. "Delicious. Allow me to return the favor, My Lord St. Aubery."

The oysters disappeared, and still Hero wondered if she could ask her question again. She felt that William was deliberately distracting her, which, she had to admit, was working beautifully. But it left her with an empty feeling lurking somewhere beneath the glorious and seemingly endless

peaks of that long evening in the firelit
chamber on Half Moon Street.

SEVENTEEN

It was still dark, although the first faint glimmer of gray showed in the eastern sky when William and Hero left the house on Half Moon Street. The streets were still quiet, although it would not be long before the first costermongers, milkmaids, and barrow boys made their appearance. At the end of Half Moon Street on the corner of Curzon Street, a carriage waited, bearing the Bruton arms. Hero didn't inquire how or when the mews had been told to send the carriage for her at precisely four thirty in the morning. William would have arranged it in his usual seamless fashion.

He handed her up into the carriage and stood for a moment, one boot resting on the footstep, his arm along the edge of the open window. "I'll see you this evening." His eyes still held the residual glow of the passionate hours they had just passed.

"At seven o'clock." She smiled, leaned

through the window, and lightly kissed his mouth.

"Go," he said, stepping back hastily, casting a quick glance around.

Hero grinned. "Oh, so cautious," she mocked. "Every right-thinking person is tucked up in his bed at this hour."

He said nothing, but his face closed, and he turned away without a further gesture of farewell. The coachman's whip cracked, and the carriage moved off in the direction of Grosvenor Square.

William walked home, wondering what hold Hero had over him that she could so easily overcome his hard-fought resolution. His fears for her reputation were one thing, but now he had Everard Dubois to add to the equation. If the Lizard was playing in the open now, it would be to disarm his quarry. But William couldn't see how his old enemy thought he could do that just by making himself visible. But he was up to something, and that meant that William and every one of his associates would have to be even more alert. And that included Hero, since, as seemed obvious, he had so spectacularly failed to exclude her from his life.

Every inch of him was resistant to involving her in that world again, whatever her brother had said, but the minute he took her into his confidence, she would see herself as involved, and he knew her well enough to know that she would embrace that involvement with open arms. But if he said nothing to her, she would continue to behave with her habitual reckless disregard for convention and would inevitably come to the notice of the Lizard and his cohorts.

His alternative, of course, was to follow Alec's advice and make use of her as he had done in Paris. If he had to take her into his confidence, then why not make the most of what she had to offer? Not only was she clever, resourceful, careful when she recognized the need to be, and quick to respond to danger, but she was perfectly placed to do what needed to be done. On the whole, he decided, she would be safer being a part of his enterprise. There was no knowing what she would get mired in if left to her own devices, and at least if she was working with him, she would accept his leadership.

He would put her to work at a task that would be quite natural for her, would be perfectly safe, and should keep her satisfied and out of trouble.

His mind made up, his step lightened as he reached Half Moon Street in search of his bed. He was in dire need of a few hours of uninterrupted sleep.

■ ■ ■ ■

Hero greeted the night doorman sleepily as he let her into the darkened house. It was still too early for any of the household to be up. She hurried up to her own bedchamber, yawning. The candle was burning low on the bedside table when she entered the chamber, and the fire was little more than glowing embers. She lit a fresh candle from the guttering one and threw more wood on the fire.

Her nightgown was lying ready for her on the bed, the heavy damask curtains drawn across the long windows. The water in the ewer was, of course, cold. Her note to Alec had asked him to tell Maisie, her maid, not to wait up for her, and Hero knew the girl would not disturb her until she rang for her in the morning. For the moment, all she wanted was sleep. Her body ached in the most pleasurable way, but her limbs were heavy and resistant to any kind of energetic movement. She discarded her gown, chemise, and petticoats and dropped the nightgown over her head. Ordinarily, she would have washed her face and brushed her teeth and hair, but such activities were beyond her. She fell into bed and was almost

259

instantly asleep.

The sun was high when Hero awoke, a gleam of light creeping through a crack in the curtains. She swam upwards slowly from the depths of a dreamless sleep and lay reordering her thoughts before lazily reaching for the bell pull beside the bed.

"Good morning, my lady." Maisie came in with her usual sunny smile and a silver tray with a pot of hot chocolate, a plate of bread and butter, and a small pile of billets-doux. She set the tray on the bedside table and went to draw back the curtains. Golden autumn sunlight flooded across the rich Aubusson carpet, and Hero hitched herself up against the pillows, looking around rather blearily.

"Good morning, Maisie. Is it still morning?"

"Just after eleven, madam." Maisie poured a fragrant stream of hot chocolate into the wide, shallow porcelain cup. "You must've come in late." She handed the cup to Hero and picked up the discarded clothes from the chair where Hero had dropped them.

"About half past four, I think." Hero sipped her chocolate and opened one of the envelopes the girl had set on the coverlet beside her. She read the contents with a little frown and laid it aside. Her suitors, if they could be called such, tended to be fulsome with their compliments and sometimes overly demanding in their invitations. She picked up a dainty nosegay with a ribbon-attached note and smiled appreciatively. The handwriting belonged to Sir Marcus Gosford, and the nosegay was exactly the delicate gesture she had learned to expect from him in the few weeks since they had met in London again after Paris.

He was a lighthearted friend and an easy companion, as comfortable with Hero as he was with Alec. He was always willing to step in as an escort when she needed one, and he had never shown the slightest inclination to move beyond friendship, for which she was grateful. It was pleasantly refreshing to have such a natural, unpressured friendship. He had returned to London almost a year after they had parted on the banks of the Seine after that dreadful journey through the city sewers, and he never said where he had been or what he had been doing. Alec and Hero didn't ask; they knew the rules of that world too well. And somehow Hero had found it impossible to ask him about William. A casual inquiry should have been natural enough, but for some reason, such a question seemed taboo, and he had never been mentioned between them.

Marcus was suggesting a ride to Richmond Park that afternoon, and Hero's first thought was that now she could casually mention that she'd met William again very recently and see if Marcus could throw any light on his presence in London and, even more, any inkling of his peculiar fixation on that bugbear, *reputation.* She had no illusions, however, that Marcus would be any more likely than her brother to tell her anything important without William's permission. And if he hadn't given it to Alec, he wouldn't have given it to Marcus. However, Hero was an eternal optimist, and there was no telling what she might inadvertently discover about his past that might explain some aspect of his present. At the very least, she would enjoy a long ride in pleasant company on such a glorious day.

"Lay out my riding habit, Maisie. And when I return later this afternoon, I'd like to have a bath before dinner." She threw aside the covers and got up with a surge of energy, stretching deeply and rolling her shoulders. She sat at the secretaire and penned a quick note of acceptance to Marcus, and informing him of the exciting news in Grosvenor Square. Alec would have sent the obligatory notice of the baby's birth to the *London Gazette,* but Marcus may not have read it as yet.

She folded the note and sealed it, handing it to Maisie. "I'll just go and see how Lady Bruton and the baby are this morning. Could you have this sent to Sir Marcus right away?"

She made her way to Marie Claire's apartments across the landing and knocked. The door was instantly opened by Nan, who gave her erstwhile nurseling a searching, all-seeing look. "Just getting up, are we?" she stated with clear disapproval. "The day's half gone."

"I didn't get to my bed until this morning, Nan," Hero protested.

"All this gadding about doesn't do a body any good."

Hero chuckled and ducked past the elderly woman to go to the bedside. Marie Claire was sitting up, looking rested and happy, her baby nestled against her breast. Hero bent to kiss her sister-in-law and then the baby's soft cheek. "She grows prettier by the minute."

"Just like her mother." The adoring comment came from Alec, who entered the room from his dressing room, toweling his wet hair. "Aren't they beautiful?"

"Utterly," Hero agreed, perching on the edge of the bed. "Have you only just got

263

up, too?"

"Not a bit of it. I've been out riding since six," he declared. "It's too beautiful a day to waste."

"I'll leave you to it," Nan stated, nodding at the group by the bed. She looked rather self-satisfied, Hero thought, smiling as the nurse left the chamber.

"So you were with William last night?" Alec sat beside her, taking his baby daughter from her mother's arms and cradling her in the crook of his elbow.

"Yes," she said. "He's coming to dinner tonight."

"I should like to see him," Marie Claire said in her soft voice. "We have a question to ask him, do we not, Alec?"

He nodded and brushed the baby's wrinkled forehead with a tip of his finger. "Yes, we do." He looked at his sister. "Did he talk to you?"

"Not in the way you mean, no," she said with a shake of her head. "It's so infuriating."

"Talk about what?" Marie Claire inquired.

"That's the problem, my dear. I don't know," Hero said. "He's here on some kind of business, the usual kind for him, I suppose. He's told Alec but swore Alec to secrecy, and although I spent all evening and night with him, he told me nothing. I'd like to strangle him sometimes."

Marie Claire's smile was a little wistful. Even after the close bonds they had forged during their long journey down the river and out of France, she still found the thought of William and Hero's relationship both puzzling and a little shocking. She was still in awe of William, and Hero's willingness to oppose him whenever it felt right to her remained a source of wonder to Marie Claire's gentler, more accommodating soul. "He probably wants to keep you out of danger," she ventured.

"Exactly," Hero responded vehemently. "And I cannot get him to understand that I don't want to be kept out of it. I don't need to be. If I can be useful, then I'd like to be. He has some misguided misgivings about my reputation, would you believe?"

Alec gave a shout of laughter, and even Marie Claire managed a chuckle. "I'd have thought he'd recognize a lost cause when he saw it," Alec said, getting up to answer a discreet tap at the door. "Aunt Emily, come in. See how well they both are."

"Oh, I'm so pleased." Emily wafted in her cloud of shawls and sal volatile to the bedside. "How well you're looking, my dear, and after such an ordeal." She shook her head with an air of astonishment. "I don't know how you young ladies manage it. Indeed, I don't."

Hero winked at Marie Claire. "I'm not sure there's any choice once conception has taken place, ma'am."

"Oh, dear me, Hero, must you talk like that? It's so indecorous." Emily waved her fan vigorously, as if to banish Hero's outrageous bluntness. "I don't know what your dear mother would have said."

"I rather think she would have agreed with me," Hero responded, rising to her feet. "I must go and dress. I'm riding to Richmond with Marcus a bit later."

Marcus rode up to the doorway precisely at one o'clock, and Hero was watching for him from the salon window. She ran downstairs just as Jackson was crossing the hall to greet the visitor as the footman opened the door.

"Good afternoon, Hero." Marcus bowed, his gaze running appreciatively over her. She wore a riding habit of deep bronze velvet edged with gold braid, the skirt swept up to one side, and a golden feather in her hat, its brim turned up rakishly on one side. He offered his arm and escorted her down to the pavement where her horse was waiting with a groom at its head.

"I must say, it's hard to imagine you as you were when I first met you," he remarked with a laugh. "You clean up remarkably well."

"I might say the same about you," she retorted, taking the reins and bending her knee for the groom to hoist her up into the saddle. It was true. Marcus cut a very fine figure of an English gentleman-about-town in his dove-gray riding britches, close-fitting black coat, and immaculately starched white stock. His high-crowned beaver hat sported a black plume, and his boots shone like glass.

He laughed. "We've come a long way since then."

"Yes," she agreed, and for a moment, they were both silent, their expressions grave. The memories of those grim days were not easily banished.

"How are Marie Claire and the baby?" he asked after a while. "Alec must be over the moon."

"He is, and they're all doing splendidly," she responded, before adding, "I saw William yesterday." She shot him a sideways glance as they trotted around the square.

"Ah." His tone was noncommittal. "Yes, he's been in town for a couple of weeks."

"I ran into him the other night at a ridotto

at Ranelagh." She paused for an instant before saying, "He wasn't best pleased. He seemed to think I should be living the life of a maiden on the marriage mart, which struck me as a little strange in the circumstances."

Marcus's expression didn't change. "William has many different facets, I've noticed over the time I've known him. The Guillaume of Paris might view life and its rules very differently from the Viscount St. Aubery in the midst of London Society."

"I suppose so." She sounded doubtful. "But can you think of a reason why he should become so exercised about *my* reputation?"

"He cares for you, Hero. You know that well enough."

She was silent again as they started to leave the busy streets of the city behind them, riding alongside the Thames towards Richmond Park. "Sometimes," she observed slowly after some time, "he makes it difficult to believe that."

Marcus sighed. "Hero, my dear girl, I don't understand William very well, either. He holds his past and his secrets close to his chest, and he has never confided in me anything that was not related to the work he does."

"I understand, and we'll leave the subject alone, unless, of course . . ." She shot him a mischievous glance from under her lashes. "You would care to tell me what business he has in London at present."

Marcus laughed. "You really are an outrageous creature, Hero. You know perfectly well I cannot divulge anything I know about that. If you want to know, ask him yourself."

"I tried that," she said glumly. "For some reason, he wouldn't tell me." They turned through the gates of the vast expanse of Richmond Park. "Let us gallop. Petra has been itching to get her head since we left the roadway."

"Then give it to her." He held back for a moment as Hero relaxed the reins a fraction and nudged the mare with her heels. Petra shot off like a bolt from a cannon, and Marcus followed on his gray gelding, galloping along the broad ride between the trees.

The subject of William did not come up again during the three hours of their ride, and it was close to five o'clock in the gathering dusk when they returned to Grosvenor Square. Hero was exhilarated as Marcus helped her dismount, and she gave the reins to the groom, instructing, "Rub her down well and give her a bran mash. She's had a long and hard ride."

"Aye, m'lady." The man touched his forelock and led the horse away to the mews at the rear of the house.

Hero turned to Marcus with a warm smile, her hand extended. "Thank you for that, Marcus. It was just what I needed."

He lifted her hand to his lips and kissed. "Your company, as always, dear girl, was pure delight."

"If you have nothing better to do this evening, would you come for dinner? William is joining us. We're celebrating the baby. Actually, we're celebrating the baby every minute of the day at the moment," she added with a laugh. "But if you would join us, it would be an even greater celebration."

Marcus bowed. "I would be delighted. Are you sure I won't be in the way?"

"No, of course not. Aunt Emily will preside, of course, but she always excuses herself early, so we can have a cozy evening. Not quite the old days but . . ." She shrugged, her head to one side in a quizzical question mark. "At seven o'clock?"

"At seven o'clock. Give Alec and Marie Claire my congratulations until then." He bowed again and remounted, waiting until Hero had vanished into the house.

Hero ran upstairs to her bedchamber, unpinning her hat, her mind occupied with thoughts of washing her hair in a hot bath before the fire. The ride had exercised rather different muscles from those that had been used to such good effect the preceding night, but her entire body craved a long soak in warm water.

EIGHTEEN

Hero looked at herself in the cheval glass, extending one daintily shod foot to reveal her silk-stockinged ankle. Her gown was simple enough, silver-threaded rose-pink damask, caught under her breasts with a silver band, the little puff sleeves and low neckline edged in silver lace. The Directoire style suited her tall, slender frame better than the stiffened petticoats and tight bodices fashionable a mere ten years earlier, and her bosom was high and full enough to support the low neckline without additional corseting.

Maisie fastened the diamond collar around her throat as Hero screwed in the small diamond ear drops. Her freshly washed hair, fragrant with orange flower water, was drawn up into a rich knot on top of her head, carefully curled side ringlets clustered casually around her face, and a silver fillet banded her forehead. It was exactly the impression of artful carelessness she had been aiming for, she decided, smiling a rather complacent smile. Somehow it seemed very important tonight that her appearance be a statement both alluring and elegant.

She picked up her ivory fan, and Maisie draped a shawl of gossamer silk over her elbows. The maid stood back to assess the effect and nodded significantly. "You look lovely, Lady Hero. There'll be lucky gentlemen downstairs tonight."

Hero's answering grin was complicit. "There's only one I'm trying to impress, Maisie, and I think this might do it."

Maisie grinned back. Over the years since she had started to wait upon Lady Hero, when they were both barely out of childhood, she had quickly succumbed to her mistress's easy ways and frank confidences. It had taken a while for the official constraints of the mistress-servant relationship to develop these deeper ties, but Hero still remembered how it had felt when she first realized how much she needed another woman of her own age to confide in. Maisie never overstepped the line, and Hero was always careful not to involve her directly in anything that would cause the girl trouble, but the company of a trusted confidante was something she treasured.

"You need not wait up for me, Maisie," she now said. "But would you make sure there are plenty of candles, the fire is well lit, and there's more wood in the basket? Also decanters of port and cognac and a basket of those Florentine biscuits that Cook makes."

Maisie's expression didn't change. She bobbed a curtsy with a murmured, "Of course, m'lady," and went to open the door for Hero.

Hero hesitated for a moment at the top of the sweep of stairs leading down to the ground floor. Jackson was greeting the evening's guests at the doorway. William's voice rose clearly, Marcus's an instant after, so they must have arrived together.

She laid a hand on the polished banister and began to descend the stairs. "Good evening, gentlemen. I bid you welcome." She paused for effect halfway down.

"Lady Hero." Marcus bowed deeply.

"Hero." William's greeting was more amused than anything, an eyebrow raised, a twitch of his lips, as he moved to the base of the stairs and held out his hand to her as she continued her descent. "You look magnificent, my dear."

"I was wondering if you'd notice," she

muttered, taking his hand, rather spoiling the effect of her splendid entrance.

He laughed, raising her hand to his lips. "How could I not?"

She gave him a mock pout and turned back to the stairs. "Alec and my aunt are in the drawing room. Won't you come up?"

Jackson moved ahead of her on the stairs and led the way, flinging open the double doors to the drawing room with a flourish. "Viscount St. Aubery and Sir Marcus Gosford, my lady."

Emily fluttered towards the visitors, a welcoming smile on her sweet-natured face. "Gentlemen, I bid you most welcome."

Alec moved to the sideboard and poured two glasses of sherry for his guests. The preliminaries over, he said, "Marcus, would you mind if I extracted William for a few minutes? Marie Claire wishes to see him, but she's not really up to general visiting yet."

"Good Lord, no, not at all. Give her my best love." Marcus took a seat next to Emily on a sofa. "Lady Emily and I shall have a most comfortable chat, shall we not, ma'am?"

Hero followed William and her brother from the drawing room. She knew what Marie Claire and Alec were going to ask William and was most curious to see how he would respond.

Marie Claire was propped up against cushions on a daybed beside the fire. She wore a loose embroidered dressing robe, a cashmere rug draped across her knees, the baby lying swaddled in shawls in her cradle beside her. Marie Claire held out her hand to William as he came in and went instantly to her side, kissing her hand and then lightly kissing her cheek.

"Congratulations, my dear. You look remarkably well."

"Thank you. You're too kind, as always."

"As always?" He raised a quizzical eyebrow. "I dare swear there have been occasions when you did not believe that."

She laughed a little self-consciously. "Well, perhaps once or twice. But I always knew there was no choice. Would you care to hold little Fleur?"

William looked down into the cradle at the baby, whose eyes were wide open, the bright blue of her mother's, but the scrappy fringe of hair on her forehead had glints of her father's chestnut. He bent and lifted the infant with a practiced ease that surprised his audience.

Hero watched, fascinated. William held the baby as if he had been holding infants

276

for years. He gave her his little finger, and her fat, dimpled fist closed over it. He smiled and lifted her, kissing the tip of her smudge of a nose.

"She's lovely, my dears. I congratulate you both." His voice was warm, his eyes soft, as he smiled down at the baby. He held her easily in the crook of his arm, and she gazed up at him with a curious intensity.

"William, Alec and I would like you to stand godfather to Fleur," Marie Claire said softly, almost hesitantly. "Would you agree? It would make us so happy."

William's expression changed, became somber, the muscles of his cheek tightening. "You do me too much honor, Marie Claire. Be honest, now, do you both really think I am the right person for such a responsibility?"

"Without you, Fleur would not have been born," Marie Claire stated with unusual stubbornness. "I would not have been alive. We *know* you are the right person. Hero has agreed to stand godmother, and we know that the two of you will protect her whatever happens."

"Indeed, William, you *must* agree," Alec said. "For friendship's sake. After all we have been through together, there is no one

277

else but you we would trust to take care of Fleur."

William held the child, looking down at her face, at the unblinking stare. And he fought the surge of emotion, of loss, of inadequacy, that hit him sometimes with breathtaking force. How could he possibly accept responsibility for this fragile life, yet another fragile life, when he had so little to give?

Hero put her hand on his arm. Her voice was soft. She did not understand the meaning of his expression, only the profound emotional loss it showed. "My love, you and I together, we can do this. We can stand up for Fleur. It means so much to Marie Claire, to Alec."

The silence seemed to last forever, and finally, William bent over and placed the baby back in her cradle. "Very well. If you trust me, then I must trust myself. I am deeply honored." He kissed Marie Claire again and extended his hand to Alec. "I swear I will do everything in my power to honor my commitment to this little one."

And once again, the ordinary burdens of an ordinary life settled on his shoulders, together with all the unordinary burdens of a dangerous and difficult existence, one that he had freely chosen. As he had freely chosen all his responsibilities.

Except for Hero. He didn't think he had had any choice at all when it came to accepting Hero as his love and his responsibility.

"We must go down to Marcus, my dear," Alec said, leaning over his wife, adjusting the rug over her knees. "We cannot leave him alone with Emily for too much longer."

"No, of course not." She smiled up at her husband. "And thank him again for me for the beautiful flowers." She gestured to the lavish display of winter jasmine on the mantelpiece. "So delicate and such a delicious fragrance. I did write to thank him, but if you could . . ."

"Of course. Rest now, sweetheart. Shall I ring for Nan to put you back to bed?"

"No, I shall stay here a little longer. I have grown tired of my bed. Tomorrow I shall come downstairs."

"We'll discuss that with Nan and Dr. Barrett," Alec stated firmly.

Marie Claire wrinkled her nose at him, and he laughed, blowing her a kiss as he followed William and Hero downstairs to the drawing room.

Aunt Emily presided over the dinner table with her customary air of bemused amiability. Her dining companions were scrupulously courteous, keeping the conversation as general as possible for such a close-knit group, with such a shared past. But it was with relief that Hero rose with her chaperone when Emily gave her a significant nod as the dishes for the last course were cleared away.

"We will see you in the drawing room for coffee, gentlemen," Emily said gently, as William beside her rose to draw back her chair. "Thank you, sir." She bestowed a smile upon him. "I shall seek my bed soon, so don't sit too long over the port, Alec."

"We'll be in soon, ma'am." Alec and Marcus both stood up, waiting until the ladies had withdrawn, not without Hero shooting her brother a warning look over her shoulder as she went out of the room.

"Ten minutes," she mouthed at him.

"Hero is not going to be best pleased if we don't follow them quickly," her brother remarked as he fetched the port decanter from the sideboard and filled his guests' glasses. "Do we have further news of the Lizard?"

"Not a sign of him since I saw him in White's." William twisted the stem of his glass between his fingers. "And it's the oddest sensation, but I have no feeling whatsoever that I am being watched. What of you,

Marcus?"

Marcus shook his head. "No, all quiet. If I didn't know better, I'd say he's not even noticed I'm back in England."

"Oh, you can be sure he has," William said. "After that narrow escape in Austria."

"I don't know about that," Alec said, leaning forward a little. "What narrow escape?"

"Yes, indeed, what narrow escape?" Hero's voice preceded her as she emerged from behind a tapestry screen that concealed the door to the butler's pantry beside the dining room. "You cannot have interesting conversations like this that exclude me. It's really not just." She helped herself to a glass of port and resumed her seat at the table, looking at the three men expectantly.

"Have you abandoned Emily?" Alec asked.

"No, of course not. She decided she had a headache coming on, a touch of her neuralgia, so I persuaded her that you would not consider her in the least discourteous if she took herself to bed in the capable hands of Harper," his sister informed him. "And since I have no interest in sitting alone behind the coffee cups, I came to join you." She sipped her port. "So what happened in Austria?"

"The Duc d'Enghien is raising an émigré army to go back into France and attack the

281

Directory," William explained, reflecting that there was no time like the present to do what he had already resigned himself to doing. If Hero was going to be involved willy-nilly, then so be it. "We were in Austria, gathering supplies and revenue for the émigré army. The Lizard was not there, but his agents were all over Vienna, ferreting about for information about the size and efficacy of the army, whether it would become strong enough to invade France. The Royalist uprisings in Paris were being put down savagely whenever one raised its head aboveground, so any force strong enough for an invasion had to be massed and supplied from beyond the borders."

"French agents were crawling all over Vienna and the surrounding countryside," Marcus put in. "William discovered a plot to capture the Duke and three other leaders of the army when they gathered one night in an inn close to the French border. We managed to warn Enghien and his men and got them out of the inn just as the French agents entered the inn through the back way. It was something of a mad scramble," he added with a rueful headshake. "William and two others fought hand-to-hand while we got the Duke and his retinue into the surrounding forest. By the time I got back to help, the French agents had fallen back, licking their wounds, and we just made it out of Austria into Italy ahead of them."

"I wish I'd been there," Hero said.

"Well, I, for one, am very glad you were not," William declared. "However, we could use your help now, but on one condition." His golden gaze held hers with a hard steadiness.

"And what's that?" Hero asked carefully. She took a macaroon from a platter and nibbled its edge, returning his stare.

"You confine yourself only to the task you are given," he stated. "Once again, you will follow orders, *my* orders. Do we understand each other?"

"You drive a hard bargain, sir." She dipped her macaroon into her port and savored the moist morsel, frowning thoughtfully. She had every intention of agreeing to his demands, whatever they were, if that was the price of admission, but a touch of stubborn pride kept her from capitulating for just a moment longer. Then she shook her head. "Oh, what the hell. Of course we do. So tell me how I can help."

William crossed his arms and rested them on the table, regarding her with the same concentration. "First, I need you to make contact with certain émigré families in

London and try to discover which of them would be prepared to support another Royalist uprising. We need money, and we need men. Second, I have the names of some families already, and I need to discover if French agents have their sights upon them. Is the Lizard watching them? Or, indeed, have they noticed any untoward folk in their neighborhood? But you have to discover this subtly. If they are under observation by the Lizard, I don't want them to run scared. They are all novices, frightened enough by events already and by the circumstances of their escape. Some have money; many do not."

He paused and sipped his port, watching her expression all the while. "You should be able to accomplish this without drawing any attention to yourself. You will simply go about your daily round of calls, rout parties, balls, and visits to milliners, dressmakers, shoemakers. There are many émigrés among the latter, struggling to earn a living. They will know others. The circles of émigrés in different situations are quite tight. A word to one could well bring useful information from another."

Hero nodded. "It seems simple enough."

"Less so than you think," he corrected a little sharply. "I would do it myself, but I don't have the time. It's a very important piece of work, Hero."

"I would do it myself, Hero," Alec put in. "But I want to take Marie Claire to the country, at least until after Christmas. The air in Hampshire is cleaner, and it's so much more peaceful without the sounds of cart wheels rattling beneath her windows night and day. She and Fleur need to rest and grow strong."

"Of course, love." She put out a hand to cover his. "I think it's a splendid idea. And you may be sure Nan will approve." She smiled at him. "I wouldn't leave the lights of London for anything at the moment. There's far too much excitement, and I shall have Emily to chaperone me. And in addition," she added, giving William her most brilliant smile, "I shall have the Viscount St. Aubery to guide my every move. You may be sure he will safeguard my reputation. Is that not so, sir?"

"Once again, dear girl, you are on perilous ground," William said, draining his glass. "It's never wise to seize the tiger by the tail."

"Oh, I've always rather liked the idea of riding the tiger," she returned instantly.

"D'you care for a game of billiards, Marcus?" Alec asked, pushing back his chair.

"Yes, of course." Marcus followed suit, his amused gaze flicking between the clearly annoyed William and the somewhat flushed Hero. "We'll leave you to it, shall we?"

"I beg your pardon," Hero said. "I was forgetting for a moment that we weren't in the kitchen in Rue St. André." She shot a half-apologetic, half-conspiratorial look at William, whose expression was steadfastly impassive.

"Well, we'll leave the two of you to reminisce in peace," Alec stated, going to the door, Marcus on his heels.

"Oh, dear, you're cross again," Hero said as the door closed behind them.

William shook his head. "No, not really." He rubbed the frown lines between his brows with a finger. "If only I could be sure you'd keep your indiscretion to the appropriate company."

"You know perfectly well I can," she said quietly. "I have never betrayed any of us with an accidental indiscretion."

"No." He reached a hand across the table to cover hers. "I know you would never risk anyone but yourself, Hero. And that is what worries me." His fingers tightened over hers for a moment, before he said in a different tone, "And somehow I think you have further plans for this evening."

"Oh, yes." She rose, pulling him with her. "Be pleased to follow me, sir."

NINETEEN

Everard Dubois entered the coffeehouse on Curzon Street with all the jauntiness of a man without a care in the world. He threaded his way through the tables to where two men sat over cups of hot chocolate. *"Bonjour, mes amis."* He pulled out a stool and sat down, signaling to a waiter to bring him hot chocolate.

His friends responded with nods, and they exchanged a few words of small talk while they waited for Dubois to get his chocolate. The waiter moved away, and the Lizard leaned forward on his stool, his voice dropping. "So? Reports?"

"Does the name Bruton mean anything to you?" one of his companions inquired, breaking a sweet biscuit in half and examining it critically before taking a bite.

"Fanshawe, yes. He's the Marquis of Bruton," Dubois said, taking a biscuit for himself. "What of him, Luc?"

"Does the name St. Julien mean anything?" the other man asked, exchanging a quick complicit glance with his companion. It was rare to spring a surprise on Everard Dubois, who prided himself on being a step ahead of any of his fellow agents.

Dubois frowned, sensing that he was about to find himself at a disadvantage. "The family went to the guillotine," he stated. "Do you know otherwise, François?"

"The girl's head was not accounted for," François responded. "The parents paid the price the day before, and the girl was scheduled for execution the following afternoon. Somehow, when the heads were counted, they were one short. The only name with a mark against it that was not accounted for was that of Marie Claire St. Julien." He smiled at his clearly discomfited colleague.

"And Marie Claire St. Julien is now the wife of Alec Fanshawe, Marquis of Bruton," Luc finished for him with a gesture of salute. "Something I venture you were not aware of, Dubois."

Everard stared into his rapidly cooling hot chocolate. "No," he admitted finally. "No, I was not." He broke off another piece of biscuit, crumbling it between his fingers. "Are we to assume, then, that Fanshawe was

289

in Paris with Ducasse?"

Luc shrugged. "It seems the logical conclusion that he was part of the effort to rescue the St. Julien girl from the guillotine, got her out of France, married her, and she is now here, in the Bruton mansion on Grosvenor Square."

Everard considered this for a moment. "The Marquis has a sister."

"Lady Hermione Fanshawe," François responded. "A lady of . . ." He coughed. "Of somewhat eccentric reputation, as I understand it."

"How so?" Dubois pushed aside his cup and leaned closer. Any hint of scandal was always fruitful ground.

"Nothing much . . . nothing concrete. She's from such an impeccable background, has considerable wealth in her own right, very little scandal can stick to her. But she's careless, frequents places that are not always socially acceptable."

"In short, she has the name for being somewhat careless of her reputation, indiscreet, even," Luc finished.

"Which makes her very useful to us," Dubois murmured. He leaned back and beckoned the waiter. "Brandy . . . three cups."

The waiter nodded and vanished into the

throng. "So, if Ducasse was involved with the escape of the St. Julien girl, who is now the wife of Fanshawe, then it seems reasonable to conclude that Ducasse and Fanshawe are more than acquainted." Dubois paused, leaning back as the waiter set three cups of brandy on the table. When the man had gone, he leaned forward again. "So that leaves the Lady Hermione as a possible crack to be opened. One has to assume she knows something of her sister-in-law's history. It's likely that she is acquainted with Ducasse through her brother's connection."

"We should set someone on her," Luc said with a slight questioning inflection.

"Definitely. But I think I will take on that task myself. I will set Gilles to watch the house. He's the best we have, and he already reports directly to me." Dubois drank down his cognac in one deep swallow. "And since I have the right entrées to Society, I shall cultivate the Lady Hermione personally and see where that leads us . . . if anywhere," he added, rising from the table. "Gentlemen, continue the good work. We shall meet as usual at the Fox and Hounds in Whitechapel next week." He picked up his hat, tossed a handful of coins onto the table, and strolled away with the same casual ease with which he had entered.

"Bastard," Luc muttered into his brandy. "Never credits anyone with anything."

"Does he need to?" his companion asked with a dour smile as he gestured to the waiter to refill their brandy cups.

William awoke before dawn in Hero's bed, aware of a sensation as delicious as it was unexpected. His body rose to full awareness as his sex flickered to life under the delicate, moist strokes of Hero's tongue. She was lying alongside him, her feet close to his head, her mouth encompassing his penis. He ran his hands along her calves and thighs, palming her bottom, relishing the smooth, muscular curves, which tightened against his hand. He let his eyes close and gave himself up to pure sensation. As his climax approached, Hero clenched and flexed her feet in an involuntary movement as she intensified her attentions. His fingers curled into her buttocks as he yielded to the flood of delight, a low moan escaping him, and when the moment had passed, he lay awash in fulfillment, his hands flat upon her bottom as she rested her turned cheek against his thigh, one hand loosely enclosing his still-throbbing penis.

"Did you enjoy that?" Hero murmured with a mischievous little chuckle. "I think you did."

"Yes, you wicked witch, I did. Come up here." He patted her hip encouragingly, and she folded over to appear from beneath the covers with her flushed face against his shoulder.

"Indiscretion has its place," she said, kissing the hollow of his shoulder.

"Indeed," he responded. "And in a moment, when I've recovered myself, I shall return the indiscretion."

It was still dark when Hero opened the side door for William. It led into the narrow cobbled alley, which gave access to the mews behind the house. He paused as usual, assessing his surroundings, then stepped into the alley. "Don't make any attempt to contact me, Hero. I will contact you first. Later this morning, I will send you a list of the families who may be responsive to our needs and who may have other contacts we can follow up. But whatever you do, stay away from me until I say it's safe. Is that clear?"

She nodded. "Crystal. But don't wait too long, William."

He smiled and touched his hat. "No, ma'am. Not a moment longer than necessary."

Hero stepped back and closed the door,

bolting it, before speeding up the back stairs to her own chamber. It had been a long and generally sleepless night.

William's list arrived as promised much later that morning. Hero read through the names, looking for any that might be familiar to her. Some of the wealthier French aristocratic émigrés had been familiar figures in court circles in England during the years before the revolution, as comfortable among their English counterparts in the palaces of the English royal family as the English had been at Versailles, and many of them, those who had managed to get their assets out of France in time, were now established in London. But there were no familiar names on this list and no immediately recognizable addresses. William had probably approached the most obvious and accessible already, she decided. Finding these others was a task more suited to a lowlier member of his band.

The reflection didn't trouble her any more than it would have done during their time in Paris. Viscount St. Aubery was the unquestioned leader of any enterprise he undertook. It interested her a little, though, that she actively disputed any authority he assumed in other areas of their unconventional relationship.

She decided to try an address on Holland Street first, where several names were grouped together. "Maisie, do you know where Holland Street is?"

The maid paused in her work of selecting gowns in the armoire that required the pressing iron. "Somewhere across the river, I think, m'lady. Cook was talking about a milliner there who does fine work and don't charge an arm and a leg for it, neither."

"Then I had best take a hackney." Hero rose from her dressing stool. It would be a less conspicuous visitation than rolling up in the Bruton carriage.

"Should I be coming with you, ma'am?" Maisie looked a little alarmed at the idea of Lady Hero venturing alone into the foreign realms south of the river.

"No, there's no need," Hero said, reaching for a long hooded cloak at the back of the armoire. "I'm sure it's not dangerous if Cook sees a milliner there."

Maisie shook her head but didn't attempt further dissuasion. "I'll run down and tell the footman to fetch a hackney, then."

"Tell him to ask the cab to wait at the corner of Brook Street."

Hero examined her reflection in the cheval glass and decided she looked anonymous enough in the long dark cloak, particularly when she put the hood up. *A mysterious dark lady,* she thought with a chuckle, enjoying the frisson of excitement afforded by the prospect of this little adventure. She hurried down to the hall where the footman waited to escort her to the summoned hackney. If he wondered why the cab had been ordered to wait on the far side of the square, he didn't ask.

"Where should I direct the driver, ma'am?" He held open the carriage door for her.

"Sixty-two Holland Street," she said blithely, settling gingerly against the cracked, stained leather bench. She kept back from the window as the hackney moved away down Brook Street. The precautions were rudimentary, she knew, but she had never had the sense of being followed in London and relied to a certain extent on her instincts. Simple watchfulness should be sufficient to alert her to anything suspicious.

"Tante Jeanne . . . Tante Jeanne . . ."
Jeanne turned from her cooking pots as Marguerite exploded into the kitchen. "What is it, *petite*?" She smiled at the flushed and excited child.

"Come and see." The little girl grabbed Jeanne's hand and tried to drag her from the kitchen. "There's a man in the street . . . he has a pack and a tray with so many things on it. Ribbons and silvery things and dolls. And a spinning top . . . oh, come and see. He's going to all the houses."

Jeanne allowed herself to be pulled out to the front garden. The usually quiet lane was a hive of activity. Women and children crowded the lane, examining the peddler's wares, the women arguing prices with the fierce determination of those who didn't have too many half-pennies to spend on fripperies, the children clamoring for the brightly painted toys. Marguerite tugged her to the gate.

"Please, Tante Jeanne, please, may I have something?" Marguerite pulled at the latch of the gate.

Jeanne hesitated. Every instinct told her that to step into the lane, to engage with a stranger, however seemingly harmless with his bright streamers and cheerful toys, made them conspicuous. But how could she deny the little girl such a treat when every child in the village was crowded around the pack-man, picking and choosing under the rarely benevolent eye of a harried parent?

"Wait here, child." She hurried back to

the cottage for her purse and returned to find Marguerite already in the lane, jumping up and down to see what the packman had on his tray. The gate was swinging wide open, and Jeanne quashed the moment of alarm fueled by so many lessons from the past and William's oft-repeated strictures. She pushed the gate wider and went up to Marguerite. She felt as if every eye was upon her — she and the child were so rarely seen on the lane — and tried to deflect attention with smiles and cheerful greetings as she examined the packman's wares with Marguerite.

"I want this," Marguerite declared, pointing to the garishly striped spinning top. "Please, may I have it? Uncle Guillaume would let me have it, I know he would." She hung from Jeanne's arm, her glowing eyes huge and pleading as she produced the one argument that she was certain would carry weight with her aunt.

"Come now, Mama, how can you resist such big eyes?" the peddler asked, holding up the top. "Just sixpence for such a pretty little girl."

"Oh, she's not my mama," Marguerite stated, with a child's stubborn need for accuracy. "This is Tante Jeanne, she's my aunt."

298

"Then I'm sure your auntie will buy it for you as a special treat." The packman fixed Jeanne with a determined smile, extending the top. "See how well it's painted, ma'am. No chips, and the string's good and strong."

"Yes . . . yes, we'll have it." Hastily now, more and more conscious of the curious eyes upon them, Jeanne took out a handful of coins. She knew she should bargain like any other village woman, but she felt an overpowering need to get Marguerite back into the cottage, away from prying eyes, before she gave away any more details of their circumstances. She gave the peddler sixpence, and as Marguerite flourished her prize in triumph, hurried her charge back into the cottage, locking the door behind her with a sigh of relief.

It was no way to live, she thought, leaning against the securely closed door as Marguerite danced into the parlor, already winding the string that would set her top spinning. This constant underpinning of fear, every knock at the door, every stranger on the street, set the alarm bells ringing. There had to be somewhere in this world where she and the child could live without this constant sense of threat. Marguerite didn't seem too aware of it, which was a significant mercy, but she was little more than a baby.

Soon she would begin to question this seclusion of their lives. And how would Guillaume deal with that? Jeanne felt a flare of resentment. It was too easy for him to dictate the necessities of their lives when he didn't have to live with their consequences.

Almost immediately, Jeanne felt regret at the reflection. Guillaume lived his own life on the edge of terror, and that terror encompassed the dangers affecting his nearest and dearest. She must simply remain constantly on the alert but reasonably so. There could be no harm in a gypsy peddler after all. The entire village had been his customers.

Hero's cab trundled across the crowded Blackfriars Bridge, and here she risked pushing aside the leather flap to look out at the unfamiliar surroundings. There was quite a different atmosphere away from the elegant streets and squares of Society London. The air smelled different, the street noises seemed different, and a haze of evil-smelling sea coal smoke shrouded the gray buildings and warehouses lining the river. This city seemed to bear little relation to the one Hero inhabited.

The hackney drew up outside a tall, narrow, run-down house in a long row of indistinguishable buildings. "Number sixty-two," he called down at her.

Hero opened the door and stepped out onto slimy cobbles, the gutters thick with refuse. Her nose wrinkled unconsciously at the sewer stench of garbage. "Wait for me," she instructed the cabdriver, who didn't look best pleased but without payment had little choice. Hero walked up to the door and, in the absence of a knocker, banged with her closed fist.

It was opened after a moment by a small girl, who peered around it, her cornflower-blue eyes round in a small, pale face.

Hero spoke in French as she asked the child if her mother or father was at home. The child nodded solemnly just as a man appeared behind her. He looked thin and worried as he regarded the visitor. *"Oui, madame?"*

"Monsieur le Vicomte Saulinac?" she asked, and when he nodded, she continued, "My name is Hero Fanshawe. Guillaume Ducasse sent me to you." She was instantly relieved by the smile that broke across his sallow countenance.

"Entrez . . . entrez, madame, je vous en prie." He stepped back with a wide, welcoming gesture. "Come in, come in, I beg you."

Hero stepped, smiling, into the narrow hallway. He closed the door firmly, plunging the narrow space into gloom, and called, "Therese? Therese, we have a visitor from Guillaume."

A woman appeared instantly from the corridor behind the steep staircase, her expression a mixture of anxiety and hesitant expectancy. "Madame?"

"Forgive the intrusion, Madame Saulinac," Hero said, extending her hand. "My name is Hero. Guillaume asked me to come, to see how you are."

"Well enough, we manage," the woman said, opening a door to the side of the hall. "Please, madame, will you come in?"

Hero went into a sparsely furnished parlor. It was clean and tidy, with a small sea coal fire burning in the hearth.

"Please, madame, be seated." The man pushed a chair forward. "How is Guillaume?"

"He is very well," Hero responded, taking the proffered seat. "I understand there are other émigré families living here, too." She consulted her list. "Chevalier and Madame Lesquet and Monsieur and Madame Junot."

"Ah, yes, of course. Sylvie, run upstairs and ask them to join us," the Viscount instructed the child, who disappeared at a run. "Such a pleasure this is, Madame Fanshawe."

"Hero, please," she said. "I was with Guillaume in Paris last year," she added, hoping that would enhance her credentials. Viscountess Saulinac seemed still a little hesitant. "My brother's fiancée, now his wife, was Marie Claire St. Julien."

They both nodded gravely. "She escaped Paris?"

Hero told them the story, and they listened intently. As she talked, she became aware of other people entering quietly, but no one interrupted her until she finished, saying, "That is the story. One I'm sure you know all too well."

"Indeed, we do. Please, meet our compatriots." Therese indicated the four people who had just entered, introducing them. A small group of children gathered in the doorway behind their parents, gazing with wide-eyed fascination at their visitor.

"Coffee, Hero. You will take coffee with us," Therese said, getting to her feet.

Hero hesitated. It was clear to her that these people had little enough of anything for themselves without sharing it with strangers, but then she reflected that to refuse their hospitality would be discourteous, tantamount to pointing out their poverty. She smiled her thanks.

The conversation became general for a

few minutes while she tried to think of a way to explain why William had sent her to them. It seemed callous to ask them for help supporting an émigré army when they seemed to need help and support themselves so badly. But it was the Viscount who gave her the opening. "We hear that d'Enghien is raising a Royalist army for another attempt to take back France. Does Guillaume have any further news?"

Hero took a breath and jumped in. "They need money and men," she said bluntly. "Guillaume is attempting to raise both from any who can manage to help."

Silence fell over the room. Hero sipped her coffee, a thin and bitter brew that tasted a bit like she imagined acorns might.

After a moment, one of the men said, "We have little enough money for ourselves. My wife and Therese both work as milliners, and when times are really hard, they take in laundry. We . . ." He gestured inclusively to the men. "We take what work we can find." He shrugged. "It is hard when one is unaccustomed to earning a living. None of us has been trained to do anything worthwhile." His voice was bitter. "I work occasionally cleaning out the stables at the King's Arms inn at Bankside. Saulinac mends shoes. We turn nothing away, but it is still a struggle to put food on the table and shoes on our children's feet."

"I understand," she said quietly. "I believe Guillaume understands your struggles, too."

"We have sons," Therese said, as if the words were dragged from her. "They are of an age to offer their services to the cause."

Hero glanced askance at the small children still crowding the doorway.

"We all have older sons," the Viscount said. "They, too, work where they can and at what they can. Therese is right. Both of our sons, Jacques and Marc, are anxious to do more. They complain about sitting on their hands while other young men are fighting for the cause." He looked at his wife and then around at the others in the parlor. "Their mothers have been unwilling to let them go."

"With good reason," Madame Junot said, her face very pale. "We barely got out of there alive. You would have us give them back to the carnage? Guillaume would ask that of us?"

William would ask anything of anyone, Hero thought, just as he set no limits on what he demanded of himself. She had no answer to the woman's question but privately decided that this particular work William would have to do for himself next time.

She would infinitely prefer to be paddling though a Parisian sewer rather than asking such a sacrifice from these people.

"Tell Guillaume that we will consider the matter," the Viscount said into the silence. "We will talk with our sons. Where can we send a message?"

"To White's in St. James's Street," Hero told them. It had seemed to her a very public and vulnerable poste restante for delicate communications, but William had simply said that the best place for secrets was in the open. And she could see his point. "If you think you can help in any way, however small, just send a message, and he will come to you himself." She set down her coffee cup just as a loud banging came from the front door. "Oh, dear, that'll be the cabdriver. He has grown impatient, and indeed, I have kept you long enough. My thanks for the coffee."

The Viscount escorted her to the door, where the hackney driver stood fulminating, his fist raised for another round of knocking. " 'Bout time," he muttered as Hero appeared. "Wastin' time and money 'angin' around out 'ere."

"You'll be well paid, I assure you," Hero said haughtily, before turning to take her leave of her host. She wanted to give him

306

money but knew it would be seen as an insufferable insult, so she contented herself with a warm handshake and the resolve that she would send presents for the children, winter coats, perhaps. That would not come amiss, she was sure.

TWENTY

Alec left for Hampshire with his wife and baby a few days later, when Dr. Barrett pronounced Marie Claire fit for the coach ride. Nan accompanied them, and Hero waved them away from the front steps, feeling both bereft and liberated. It was difficult to share a house with another family, for all that she and Alec were closer than most siblings, but sometimes she felt like an intruder in their marriage, and now, with the baby, she could see it might feel even more so. But for the present, she had a mission, a sense of life-affirming purpose, and a man whose presence was somehow essential for her happiness. She didn't dare call it love even to herself; somehow she felt that such a definitive emotion could only exist if it were openly reciprocated. It was certainly lust, but it went much deeper than mere lust, she knew that, and it suffused her with energy, the lethargic indifference she had felt since Tom's death banished, for the present. She would not think about the future, better . . . safer . . . always to live in and for the moment.

She didn't notice the carriage trotting slowly past the front door of the mansion as she turned to go back inside.

"If his intention is to make me anxious, he's succeeding better than his wildest dreams," William muttered into his claret. "Look at him, all complacent smiles, while we both know he's just waiting for the moment to strike."

"The proverbial snake in the grass, except that he's not hiding," Marcus observed, refilling his glass from the decanter on the table between them. His eyes flicked across the salon at White's to where Everard Dubois sat at his ease, legs crossed, seemingly engaged in a spirited game of piquet with one of the eager young lordlings who frequented the club, confident that they could fleece any older member unwise enough to take up the cards against them. This particular lordling was looking increasingly troubled, William noticed, unable to resist giving his nemesis a silent cheer for putting the arrogant young man in his place.

"So what is he up to?" William muttered

again. The Lizard seemed to be everywhere, just taking up space, showing no particular interest in Ducasse beyond a raised glass, a nod of acknowledgment as between casual acquaintances. But there was nothing benign about his presence, and William found it utterly disconcerting to have his enemy constantly in his sights.

"I don't think anyone's following me, either," Marcus said thoughtfully. "Once or twice, I've had a sense, but every counter-move I make reveals no one. Either they're becoming superhuman at surveillance, or they've lost interest in us."

William shook his head. "Not the latter, I assure you. He's changed tactics, but I'm damned if I know what to. And that, my friend, makes me very uneasy indeed."

"Did Hero have any success on her visits?" Marcus moved the subject on a slightly different tack.

"Only to the extent that she told me roundly that I could do my own dirty work in future," William responded with a rueful half smile. "She considers it an outrage to ask people to contribute who already have nothing to live on. She's right, of course," he added. "But she did say that none of them was aware of any unusual interest in their movements, so it seems as if Dubois

310

and his friends are not actively watching them."

"And Hero's not aware of surveillance?"

"She says not . . . at least, not so far." William's expression darkened. "If the Lizard makes the connection between us, however . . ." He left the rest of the thought unspoken.

"Hero knows what the stakes are," Marcus offered. "She'll have her wits about her. After Paris, just the thought of the Lizard should put the fear of God into her."

"Into Hero?" William gave a short laugh. "If you could tell me something that would make Hero afraid, I'd be delighted to hear it. She cares nothing for Society's censure, and while I'm certain she would not deliberately put anyone else in danger by her actions, for herself, she seems not to give a damn."

"She cares about you," Marcus pointed out quietly. "She cares about your opinion."

"She accepts my authority when it comes to our work," William responded. "A quite different matter, Marcus. I just wish I could get her to care about herself." He pushed his glass away and rose to his feet. "I have an appointment to cross swords with Maître Raoul. He has a new move with the épée that I would like to master."

"I must drop by his studio and take a lesson myself." Marcus picked up his glass with a nod of farewell. He watched as William sauntered across the room towards Everard Dubois's card table, where he paused with a polite bow.

"Chevalier Dubois." William smiled courteously. "I trust you're enjoying your game."

The Lizard's smile flickered. "Oh, yes, indeed, Viscount, I find it most enjoyable. Matching wits with a worthy opponent is always a pleasure, don't you find?"

"Most certainly, I do," William responded smoothly. "I am sure the better player will win." His gaze flicked disdainfully to the young lordling before he turned it full upon Dubois. "It is generally the case, is it not, Chevalier?" The smile remained on his lips, but his eyes were narrow and hard, the challenge given and accepted.

The Lizard inclined his head in acknowledgment. "It is always a pleasure to see you, Viscount. Will you perhaps be attending the ball at Almack's this evening?"

"I think it unlikely," William responded. At no point in his career had he ventured through the august portals of Almack's Assembly Rooms, and he had no intention of starting now. The entertainment was insipid, the refreshments lamentable, and he had no desire to be included among the exclusive elite who frequented the weekly balls. He offered another short bow and moved away to the door.

Dubois smiled to himself and laid down a card. "A Rubicon, I believe," he declared, running his eye down the figures on the paper beside him. "That brings your losses to six hundred, my lord. When will it be convenient for you to settle the debt?"

The young man looked around uncomfortably. "Perhaps you would be good enough to wait until next quarter day, Chevalier."

Dubois quirked his strangely shaped eyebrow, saying gently, "I am sure you are aware, sir, that a gentleman settles his gambling debts immediately."

His opponent flushed darkly. "Yes . . . yes, of course. If you will take my IOU now, I will present myself at your lodgings tomorrow to settle up."

Dubois smiled again. "That will be agreeable, sir. Shall we say at ten in the morning?" He rose, bowed, and strolled away, leaving his discomfited opponent staring dismally at the unpalatable sum in front of him.

That evening, Hero dressed without much

enthusiasm for Almack's weekly ball. She attended only when she could not possibly avoid it, and tonight was one of those nights. Aunt Emily had decided on impulse to indulge in a little light dissipation, and of course, Hero was obliged to accompany her. Emily's dissipation would consist of sitting against the wall sipping tea, nibbling bread and butter, and engaging in idle gossipy chatter with the dowagers who made up her social circle, while Hero would be obliged to dance and make small talk with whichever gentlemen chose to honor her with their hands in the dance. Almack's was no better than a marriage mart for debutantes, Hero had declared on several occasions to her amused but sympathetic brother. However, when duty called, it must be obeyed.

"Maisie, I think I'll wear the topaz set with this gown," she said, examining herself critically in the long mirror. Her gown was of a very dark gray silk with an almost opalescent sheen, and the deep golden hues of the topaz would provide a dramatic contrast. The color reminded her of William's tawny gold gaze, and she felt that familiar jolt of lust in her belly whenever she thought of him. He wouldn't be there, of course. It was impossible to imagine him moving with that leonine stride through those rooms full of preening beaux and simpering maidens. Her lip curled unconsciously. It was all so pointless when there was so much suffering, so much work to be done in the world.

A tap at the door brought Aunt Emily into her chamber. "Oh, Hero, dear, you look lovely," she said, smiling and nodding, setting the plumes on her rather elaborate headdress bobbing frantically. "I wonder whose eye you will catch tonight, my dear. I do so wish . . ." Her voice trailed away, and she seemed visibly to shake herself. "Well, I'm sure you know your own business best. The carriage is at the door. I won't wish to be out late, but the carriage can return for you if you wish to stay and enjoy yourself."

"I'm sure I shall be more than happy to return with you, Aunt," Hero responded with some feeling. She turned so that Maisie could drape a cashmere wrap over her shoulders. "Shall we go, ma'am?" She gestured to the door, and Aunt Emily sailed ahead of her, the stiff folds of her rather old-fashioned damask gown rustling around her.

The windows of the Assembly Rooms were brilliantly lit as the Bruton town carriage drew up to the door, easing its way forward as the long line of vehicles moved up to deposit their occupants in turn. Hero had the sudden vivid image of the tumbrels in Place de la Révolution moving forward one by one to disgorge their victims at the steps to the guillotine. She shuddered, wrapping the shawl more tightly around her shoulders. They were images that she knew would stay with her for the rest of her life.

"Are you cold, dearest?" Emily looked at her in concern. "I do wish you young girls would wear more clothes. That dress is so flimsy, it's a wonder you don't all catch a consumption."

"I'm not in the least cold, Aunt. It's quite a warm evening." Hero urged her aunt up the steps to the grand hall. They discarded their outer garments, which in Emily's case took quite a while, and then climbed the wide flight of stairs to the upper salons. Hero's heart sank as it always did at the familiar faces, the scene that never seemed to change. The orchestra was playing a country dance as they entered the ballroom.

"Oh, there's dear Lady Hammond," Emily declared, her eyes surprisingly sharp as they swept the room. "I must congratulate her on her niece's marriage . . . such a grand affair that was. Come, Hero." She took Hero's arm in a surprisingly determined grip and took off around the side of the room to where a group of matrons was

316

gathered in cozy congress.

Hero played the part expected of her and took a seat beside her aunt among the chaperones, waiting for the inevitable moment when one of the patronesses would present her with a partner. She was playing idly with the tassels on her fan, her eyes gazing absently at the delicately painted chicken skin between the ivory sticks, when a voice said, "Lady Hermione, may I present Chevalier Dubois. He has asked to be presented to you."

Hero looked up, unsurprised, as she'd expected the interruption to her thoughts at any moment. Lady Jersey was smilingly gesturing to a man with a strangely shaped eyebrow. He bowed, extended his hand. "An honor, Lady Hermione."

A thin smile flickered across the Lizard's thin lips, and for one dreadful moment that seemed to last for an eternity, Hero felt the room spin and she heard again the roar of the blood-mad crowds in Place de la Révolution.

Somehow she managed to go through the motions, grateful suddenly for a routine that, while irksome, was so familiar she could respond without thought. "Chevalier, I'm delighted to make your acquaintance." She gave him her gloved hand. He lifted it

317

to his lips and looked at her with a smile that contained neither warmth nor humor. His eyes, so pale as to be almost colorless, were as flat and impersonal as a dinner plate.

"Charming . . . quite charming. May I entice you onto the floor, ma'am?"

She rose instantly, her body automatically obeying the rules of the game. Had she shown her surprise, that instant of fearful recognition? Hero didn't know what her eyes had given away in those first moments, but now she was back in control, allowing him to lead her to the dance floor, where a cotillion was forming.

"I haven't seen you in town before, Chevalier. Have you recently arrived?" she asked as she curtsied deeply at the beginning of the movement.

He returned her curtsy with a deep, ceremonial bow. "I've been in London for several weeks, but business has unfortunately prevented me from enoying many such delightful social occasions." He gestured to their surroundings as they moved through the opening steps.

"Business?" Her eyebrows lifted as she gave a little laugh. "How very tiresome for you, sir."

"The affairs of my unfortunate country

are perhaps tiresome to those not directly involved in them," he returned. "I would hardly expect them to impinge upon Society's pleasures."

"That sounds suspiciously like a rebuke for our thoughtless indulgences, Chevalier." As Hero turned away from him in the dance, moving around the square, she was aware of a rush of excitement, a thrill of danger, the sense of walking on a knife-edge. The Lizard would not outwit her. It was possible this meeting was mere chance, but it was also possible there was a more sinister motive behind it. The fact that she had not seen him in the last weeks did not mean that he had not seen her. But why would he be interested in her . . . unless he had seen her with William?

They had been together in public on very few occasions — the time at Ranelagh, the conker game in the square garden — but William had asserted that he was certain he was not under surveillance. When he had visited the house with Marcus on that one occasion before Alec and Marie Claire had left for the country, both of them would have ensured they had no followers. And yet she could not be sure. Whatever else she had learned from William, she had learned that there was no such thing as an assumption of safety.

"Forgive me, Lady Hero, I would never be so presumptuous as to imply any such thing." He resumed the conversation as if it had never been interrupted when the dance brought them back together. "There is no reason you and your compatriots should think twice about the travails of my countrymen. You have all been more than hospitable, and we are pathetically grateful for whatever crusts you may offer us exiles."

"That, sir, sounds remarkably like another put-down," she stated, flicking a smile at him from beneath her eyelashes. "We are perhaps rather too preoccupied with our own little affairs, but, indeed, life is so full of diversions it's hard to find time for the more serious and unpleasant facts." She sounded so *silly,* Hero thought with satisfaction. An empty-headed little fool who could not think beyond her next party or her next flirtation.

The Lizard's expression didn't change. He passed her along the dance again and gave his attention to his new partner, a damsel Hero knew to be capable of eye-watering inanity. She must pay more attention to Lady Millicent and take some lessons, she thought, still bubbling with that thrill of danger.

When they came back together, Dubois kept the conversation to the smallest of small talk, and Hero responded in the same way, and when the dance concluded, she curtsied with a smile of thanks as he bowed in return. "May I fetch you a glass of lemonade?" He offered his arm to lead her off the floor.

"If it cannot be champagne, then I would be glad of a glass, thank you, Chevalier." Again, she gave him that up-from-under, slightly flirtatious little glance.

He led her into a window embrasure, where two chairs offered an invitation. "Pray wait there, ma'am, and I will be back in a moment." He moved off towards the refreshment room, and Hero gathered herself together.

She had to be careful. She could not allow this frisson of danger to trump her sense of caution. There were others involved, and if she took risks just for the pleasure of the game, she would endanger them. William would probably be livid if he knew that she was engaging his nemesis on any level. It would have been so easy to have danced with him and then excused herself to sit quietly again with the chaperones. A new partner would have presented himself quickly, and that would have been the end of it.

"Madame . . ." The Chevalier stood before her, two tall glasses of lemonade in hand. He set them down on the windowsill and glanced once over his shoulder before, with a quick, conspiratorial smile, he reached into the inside pocket of his black coat and withdrew a silver flask. He opened it, and the heady aroma of cognac filled the air as he poured a generous measure into their glasses. The flask disappeared into his coat again, and he handed her a glass. "This might improve the shining hour, my lady."

Absently, Hero took a generous sip, wondering now how to proceed. Clearly, her performance as a silly, empty-headed debutante had not impressed him. One did not offer doctored lemonade to such maidens. So what persona should she assume now? Before she could decide, his next words put paid to any sense of excitement she might have felt.

"I have the strangest feeling we have met before, Lady Hermione." He regarded her closely over the lip of his glass. "Somewhere most unlikely . . . and yet I just can't think of it." He set down his glass and reached for her fan, taking it from her suddenly nerveless fingers. "Allow me, ma'am. It is very warm in here, and you look a little

322

heated." He wafted the fan in front of her flushed face.

Hero cursed her inexperience, the overweening sense of confidence that had somehow led her to believe she could play with fire and remain unscorched. She took another sip from her glass and coughed and sputtered a little. "Oh, forgive me, sir. I am not accustomed to cognac. So silly of me . . . I had just thought to try a little, but it burns one's throat so."

"My error." Smoothly, he removed the glass from her hand while continuing to waft the fan. "I had thought perhaps . . ."

Hero remembered abruptly how on that voyage in the fishing boat across the Channel, a flask of rough apple brandy had been passed among the crew and offered to their two passengers. She had accepted the flask eagerly, hoping it would combat the cold and the damp. "No, I assure you, sir, I am accustomed only to a little champagne or ratafia on occasion." She tried for an ingenuous and flustered smile. "I feel so foolish . . . if you would excuse me, I must return to my aunt." She stood up so abruptly her chair skittered away from her, and with another inane titter, she hustled her way towards her aunt and the chaperones.

Dubois remained where he was for a moment, watching her hasty departure, tapping her closed fan against his palm. She had fallen so neatly into that little trap with the cognac. Any other young lady in the Assembly Rooms would have been horrified at such an addition to Almack's insipid lemonade, and Lady Hermione hadn't given it a moment's thought, tossing it back as easily as the silent young lad in the fishing boat all those many months ago. And those vivid green eyes were unmistakable, even though he had only glimpsed them briefly that night on the waters of the Channel.

He was forced to admit, however, that if he hadn't been alerted to the St. Julien connection, which led inexorably to Ducasse, he probably would not have given Lady Hermione a second glance. And for that, he had only himself to blame. He had been too occupied with the urgent business taking him to Paris that night of the Channel crossing to pay much attention to the boy accompanying them. In different circumstances, he would have made inquiries of the boat's captain and would have certainly watched to see what his fellow passenger did when they got to Calais. But his coach had been waiting for him at the quay. Robespierre had sent for him, and a man did not gainsay Robespierre at the height of his powers. A few months later, the all-powerful tyrant would lose his own head to Madame Guillotine, but at that time, his rule of terror was still absolute.

Lady Hermione *was* very striking, however, with a boldness to her that was barely concealed by that ridiculous show of debutante inanity. A rather unpleasant smile lurked behind his pale eyes. Unless he was much mistaken, this path to Ducasse might well afford a satisfying challenge on the way. He had been watching her for a week now, with the best man among his deputies keeping a close eye on the house in Grosvenor Square. He himself had been observing her social movements from a distance, until tonight, and apart from a certain air of bored distraction, he had seen nothing particularly out of the ordinary, but tonight had revealed a different side to the lady.

He made his way around the floor to where she now sat decorously amidst the chaperones. "Your fan, Lady Hermione." He bowed before her, presenting the article to her on his crooked arm with an elaborate gesture. "And my thanks for a most enjoyable dance."

"The pleasure was all mine, sir," she returned, taking the fan but keeping her eyes lowered to her lap. "Ma'am, allow me to introduce Chevalier Dubois." She turned slightly to her aunt, who offered the Chevalier her usual blandly amiable smile, extending her fingertips. "Lady Emily Harrington." Hero performed the second part of the introduction, aware that her tongue seemed rather thick.

Dubois bowed over Lady Emily's hand, raising it to his lips in a courtly gesture. "An honor, madame." He turned with a smile and walked away.

"I think, my dear Hero, that I am ready to go home," Emily declared. "Should I send the carriage back for you?"

"No . . . no, indeed not, ma'am." Hero jumped readily to her feet. "I will send a servant at once to summon the carriage and fetch our wraps." She could not wait to get away from the overheated room. The brilliance of the candles was hurting her eyes, but nothing was as hurt as her pride. She had made a complete and utter fool of herself, and the sooner she could leave the scene of her humiliation, the sooner she could lick her wounds and try to decide how much damage she had caused.

TWENTY-ONE

"What a most pleasant evening," Emily declared with a little sigh of satisfaction, settling into the coach. "Did you not find it so, my dear?"

"Pleasant enough, Aunt," Hero managed. "Did you enjoy a comfortable chat with Lady Hammond?"

"Oh, yes, delightful. The wedding sounds to have been a most congenial affair." Emily nodded her head. "The Chevalier appears to be a delightful gentleman. I wonder I have not met him before. One of those poor émigrés from that dreadful revolution, I daresay." She shuddered. "So shockingly uncivilized of a country to have a revolution, one always thinks."

Despite her inner turmoil and general dismay, Hero was hard pressed not to laugh, even as she had to bite her tongue on a sharp response. Emily knew nothing of the world outside her own sheltered, pampered existence. She would have an apoplexy if she had the slightest hint of what her supposedly gently brought-up young relative had witnessed and experienced.

"I daresay you're fatigued, ma'am," she offered, knowing Emily's mind would immediately switch to her own concerns.

"Oh, yes, I'm sure after such dissipation, I shall be obliged to keep to my chamber tomorrow. A day of rest with a little light broth and tea and toast will be the most restorative." She smiled and nodded, her eyelids drooping as the carriage turned into Grosvenor Square.

Hero accompanied her aunt to her bedchamber and gave her into Harper's waiting hands. The lady's maid murmured comfortingly as she fussed over her mistress, urging her to the fire with promises of a hot posset to restore her after the exertions of the evening.

Hero made her way to her own chamber, thankful that she had told Maisie not to wait up for her. She couldn't bear the prospect of responding to anyone at the moment. Her head felt as if it would burst as the stupidity of what she had done seemed to grow like some evil black fog, obscuring all clarity of thought.

Huddled in the cashmere wrap, she sat on

a low ottoman in front of the fire and tried to think. How bad was it? But she could not banish the image of those pale eyes, the faint hint of triumph skidding across their flat surface as she had realized her mistake with the cognac. She could not banish his voice, the French accent quite pronounced, although his command of English seemed impeccable. The insinuating twists and turns of his conversational gambits had seemed like a challenge she couldn't resist, and her arrogant overconfidence had led her to cross swords with a master, to tangle with a man who could extinguish her with his little finger. And not just her, although he would need more than his little finger to extinguish William.

That thought somehow did not give her the reassurance she had hoped for. She shuddered suddenly, an instinctive convulsion of pure fear filled with the memory of the gray, heaving waters of the Channel, the cold, pale eyes she could feel again on her face, taking her in despite the darkness of the night and the thick hooded cloak that obscured much of her face. She hadn't thought at the time that he had even noticed her particularly, but now she knew differently. The memory of every moment of that voyage was suddenly as vivid as if she was

329

reliving it.

And Hero knew at her very core that she had not the skills to combat the Lizard. She had thought herself invincible, hardened by her experiences in Paris, a worthy opponent for any French agent, but now she knew herself to be a rank amateur, a pathetic novice in the arena of blood and death where men like the Lizard and William fought.

Now she had to tell William about the foolishness, the reckless pride that had led her to cross swords with such an enemy. She dreaded his condemnation, dreaded the cold contempt in his gaze as she laid it before him. His anger would be welcome, cleansing almost, but she was afraid his reaction would go well beyond anger. She had endangered not only him but everyone who worked with him. Herself, too, of course, but somehow that didn't seem to matter.

She glanced up at the pretty ormolu clock on the mantel. It was one o'clock in the morning. William could be asleep, entertaining, out with friends, or on business. She couldn't go in search of him now, but she would walk to Half Moon Street at sunrise.

Wearily, she shrugged off the cashmere shawl and undressed, pulling her nightgown over her head, her body chilled and achy.

She washed her face and cleaned her teeth in desultory fashion, unpinned her hair and pulled the brush through it a couple of times, and crawled into bed, snuffing the bedside candle. The warming pan had long lost its usefulness, and she kicked it out of the bed, lying wide-eyed and sleepless between the cold sheets, staring into the darkness.

William awoke instantly, every sense alert at the sound of his chamber door opening. His hand instinctively slipped beneath his pillow to curl over the handle of his pistol, but almost immediately, he registered the familiar presence, and his grip relaxed. He hauled himself up against the pillows. "What is it, André?"

"A message, my lord." The manservant straightened from the embers of the fire, a lit spill in his hand. Yellow light flared as he lit the wick of the candle on the mantel. "From Knightsbridge."

William was out of bed on the instant, reaching for his brocade dressing gown. He took the folded sheet André held out to him. "What time is it?"

"Almost five, my lord." André threw fresh kindling onto the embers. "Shall I fetch coffee?"

331

"Mmm." William nodded as he broke the seal and unfolded the sheet. Outwardly, he was calm, but fear clutched at his heart. *Jeanne and Marguerite.* The missive was dated the previous evening.

William, this will probably reach you at dawn, so please forgive me for disturbing you at such an hour, but I have been wrestling with myself all evening. I do not know if I'm imagining things. I could so easily be; living as we do in such a state of permanent awareness, it's all too easy to create bugbears out of thin air, but there have been two unusual visitors to the village in the last few days. First a packman and then a knife grinder. As a rule, we only get such visits around Christmas and occasionally at harvesttime, so two different itinerants in one week caused general surprise. Marguerite was so excited by the peddler and insisted we go into the lane to buy something from him. She informed him and most of our neighbors, who were all gathered there, that I was not her mother but her aunt. I don't know whether that confidence matters in the village or not, but I would have preferred her not to have said it. The peddler went on his way, and no one seemed to pay us any more attention than usual, so I decided it wasn't significant, until the knife grinder paid us a visit. He came to the door and seemed very anxious to be invited into the kitchen to examine my pots and pans and see if any needed soldering and if any knives required his grindstone. I managed to send him on his way eventually, despite his insistent manner, but the more I think about it, the more anxious I become. I decided I would never rest easy if I didn't tell you, even if it's of no significance. You have always stressed that we must be alert to anything out of the ordinary, however innocent it might seem. Forgive me if I have troubled you unnecessarily, but if you could visit in the next day or two, it would be a great relief to me and, of course, a delight to Marguerite. The child goes on well but talks of you every day.

Amitié, J.

William reread the letter, then tossed it onto the now blazing fire. He glanced at André, who was coming back into the room with a tray of coffee. "Who brought this?"

"The ostler from the Blue Duck in Charing Cross, my lord." He set the tray on the dresser.

William nodded, satisfied. He had set up a postal service for Jeanne to use in emergencies. The wagoner left his farm with his produce for London in the early hours of the morning and always stopped at the Red Fox in Knightsbridge to collect any fee-paying passengers or parcels destined for the city. These he would leave at the Blue Duck in Charing Cross a couple of hours later. The ostler there was well paid to bring any missives addressed to Half Moon Street. No method was fail-safe, of course, but there were enough strands to this courier path that William was reasonably sure it would escape surveillance.

He drank his coffee hastily. Ordinarily, he would ride to Knightsbridge, but if it was necessary to move Jeanne and Marguerite immediately, he would need a carriage. He drew aside the curtain and looked out at the graying light. He was still positive, since the Lizard had changed his game, that there were no watchers on the house, but if he was mistaken, pursuit would be easy enough to detect in the semideserted streets at this hour of the morning.

He dressed rapidly, instructing André to summon a hackney. "Find one as respectable-looking as possible, and tell the jarvey I'll need him for the whole morning, but he can expect six guineas in payment."

André went off, and William pulled on his boots, slung his riding cloak around his shoulders, and ran downstairs. The hackney stood at the door, the horse's breath steaming in the early-morning chill. The animal looked glossy and well cared for, and the jarvey jumped down from his box as William appeared, opening the door with a flourish of his cap.

"My lord, an honor."

"Knightsbridge, Primrose Lane," William responded. "There's no great hurry, so don't draw attention to yourself with any fancy tricks with the whip."

The driver looked a little disappointed, but he slammed the door on William, crammed his cap back on his head, and jumped back onto the box, whistling up his horse.

Deep in the shadows of the neighboring alleyway leading to the mews, Hero kept close to the wall, her heart pounding. After sleepless hours going over and over the encounter with the Lizard, she had steeled herself to tell William the whole sorry story. The minute a peek of gray had shown in the

335

eastern sky, she had dressed and let herself out of the still-sleeping house by a side door, knowing that if she put it off for even an hour her courage would fail her. But just as she'd turned the corner of Curzon Street, the hackney had pulled up outside the house. Instinctively, she had darted into the mews alley, conscious of how conspicuous she must look at this hour of the morning on the deserted street. As she cowered in the shadows, William emerged onto the street.

She peeped cautiously around the corner as he stopped to talk to the jarvey. William looked tense and worried, an expression she didn't remember ever seeing before, even at the direst moments in Paris, and for the life of her, she could not summon the courage to step up to him now. Whatever was troubling him, this was not the moment to add to it with her own confession. But she knew it couldn't wait long. He needed to know everything there was to know. If she'd understood anything in the time they'd been in Paris, Hero understood that. She strained to hear what he was saying. His voice was low, but she distinctly heard his instructions to the jarvey: Primrose Lane, Knightsbridge.

Hero withdrew her head, pressing herself

back against the wall as the hackney passed the entrance to the alley. What could there be in such an out-of-the-way spot that would draw him at such an ungodly hour?

Something to do with his present business for the émigré army, presumably. Maybe there was an émigré family in Knightsbridge whose support he wanted. But why would he go on such an errand at dawn? And in a hired hackney? From what little she knew of Knightsbridge, it was where wealthier tradesmen, men who worked in banking or other such professions, had their residences. Solid burghers with whom William could have little or nothing in common.

But even as she thought that, Hero knew it sprang from her own world of aristocratic privilege, and William had no time for that world and its prejudices. She hadn't thought she had, either, she reflected ruefully, but upbringing laid deep roots, it seemed.

Once she was sure the carriage had turned off Half Moon Street, Hero abandoned her hiding place and began to walk home. Why had he looked so worried? Was he in danger? And then the obvious question: Could she help him?

But she would be discreet. She would wait for an hour or two before taking her own anonymous hackney to Knightsbridge.

Once there, she could take a covert look at Primrose Lane. If William was under threat, then maybe she could do something to help. And if he wasn't, if his business in Knightsbridge was clearly none of hers, then she would retreat, and no one would be any the wiser. A little voice niggled: *Why would he have business in such an out-of-the-way place that was none of my business?*

There was so much about him that she didn't know. Great acres of his past life, of his childhood and growing, that he had never confided. In fact, Hero reflected, he had never confided anything personal to her really at all. Just that one thing about the dangers of losing one's reputation, one's place in the world. But even that had simply been issued as a warning without background explanation. It had involved something personal, someone he had loved, but he had closed the subject down, leaving her tantalized but none the wiser. Hero knew it had something, if not everything, to do with that wretched rejection at Yarmouth, but their renewed loving still felt so fragile, as if anything could bring it to another awful, senseless ending, that she had not dared to question him again. Somehow she had hoped that as their ties grew stronger, more secure, that story would reveal itself quite naturally as a simple progression of their loving intimacy.

But she knew in the deepest part of her soul that if there was ever to be a future for her in this relationship, then she had to have the answer to that rejection. If that meant pushing the boundaries that William had set so firmly for them, then so be it. And suddenly, Hero realized that the uncertainty, the dreadful anxiety of walking on eggshells around him all the time, was too much. It was no way to conduct a love affair. William *must* trust her with his self, with his past, with the hopes and fears, the joys and terrors that informed the person he was. If he couldn't, *wouldn't,* then there could never be a future for her with him. She could not subdue her own essential self to the narrow confines of physical intimacy with which William seemed comfortable.

TWENTY-TWO

The man, Gilles, arrived to take up his position in the square garden soon after dawn. It was boring work, and he huddled into his woolen driving cloak against the dank morning chill. The grand double-fronted house opposite was just coming to life, the curtains in the front of the house opening, smoke from the revived fires gusting from the several chimneys. A maid appeared on the front step and threw a bucket of water down the steps to clear away any debris from the night.

Only one person appeared on the street itself, a cloaked figure walking quickly up to the door. The watcher frowned as he recognized the object of his surveillance, Lady Hermione Fanshawe. Quite apart from the strangeness of her being out in the street at this hour, there was something unusual about her clothing. He was used to seeing her in the most fashionable of dress, but this morning, in a plain wool cloak and half boots, her hair tied back in a simple knot, she could have passed for a parlor maid.

Where had she been all night? No, not all night, he amended. His colleague had watched her return from her evening's amusement just before one o'clock in the morning. They had no instructions to watch the house all night, and Alain had gone to his own bed after noting the time of her return on the report sheet in the lodging he shared with Gilles. Sometime between then and now, when Gilles took over the surveillance, it seemed the lady had gone out again.

He hesitated, reasoning that if she'd just come back, she wouldn't be leaving again for a while. Not within the hour, at least. Time enough to report her nighttime activities to his master. It was sufficiently unusual to arouse suspicion, and his orders were absolute. Citizen Dubois was to be informed immediately of anything out of the ordinary. He hurried across the square and flagged down a hackney, its driver nodding sleepily on his box, blue smoke from his pipe curling in the early mist.

"Jermyn Street." The man clambered in as the jarvey cracked his whip.

They reached his destination in ten minutes on the still-quiet residential streets, and Gilles knocked a rapid rhythm on the blue-painted front door. It swung open as if of its own accord, and he stepped into a narrow hallway. The door closed behind him, and Everard Dubois emerged from the shadow, sheathing his knife. It was a simple precaution and one the Lizard maintained with utter dedication. One could never be absolutely certain who was on the other side of a street door, even when the correct signal had been given.

"You've left your post . . . why?" he demanded of his visitor, stepping into a cramped parlor to the left of the door.

"She just came back," was the succinct response.

"Back . . . from where?"

"I don't know, *citoyen*. I'd just gone on duty, and she came walking down the street. Let herself into the house just after six."

Dubois frowned and kicked at a falling log in the small hearth. "She left Almack's with her aunt just before one. When did she go out again?"

It was a question to which his agent had no answer and didn't offer one. Dubois swore vigorously, and Gilles took an instinctive step back, but the Lizard's wrath was directed at himself. He had neglected to keep watch on the house overnight. Somehow he had not considered that Lady Hermione Fanshawe might be roaming the streets of London during the dark of the moon. But then, until that moment at Almack's when he realized the lady and the lad on the fishing boat in the Channel were one and the same, he had underestimated her. He had still foolishly thought her bound by the conventions of her upbringing while she was living the life that upbringing dictated. Her brother had been in Paris, but that was no reason to suspect his sister of being part of that deadly operation. Now he knew better.

He thought rapidly, then instructed in crisp tones, "Very well, she's clearly unpredictable. We need to step up our surveillance so we're prepared for anything. We'll bring the hackney into play in case she decides to use one the next time she leaves. You'll be in charge there, and I'll send Alain back to watch the house."

The agent nodded. *"Oui, citoyen."* He left at once, and Everard Dubois stood before the fire, gazing sightlessly into the flames, wondering where this path was going to take him next.

The house was up and about when Hero let

343

herself in. A startled parlor maid scurried past her with a scuttle of coals for the drawing room fire as she headed for the stairs to the bedchamber floor, and another young girl, on her knees brushing the staircase, pressed herself against the banister with a little yelp of surprise.

Hero offered her apologies as she stepped carefully to the side of the stair. In her own chamber, she rang for Maisie and discarded her cloak and gloves.

"Lord love us, Lady Hero, what have you been doing, up and about at this hour, all dressed like, and not even ringing for me?" Maisie exclaimed as she took in Hero's outdoor garments.

"I woke early and was feeling restless, so I went for a walk in the square," Hero responded, sitting down to unlace her boots. "Would you be a dear and bring me some breakfast? A boiled egg, some toast, and hot chocolate would do. I have to go out again within the hour."

Maisie clucked a little with the license of a confidential retainer. "And will you be changing your clothes, my lady?" she asked rather pointedly.

Hero had not considered her outfit when she'd dressed in such haste earlier, wishing merely to look as inconspicuous as possible.

344

Beneath her wool cloak, she was wearing a plain serge gown that she would have worn at the estate in Hampshire for roaming around the countryside or fishing in the Beaulieu River. It was quite unsuited to the streets of fashionable London. But then, her errand wasn't taking her out and about in fashionable London. She needed to be as discreet as possible, and if she could pass as an upper servant, so much the better.

"No, I'll stay just as I am, Maisie. I'm going on a private errand."

Maisie said nothing more but went off to see about breakfast. Hero laced up her boots again. She should let Aunt Emily know she was going to be out for the rest of the day, but if she showed herself in this garb at the lady's bedchamber, there would have to be explanations. She went to the secretaire to write a note, explaining that as it was early in the day and she knew dear Aunt Emily wished to keep to her room after the excitements of Almack's the previous evening, she thought it best not to disturb her. She would be home in the early afternoon. Hero signed the note with a flourish, sanded it, and folded it just as Maisie returned with the breakfast tray.

"Will you be wanting me to accompany you, Lady Hero?"

Hero shook her head and cracked the top of her egg with a tiny silver spoon. "No, there's no need, Maisie. Why don't you take the morning to yourself? I doubt I'll be back before this afternoon."

Maisie looked gratified. Free time was a rare commodity. "Well, thank you, Lady Hero. I own I'd be glad of a chance to visit my sister. She's housemaid at Lady Denizon's in Brooke Street."

"Then you must certainly do that." Hero dipped a finger of toast into her egg and carried the dripping morsel to her lips. "Could you ask Jackson to send a footman to fetch a hackney for me?"

"I'll tell him to bring it in five minutes, ma'am. So you can finish your breakfast."

Hero controlled her irritation at Maisie's well-meant solicitude and finished her egg with a little less haste. But after a few minutes, she drained her chocolate even as she stood up, impatient now to be on her way. She hurried down to the hall, where Jackson stood at the front door waiting for her.

"Your carriage is outside, Lady Hero," he declared in customary stately tones. "What direction should the footman give the driver?"

"Oh, just to Piccadilly, Jackson," Hero

responded with a careless smile. Keeping her destination a secret was a simple precaution but a necessary one. William could with good reason accuse her of prying into his private business, but she was determined he would have no further justification for accusing her of carelessly endangering him or his business.

She ran down the steps to where the cab waited in the street. It promised to be a beautiful autumn morning, with crisp air and copper leaves sharp against a bright blue sky. "Thank you, Fred," she said cheerfully to the footman who stood at the door of the cab. She stepped into the hackney, giving the driver on his box barely a glance, and the vehicle started off. Once they were safely around the far side of the square, she moved aside the leather curtain at the window and leaned out. "Driver?"

The man slowed his horse and peered down and around from the box. "Aye?"

"I've changed my mind. I want you to take me to Knightsbridge . . . Primrose Lane." Hero had expected a protest at such an out-of-the-way destination and was surprised when the jarvey merely withdrew his head and snapped the reins, setting his horse into a brisk trot.

She sat back against the unusually clean

leather squabs of the cab, reflecting idly that it felt almost like a new vehicle, unlike the majority of the hackneys plying the streets of London, which for the most part smelled of sweat, tobacco smoke, and frequently, for some unknown reason, boiled onions.

She knitted her gloved fingers together in her lap, wondering if she was doing the right thing. Whatever business was occupying William at the moment, it was imperative that he know about her reckless indiscretion with the Lizard. It would affect every plan he had made. And behind that grim knowledge lay the image of his worried, tense expression. Something lay on Primrose Lane that concerned him so deeply it broke through his normally calm, controlled exterior. She loved him, and it was so hard to accept that he still withheld so much of his essential self from her.

Hero pushed aside the curtain again and watched the streets slide past. It was still quite early, and few of the fashionable set were out and about, one or two energetic riders on the tan in Hyde Park and the occasional drunken young buck swaying down the street in search of his bed after a night's debauchery in the brothels and deep gambling dens under the arches of Covent Garden.

The streetscape began to change, the streets becoming wider, the paving less even, and Hero glimpsed the occasional green field in the distance. Some of the houses were large and solid, set around leafy squares with neat front gardens. It was curiously peaceful after the smoky bustle of London. Private barouches bowled past her on their way into the city, presumably carrying the businessmen and substantial tradesmen who lived in the large solid houses. Children played in the squares under the watchful eyes of nursemaids, and servants carrying laden shopping baskets hurried down the streets.

The hackney slowed and came to a stop at a crossroads. Hero leaned out. "Are we there?"

"This is Knightsbridge, ma'am. No idea where Primrose Lane is. Which way?" The driver's voice was muffled by his thick woolen scarf as he gestured from side to side with his whip.

"I don't know, either." She looked up the street. A woman was tending a garden a few houses down. "I'll go and ask." She opened the door and jumped down to the lane. "Excuse me, ma'am, but we're looking for Primrose Lane."

The woman straightened up from her cabbages and wiped her hands on her apron. She looked curiously at Hero. "Don't see many strangers around here." She pushed a straggle of gray hair back under her kerchief. "Primrose Lane's that-a-way. Take the next turn on the left." She gestured ahead down the lane.

"My thanks, ma'am." Hero hurried back to the hackney. There was no need for the driver to know her final destination. "Go back to the inn we saw on the village green. I'll find you there when I'm ready to go back."

The driver merely raised a hand in acknowledgment and turned the hackney on the narrow puddled lane.

Hero didn't give him another thought. She followed the woman's directions and found Primrose Lane. She walked carefully down its length, looking at the cottages. They all looked the same to her, but presumably everyone knew their neighbors.

At the end of the lane, she stopped at a small, whitewashed cottage with a neatly thatched roof, a carefully tended front garden dominated by an apple tree, and, most unusually, a gate with a low stone wall separating the garden from the lane. She was suddenly at a loss. Impulse had brought her this far, but what now? There was no sign of the cottage's occupants, no one to ask. The lane was quiet, just the quiet, rhythmic sounds of the farm animals. No sign, either, of William's hackney.

"I'm sorry, William, if I've brought you out on a fool's errand." Jeanne brought the coffeepot to the table. "But I was anxious . . . and now you're here, I feel as if I overreacted."

"No, you did right to send for me, Jeanne." William broke bread into the runny yolks of the eggs on the plate in front of him. "Would you feel safer if I move you and Marguerite to somewhere further in the country?"

Jeanne shook her head vigorously, taking a sip of her own coffee. "I don't think it would be good for the child to move her again, as I've said before. Not without some concrete evidence of danger. And there's been no sign of the itinerants since the knife grinder." She shrugged, an elegant movement of her shoulders beneath the cashmere shawl. "I didn't have that absolute feeling of danger, just a nervous, crawling sense . . . I don't know how to describe it."

"It's called gut intuition," William said grimly. He took up his coffee. "I would never discount it, but if you don't think it

351

wise to move now, then I'll put a man to watch you."

"He couldn't stay here," Jeanne exclaimed, horrified. "What would the village say?"

William shook his head. "No, my dear, of course he couldn't. But my men are trained to be unobtrusive. You wouldn't see him, and neither would anyone else. But you would always know that he was there. Would that give you peace of mind?"

"Immensely," Jeanne said. "He would be armed, of course?"

"Of course." He raised a quizzical eyebrow. "You know as well as I do, my dear, that fire can only be fought with fire."

Jeanne shook her head, doubt in her eyes. "This is such a peaceful village, and Marguerite knows nothing of such evil. Isabelle would not have wanted it."

"No," he agreed, his mouth twisting. "She would have hated it. And look where that took us all."

Into the moment of uncomfortable silence, a voice called from beyond the kitchen door, "Tante Jeanne . . . Tante Jeanne . . ." And Marguerite burst into the room, her muslin nightgown billowing about her skinny frame. "Oh, Uncle Guillaume, no one said you were coming. Why did no one tell me you were coming?" She directed an accusing glare at her aunt.

"Because it was a surprise, *ma petite,*" William said, making room for her on his lap. "I happened to be passing and decided to drop in and see you."

"But I was asleep," Marguerite objected, dipping a piece of his bread into his egg. "I would like an egg. May I have an egg, Tante Jeanne?"

"Certainly you may," Jeanne said. "But you need to fetch it from the henhouse. Take the basket, and collect as many as they've laid this morning."

In answer, Marguerite waved her bare feet at her aunt. William lifted her off his lap. "Put on your boots and your cloak, and collect the eggs. It's not cold outside." For a moment, Marguerite didn't move, her lower lip extended in a distinct pout. William held her gaze in silence, and then she turned and went to get her boots.

"She needs you," Jeanne said softly, almost under her breath.

"She'll do well enough as long as she's safe." His voice was harsh, but Jeanne understood why, and her own heart ached for William . . . for all of them.

Standing at the gate, looking at the deserted lane, the cottage's closed door, Hero had the feeling that nothing of significance could ever happen here. And yet, deep in her inner self, she knew that here in this unremarkable cottage on this unremarkable lane lay the secret to William's heart.

But unlocking that secret was less important than making sure he knew what had happened with Dubois. The Lizard could be plotting anything at this point and William needed to be on guard. She'd taken a risk coming here, but it was an acceptable one, given how careful she had been, and the degree of emergency. She put a hand on the latch of the gate, and the door opened as she did so.

TWENTY-THREE

William carried Marguerite on his hip as he stepped through the front door, his head turned towards Jeanne, who was following him out.

Hero stood transfixed, her hand still on the garden gate as she prepared to shut it behind her. She didn't know what to do next. The quiet intimacy of the three people in the doorway shook her to her core. She hadn't realized William was capable of being part of such an ordinary tableau. A man, a child, a woman, held in a circle that shouted familial understanding. The woman laid a hand on his shoulder, leaned in to kiss his cheek, and the child's arms around his neck seemed to clutch tighter. And then he turned, a half smile on his lips, and saw Hero. The smile vanished as if it had been erased on paper. His face whitened.

She didn't move, watching as William came towards her, still carrying the child.

"How did you get here?" His voice was cold and impersonal, as if he was talking to a stranger on the street.

Hero said calmly, "Hackney. I came in a hackney. I told the jarvey to wait at the inn. There's something I need to tell you."

"Go back to the inn and pay him off. Wait for me there." Nothing in his tone or expression gave any indication that she was anything more to him than an ill-met chance acquaintance.

"Who is the lady, Uncle Guillaume?" the little girl demanded, pushing against him in an effort to get down.

"No one you need concern yourself with, Marguerite." He held on to her wriggling body and turned his back on Hero. Jeanne had stepped closer on the path, her eyes fixed on Hero with unabashed curiosity. Over William's shoulder, the little girl gazed open-eyed at the stranger.

Hero turned away back to the lane and walked towards the village green and the inn, her skirts gathered above her ankles as she negotiated the puddles. Her mind was alive with questions but she also understood that she had stepped into forbidden territory. William's boundaries were absolute. He had never made any secret of that. But maybe, just maybe, he might learn to understand that those boundaries forbade the emotional commitment that was the only way to any kind of a future for them.

The hackney was drawn up outside the small inn, the jarvey leaning against the traces, his face obscured with his muffler as he picked at his nails with a sharp twig. He glanced up as Hero came close.

"We off, then?" He sounded thick, as if he had a cold.

She shook her head. "No, I'm staying. You may return. What do I owe you?"

"Two shilling." He held out his gloved hand to receive the two silver coins she produced from her coin purse. "Thankee." He touched his cap, climbed back onto the box, and drove away.

Hero watched him go. This was not the moment to run scared. William needed to know what had brought her here. His hackney was standing to one side of the inn, the horse chewing contentedly on a nose bag, a youth in attendance, sitting on a water butt idly sucking on a straw, regarding Hero with a degree of interest.

And William owed her some truth, Hero thought, the image of the man, woman, and child vividly alive in her imagination. After everything they had been through together, after the hours of loving and companionship, she knew two Williams, and if this moment gave her the opportunity to marry the two and discover the one true man, then it was to be embraced.

She walked back down the lane. When she reached the garden gate again, William was deep in conversation with the woman, and the child was picking daisies on the small lawn. She looked up as Hero approached, and ran to the gate.

"Can you make a daisy chain? Aunt Jeanne can." She indicated the woman talking with William.

"I used to be able to," Hero responded, leaning over the gate to take the crumpled flowers from the little girl. For some reason, she wasn't able to make herself open the gate.

William spun around at the sound of her voice, and a strange expression crossed his face as he saw what she was doing. He took half a step towards the gate, and then Jeanne laid a hand on his arm and he stopped, turned back to her, leaving Hero and Marguerite to their flowery construction.

Patiently, Hero split the daisy stems with her fingernail and threaded them together until she had a passable chain, while the child looked on, head tilted with a slightly critical appraisal of her handiwork. "There."

Hero held up the necklace she had made. "May I put it on?"

Marguerite ducked her head as Hero dropped the delicate chain over her. "That's so pretty. What's your name?"

"Marguerite," said the girl, her head lowered as she lifted her necklace and examined it carefully. "That means daisy."

"Yes," said Hero, smiling. She stretched a hand over the gate. "Show me how it looks." With a forefinger, she tipped the child's chin, and a pair of glowing golden eyes gazed up at her. The jolt of recognition almost took her breath away, but she managed to say easily, "A daisy chain for a daisy."

Marguerite laughed and clapped her hands. She turned and ran up to William and Jeanne. "See, Uncle Guillaume. I have a daisy chain to match my name. A daisy chain for a daisy, the lady said."

"Did she?" William voice was flat. Her lifted Marguerite and kissed her, lingering for a moment to inhale the sweet child fragrance of her skin and hair before setting her on her feet again. "Be good, now. I'll be back soon." He kissed Jeanne on both cheeks.

She took his hand for a moment, but her eyes were on Hero, still standing outside

359

the gate. "You have lost so much, my dear," she said softly. "Be careful you don't lose any possibility of happiness."

He seemed to freeze, then shook his head. "I have to do what has to be done, Jeanne. You know that."

"I know only that you have to do what you *believe* you have to do, Guillaume," she returned, before taking Marguerite's hand. "I'll look for your guard, but of course, I know I won't see him." A smile touched her lips before she urged the child inside, and William turned back to the gate, where Hero stood waiting.

"I told you to wait at the inn," he said, opening the gate. He brushed past her where she stood in the lane, and walked briskly in the direction of the inn.

Hero followed, refusing to run to keep up with his fast stride. She felt her resistance to his anger growing by the moment.

The innkeeper emerged from within at the first sound of their arrival in the yard. "A pot of coffee for your lordship," he said, with a bow and an inviting wave through the door behind him. "And madam, I'm sure, would be glad of some refreshment." His gaze was greedily inquisitive as he looked at Hero. It was clear he didn't know where to place her on the social spectrum, but her confident manner suggested a position somewhat at odds with her ordinary dress. Hackney carriages and their passengers were rare visitors to his establishment. It was too close to town for a refreshment stop on a long journey and too undistinguished for a pleasure trip.

"We have no need of anything," William stated curtly.

The man looked put out. "And what of the horse's feed, sir, and the jarvey had a pot of ale and a cheese pasty?"

William merely handed the man a guinea and turned away to open the cab door. Wordlessly, he offered his hand to Hero to assist her up into the carriage, then followed her, pulling the door closed behind him with what struck Hero as unnecessary vigor.

He sat opposite her and fixed her with a blazing stare. "How and why?"

Hero folded her hands in her lap and returned his stare as steadily as she could. "I had something to tell you that I didn't think could wait, so I came to Half Moon Street at dawn. I reached your house just as you were getting in a hackney. I overheard you tell the jarvey where to go. You looked worried . . ." Her voice faded for a moment. "I have never seen you look worried before. So, I decided to follow you, but only when

I'd made sure it was safe to do so. I went home, waited for an hour, and then I took a cab . . . No one knows where I am or where I was going because I didn't give the jarvey the direction until we were well away from Grosvenor Square." She paused for a moment under his cold-eyed stare, then repeated quietly, "I had something you needed to know."

William's gaze was suddenly sharply attentive. "Go on."

Hero took a deep breath and jumped in. "Last night I met the Lizard at Almack's. I'd never come across him before, I didn't even know he was in London. He asked for an introduction and we danced." She stopped, twisting her fingers together. "I may have been a little indiscreet and I'm afraid he recognized me from the fishing boat."

William's eyes closed briefly in the dimly lit carriage. "Indiscreet how?"

She told him, saying at the conclusion of her sorry tale, "I was a fool to think I could match wits with him. I am sorry."

His moderate response surprised her. "You're not the first, and unless I can do something about it, you won't be the last."

There was an uneasy silence for a few moments before Hero said with quiet vehemence, "I'm sure no one followed me to Knightsbridge. I would have noticed a horseman or another carriage, but I could swear there were no other travelers. They would have to have followed me from Grosvenor Square and that couldn't be done on foot. So I don't see how there could be any danger at the moment."

There was sense in it, William was forced to admit, and if they had managed to avert danger this time then he would be doubly prepared for it from now on. Hero was clearly now in danger, and also posed a danger to every other of his associates. But what was he to do with her? If he sent her to Hampshire, she would merely endanger Alec, Marie Claire, and the baby. But there were other places.

"You're going to have to go away for a while," he said.

"Go away? Why? Where?"

"You know perfectly well why. I don't know where yet, but I'll put a plan together as soon as I can."

Hero looked at him, clear-eyed and resolute. "You don't have the right to send me away. I don't belong to you. You've made that abundantly clear, William."

"And you've made it abundantly clear that you will have no hesitation in interfering in my most private business," he returned, his voice once more frigid, cold and flat. "What made you think you had the right to follow me, Hero?"

"I love you." The statement seemed to make itself, the words she had withheld for so long. She shook her head with a gesture of resigned disbelief. "You were in trouble. I wanted to help if I could."

She could not interpret the look that flashed across his golden eyes, but when he said nothing, she continued in the same quiet tone, "She's your child, isn't she, William? The likeness, the eyes, it's unmistakable. Marguerite is yours."

He said nothing, and that silence was affirmation enough.

"She said the woman with her was her aunt, so where is her mother?" She hesitated for a second and then declared, "I have a right to the answer, William."

"Her mother is dead." It was a flat and brutal statement.

Hero absorbed the implications of this. "So you were married?"

William gave a short laugh. "What makes you think that? I hadn't thought you so naïve, Hero." His eyes flared with anger again. "Why do you always appear where you are not wanted, where you can only make trouble?" He seemed to fling the words at her, and she felt them like a body blow.

There was suddenly no more to be said. She had spoken the only truth she had and once again he had rejected her. Winded, Hero turned from him, moving aside the curtain at the window, trying to conceal the depths of her shocked distress. They were so far apart now that there was no possibility of common ground. And Hero didn't know how it had happened, how so much love and promise could so quickly become a mere chimera. A figment of her naïve and overactive imagination.

Twenty-Four

Nothing more was said until they reached the center of town. William knocked on the roof, and the hackney drew to a halt at the top of Piccadilly. "He'll take you home. You'll hear from me later today. If you can manage to do it, would you please stay within doors until you get my instructions?" His voice was flat. Without a word of farewell, he opened the door and jumped down, closing it firmly behind him.

Hero heard him talking to the jarvey, then the carriage lurched forward again, and when she looked through the window, she saw William walking away, his stride long, in the direction of Half Moon Street. She let the leather curtain drop again and sat back, cold and shivering a little, although the day was mild enough. It was as if something inside her was broken, a snapped string that made her nerves jangle. The world was unharmonious, and she seemed to have lost the ability to make it play in tune again. Once upon a time, their quarrels would end in a different kind of passionate encounter, but this time, there had been only a vast, icy chasm between them, not a spark of fire to be felt.

The hackney drew up at Grosvenor Square, and she flung open the door, jumping unceremoniously to the ground, almost losing her step. She turned to pay the jarvey, but he merely touched his forelock and drove off. Presumably, William had paid him. She paused on the pavement, looking around her, her senses alert for some sign of a watcher, but everything seemed normal. The sounds of children playing in the square garden, a maid scrubbing the steps of a house, an errand boy whistling as he went past. But if there was anyone there, Hero wasn't going to know about it, she reflected grimly. All her confidence seemed to have been leached from her.

She hurried up the steps as the door opened, and Jackson greeted her with a solemn bow. Hero murmured a response and hastened to the solitude of her own chamber, closing the door and leaning against it, breathless, her heart beating rapidly in her throat as if she'd run a marathon.

Everard Dubois sat back in his chair, one leg crossed over the other, his booted foot swinging casually. He looked reflectively into the contents of his wineglass. "So I wonder who or what took Lady Hero to Knightsbridge? She gave you no clue?"

"No, sir. I went to the inn as she'd instructed. I didn't want to arouse her suspicions by making inquiries at the inn, in case she accidentally heard of my interest when she came back."

"And you said there was another hackney waiting at the inn?"

"Aye. The jarvey said he was waiting for a gentleman who was paying him generously for a morning's work. Pleased as punch, he was. Said he'd picked up the gentleman in Half Moon Street. It could have been Ducasse."

"Given what we know of the connection between the lady and that gentleman, that seems a reasonable assumption. So first, we need to know who lives in Knightsbridge and then what connection they have with our friend. I want you to stay on Lady Hero. I'll send someone else to Knightsbridge. Go to Grosvenor Square and debrief Alain.

Find out if she's back yet, and if so, when and how, then send Alain back here."

Gilles nodded and left at once.

Everard sipped his wine, a slight smile on his thin lips. He was getting closer, and his old enemy's seemingly impervious existence was beginning to hint at vulnerabilites. If he could insert a fingernail in one, then he could split it wide open. He debated putting a closer watch on his quarry and then decided against it. The less Ducasse felt himself under surveillance, the easier he would be to trap when the time came.

But he could, however, see for himself what had taken Ducasse to Knightsbridge. He stood up abruptly. He didn't usually do his own dirty work, but he had a sudden imperative need to investigate the mystery of Knightsbridge immediately and with his own eyes. He shouted for his servant and when the man appeared sent him to the mews to fetch the closed carriage to the front door. Everard's London operation was well equipped, with the hackney, a closed carriage, and both riding and carriage horses. The Directory in Paris was not short of funds when it came to supplying the needs of its outposts abroad.

The door to the house on Half Moon Street

closed with a slam, and André jumped, the blacking cloth he was using to polish his master's riding boots smearing his leather apron. Hastily, he put aside the boots and cloth and went out of the kitchen into the hall.

William was taking off his cloak, his beaver hat tossed carelessly onto a stool. He turned as André came through the baize door from the kitchen. "Bring me sherry, in the parlor," he demanded, swinging aside into the square salon beside the front door.

André frowned. He had worked closely with Viscount St. Aubery for many years, both as a personal servant and, when required, as a courier or in whatever role his master's clandestine business needed. It was not the Viscount's habit to be so peremptory with those who worked for him, but something had seriously put him out of countenance. His expression had been hard and tight, his jaw clenched, all most unusual for a man who rarely lost his composure. It was not unheard of for the Viscount to respond to an urgent summons at whatever hour of the day or night, but something about today's dawn errand must have gone wrong. André was not in the Viscount's confidence about everything, and the situation in Knightsbridge was one area where he knew almost nothing. Messages arrived occasionally via the courier service through the posting inn, and André knew it was vital to deliver them as immediately as he could, but who sent them remained his master's secret.

He went back to the kitchen to discard his apron and fetch the sherry decanter, and carried the tray into the parlor. William turned from the fire, where he had been gazing into the flames. For a moment, he seemed surprised to see André, then gave a little shake of his head as if bringing his mind back to the present. "Oh, thank you, André."

André felt a twitch of relief at this return to ordinary courtesy. He set down the tray and poured a glass of the pale liquid, asking tentatively, "How was your morning, sir?"

"Could have been better." William took the glass. "I need you to carry some messages for me, André. Bring me paper and refill the inkstand, will you? It's dry as a bone."

André took the inkstand and went off, returning with the refilled inkstand and paper within a few minutes. William was sitting now by the fire, legs crossed at the ankle, lifting his newly refreshed glass to his lips. He nodded his thanks at André, who arranged the secretaire neatly, lighting a candle and setting sealing wax ready beside it. "Will that be all, sir?"

"For the moment. I'll call when I need you."

The door closed softly behind André, and William, remaining where he was, pondered his various options. Hero had to go somewhere where she would be safe and he could keep an eye on her. It seemed to him there was only one real answer. The only possible way he could be certain she was safe and not rushing headlong into more trouble would be to keep her under his own roof, where he could watch her until he had finally taken care of the Lizard.

But how could he do that, have her so close to him and yet still manage to keep the necessary distance between them? Their liaison was over; it had to be. He had tried once to bring it to a close, and he still regretted the brutality of that parting in Yarmouth, but he hadn't known how else to make it happen when every ounce of his being revolted at the prospect of never seeing her again, of losing her once and for all. If he had hesitated, tried for the slightest softness, his resolve would have weakened, melted like butter in the sun.

And then he had the stunning thought

that it was quite possible that Hero herself
had no interest in continuing their affair
after this morning's revelations. Somehow
that had not occurred to him, but it would
be perfectly reasonable for her to decide she
couldn't stay in an intimate relationship
with a man who had concealed his own
daughter's existence from her. It could
certainly be seen as a betrayal of trust, and
loyalty and trust were as deeply ingrained
in Hero's character as they were in her
twin's. She had followed him because she
had made a mistake and, quite rightly, she
believed he needed to know it. If underneath
that primary motive had lurked her need to
understand what lay behind the distance he
maintained between them, then he could
force himself to face that knowledge. William knew he lived too much in his own self-
controlled world. He chose to ignore the
past that had made him as he was. And he
understood now, as he had understood only
distantly in the past, that Hero could not
accept that about him.

The idea that with this betrayal he had
killed all her feelings for him distressed him
more than he could ever have imagined, and
yet, he told himself, it would be a relief if it
were so. Once the immediate crisis was over,
Hero would be free to find her own path to

love and happiness on a conventional track. She would be so much happier when she was able to have straightforward feelings towards a man . . . a lover . . . a husband.

But no, such reflections were like rubbing salt into a wound. And they muddled the clarity of mind he needed to deal with the various strands of the present situation. His first task was to arrange a guard for Jeanne and Marguerite. He would much prefer to move them again, but Jeanne was right about the disruption for the child. Marguerite had been moved from pillar to post most of her short life because of her father, the man responsible for her mother's death. It was his duty at the very least to ensure her stability and safety.

For as long as only he and Jeanne knew the truth about Marguerite, he had felt confident that he could keep her safe, but now someone else knew. Hero knew Marguerite was his child, and the first crack had appeared in the seamless shell encasing his secret history. He hadn't been able to deny it when she'd challenged him; it would have been futile. Hero had seen what she had seen. Her eyes were too sharp, her mind too acute, not to have drawn the obvious conclusion once she had penetrated his private world. She would not deliberately betray him, he was certain of that, but she was not invincible, not proof against the kind of pressure the Lizard could bring to bear.

He sighed heavily and drank down the contents of his glass. Why did everyone associated with him have to suffer for it? It was a pointless question, he knew. He had made his choices long since and accepted with cold clarity that there would be collateral damage as he fought the wider battle. Now, as he was getting closer to the end, was not the moment to have second thoughts, to back away from the front line.

He had to change his focus. Instead of being merely content to evade the Lizard and his cohorts while he raised support for the émigré Army of Condé, he must take the fight to Dubois. He and everyone associated with him would not be secure until he had got rid of the Lizard. Once he was out of the picture, he could complete his work and rejoin the army, and they would take back France. Maybe then . . . then he could step back and imagine a quiet life where he could have friends and family without putting them in harm's way.

But in his heart, William knew that such a dream would not be possible for him. He wasn't made to live a peaceful life.

Wearily, he got up and went to the secretaire, sharpening the quill before pulling several sheets of paper towards him. He would consult Marcus about Hero. He was the one person to whom William could talk with relative openness about their relationship.

He wrote rapidly, pressed his ring into the hot wax to seal it, and then hastily scribbled a cryptic line on another sheet, folding and sealing it similarly. He called for André. "I need you to take this letter to Sir Marcus Gosford. If he's not at home in Albermarle Street, then try White's and Brook's. You'll find him in one of his usual haunts; I know he's not left town. But first take this note to the usual spot in St. Giles churchyard."

André nodded his comprehension, tucking the two sealed letters inside his jacket. He left the house at once, and William, after a moment's thought, went upstairs. His own bedchamber was at the front of the narrow house; André slept in a small attic chamber under the eaves. The spare bedroom was behind William's. He opened the door and examined the room. It was perfectly pleasant, with a small window looking over the small kitchen garden and the mews alley beyond. Hero would be perfectly comfortable here, except that he would have to insist on keeping her a virtual prisoner.

There was no sugarcoating that unpalatable fact. She would not give up her freedom willingly, either, whatever her present feelings about himself.

His mind flippped back to that afternoon in the prison of La Force, to the moment when that scrappy bundle of grimy rags had burst into his life. If he had known then what he knew now, he would have . . . would have what? William shook his head, knowing full well that he would not have changed one iota of the events that followed.

Hero had happened to him.

But maybe when this was all over, he'd find a quiet monastery somewhere and assume the chaste existence of a monastic order, preferably a silent one.

And the moon was made of Camembert. A sardonic smile hovered over his lips as he left the small bedchamber.

Alain was on the doorstep of Everard's lodgings on Jermyn Street at the moment the Lizard let himself out. "You sent for me, sir."

"Yes . . . yes, I did." Everard looked at his agent with a frown. "I was going to go on my own, but you can come with me. You might be useful."

"Go where, sir? Come where?"

"Never mind. You can drive the closed carriage. Are you well armed?"

"Aye, sir. Are we expecting an attack?" Alain followed his master to the vehicle waiting with the footstep already lowered in the street.

Everard shook his head brusquely. "No, but it's as well to be prepared." Particularly if you were dabbling in waters where William Ducasse swam. But that thought he kept to himself. "Did you see Lady Hero return this morning?"

"Aye, sir. In a hackney, about eight o'clock."

"Good." The Lizard hopped up the red-carpeted footstep and took his seat inside the carriage. "You're driving to Knightsbridge," he informed Alain, who stood at the open door awaiting instruction. "Go through the park. Then pass through the main part of the village, and on the outskirts is a hamlet with a green and an inn. We'll stop there."

Alain touched his cap in acknowledgment and climbed into the swaying driver's seat, flicking his whip at the horses while Everard sat at his ease within, smiling a little as he considered his approach to whatever secret Ducasse held in this out-of-the-way spot.

The keeper of the Red Fox in Knightsbridge was gratified at the arrival of a third carriage visitor into his yard in one day. And a very smart gentleman's carriage it was. He emerged from the inn to greet the new arrivals, beaming.

Everard stepped down and looked around with a rather haughty air. His eye fell on the innkeeper, who bowed several times in quick succession. "Will your lordship be pleased to enter my humble hostelry? I can offer a fine repast, some excellent claret or, if your lordship would prefer, a goodly tankard of the very best October ale."

Everard nodded and walked past the man towards the inn door. "See that the horses are watered, and bring me ale." Inside, he turned towards the taproom, where several men leaned against the bar cradling tankards of ale and porter. He ignored them and took a seat at a small scarred table in the window, drawing off his gloves as he did so.

Alain came in a few minutes later and took a seat at the table opposite the Lizard. "Go and investigate this Primrose Lane," Everard instructed, his voice low. "I don't know which house has the lure, but see what you can gather. I don't need to tell you to be discreet."

Alain cast a longing eye at the foaming

tankard of ale the innkeeper set on the table but rose to his feet without demur and headed back outside. It was early afternoon, a light breeze sending the last of the autumn leaves fluttering to the ground, a pale sun peeping through scudding clouds. A stable boy had taken the horses from their traces and was watering them at the trough. "Where's Primrose Lane?" Alain asked gruffly, muffling his voice with his scarf. The less noticeable his accent, the better.

"Over yonder." The lad pointed back to the green. "T'other side next to the church."

Alain strolled away, nothing about his manner or pace indicating any kind of urgency or a need beyond the urge to stretch his legs. He crossed the green and stood at the head of the lane by the church. It was narrow, deeply rutted, with fields on one side, cottages on the other. After a moment's thought, he entered the church-yard and strolled around to the back, look-ing at gravestones with an air of interest, as if trying to find a particular name. As he'd suspected, the rear of the churchyard merged into the fields, and it was a simple matter to slip alongside a tall bramble hedge that ran the length of the lane separating it from the fields.

Through regular gaps in the hedge, he had

a good sight line of the cottages across the lane. They were neatly kept for the most part but humble dwellings. He saw several of their occupants working in the small front gardens, women with small children clinging to their homespun skirts, and he noted how few young, able-bodied men there were to be seen. Presumably, they were all working on the surrounding farms, leaving their womenfolk, children, and the old men to mind hearth and home. At the very end of the lane, where the rutted, hard-packed earth halted at a stile that gave entrance to an apple orchard, he stopped to look at the last cottage. It looked just like all the others, except that it was perhaps a little larger and the front garden had flowers as well as vegetables, an indication that its residents were not solely occupied with the day-to-day business of existence. Anyone who had time and space to plant and cultivate flowers did not need to grow their own cabbages.

He settled into a small ditch, where a gap in the hedge gave him a clear view of the cottage, and waited. His patience was rewarded within a few minutes. The door opened, and a child in a blue pinafore emerged with a shallow trug. She pranced to the flowerbeds and knelt to pick bright orange chrysanthemums, laying each bloom carefully in the trug.

"Marguerite, petite, viens ici." The soft voice was followed immediately by the appearance of a woman in the doorway. Even if she had not spoken French, Alain would have known that this woman didn't quite fit her surroundings. Her clothes were simple enough, but there was an elegance to her posture, to the tilt of her head, to the delicacy of her frame, that made her stand out among the women he had seen in other gardens down the lane.

The child scrambled to her feet and ran to obey the summons, clutching her trug, and after another few minutes, Alain made his way back to the inn. This time, a tankard of ale awaited him on the table, and Everard was eating a thick meat pasty with an air of mild distaste. "Would you like one?" he asked. "It's food, that's about all you can say for it."

Alain was ravenous. He had had barely two hours' sleep before being woken by Gilles and sent breakfastless to Jermyn Street. He accepted the offer eagerly and took a deep gulp from his tankard. Everard did not hurry him. The Lizard rarely hurried; undue haste encouraged mistakes. He pushed the remnants of his pasty to one side, sipped his ale, and waited.

Alain took a large bite from the greasy offering in front of him and chewed, wiping his mouth with the back of his hand before washing the mouthful down with ale. "There's a woman and a child in the last cottage," he said finally. "French — at least, the woman is. The child certainly understands it."

"Hmm." Everard digested this for moment. "Ducasse has no sisters. How old was the woman?"

"Hard to tell. Thirty-something, perhaps. Not what you'd call young."

"And the child?"

"Small, three . . . four." Alain shrugged. "I don't know children. I can't tell how big they're supposed to be at what age."

Everard rubbed his lips with his fingertips, frowning in thought, before saying, "I'll stay here and see for myself. Leave the carriage. I'm sure this miserable hostelry has a jobbing horse you can hire to go back to London. Fetch Gilles, and return here first thing in the morning. Make sure you are both well armed."

He remained at the table after Alain had left, then summoned the innkeeper and asked if he had a bedchamber for the night.

"Why, yes, indeed, sir. The best bed you'll

find between here and town, sir. Good, clean sheets, no vermin, I'll swear, and I can offer you a nice shoulder of mutton for your dinner."

Somewhat wanly, Everard accepted these offers. Sometimes his work required supreme sacrifice.

TWENTY-FIVE

"Oh, you're back, then, Lady Hero." Maisie came into Hero's bedchamber with an armful of freshly ironed petticoats. "I wonder you didn't ring for me." She sounded faintly disapproving as she laid the crisp white muslins over the back of a chaise before hanging them in the linen press.

"I didn't need anything, Maisie," Hero responded. In truth, she had not wanted to see or talk to anyone. "I thought you were going to visit your sister."

"She couldn't get free time. Lady Denizon is having a rout party this evening, so I didn't stay." She looked critically around the chamber. "The fire needs making up." She abandoned her task and went to poke the sluggish flames in the grate. "Lord, I wonder you didn't notice." She glanced curiously at her mistress. "Are you feeling quite well, ma'am? You look a bit peaky. Should I fetch a posset or ask Lady Emily for some of that tonic she swears by?"

Hero shook her head against the embroidered back of her chair. "I'm quite well, just a little tired, perhaps."

"Hardly surprising, getting up so early." Maisie returned to hanging petticoats. "Why don't I bring you up a spot of nuncheon? A little chicken, a slice of ham . . ."

"I'm not in the least hungry," Hero stated firmly. "I may just rest a little this afternoon. Has Lady Emily left her chamber?"

"Oh, no, m'lady. Harper's been making up gruel and a hot mustard bath for her ladyship. She fears a quinsy after being out so late last evening."

Hero's smile was faint. "I daresay she'll not come down to dine, then."

"Will you be staying in yourself tonight?" Maisie smoothed down the folds of the last petticoat and closed the linen press.

Hero's gaze flicked to the mantel, where an engraved invitation to Lady Denizon's rout party was propped against the mirror. Even in different circumstances, she would have been reluctant to attend, knowing her absence would be barely noticed among the crowds flocking the salons of the mansion in Brook Street. Tony Cardew had offered to escort her, but she had declined his company, knowing he would disappear into the card rooms the minute they arrived and she wouldn't see him for the rest of the evening.

"Probably," she replied. "For now, I think I'll rest a little."

Maisie bobbed a curtsy and left Hero to her thoughts, dismal and confused as they were. She wasn't left alone with them for long, however. Maisie returned with a sealed envelope. "This just arrived for you, Lady Hero. The messenger is waiting for a reply."

Hero recognized the writing instantly, and her stomach plunged and then righted itself. He'd told her to await his instructions, just as she had been. She slit the wax with her finger and opened the sheet.

Attend the Denizons' rout party this evening.

She stared down at the script. No salutation, just a curt order. Was she going to obey it?

It was an interesting question. But one to which there was only one answer. She went to the dainty secretaire in the window embrasure and wrote: *As you wish.* She folded the sheet, sealed it, scratching her initials into the hot wax, then handed the paper to Maisie. "It seems I shall be going out this evening after all, Maisie. When you've given this to the messenger, could you come back, and we'll decide what dress I should wear to the Denizons' party?"

A thronged salon, bright lights, music, cards — it was a perfect venue for secret conversations. Would the Lizard be there? Now, that would be interesting. A little ripple of excitement seemed to wake Hero from her slough of despond. The game was still there to be played. She would not leave town on William's say-so. But she would not refuse to listen to him.

She went to the armoire and flung open the double doors, examining the contents. Red, she decided, turning at the sound of Maisie's return. "The crimson silk, I think. It's so luscious. I'll wear it with the gold tissue shawl and the emerald set."

Maisie's eyes lit up. "You'll wear the tiara, m'lady?"

Hero hesitated. She almost never wore it except at court, but tonight she was in the mood to stand out. She nodded. "Yes, the tiara."

She would arrive without an escort, ascend the staircase alone, and make her entrance alone. Everything about this evening was going to establish that she stood alone, regardless of William and whatever secrets he held, and fearless of any threat of the Lizard's.

At nine o'clock that night, Hero stepped into the Bruton town carriage, with Maisie holding the small train of her crimson gown. Maisie arranged the gown carefully before stepping up beside her mistress. Denizon House was brilliant with light, the pavement outside lit by sconces at regular intervals, link boys carrying torches running between arriving carriages and the double front doors.

A liveried footman, recognizing the Bruton carriage, came to open the door for Lady Hero and her maid. Maisie fussed over the train as Hero stepped down to the pavement, and then hurried after her ladyship a discreet few footsteps behind while the footman led the way along the red carpet to the open doors. In the marble foyer, Maisie made final adjustments to Hero's gown, took her outer wrap, and stepped back against the wall as Hero advanced to the wide staircase. At its head stood Lord and Lady Denizon, waiting to greet their guests, beside them their majordomo, who announced in ringing tones, "Lady Hermione Fanshawe."

"Hero, my dear, how delightful to see you. How is dear Lady Bruton? So sad that town has to lose her and Lord Bruton at such a point in the Season."

"Babies can be disruptive, Amelia," Hero said with a smile, leaning forward to exchange brushing kisses before holding out her hand to Lord Denizon with a small curtsy. He bowed over her hand and muttered his own greeting, looking impatiently over her shoulder to see how many more guests he must greet before he could escape to the card rooms.

Hero left her hosts and walked to the doors open to the first salon. She stood for a moment in the doorway, assessing the crowd, perfectly at her ease. She was not alone for long. Young men swarmed to her side, begging for a dance or to take her into supper. She responded lightly to them all, flirting delicately, waiting for William to show himself.

But it wasn't until supper that he made an appearance. She had danced, flirted, and chatted inconsequentially until she thought her head would burst and had finally allowed herself to be led to the supper room, to be plied with champagne, oyster patties, and lobster mousse, before she saw William enter the supper room. He appeared to stand a head taller than the other men, but Hero knew it to be an illusion. It had everything to do with the way he stood, the way he wore the black knee britches and tailored coat, a single diamond glittering in his starched white stock, the way he held his head, the self-containment evident in every move he made. And her stomach did its customary lurch of desire despite everything, despite the certainty that she had hardened herself against this involuntary yearning.

William surveyed the room, a glass of claret in his hand, and when his eye fell upon Hero, sitting at a table with two men and a woman, he nodded infinitesimally and began to make his way over to them, unhurried, pausing to exchange a few words with knots of people who greeted him as he passed.

At Hero's table, he stopped. His smile was bland as he bowed to Miss Susan Armstrong, who fluttered her fan and peeped up at him through luxurious black eyelashes, and greeted her escort and a somewhat inebriated Tony Cardew, who had dragged himself from the card tables to take Hero into supper.

"Miss Armstong, Lady Hero, gentlemen."

"Don't expect to find you at these kinds of occasions, Ducasse," Tony said with a touch of belligerence. He was still smarting from his acerbic encounter with William at Ranelagh Gardens a few weeks earlier.

"I can't imagine why not, Cardew," William said easily. He turned to Hero. "Could I entice you from the supper room, Lady Hero? There is a full moon and a lovely view of it from the terrace."

"I own a breath of fresh air would be pleasant," Hero said, rising from the table. "It's quite warm in here." She took his proffered arm.

William threaded an adroit path through the thronged supper room and the noisy salons out onto the long terrace that stretched across the back of the mansion, overlooking a garden, lush in spring and summer, now in an autumnal decline. There was, however, a full golden moon.

Hero drew her thin shawl closer around her shoulders at the chill in the late-evening air as she walked to the low parapet overhanging the garden. "So?"

"So." William came up beside her, and she could feel his body warmth against her. "Marcus will come tomorrow morning to take you for a drive to Richmond. Bring with you any personal necessities you cannot do without for a week or two. You will not be going out for the duration of your stay, so you will need very little —"

"Not going out from where?" Hero interrupted.

"My house. Marcus will bring you to Half Moon Street when he judges it safe to do so. You will need to inform your chaperone and whomever else you deem necessary that you are going on a short visit to relatives or whatever your imagination decides is most plausible."

"I'm to stay with you?"

"I think it's the best and safest option at the moment. I have a more than adequate bedchamber for you. André will take care of you. You need have no fears for your safety."

"I have no such fears now," Hero stated, taking a step away from him. He was intending to imprison her in a spare bedchamber in his house. It was another body blow, and she was momentarily breathless at the sheer impossibility of such a prospect. The sheer lack of consideration, of understanding, of any kind of shared rapport. How could he even think of such a thing after everything they had shared, every glorious moment of their loving? Could he really click his fingers and all those memories would disappear for him?

"I'm leaving now," she stated, turning away from him, back to the music and the brilliant lights inside.

William, for a moment speechless at this abrupt departure, stared at her retreating back, struck by her erect posture, the elegance of her neck, the set of her head. "Hermione?"

She stopped, turned to face him again, the fire in her vivid green eyes matched by the emerald sparks of the gems in her rich, multihued hair, nestling in the hollow of her throat, accentuating the creamy lobes of her delicate ears. She merely looked at him, and he saw beneath the blaze of anger in her eyes a bitter well of disappointment. Then she turned again and walked away, the crimson silk of her gown moving sinuously with every step.

William felt a cold emptiness where before there had been only calm resolution and the certainty he was doing the only possible thing. How, he wondered, could he keep hurting her in this way? How could he do it in the first place, when all he wanted was to have her at his side, fighting his fight, loving him? But something made him throw a poisoned javelin into the heart of this love, and for the first time he doubted himself and the rightness of what he was doing. He moved to follow her, to catch up with her, to try to explain, but a group of overheated, chattering dancers stepped out onto the terrace as he headed for the door, and it took a precious few minutes for him to weave his way through them. When he reentered the supper room, he could just glimpse her gleaming head at the far end returning to the ballroom, where the orchestra was just beginning a lively Sir Roger de Coverley.

When he reentered the ballroom, there was no sign of her. The dancers were lined up facing each other, the chaperones nodding in their gilt chairs along the walls, but Hermione was gone. And for once in his life, William Ducasse, Viscount St. Aubery, was at a loss.

Maisie was surprised to see her mistress descend the staircase so early in the evening; it was barely past midnight. But when she saw Hero's cold, set expression, she refrained from comment, merely fetched her evening wrap from the cloakroom while a footman went outside to summon the Bruton carriage.

Hero was silent throughout the short carriage ride and offered only a distracted smile in her bedchamber as Maisie helped her out of the red silk gown. She sat at the dresser mirror to remove the emeralds, laying the set carefully back in the jewel casket, while Maisie unpinned her hair and brushed it in long, careful sweeps so that the honey-caramel strands fell in a rich curtain over her shoulders.

"Are you quite well, m'lady?" Maisie asked a little hesitantly as she dropped the folds of her white cambric nightgown over her head. "You don't seem quite yourself tonight."

"I'm a little tired. Too much dancing, I expect," Hero responded with another faint smile as she buttoned the tiny pearl studs at the front of the gown. "Would you bring me up a cup of hot spiced wine? I shall sit up by the fire for a little."

Maisie went off immediately, and Hero sat down in the armchair by the fire, her gaze fixed upon the bright flames although she was not really seeing them. She rested one bare foot on the copper fender, curling her toes against the fire's warmth as her thoughts slowly solidified, purpose now dominating the hurt bewilderment.

"Oh, thank you, Maisie." She nodded at the maid, who set the steaming, aromatic pewter tankard on a little table beside her with a plate of shortbread biscuits. "I shan't need you again tonight. And I may decide to go for a ride early tomorrow. I won't ring for you until I return, probably by midday."

Maisie bobbed a curtsy of acquiescence, although her expression said very clearly what she thought of Lady Hero's sudden habit of disappearing from the house before the household was up and about. "Whatever you say, ma'am. I'll bid you good night, then."

"Good night, Maisie." Hero took up the tankard and inhaled the rich, spicy aroma of nutmeg and cloves. It soothed and warmed her. She nibbled a biscuit and re-examined the questions she had been mulling since she'd left Brook Street.

Was she prepared to fight for William any longer? Had he finally caused too much damage for there ever to be anything more between them again? In the end, it came down to how much pain one person could cause another and still be forgiven. She understood so much about him but not enough, because he withheld his trust. She had tried so hard to understand and respect his passionate undertakings for the causes he believed in, but the part of himself that he withheld from her was beyond her understanding.

He had a child. The child's mother was dead. She had not been his wife. Those were straightforward, stark facts, and Hero had no difficulty understanding any of them. But why wouldn't he tell her anything about his past beyond those bare facts? There was so much more, she knew, and she was also

397

certain that it was that "much more" that held him back from her.

Was she prepared to risk rejection once more? She sipped the spiced wine, savoring the taste and fragrance in the tankard. It couldn't be any worse than any other time he had pushed her away.

She rose from her chair and went to the long window overlooking the street and the square, moving the heavy damask curtain aside just enough to see out. Was there a watcher out there, his eyes fixed upon the house?

She let the curtain drop again, reflecting that all things considered, there probably was. The Lizard was by no means done with her. Not after her careless revelation at Almack's. He had almost certainly increased surveillance. The question was whether he was watching the rear of the house as well as the front.

She would know soon enough once she ventured forth, Hero decided, returning to her chair. If anyone had the answers she sought, it would be the woman Jeanne, Marguerite's aunt. Maybe she wasn't the child's aunt and it was just a convenient familiarity, but it had been clear from her observations that morning that she and William were close. If she was looking after William's child, then it stood to reason she knew the child's history. Whether she would talk to Hero was another matter altogether, but it was her last chance to salvage anything from this relationship.

Her mind made up, Hero finished the contents of her tankard and went to bed, surprised at how quickly she fell asleep.

TWENTY-SIX

Hero awoke with the first chirps of the dawn chorus. She felt surprisingly refreshed after a few hours of sleep, and her resolution had not wavered. She would try one last time to penetrate the thicket of thorns William had erected around his deepest feelings, his past, all that made him who he was. If she failed, then nothing could be worse than the present.

She left the curtains drawn tightly at the window for the sake of any watcher in the street and dressed by the light of a single candle. If the Lizard kept a watcher on her twenty-four hours a day, she didn't want him to know that she was awake betimes. She fastened the braided looped buttons on her high-collared riding jacket and pulled on her boots, took up her gauntleted gloves, and softly let herself out of her chamber into the dimly lit hallway.

She took the back stairs down to the

kitchen regions. The servants' hall was deserted, the vast kitchen equally so, although the banked-up fire in the big kitchen range offered a dull glow. Before unbolting the back door, she took an apple from a barrel in the pantry, then slipped out into the distinctly cold air of early morning. The evening star still shone in the gradually lightening sky, and she shivered as a gust of wind blew the dry autumn leaves from the twin giant oaks against the far wall of the garden. As small children, she and Alec had claimed the trees for themselves, christening them with their own names. They had spent many hours together, each crouched in a tree, listening to the sounds of exasperated nursemaids and governesses searching for them. Often, when the pursuit died down, they would drop over the wall from the overhanging branches and into the mews behind, where they would hide in the hayloft with a pile of windfalls between them, vicariously enjoying the busy life of the stables below.

Hero crossed the lawn, her feet leaving imprints in the thick dew, and let herself out through the small gate in the wall at the rear of the garden, which opened directly into the mews. Apart from the snufflings and rustlings of the horses, there was no sign of life.

Hero took Petra out of her stall, and the mare sniffed the cold morning with a rather dubious air. But she took the apple eagerly enough and stood patiently as Hero threw the saddle over her back and tightened the girth, adjusting the stirrup lengths before slipping the bridle over the mare's head and leading her to the mounting block.

"It's a strange time to be out and about, I know," Hero murmured, stroking the animal's velvety neck, pulling her ears lightly, before swinging into the saddle. "But it's easier to keep our business to ourselves at this hour." She nudged Petra towards the cobbled lane that led into Adam's Row behind the mews and away from Grosvenor Square. There was no one around and nowhere to hide, at least as far as she could see. And if anyone did follow her in these deserted streets, she would surely be aware of it.

The easiest route to Knightsbridge lay through the park. It was getting lighter now, and to be on the safe side, Hero took a few maneuvers designed to disclose pursuit if there was someone on her tail. But stopping occasionally, retracing her steps once or twice, and taking small detours from her route revealed no pursuer, and she entered the park from a small gate at South Street, as confident as she could be that she was unobserved. She took the carriage drive around, hoping she wouldn't meet any early-morning riders who might recognize her. But her luck held, and within half an hour, she found herself in Knightsbridge.

There were more people around now, laden drays and farmers' carts taking their goods to the markets in town, a few servants hurrying to start their day in the merchants' houses, day laborers hauling coal and wood for the gentry's fireplaces and cooking ranges. No one seemed to take any notice of her as she rode around the village green and turned onto Primrose Lane. She drew up outside the last cottage on the lane, dismounted, opened the gate, and led Petra up the path to the front door. Hoping she wouldn't be waking the inhabitants from a sound sleep, she knocked once and almost immediately heard the sound of the bolt being drawn back. The door was pulled open with some effort, and Marguerite stood there in her nightgown, looking up at Hero.

The child called excitedly, "Tante Jeanne, the lady who makes daisy chains is here, and she's brought a horse. Can I ride him? Please, I want to ride him. Uncle Guillaume lets me ride his horse." She pranced on her tiptoes as the words poured forth.

Jeanne emerged from a door at the rear of the small hall. She looked at Hero, her eyes a little narrowed, her gaze speculative but not hostile. Then she said, "I'm glad you came. It would be wise to take your horse around the side to the kitchen garden. It will be less conspicuous there."

"Of course, at once." Comforted by her welcome, Hero stepped back from the door, and it closed instantly on Marguerite's voice rising in complaint. She tethered Petra to the fence enclosing a small kitchen garden, loosened the girth and knotted the reins, then made her way to the kitchen door, which now stood open, Jeanne standing within, a plaid shawl wrapped tightly around her nightgown.

"Come in, please." She held the door wider in invitation. "Marguerite and I were about to have breakfast. I hope you'll join us."

"Thank you." Hero felt as if this was all taking place in a dream; it felt so unreal. She took off her gloves as she stepped into the warm, homey kitchen.

"Marguerite, would you let the hens out of the henhouse and fetch the eggs, please?" Jeanne handed the child a basket.

"Can I give the horse some apples, too,

and a carrot? Please, may I?"

Jeanne glanced at Hero, who said swiftly, "Petra would love just one apple and one carrot, Marguerite. Thank you so much."

Beaming, Marguerite danced off with her basket to pull a carrot from the vegetable patch and pick a windfall from beneath the apple tree. Hero watched from the small latticed window for a moment. Petra was not particularly skittish, but if the child approached her too suddenly, she might be unpredictable.

"It's all right. Marguerite knows how to be around horses. William taught her sometime ago." Jeanne set a mug on the table. "Coffee?"

"Thank you." Hero sat at the table, cupping her cold hands around the mug. "I'm sorry to burst in upon you like this," she began.

Jeanne interrupted her. "No, don't apologize. I'm glad you did," she repeated, and a rather sad smile touched her lips. "William is not very good at helping himself, as I expect you've noticed, so it's incumbent on those who care for him to do it for him."

Hero was silent for a moment. "I don't know whether I'm betraying him by coming here, but I think it's our last chance . . . . his and mine."

"Petra ate the carrot *and* the apple, although it might have been a bit maggoty," Marguerite announced from the door, letting in a blast of chill air. "And there are six eggs." She set down her basket and sat to haul off her boots. "Petra is a girl's name, isn't it?"

"Yes, Petra is a mare." Hero sipped her coffee, wondering how she and Jeanne were to have a conversation in the child's company.

But she needn't have worried. Jeanne said, "Go and get dressed, *petite,* and then you can take some bread and jam outside and talk to Petra some more while I prepare the eggs." Marguerite went off with her usual dancing step, and Jeanne said, "I don't even know your name."

"Hermione Fanshawe, but I'm always called Hero. I met William in Paris. Forgive me, but are you related to William . . . his sister? I know Marguerite is his daughter; it's impossible to miss."

"The eyes, yes," Jeanne agreed. "I am her aunt. Her mother was my sister. She and William fell deeply in love about six years ago. Her parents felt she was too young for marriage, although I think they hoped she would find someone at the court of Versailles of more august lineage than a mere viscount, although the St. Aubery name is venerable enough and there's wealth enough. But my family, my father in particular, always had an inflated sense of family pride. He didn't forbid the marriage outright but insisted that they wait for twelve months."

She gazed over Hero's head through the window to the gray morning sky. "Isabelle, my sister, was never one to wait for something she wanted. She didn't care much for the rules and societal regulations imposed upon our class."

Hero was beginning to see a glimmer of light. "William seems to care overmuch for such things," she commented.

"Now, perhaps. Not so much then." Jeanne got up to fetch the coffeepot from the range. She refilled their mugs. "They were not alone at court in violating the rules," she added. She shook her head. "It was a passion I had never seen between two people. It seemed to swallow them whole. They saw no one but each other . . . I'm sorry, I don't mean to imply that you and —"

Hero waved her hands in dismissal. "No, please, I understand. You see, it was like that for William and myself for a while, and then he ripped us apart. It was so savage, so brutal, and I had no explanation, and he still will not give me one, but I know in my heart, my *self,* that it is the same for him as it is for me. I can't let him go without one more fight for us both."

Jeanne leaned her elbows on the table, her hands cupped around her mug, and her eyes met Hero's with a straightforward gaze. "Isabelle became pregnant. Such matters are often dealt with by a strategic illness and an absence from court for the necessary time, and the child is fostered at birth. Our family was prepared to protect the family honor in such manner, although my father insisted that Isabelle was so disgraced she would have to take the veil as soon as the child was born. Until then, she would be held in seclusion in the country."

"William . . ." Hero prompted into the sudden silence.

Jeanne made a visible effort to concentrate on her story. "William was in Italy. His father had been France's ambassador to Rome, and he hoped that William would follow in his footsteps. He had arranged for him to spend a summer at the embassy and tour the country. William was reluctant, but his father was no tyrant, and he and his son were close. Isabelle did not know she was pregnant at that time, and they both agreed that while it would be hard for them to part, it might make the year go more quickly. Also, their risk taking had become increasingly reckless, and they both knew it."

Hero winced a little as the glimmer of light grew brighter. She waited, unwilling to prompt Jeanne. However, the reappearance of William's daughter put a temporary stop to the story, and Jeanne rose to fry eggs and bacon, chatting inconsequentially the while. Hero did her part, telling her hostess and Marguerite about her own family, her brother and the new baby. She touched briefly on Marie Claire's experiences in Paris without sharing her own part in them. That would come later, when there were no little ears to hear.

Hero was hungry for the first time in a long time, it seemed, and she finished her plate with relish. As soon as the child had disappeared again to talk to Petra and give her more apples, Jeanne resumed her history.

"So, with William away, poor Isabelle had little choice but to obey our father's edict and remain immured on our country estate, kept away from neighbors, not even permitted to attend church. It was said she was dangerously ill with smallpox, and that was sufficient to keep the local families well away." Jeanne's mouth twisted in a grimace of disgust. "I was permitted to leave the convent that I had just joined as a novice and allowed to stay with her, to look after her until the birth. Since my life was already dedicated to the church, it seemed reasonable to the world in general that it shouldn't matter if I caught the disease and was pockmarked for life. I was not destined for the marriage bed."

Hero could almost hear William's dry cynicism in his sister-in-law's tones — sister-in-law in all but name.

"Isabelle and I concocted a plan that I would take the baby and tell everyone the child had died at birth." She shrugged. "It was an old and tried story, after all. As long as we could keep meddling midwives out of the birth chamber, it would work. Throughout the nine months, Isabelle heard nothing from William. She wrote to him constantly, told him of the pregnancy and the plan she and I had made for the baby and for herself. As soon as she was ready to leave her bed, I would get her away from the house, and together we would leave France with the baby. She asked William over and over where she should go and when he would arrive. They would marry without her father's blessing and make a life for themselves and their child."

Hero was staring steadily at Jeanne as she talked, an almost pitiless stare as she absorbed every word.

"But she never heard anything from William." Jeanne spoke with finality. "Not a single letter, not a message, nothing in the entire nine months. I myself ensured her letters went to the embassy in Rome without our father's knowing anything of it, but there was never a reply. Isabelle was in despair. She couldn't understand why he wouldn't even acknowledge the pregnancy, the fact that she carried his child. It was a difficult pregnancy, as much because of her dreadful anxiety as anything, I think. Our parents said her suffering was well-deserved punishment for her sins," she added with a caustic smile. "Their religious fervor was acclaimed throughout the region."

"The proverbial whited sepulchre," Hero murmured.

"Indeed," Jeanne responded. "Anyway, I took Marguerite as soon as she was born, as we'd agreed, and fostered her initially with a family attached to the convent. Then I went back to the country. Isabelle was very ill and had fallen into an even darker depression. She was physically very weak, and our parents both harangued her constantly about her disgrace, her own dishonor and the dreadful dishonor she had brought upon the family. They told her she could never show her face in public again, and they put it about that she was so severely disfigured with the smallpox that her only recourse was to enter a convent.

"And still William never wrote." She laid her hands palms up on the table in a gesture of defeat. "One night, Isabelle left the house and threw herself into the river from the stone bridge that gave entrance to our estate. The river flowed very fast at that point. They found her body five miles downriver two days later."

Hero closed her eyes, the better to absorb the full horror of this story. "Why?" she asked after a moment. "Why didn't William write?" Even though she knew he was capable of hurting those he loved if he felt a greater good, by his lights, would be served by it, this horror did not fit with the conflicted man she knew and loved.

"He wrote," Jeanne said flatly. "But he never received Isabelle's letters. Our father had written himself to the ambassador and explained that his daughter and William were engaged in a clandestine correspondence of which he disapproved and asked that the ambassador ensure that William received no letters from anyone but himself. The ambassador, who had daughters of his own and presumably responded with paternal fellow feeling, did his work beautifully. William wrote nevertheless, but of course, our father merely burned the letters as they arrived. I had written myself, telling him to direct his letters to the nurse Isabelle and I had had as a child, but he didn't get that one, either. So he wrote to the only address he knew."

"What happened when he came back?" Hero asked, although she could guess the rest of the story, just as she now understood William's seemingly illogical obsession with her reputation. It came from love, from the fearful reminder of his own loss because of Society's judgment. And that judgment was real enough; she'd heard enough stories, seen the consequences among her own circle often enough, not to discount it. But since Tom's death, she hadn't cared twopence for the consequences of flouting the rules.

"When he was on his way home, he wrote to me at the convent where I had returned with Marguerite. I was looking after the baby there with the Mother Superior's rather reluctant consent, although I knew I would have to make other arrangements soon enough. William's letter was the answer to a prayer. I was finally able to write and tell him the whole dreadful story. He got my letter in Genoa, where he was staying with friends, and drove night and day to find me and his child. Since then, he has taken care of us both."

She got up and took the dirty plates to the sink. "Of course, soon after his return, he threw himself into the revolution, at first on the side of the Fourth Estate, and then, when the Terror started, he turned his focus to rescue. His life has been in danger ever since he set himself up against the various regimes that have terrorized the country and still do. He worries constantly that anyone close to him is also in danger. He has stationed a guard to keep watch on the cottage even now."

"Which means he'll know I'm here," Hero said with a wry grimace. "Even if I wanted to keep it a secret. He won't be best pleased, that much I do know."

"Tell me the whole." Jeanne came back to the table. "Maybe I can help."

TWENTY-SEVEN

Everard Dubois had not enjoyed his night's sleep at the inn. Despite the landlord's insistence on the cleanliness of his bed linen, he was convinced there were vermin crawling among the feathers in the mattress. As a consequence, he was in a foul mood when he awoke just after dawn. He was breaking his fast in the taproom when Gilles and Alain arrived from town.

"Alain, go and check on Primrose Lane. See if anything's changed. It was quiet enough when I took a look before going to bed," Everard instructed, his tone curt. He looked with distaste at the plate of fat bacon in front of him.

Alain went off without a word, and Everard gestured to Gilles to take the seat opposite him. "The coffee's vile; you'd do better with ale," he stated, waving at the landlord. "Two tankards of ale." He pushed aside his untouched plate with a shudder.

"Barbarous nation. I'll never get used to the food. So, no movement in Grosvenor Square? Did she go out last night?"

Gilles shook his head. "Luc was on watch in the garden all night, said no one came in and no one went out. The curtains at the window of what we believe is her bedchamber were still drawn when he was relieved an hour ago."

Dubois nodded and took a draught of the ale the landlord set down in front of him. "I made a few discreet inquiries about the woman and child, but no one seems to know much about them. They arrived in the village about nine months ago, renting the cottage from a farmer. They keep themselves to themselves, occasionally have a visitor . . . a gentleman visitor." A smile flickered across his thin lips. "Ducasse, one assumes."

"No other village gossip?" Gilles asked. "Villagers love to gossip."

"Not this village," Everard responded. "All I gathered was the gentleman only ever stays for a couple of hours, and he's often seen outside playing with the child."

"Is the woman his mistress?" Tentatively, Gilles took a piece of cooling bacon from the Lizard's discarded plate.

"One would assume so. But the nature of their relationship is immaterial . . . Is that edible?"

Gilles shrugged and took another piece. "I've not broken my fast this morning."

Everard shook his head before returning to his subject. "Lovers or not, she's clearly important to Ducasse, and that's all that matters. The woman and child make him vulnerable, so we take them, and we have him . . . Ah, here's Alain."

Alain hooked a stool over to the table with his foot. "The woman's there," he stated, thumping down on the stool.

"She lives there," Gilles said through a mouthful of bacon.

"Not that one, the other one." Alain was a man of few words.

"Lady Hero?" Everard's expression offered no sign of the quick thrill of anticipation. "The Fanshawe woman, is that who you mean?"

"Aye. That's the one." Alain took up the tankard the innkeeper had brought over. "There's a horse tethered in the back. The woman's inside. I saw her through the kitchen window."

"How did Luc miss her leaving?" Gilles muttered.

"That doesn't matter now." The Lizard brushed the issue aside with an impatient

417

gesture. "We have all three of them to-gether."

"Only problem, there's a guard on watch," Alain said. "In the orchard."

"One man?"

Alain nodded and absently took the last piece of bacon. "Well armed, as far as I could see."

"Did he see you?" Dubois asked sharply.

Alain shook his head. "Dozy bugger was nodding off. I slipped around him in the trees."

"No problem, then," Gilles stated. "Even if he's one of Ducasse's best, one against three is no match."

Dubois nodded. He was thinking, and his companions knew better than to interrupt the master's reflections. It couldn't have been more perfect, Dubois thought. Hero, the mystery woman, and the child, together, just ripe for the plucking. "There's a back entrance, you say."

"All the cottages have one."

"How do we get them out in broad day-light without alerting the neighbors?" Eve-rard mused. "We have no time to waste. There's no knowing how long the Fanshawe woman will stay, and I want all three of them. What a gift." Unconsciously, he rubbed his hands together, his evil mood vanished. "Gilles, there's an apothecary in the village. I need you to get laudanum. Alain and I will deal with Ducasse's man while you do that. Pay the shot here, and bring the carriage outside the lych-gate of the church. We'll meet you there when we have them."

"All three of them?" Gilles frowned. "The carriage only has seats for two."

"We take the child and the Fanshawe woman. The other will provide a most eloquent ransom note." Dubois was already on his feet. "We need rope. Alain, find some in the stable yard."

He strode from the taproom and up to his chamber, where he assembled his armory. Two stiletto knives, a silver-mounted pistol, his rapier sheathed at his waist. Gilles and Alain would both have knives and pistols. The Lizard preferred knives for such operations, as they did their work silently. He threw his thick riding cloak around his shoulders, dropped his heavy purse into the deep pocket of his coat, and left the chamber. Alain awaited him outside the front door, a coil of rope secured around his waist beneath his coat.

They strolled across the green to the church and entered the churchyard beneath the lych-gate. Again without apparent haste, they wandered around the church to the rear and slipped into the shadow of the hedge, keeping to the ditch as they made their way the length of the lane to the orchard at the end. The day was uninviting, cold and overcast, and the morning was still early enough for there to be few people around. A woman opened the door of one cottage and shook out a rag rug before returning inside. An elderly woman with a kerchief around her head walked in a stoop along the lane, picking up twigs for kindling.

When they reached the orchard, Alain stopped and gestured to a group of pear trees close to the edge of the orchard. It was a position that offered a good view of the cottage. A man sat with his back against one tree, half concealed from the Frenchmen by a black currant bush. His eyes were half closed, but he was far from asleep. He'd seen the other woman arrive some half hour earlier, and despite his sleepy appearance, he was alert and waiting to see what would happen next.

Everard took a weighted string from his pocket and exchanged a look with Alain, who nodded in silent comprehension. They approached the tree from the rear, their steps muffled by the damp, mossy ground until a hidden twig cracked under Alain's foot. The man under the tree jumped to his feet instantly and looked around. He didn't see the string as it swung across his throat, the weighted ends held fast in Everard's strong hands. William's man was aware of a blinding flash of terror as the garotte cut into his throat; then it jerked hard once, and a strange noise escaped him.

Alain lowered the body to the ground as Everard released the garotte. They rolled the man into the ditch and kicked fallen leaves over him. Everard had no intention of hiding the body properly; he wanted it to be found by the man's relief as soon as he arrived. But he didn't want any villagers tripping over it by accident before then.

Still in silence, they crept through the orchard around to the back of the cottage. A horse was tethered to the fence, grazing contentedly on the grass. The child was staring into the water butt, intent on the antics of a water beetle. She didn't hear the small click as Alain opened the gate, but something made her straighten and look over her shoulder. As she did so, she was smothered in darkness, thick, musky-smelling blackness. She tried to cry out, but a hand clamped the heavy material against her throat as she was lifted off her feet, the folds of Everard's cloak trapping her legs as she fought against the stifling blackness.

Alain pushed open the door into the kitchen, where two women sat talking across from each other at a pine table, mugs of coffee between them. They both turned, startled at the sound of the door.

"Quiet," the Lizard snapped. "Make a sound, and the child will suffocate." He pressed the cloth harder against Marguerite's mouth, and her frantic kicking accentuated the threat.

Jeanne felt the shaft of pure terror push deep inside her, but she fought for outward calm, and when she looked at Hero, she saw that the other woman, although now very pale, was showing no sign of panic. Neither of them spoke, and they both gazed at the small bundled figure struggling in the Lizard's hold.

"Good . . . now, tell the child to be still and keep quiet, and I'll loosen the cloak."

Jeanne stepped forward, placing her hand on Marguerite's back. "Be still now, *petite,* it's all going to be all right. The man is going to let you go, but you mustn't make any noise." Marguerite stopped kicking, and Jeanne looked coldly at Dubois, who relaxed his hold a little and loosened the cloth around the little girl's face. She emerged red and gasping, panic filling her eyes as they looked for Jeanne, who touched her cheek gently and whispered, "That's a good girl, now. Be still, and don't make a sound."

A little sob escaped Marguerite but nothing else. Dubois looked closely at her. "What is she to Ducasse?"

When Jeanne did not answer, Alain swung his hand in a vicous backhanded slap against her cheek. She stumbled against the table, and Hero rushed forward to steady her. Marguerite gave a little cry of terror. Jeanne sat down unsteadily, her cheek already swelling.

"She's his child," Hero said. There seemed little point in denying the truth and subjecting all of them to more brutality. Marguerite was their weak spot; the Lizard knew it, and they knew it. Somehow they had to protect her. Oddly, she had felt pure panic for only an instant when the two men had burst into the kitchen. She was afraid, very afraid — she knew too much about the Lizard to feel otherwise — but a curious calm, a cold detachment from that fear, was giving her strength.

"Ah." The Lizard held the child away from him a little, examining her. "Yes, I see it now. How very interesting. And are you her mother?"

Jeanne shook her head, still mute, her

hand cradling her cheek.

"Even more interesting," Dubois said. "But not particularly important. Alain, tie the woman to the chair. If she makes a move, hit her again . . . knock her out if necessary." He turned to Hero. "Are you going to cooperate, Lady Hero, or do I have to persuade you?" He glanced pointedly at Marguerite.

"Cooperate how?" She looked at Alain, who had uncoiled the rope from his waist and was binding Jeanne to her chair. Jeanne stared straight ahead, unresisting, as he tied her hands at her back behind the chair.

"You're going to walk out of here with the child. I shall be behind you, Alain will be next to you. I shall have a knife at the child's back. One false move, and I shall use it."

Hero couldn't see any alternative to obedience. Maybe an opportunity would show itself once they were on the move, but she was in no doubt that the Lizard would do what he threatened without compunction. She looked at Jeanne again, and the older woman nodded in silent agreement.

"As you wish," Hero said without expression.

Jeanne spoke finally. "Please take some things for Marguerite, Hero. Her favorite doll, she won't sleep properly without it,

424

and her nightgown, a change of clothes . . ." She fell silent abruptly as Alain took a menacing step towards her.

"It would be better to keep the child as comfortable as possible," Hero said swiftly. "She will be much easier to handle if she's not as fearful."

Dubois shrugged. "It matters not to me. Alain, go with her to get whatever she thinks the girl needs. Only bring what the woman can carry easily." He shifted Marguerite against his shoulder. She was no longer struggling, but her little body was shaking with sobs. "Hurry," he said harshly. "I'm tired of holding her."

Alain gestured with his knife to Hero that she should precede him out of the kitchen and up the narrow flight of stairs to a bedchamber that Jeanne shared with Marguerite. Hero looked around rather helplessly. She had no idea where to look, but there was a rag doll on the small truckle bed, which she presumed was Marguerite's. She found a nightgown and clean undergarments, stockings, and a dress with a holland smock in the armoire. Alain stood to one side of the window, looking out on the lane, the knife still in his hand. He growled at her to hurry up.

She gathered the garments up with the

doll and went back to the kitchen, Alain and his knife at her back. Dubois was waiting, tapping his booted foot. Jeanne was holding herself upright in her chair, her cheek badly swollen, her eye half closed. But despite the bindings, she held herself rigid.

The Lizard set Marguerite on her feet, the cloak still wrapped around her. "Take her hand," he instructed Hero. "And remember, one false move . . ." He unwound the cloak from the small figure and then walked to the chair where Jeanne was tied. He stood looking down at her for a moment, then took a handkerchief from his pocket.

He leaned over her, taking her chin between finger and thumb, forcing her to look at him. "I trust you are not too uncomfortable, madame, but I'm sure you won't be here for long. When you see Ducasse, you may tell him he will hear from the Lizard soon. Make sure he understands the situation fully." He took the handkerchief and deftly used it to gag her, before dropping her chin and straightening.

Marguerite gave a deep, shuddering sob and tugged Hero's hand, trying to reach Jeanne. Instantly, Hero knelt and held her tightly. "Hush, sweetheart. We mustn't make any noise. Jeanne will be all right, I promise. I'm going to look after you now. Hold my

426

hand, and be very quiet."

Stunned, the child did as she was told, and Alain opened the door, pushing Hero out with a hand on her shoulder. She twitched away from him and stepped out into the garden. "My mare?" she said.

Dubois merely shrugged and said nothing. His knife gleamed for a moment before it slipped up his sleeve, and his hand rested at the small of Marguerite's back. "Move."

Holding the child's hand tightly, Hero walked out of the garden and followed instructions to enter the orchard. They picked their way through the trees and then along the hedge to the churchyard. Marguerite was silent except for the little sobs that escaped her, shaking her fragile frame as if she were icy cold. Hero whispered to her, nonsense words for the most part but all she could manage as she thought frantically of a way to get away from the knives at their backs.

But it wasn't possible, not now, and all too soon, they were out of the churchyard, where a town carriage waited at the lychgate. Gilles jumped down from the box as the little party emerged. Hero and Marguerite were on the street in plain sight for barely thirty seconds before they were bundled up and into the two-seater carriage.

She tried to hear the brief exchange between the Lizard and the driver, but their voices were too low, and within a couple of minutes, he stepped up into the carriage. "Take the child on your lap." He slammed the door behind him, sitting in the seat next to her. The carriage began to move instantly.

"Where are we going?" Hero ventured after a few minutes.

"You don't need to know that," was the curt response.

"What about my horse? What about Jeanne?" she persisted, driven by a perverse desire to irritate him. She didn't really expect any answers to her questions. Marguerite began to cry in earnest.

Dubois took a small vial out of his inside pocket and uncorked it. "Hold her tight," he instructed, leaning over Marguerite with the vial.

"No . . . no, what are you giving her?" Hero exclaimed, trying to push his hand away.

He caught her wrist with his free hand and twisted it back so that she cried out with pain, and when he let her wrist go, her hand flopped into her lap like something broken. She didn't think it was broken, but it was numb and without strength. She could do nothing now to stop him forcing the vial between the child's lips as Marguerite struggled and coughed. Dubois clamped the girl's mouth shut, and she was forced to swallow, tears streaming down her eyes.

"That'll keep the brat quiet for an hour or so," he said, recorking the vial and tucking it back into his pocket. He regarded Hero with narrowed eyes. "I strongly suggest, my lady, that you do exactly as you are told in future. I will not be so gentle with you the next time."

Hero closed her lips tight and gave Marguerite the doll, rocking her as the drug took hold, singing a few words of the only lullabye she could remember from her own childhood. Dubois stared ahead at the paneling opposite, one hand resting on his knee, the tip of the knife showing through his turned-back cuff. Hero wondered where Alain was. Until now, she had found him more frightening than the Lizard, although she knew that the other man's overt brutality only made him seem more dangerous, but Dubois was by far the deadlier. He gave the orders; his minions merely obeyed them.

Hero knew she would ask no more questions. She understood that she and Marguerite were hostages and William was to be the price of their ransom. She wondered what had happened to the guard William had put on the cottage, but it wasn't hard to guess if he had encountered the Lizard and Alain. Presumably, he would be found by the man sent to relieve him, who would then discover Jeanne, and William would get the message with brutal clarity.

There was some comfort in knowing that William would soon know what had happened and the full strength of his considerable resources would be devoted to their rescue. But how could he do that without endangering Marguerite? Or herself? Hero acknowledged the bitter truth that she had walked into the Lizard's trap of her own volition, against all the warnings, and she probably deserved to be in her present predicament, but she was also responsible for Marguerite's present danger. She had to have been the weak link that led the Lizard to Knightsbridge and William's deeply held secret. It was, therefore, her responsibility to see that no harm came to his daughter from her own recklessness, just as it was unthinkable that William should be forced to give himself up to his enemies to ensure his daughter's safety because of that same recklessness.

Hero could feel the change in the road's surface beneath the wheels as they reentered the city and steeled herself for what was to come next. She didn't dare move aside the leather curtain to see where they were, but they would surely reach their destination soon, and maybe an opportunity would show itself.

But the carriage did not stop. They were surrounded by the sounds of the city, but the wheels continued to roll over the cobbles. After a long time, the sounds outside changed; the atmosphere beyond the curtained windows seemed different. It was definitely quieter, and the motion of the carriage became smoother. Hero felt another stab of fear. Where was he taking them? Somehow she had thought that on familiar ground, she might find a way to escape. She could find her way around the streets of London, but if they were going somewhere unknown, that changed everything.

She had money, at least, and they would have to stop somewhere soon. The horses would be tiring, and she was acutely aware of her own need for a privy. Marguerite was breathing noisily against her chest, still deep in the drug-induced sleep. The Lizard was still and silent, his arms folded across his chest, but his body was close enough to hers for her to feel how alert he was, how ready to move at a moment's notice.

"I have need of the privy," Hero said into

the continued silence. "Could we stop?"

The Lizard turned his head against the leather squabs and regarded her narrowly. He knocked on the ceiling, and after a few minutes, the carriage came to a halt. He leaned over her and pushed open the door on her side. "Get down, and do what you have to beside the carriage. Be quick. If you attempt to run, the child dies." He pulled Marguerite onto his lap, and Hero saw the flash of his knife in his free hand.

She weighed her desperate need for relief with the grim knowledge that she was to have no privacy, then closed her mind to the humiliation and clambered down. The carriage was drawn up close to a hedge, with a small ditch that would give her an illusion of privacy, and at least she was invisible from any traffic passing on the other side of the vehicle. As far as she could tell, they were on a country lane, but she thought she could smell the sea. The city was somewhere behind them, that was clear enough.

A horn sounded in the distance, and she frowned, wrestling as swiftly as she could with her skirts and the britches she wore beneath for riding. It was a sound she recognized, a coach blowing its horn as it approached a toll. The smell of the sea, the presence of tolls . . . there was only one possibility.

They were on the road from London to Dover. And Dover meant the English Channel, boats, France. If the Lizard succeeded in getting her and Marguerite onto a boat to France, their chances of escape would be nonexistent. And for the first time, Hero felt her courage ebb, her natural optimism fade.

TWENTY-EIGHT

Marcus Gosford arrived at Grosvenor Square in his phaeton to take Lady Hero for a morning carriage ride, or that was how it was to appear. He expected her to be ready for him, following William's instructions, as he swung down from the driver's precarious perch, handing the reins to his groom. An anticipatory smile of greeting was on his lips as he climbed the steps to the house and lifted the brass knocker.

Jackson opened the door himself and bowed. "Sir Marcus, good morning."

"Good morning, Jackson. I've come for Lady Hero. She's expecting me." He smiled at the majordomo, glancing over his shoulder into the hall, looking in vain for Hero.

"Come in, sir." Jackson held the door wider, stepping back.

Puzzled, Marcus accepted the invitation, observing, "Perhaps she is not quite ready. I'll wait here."

Jackson coughed. "Lady Hero has not rung for her maid as yet this morning, sir. If you'd care to step into the library and take a glass of sherry, I will send Maisie to inquire."

Marcus frowned, but he walked into the library, drawing off his gloves. Jackson spoke in an undertone to a footman, who scurried off into the back regions of the mansion, and the majordomo poured a glass of golden wine for the visitor. He presented it with a bow and faded out of the room, closing the double doors softly behind him.

What the devil was Hero playing at? Marcus took his glass to the fire. William's instructions had been perfectly clear, and he himself had agreed that there was no better solution to ensuring Hero's present safety. She would have understood that, so why wasn't she ready?

The door opened softly again, and he spun around. "Well?" He was aware his voice was unnaturally sharp, the question almost discourteous, and he had to remind himself that to all intents and purposes, this was purely a social engagement. Hero, as instructed, would have ensured that her chaperone would not worry about an extended absence, but the servants didn't need to be informed in person of her ladyship's plans. If Lady Emily was satisfied, then they would not question the situation.

Jackson bowed. "Forgive me, Sir Marcus, there appears to be some confusion. Lady Hero is not at home. I understand from her maid that she intended to go for an early-morning ride. She directed Maisie not to attend her this morning until she rang." He coughed into his white-gloved hand. "She has not as yet done so, sir."

Marcus set down his glass, saying easily, "Thank you, Jackson. I expect our engagement slipped her mind. When she returns, please tell her I called." He walked past the majordomo, pulling on his gloves, his mind in a turmoil. If Hero had set herself up against William, then the fur would fly. But perhaps she had intended to be back in time and something had kept her. And in that case, there was serious trouble afoot.

René Lacroix crept through the orchard just before noon. He pursed his lips and gave a soft, trilling imitation of a blackbird's call. He paused, listening. There was no answering call. He moved stealthily from tree to tree, pausing to repeat the sound. It was a small orchard and impossible to imagine his fellow agent would not hear the signal. A premonitory chill ran up his spine as he reached the last line of fruit trees without sight or sound of the man he had come to relieve. With the same stealth, he retraced his steps, examining the ground with all the attention of a bloodhound. At the base of a group of pear trees, the ground was scuffed a little, the leaves disturbed. He bent closer to the ground, moving slowly, and then his eye caught a glimmer of white in a shallow depression a few feet away. He stepped closer and sat back on his heels with a deep sigh of regret, brushing aside the scanty covering of leaves over the body.

He scrutinized the ugly neck wound carefully, reflecting that at least the garotte would have been mercifully quick. Judging by the marks and the lack of other injuries, the executioner had been an expert. Only what one would expect from Dubois or one of his agents, René thought, his nostrils flaring with apprehension as he straightened. What had they done with the woman and child?

He moved quickly now, speed, not stealth, uppermost in his mind. He approached the cottage from the rear and examined the horse tethered in the kitchen garden. The mare whinnied with a note of distress, moving restlessly, clearly uneasy. The back door yielded to his touch, and he stepped into the well-lit kitchen.

The woman bound and gagged at the table signaled frantically at him with her eyes, making a strangled sound from behind the handkerchief. René cut the ropes and untied the gag. "What happened, madame? Where is the child?"

Jeanne tried to moisten her dry mouth enough to speak. Her cheek throbbed; her wrists and arms ached from the bindings. She had been there for almost two hours, according to the grandfather clock in the corner of the kitchen.

"Take your time, madame." René filled a cup of water from the jug on the sink and brought it to her. Jeanne drank gratefully.

"The Lizard," she said. "Does that mean anything?"

He nodded grimly. "Everything. He has the child?"

"And Lady Hero. They took them about two hours ago. He said Guillaume would hear from him soon." She passed a hand over her eyes, realizing her head was aching more than her cheek now.

René dampened a cloth in the cold water in the jug and handed it to her. "Hold it against your cheek. It will help the swelling."

"I have arnica upstairs, but we must get

438

to Guillaume now, at once." In agitation, Jeanne struggled to her feet and swayed as her knees seemed unwilling to support her. She grabbed the edge of the table.

"There is time, madame. There is always time." René spoke in soothing tones. "You said *they*. How many were there?"

"I saw two. The Lizard and one other, a man he called Alain . . . . Hero was worried about her horse . . ."

"The mare is tethered in the garden. She looks well enough, and we'll take her back with us." He frowned, looking down at the woman, assessing her strength. "Could you ride her back to London?"

"Of course," Jeanne said instantly, pressing the damp cloth against her cheek.

"I'll fetch my horse from the livery stable. Stay here and rest a bit. I'll be back in a few minutes." René hurried out, wondering what was best to do with his dead colleague. The body needed to be taken back to London. He couldn't carry a body over his saddle in broad daylight, but neither could he risk its being found in the orchard. He decided to go back to the orchard and do a better job of concealing the body in the ditch, and then Guillaume would decide how to retrieve it later. For the moment, the need to get the woman and her news back to London was paramount.

When he returned to the cottage with his own horse, he was relieved to see that the woman was dressed for riding, and despite her ashen pallor, she looked determined. She carried a small portmanteau, offering in explanation, "I don't know how long I'll be gone."

Privately, René doubted she would return to the cottage at all, but he merely took the bag and strapped it to the rear of his own horse before helping her onto Petra. The mare was still skittish, but Jeanne calmed her, taking a firm hold of the reins, feeling herself steadier, now that she was no longer helpless. Hero, at least, was with Marguerite, and that was as far as Jeanne was prepared to think.

The ride to London was an ordeal. Her body was stiff from having been bound so tightly in one position, her mouth was still painfully dry, and her cheek and her head ached abominably, but Jeanne managed to stay upright, aware of the anxious glances her companion gave her every few minutes. Petra seemed relieved to be returning to the familiar sounds and smells of town and settled down beneath her rider.

René didn't hesitate but directed them to Half Moon Street. The worst had happened, so it mattered nothing now if the Lizard's men were watching Guillaume's house and saw their arrival; they were probably expecting it, anyway. Jeanne was swaying a little in the saddle as they drew rein at the house, and he half lifted her to the ground, holding her up as he hammered on the door.

It was opened by André, who took one look and then supported Jeanne into the house, calling for his master. "Tell him the Lizard has the child," René said urgently, before turning to see to the horses. As he did so, he caught the eye of a man leaning idly against an iron railing across the street. The man raised a hand in an almost mocking gesture of greeting, and René knew it was one of the Lizard's men, confirming what they had expected to happen. They had killed Guillaume's man, left the woman as a messenger, and everything now was going exactly as they had planned. It infuriated René, but he mounted his horse, took up Petra's reins, and took the horses to the mews without so much as a glance at the enemy.

William had been in his study at the back of the house but came out at a run when he heard André's urgent summons. "Jeanne." He helped her into a deep armchair before the fire in the parlor. "Your face," he murmured. "How else are you hurt?"

Jeanne managed a stiff smile, appreciating, despite everything, that he was thinking of her when she knew he would be desperate to know about Marguerite. "Nothing much —"

"René said the Lizard has the child," André interrupted.

"And Hero, too," Jeanne added faintly. She rested her head against the back of the chair and closed her eyes. The sharp smell of sal volatile beneath her nose brought her around almost immediately, and William pressed a glass of brandy to her bloodless lips.

"Drink a little," he urged. "Take your time, and tell me everything." His voice was soft and patient, concealing the roiling urgency of his thoughts.

Jeanne sipped the brandy, and a little color returned to her ashen cheeks, the bruise across her cheekbone darkening against her pallor. Her voice steady, she told him what had occurred from the moment of Hero's arrival at the cottage.

William's face was expressionless as he listened quietly, asking no questions until she fell silent. René had returned to the house during Jeanne's account and stood against the door, waiting.

"What happened to the guard?" William turned towards him as Jeanne's voice faded.

"Garotte, it looked like. Mark of the Lizard, I would have said. It'll take two of us to bring him back."

"Take André . . . Who the hell's that?" he demanded with an unusual note of irritation at the sound of the door knocker.

André went to answer it, and Marcus strode into the room. He looked startled at the sight of the bruised woman in the chair. He had never met Jeanne, and William, while not disguising from Marcus that there was an aspect of his private life that required him to be extra vigilant, did not encourage questions about it. "Who . . . ?"

"In a minute," William said dismissively. "Hero's not at home, I gather."

"No . . . how did you know?"

William sighed, shaking his head. "The Lizard has her."

"Sweet heaven," Marcus murmured.

"I doubt we'll get much help from above," William stated with a caustic smile. "Damn the woman. Why can she never do as she's told?"

"Perhaps if you did more than give her orders without an explanation, she might," Jeanne said, sounding stronger. "Be grateful she's with Marguerite."

William made no answer to the unanswerable. He stood for a moment tapping his fingers against his mouth.

"He said you'll hear from him soon," Jeanne reminded him.

"Yes . . . but I'm not sitting here waiting for that reptile to call the cards. André, you and René get back to the orchard and bring Jean Claude back. The least we can do is give him a decent burial."

"One of the Lizard's agents is on watch outside . . . thumbed his nose at me," René said.

William frowned. There would have been time since the abduction for Dubois to get a messenger to Half Moon Street. "Get him in here. Perhaps he has something to say."

André and René slipped away and Marcus went to the window, looking out onto the street. He saw the man waiting in full view across the street and watched as William's men approached him. The man seemed to object to accompanying them back to the house but he thrust a piece of paper at them, then strolled away down the street, whistling.

André returned to the house. "He said to give you this, sir." He held out the message. "René's gone to the livery stable to hire a gig. Not too conspicuous for bringing back

Jean Claude."

William nodded but his eyes were on the paper in his hand. *The Black Gull, Dover. Before the evening tide. Make sure you're alone, or the child dies first.*

Short and to the point, he reflected. He knew the inn, knew that the Lizard intended that he should deliver himself up on the quayside, practically on the deck of whatever vessel the Lizard had comandeered to take him and his prisoner across to France. So easy, no fuss, no need for secrecy, no need for all the messiness of an abduction. It was one thing to spirit a woman and child away from a sleepy country village without drawing attention to the exercise, quite another to take a grown man and an experienced swordsman from a public place without a fight.

"From the Lizard?" Marcus inquired.

William merely nodded. "It seems I am riding to Dover."

"*We* are riding to Dover," Marcus corrected.

"That is certainly *my* intention, if not the Lizard's," William said. "But it requires some subtlety as I'm sure there'll be watchers en route. We have maybe an hour." He turned to Jeanne. "My dear, will you be all right to stay here alone, just until André returns? I know it's a lot to ask after what you've been through today, but I think the Lizard has done his worst with you. I doubt he has any further interest in you."

Jeanne smiled somewhat painfully. "In truth, a little peace and solitude would be the most wonderful thing, Guillaume. Much as I love you, nothing would please me more than a dish of tea and a quiet bed." She pushed herself up from the chair. "Where is the kitchen? I'm sure you have some tea there."

"I'll make your tea," Marcus said swiftly. "Please sit down again, ma'am." He left the room before she could argue, and Jeanne sank back into her chair with a little sigh of relief.

"I have to gather some things." William settled a cushion behind her head. "Rest here, my dear." He left her and went upstairs, his brow furrowed. Hero and Marguerite were his top priority. He had to ensure their safety before making any attempt to save himself from the Lizard's trap, but he was not walking into that trap unprepared.

TWENTY-NINE

Hero strained all her senses in the gloom of the carriage, trying to guess what was happening outside, wondering how close they were to their destination. The child was heavy in her lap, her head lolling against Hero's breast, her face pale, her breathing stertorous. Hero touched her brow. It was clammy. She had no idea how much laudanum the Lizard had forced down Marguerite, but any amount could not be good for such a small child.

"I assume we're going to Dover," she finally ventured.

"It doesn't matter to you where we're going."

"I beg to differ, sir. It matters a great deal to me," she returned.

The Lizard turned his head against the squabs to regard her with his pale eyes and an air of supreme indifference. Then he resumed his original position as if she hadn't spoken at all. The silence continued until she heard voices and carriage wheels outside, and the atmosphere changed. She could smell the sea more strongly and was certain they had entered a town. She raised a hand to lift aside the curtain, but the edge of his hand chopped against her wrist. The pain was appalling, and she blinked back unbidden tears, cradling her wrist against her breast.

"You have a short memory," her captor said. "You will make no moves unless instructed to do so."

Hero bit her lip and turned her head away from him. The carriage seemed to be slowing, turning, and then came to a halt. Beyond the curtain, she could hear running feet, voices calling, wheels rattling over cobbles, all the sounds of a busy stable yard. But she didn't move.

Marguerite, however, stirred in her lap, moaned, and blinked. She tried to push up against Hero's hold, and the Lizard swiftly withdrew the vial of laudanum from his jacket, uncorking it. "Hold her still."

"No," she stated, her own fear for the moment forgotten. "You cannot give her any more." She fixed him with an unyielding stare. "Look how small she is. You will kill her with that stuff, and if you kill William's child, he will hunt you to your grave. Don't you understand? I mean nothing to him beside this child . . . a mistress, yes, but there are mistresses aplenty. He will not put himself in your hands for me. Kill me if you have to prove the power of your intention, but the only bargaining counter you have is the child. Make no mistake." Her green eyes held every spark of determination she could muster as she tried to force her words into his brain. "I mean *nothing* to him. Now, let me get her into the air."

For a moment, the issue hung in the balance, the tension in the small space almost palpable, while his cold eyes held Hero's intense and unmoving gaze and she held her breath. Then he said, tight-lipped, "At some point very soon, I shall enjoy teaching you to mind your tongue, Lady Hero." He opened the carriage door and jumped down. "Get out."

Emboldened by his capitulation, Hero felt a renewal of optimism. What would happen if she stayed where she was and screamed for help? She would attract attention, the last thing the Lizard would want. But even as she hesitated, the door on her side was opened, and rough hands hauled her out of the carriage. She felt the prick of a knife in her back, and Marguerite, tumbling with her, suddenly threw up helplessly over the cobblestones.

"God damn it." The Lizard came around from the other side of the carriage and looked in disgust at the vomiting child.

"Laudanum," Hero almost spat at him, supporting Marguerite as she bent double, retching miserably. "What do you expect when you give it to such a tiny child?"

Gilles, who had yanked her out of the carriage and still stood with the point of his knife pricking her side, looked for guidance. He was accustomed to manhandling prisoners, but vomiting children were beyond his ken.

"Bring the woman into the inn," Dubois instructed. "Don't hesitate to use the knife if she makes a sound." He swirled his cloak around Marguerite, who was crying softly against Hero, and scooped her up into his arms, swaddling her in the folds of the cloak. He strode into the inn with his burden, Gilles and Hero behind them.

The innkeeper greeted them, bowing. "Welcome to the Black Gull, sir, ma'am. Oh, the poor little one."

"Travel sick," Dubois explained curtly. "She's sick from the motion. I need a private chamber on the highest floor you have . . . the air is fresher," he added.

450

"Yes . . . yes, of course, sir. I have a nice, airy chamber at the top of the house, lovely view over the harbor, lovely sea breezes, just the thing for a touch of travel sickness. My wife will attend madame and the child." He hurried ahead of them up two flights of stairs and flung open the door onto a small bedchamber. "This will do the trick, I'll be bound. I'll just open up the window, let the sea air in." He bustled to the leaded casement and flung it wide.

"Give her to me." Hero took Marguerite, limp and unresisting in her swaddling folds, and sat down on the bed with her. She loosened the cloak. The little girl seemed to have fallen asleep again, exhausted by her bout of sickness.

"I'll fetch my wife, ma'am."

The innkeeper hastened to the door, but the Lizard spoke sharply. "There's no need for that. The child's mother knows well enough what to do."

"But perhaps some tea for the lady after the journey, a little refreshment for you, gentlemen. A tisane for the child?"

Dubois controlled his irritation; it would only draw even more attention to them. "We will ring when we've decided what we need, I thank you."

The man bowed and departed. Hero laid

451

Marguerite on the bed, smoothing her damp hair from her forehead. "So what now?" she demanded. She had felt a shift in the situation in the last five minutes. The Lizard found himself wrong-footed for once. No doubt, he had had his plan clearly formed in his mind, but they had made no allowances for a sick child. Their entrance to the inn had been conspicuous, and Hero guessed that was the last thing he wanted. Now she wondered how best to exploit the situation.

Dubois ignored her question, however. He drew Gilles over to the window, and they spoke in low tones for a few moments. Then the Lizard walked out of the chamber, and Gilles locked the door behind him. He pocketed the key and sat down in a chair by the window, his pistol across his lap, his knife on the table beside him. He regarded his prisoners with a somewhat jaundiced air.

"I would like to get some water for the child," Hero said after a moment. "There's a jug on the washstand."

He glanced at the washstand, then back at the child, inert on the narrow bed, and nodded. There was only a little water at the bottom of the jug but enough to moisten a washcloth. Hero wiped Marguerite's mouth

and cheeks. The child was once again sleeping heavily, her breathing noisy, and Hero
realized that whatever desperate plans she
might form that might give her a chance to
overpower Gilles, she could not make an
escape with Marguerite as a dead weight.
The stress of the morning was taking its
toll, and she felt an overwhelming surge of
fatigue. She lay down on the bed beside
Marguerite and closed her eyes. There was
nothing to be done for the present, and
maybe a short sleep would clear her mind.

The sun was low in the sky as Marcus approached Dover. He had ridden fast, and
his horse was tiring, but he himself was as
alert as if he'd slept the clock round. It was
a sensation he knew well, and it would last
until their present work was done. The well-
traveled London-to-Dover road was well
paved, the tolls paying for its maintenance.
It was a popular stagecoach route and well
served by inns.

The sign of the Fox and Hounds appeared
as expected about five miles outside Dover,
and Marcus took his weary mount into the
stable yard behind the inn. He dismounted
and unstrapped a small cloak bag from the
saddle as an ostler ran to take the animal.
He led him off to water and a well-earned

bag of oats while Marcus strolled into the inn with the bag. He ordered a bumper of porter in the taproom and sat down in the window embrasure, idly flicking his gloves against his knee. The man who came in a few minutes later was dressed in a plain black coat and britches, a stiff white collar, and a broad-brimmed black hat. He looked like a man of the cloth, and his request for a small glass of watered wine did nothing to alter the impression. He stood stiffly against the bar counter, as if its very proximity might taint him, and looked hesitantly around the taproom. A flicker of a glance passed between him and Marcus.

Marcus drank his porter, left a handful of coins on the table, and wandered back to the yard to fetch his horse. Ten minutes later, he rode out of the yard and once more took the road to Dover.

The man at the bar counter took his small glass of watered wine and went to sit at the table Marcus had vacated. His foot touched the cloak bag beneath. When he stood up to leave, the bag was no longer there.

The Black Gull was a prominent landmark on the quay, a whitewashed building with a red-tiled roof. Marcus left his horse in the yard and entered the taproom. He leaned

454

on the counter and rapped his fingers on the stained wooden counter.

The landlord turned from a group of sailors he was serving at the far end and came over with an unhurried air. "What can I do ye for, sir?"

"D'you have a room for the night?"

The man regarded him with more interest. "Catching a packet to France, are you?"

"No, waiting for someone. My sister and her child." Marcus rolled a coin between his fingers. "They'll need a room and a bed to rest from the voyage."

"I've got summat at the back, quiet enough away from the quay," the landlord said, his eyes following the gyrations of the coin. "Funnily enough, we've got a woman and child here already. Poor little one was sick as a dog from the coach. Don't get too many families in here, deal more with the rougher kind, sailors and the like . . . Anything I can get you?"

"Porter." Marcus spun the coin towards the man, then turned so that his back was resting against the counter, looking around the room. A fisherman came in after a few minutes, glanced around, and walked out again. Marcus drained his porter and gestured to the landlord. "Have my saddlebags taken up to my chamber. I'm going to the outhouse."

In the noisome darkness, the fisherman awaited him. "Not the most salubrious meeting place," he remarked. "But I doubt we'll be interrupted."

"The landlord said there's a woman with a sick child in the inn." Marcus tried not to breathe through his nose.

"Sick?" The note of anxiety thrummed in William's sharp question.

"Travel sick, he said."

"You stay in the inn and watch for any sign of them. I'm going to the quay. If the Lizard's been negotiating for a boat, I might pick up some information."

"You don't think he'll recognize you if he's there?"

"He might, but he's never managed it before. I've changed clothes twice since leaving London, so I'm sure there's no tail on me. He can't know for sure that I'm here." William gave an easy shrug, implying a confidence he didn't feel. He was used to worrying about the safety of people he didn't know and about his own to a lesser extent, but now he had hostages to fortune, and it had altered his perspective in a way that didn't enhance his confidence.

"I'll change my own clothes now. I daresay I can turn myself into a sailor every bit as convincing as you, my friend." Marcus slipped out, conscious once again of the thrill of the chase. The stakes were as high as any they had encountered in France, but that knowledge merely sharpened his senses and quickened his wit.

William remained in the reeking dark for a few minutes, then sauntered out himself, whistling.

Marguerite awoke with a cry, and Hero, who had been only half asleep, sat up instantly, cradling the child against her. "My head," Marguerite sobbed. "It hurts . . . I'm thirsty."

"It's that filthy laudanum," Hero said furiously to the seemingly indifferent Gilles, who was picking at his fingernails with the tip of his knife. "She needs water, and there's none left in the jug. If you won't send for some, then you must go down yourself and fetch it."

"Can't leave you," Gilles declared, barely looking up from his knife.

"Don't be ridiculous," Hero snapped. "How in the world do you think I'm going to escape from a locked room on the third floor with a sick child? She's thirsty because the laudanum has made her sick. If she doesn't get water at once, I won't answer

457

for the consequences."

Gilles stood up and came over to the bed. He looked down at the child, lying inert against Hero's breast. Marguerite was waxen, her hair limp, a blue tinge to her lips. Tears seeped from beneath her closed lids, but she seemed too weak now even to cry out. He debated with himself for a moment, before turning on his heel and heading for the door. He unlocked it, let himself out, and then locked it behind him.

Hero listened to the sound of his retreating steps on the stairs and gently laid Marguerite on the bed again. "Stay still, sweetheart. It'll be over soon." She couldn't tell whether her words had penetrated the child's stupor but went swiftly to the window. The quayside lay immediately below, fishing boats moored along the pier. The sun was almost disappearing below the horizon, and the lighthouse at the end of the jetty that guarded the harbor entrance winked slowly. There was a lot of activity along the pier and the quay as boats were prepared for the evening tide. Hero leaned as far out of the window as she dared, her eyes searching the busy scene.

Suddenly, her gaze focused. A fisherman was walking along the jetty, stopping at the various boats. He looked just like every other man on the boats, in a thick woolen jerkin, leather britches, and high waterproof boots. At one boat, it looked as if his conversation was more productive than at others, because he stood for a few minutes, leaning against a bollard, talking animatedly to a sailor who had just come up on deck. A lock of hair fell across the fisherman's forehead as he talked, and he brushed it aside in a gesture so familiar that Hero thought her heart had actually stopped for a second.

He was here. Relief filled her, but then reality intervened. William was on the dock, but she and Marguerite were marooned in a third-floor chamber. She wondered if she could attract his attention, but he was halfway along the pier, too far to hear her voice, however loud she shouted.

Where was the Lizard? She searched the crowds again and made him out at last. Just beyond where William was standing, still in conversation with the sailor, two men appeared on the gangplank of a fishing boat, rather more substantial than many, with a roofed cabin. One of them was the Lizard. As she watched, she saw him hand something to the other man before turning to leave.

Hero heard steps beyond the chamber and

flew back to the bed, bending anxiously over Marguerite as the key turned in the lock and Gilles came back with a jug of water and a cup. He cast her a suspicious glance, but she didn't seem to have stirred from her place with the child. He set the jug and the cup on the washstand. "There." Then he returned to his chair in the window.

Hero filled the cup and took some herself, aware that she was both hungry and thirsty; it seemed an eternity since Jeanne had cooked breakfast for them all that morning. She brought the cup to Marguerite, holding her up against her as she pressed the cup to her bloodless lips.

"Take a little, sweetheart, it'll help you feel better."

Marguerite drank thirstily and seemed to perk up a little. When the cup was empty, she gave a little sigh and slumped against Hero again, her eyes closing. Hero felt a moment of despair. If an opportunity arose for them to break away, Marguerite would be unable to do anything for herself. She could barely sit up unaided, let alone run.

But William was here, she told herself. And he would not be alone. He would have a plan. All she could do for the moment was to be alert and ready to move the instant she saw an opportunity or William

460

gave her a signal.

There was a sharp rap on the door, and Gilles rose instantly, the key in his hand, to let in the Lizard.

William waited until Dubois reached the end of the pier before saying to the skipper of the *Mary Jane,* "Perhaps you'll take me on next crossing, then, sir?"

"Aye, I'll look out for you. Sorry you left it a bit late today. Best time to get hired on is first thing, when we come in on the morning tide."

"I'll remember. Thanks for your time, sir." He touched his cap before turning away and sauntering over to the craft Dubois had just left. The man who had accompanied the Lizard down the gangplank was back on deck now, checking his lines. "Don't suppose you need an extra hand tonight, sir?" William called up, even as his eyes ran knowingly over the boat, noticing its shabby paintwork and rusted ironwork.

The man peered down at him. "No, I've a full crew tonight. Left it a bit late to sign on, haven't you?"

"Just got to Dover, sir." William looked along the deck. "Could do with a fresh coat of paint . . . happy to do it when you get

461

back, sir. I can turn my hand to most things."

"We haul stinking fish for the most part, not much point in fresh paint for that," the other man said, taking a pipe from his pocket and tamping down tobacco in the bowl.

"You never take passengers, then?" William leaned carelessly against a bollard, one foot resting on the gangplank.

The other man shrugged. "Depends . . . Oddly enough, I've got three of 'em for tonight's crossing to Calais." He took out a small round tinderbox from his britches pocket and after a few tries lit a brimstone match for his pipe. Blue smoke curled into the dusk. "We leave on the tide." He glanced over his shoulder to the lighthouse and the break in the harbor wall. "About eight."

William nodded. "I'll be off, then. Looks like my luck's out for today." He pushed himself off the bollard and wandered away down the pier, keeping in the moving shadows of the tethered boats.

THIRTY

Dubois closed the chamber door behind him and regarded the woman and child on the bed. "They give you any trouble?" he asked Gilles.

Gilles shook his head. "Child needed water."

"She's very weak," Hero said.

"Gilles, you'll carry her. We need to get going." Dubois went to the window, looking out on the darkening harbor. Lamps were appearing along the quay, and sailors were trimming the lanterns fore and aft the craft bobbing against the pier.

Where was Ducasse? His instructions had said to meet Dubois at the Black Gull before the tide, but he was not downstairs, and the landlord had said he'd seen no one apart from the customers in the taproom. Dubois scrutinized the boats, the men, the ambling sailors on the quay. He would be here somewhere. He *had* to be. Everard knew his enemy well after six years of their cat-and-mouse game, and he knew that Ducasse would not sacrifice the child, even if he was prepared to let the woman go. The man had a most inconvenient streak of self-sacrificial morality.

The Lizard smiled to himself. Ducasse would want a fight, of course, but this was not one he was going to get. He would have to give himself up in the end.

Hero stood back as Gilles lifted Marguerite from the bed. At some point, she had to get the little girl onto her own feet, some point between the inn and the boat at the end of the pier where she had seen the Lizard earlier.

Dubois took her arm, propelling her in front of him. "Walk steadily, look straight ahead, and don't make a sound." The sharp prick of a knife at her back reinforced the instructions.

It seemed she had no choice but to obey. Maybe when they were downstairs, surrounded by other people, an opportunity would reveal itself. They reached the hall at the bottom of the stairs, and the noise from the crowded taproom gusted on clouds of tobacco smoke and the acrid fumes from the sea coal fire. Hero stole a quick glance into the taproom as she walked past, but

464

the sharp prick of the knife drove her forward, out into the crisp evening air of the quay.

A trio of sailors sprawled on the ale bench alongside the door, calling the odds on the dice they were throwing, smoke rising from their corncob pipes. They barely glanced at the little group that emerged from the inn. But Hero felt her skin tingle. If she had not grown familiar with Marcus in the guise of a sansculottes, she would never have noticed anything about the man in the middle of the three. But something jumped out at her. The knot in the kerchief at his throat, perhaps? The off-kilter set of his cap? She didn't dare pause for a second look, but the conviction grew that the man she normally saw dressed in the attire of an English gentleman-about-town was sitting outside the Black Gull throwing dice with a pair of seamen.

Marcus was here. William was here. It was up to her now to create the opportunity for them to do their work.

As they reached the pier, she stopped, ignoring the knife, and said quietly, "Let Marguerite walk now. She needs to try to walk off the effects of the laudanum. William will need to see that she's alive and well before he gives himself up to you."

465

Dubois decided that he disliked this managing woman even more than he had so far acknowledged. But she was right, and that made it even more unpalatable. However, he would have his revenge, he reflected savagely. He would keep her for himself after all. And later, when he had Ducasse where he wanted him, he would enjoy a little play with Lady Hero. And her lover would hear and see every minute of it.

He indicated to Gilles that he should set the child on her feet, and Hero turned to steady her as she swayed. "You need to walk, sweetheart," she murmured. "Hold my hand, I won't let you fall."

Marguerite held her hand in a fierce grip and tried to lift her head. The freshening wind was reviving her a little, and she took a step forward.

"That's my girl," Hero encouraged. "Just to the end of the pier." Where was William? She couldn't see him, but she knew he was there somewhere. And Marcus was somewhere behind them. She slipped an arm around Marguerite's shoulders and encouraged her onwards.

"Stop here." They had reached the boat tied almost at the end of the pier. It was the only craft left now; the others were already tacking towards the harbor mouth on the evening tide, and the only light came from the boat's lanterns, fore and aft. Deep shadows lay across the pier and the dark water beneath. The gangplank creaked and swayed as a burly man stepped onto it from the deck and peered down at them. Hero's eyes, fixed on the unsteady gangplank, saw something at the top.

"You for the *Maiden Witch*?"

"Four of us," Dubois called back.

" 'Bout time. We've been waiting for you. Captain said there was only three."

"And now there's four." Dubois sounded impatient.

"That'll cost extra."

"Yes, I expect it to," he responded. He looked behind him. Ducasse should have shown himself by now. He couldn't get on the boat until he had Ducasse. And as he hesitated, his quarry stepped out of the shadows across the pier.

"Good evening, Everard." William stood, legs braced, his hand on a wickedly curved fish-gutting knife in his rough leather belt. He had removed his heavy waterproof boots. "You have something for me, I believe."

"Uncle Guillaume!" Marguerite at last found her voice. In that instant, Hero seized the child and spun her backwards away

467

from her, praying that William would catch her. She leapt for the gangway and in three strides had reached the top. She shut out what might be happening behind her and launched herself at the line that held the gangplank to a post on the deck rail. The line was frayed, and the loop was only partially over the top of the post. She scrabbled frantically for a second and yanked it free. The gangplank dipped beneath her, tilting violently, and she hurled herself to the other side just as the sailor grabbed her.

"Hold her fast!" Dubois yelled from the pier, attempting to put one foot on the now crazily swinging plank.

Hero jerked backwards, half turned in the startled sailor's hold, and drove her knee upwards. The air seemed to go out of him, and he bent double, his grip slackening. She put her head down and leapt for the pier as the gangplank tilted sharply, its single line stretched to the limit. Her feet touched solid ground at the same moment Dubois reached for her. She drove her head into his belly, and he fell back, giving her enough space to step aside, breathless, terrified, and yet exhilarated.

Marcus held Marguerite tight against him. He had caught her as William had imitated

Hero's movement and spun the child behind him to where he knew Marcus was lurking farther down along the pier. William now faced Gilles, while Dubois still struggled to catch his breath.

Hero slipped behind Dubois into the gloom. She had no fight left in her and knew her part was now over. She took Marguerite from Marcus, who yielded her without a word, and drew the child back into the shadows, hiding her face against her skirts.

Gilles swung around as he heard Marcus behind him. His knife flashed, but Marcus was ready for him, ducking neatly as he drove his sword deep under the other man's armpit. Gilles crumpled to the pier, and Marcus turned to assist William, but William made a quick imperative gesture that kept his friend where he was.

The Lizard belonged to Ducasse.

Dubois had straightened from his crouch and caught his breath. He drew his sword. "So, it has come to this at last, my friend."

"Indeed," William returned. He held the ugly gutting knife in his hand. "But I would not sully my sword on you, Dubois. A man who would threaten women and children is not worth good steel."

Dubois flushed with anger, but he said nothing, taking a dancing step forward, his sword point glinting in the lamplight from the fishing boat. They now had an audience, but neither man noticed it, and the crew aboard the *Maiden Witch* was only interested in the outcome. A fight was always good entertainment, and the rights and wrongs of the issues meant nothing to them.

William feinted, moved sideways, light on his stockinged feet, but he had no wish to prolong the duel. It would have an ugly end, and the sooner he brought that about, the better. Dubois's rapier was an elegant weapon, and he was wielding it with all the skill of an experienced swordsman. William had the weapon of a street fighter, and he knew how to use it. He dodged a thrust from the rapier and came in close, the vicious curved blade slashing in and up, as if he were gutting a hog.

Hero clamped Marguerite's face to her skirts even as she stared, spellbound and horror-struck, at the bloody end of it all. It was fitting that it should end in blood as it had begun, she thought, her mind filled with the vivid memories of Paris and the dreadful scenes of carnage. But it was over now. The Lizard, bent double, clutching at the hideous wound in his belly, had finally done his worst.

"Hero, take Marguerite to the inn." William spoke softly over his shoulder. The fishing boat had pulled up anchor and was now moving rapidly away from the scene, its crew anxious to be far away from the aftermath. He bent to the body at his feet, and as Hero hurried Marguerite down the darkening pier to the lights of the quay, she heard the plash of something hitting the water. It was followed almost immediately by a second one.

Marcus straightened as the body of Gilles entered the water. "Best get rid of that knife," he said, indicating the bloody gutting knife William still held.

William dropped the knife into the water and wiped his hands on his britches, his expression grim as he looked along the deserted, shadowy pier. It seemed that the silent, ugly battle at the end of the pier had drawn no attention from the quay. But then, a sailors' brawl was hardly an unusual occurrence in Dover harbor, he reflected. And it had been over very quickly.

"We need to get away from here at once," he observed. "If the tide doesn't take the bodies out beyond the harbor wall, they'll be found in the morning." He turned and looked back to the quay. Light spilled from the open door and windows of the Black Gull.

"But first," he said slowly, "I have some serious fences to mend . . . if they can be mended," he added, so softly Marcus barely heard him. "See what you can do about finding us transport back to London." He walked away towards the lights of the inn. Marcus watched him for a moment, a half smile playing over his lips, then he followed to do his own errand.

Hero was sitting on the ale bench outside the Black Gull, Marguerite in her lap, rocking her gently. The child was asleep again, and Hero, her own eyes closed, was grateful. The events of the last day had been terrifying for the little girl, but Hero hoped that sleep might help to obscure some of the worst memories. She was sure Marguerite had seen nothing of the hideous battle between her father and the Lizard, and she hoped that those few minutes at the end of the pier would merely fade into the backdrop of the day's events, all of them frightening. She would recover, with the right care.

She heard William's footsteps just as she felt his shadow fall over her where she sat in the light from the open window behind her. She opened her eyes and looked up at him.

"Will she be all right?" he asked quietly.

"I hope so. It depends on how you explain

472

what's happened," Hero responded, her voice dull. "I'm sure Jeanne will know what to do."

His heart ached as he looked at her, seeing again the sadness and disappointment in her eyes. She had given him so much, she had saved his child, his own life, just with her core of courage and honesty that in his heart he had always responded to, even as he tried to diminish it when it led her to follow a path that for his own selfish reasons didn't suit him. And fear filled him that it was too late now to put things right.

"I need you," he stated. "I need you, Hero, my love. I need you to forgive me for all the hurt I've done you. But I don't know if you can." He looked suddenly helpless, his golden eyes so deeply shadowed with sorrow they seemed to have lost all the fire and glow she loved so much. "Do you think that one day you could?"

Hero felt herself opening, unfurling to the glorious possibility that they were not lost to each other. "I love you," she said simply. "I can't seem to remember a time anymore when I didn't love you."

"But can you forgive me? I know how deeply I've hurt you, and I thought my reasons were good, were to protect you from me and from yourself. But I know better now." He still stood above her, the intensity of his expression almost painful. "I love you more than I have ever loved."

She smiled and shook her head. "There is no competition, William. Love is what it is. If you love me now, here and now, then that's all I need." The child in her arms stirred, and she shifted her into a more comfortable position.

William bent and took Marguerite from her, cradling her against him. She opened her eyes, "Uncle Guillaume?" He stroked her cheek, and her eyes closed again.

"Far be it from me to give you advice," Hero said with a half smile, "but I think it's time you and your daughter acknowledged each other properly."

"Jeanne would agree with you," he responded with a rueful smile. "I wish I could kiss you, but . . ." He glanced around at their surroundings with an expressive gesture, just as a pony and trap rounded the corner from the stable yard, Marcus's horse tethered to the back.

"May I offer anyone a ride back to town?" Marcus called down from the driver's bench.

William lifted his daughter into the trap and held out a hand to Hero. As she put her hand in his, his fingers closed tightly over hers, and he bent and kissed her ear, murmuring, "That will have to do for now."

Hero climbed up and took Marguerite's head onto her lap as William climbed up beside Marcus, and the small conveyance moved off, leaving Dover and the final residue of the Terror behind.

"What kind of a wedding do you want, sweetheart?" William asked, smoothing the caramel-striped cascade away from Hero's face as she lay with her head in the hollow of his shoulder. Mid-morning sunlight streamed through the casement window on Half Moon Street. The clothes of a fisherman lay in a heap on the floor, incongruously entangled with Hero's riding habit and britches, her undergarments strewn hither and thither.

Hero yawned involuntarily. They had exchanged the pony and trap for a fast chaise and four at a coaching inn on the road back to London and had reached Half Moon Street soon after dawn, but they had still not slept. There had been too many promises to make and to seal, but now, in the afterglow of passionate renewal, she could barely keep her eyes open.

"A big one," she stated, hiding her smile in his neck. "St. George's, Hanover Square, with Alec giving me away to a French agent in the eyes of all Society."

William groaned. "If that's what you want, my love, so be it." He felt her body quiver against him and seized her beneath the arms, pulling her on top of him. "Wretched creature, don't make mock," he scolded, pushing his hands through the veil of her hair to reveal her laughing face. "It was a serious question."

"Well, forgive me, sir. What kind do you want?"

"To be honest, I don't give a damn. I just want one."

Hero kissed him, lightly brushing his lips with the tip of her tongue, before giving him butterfly kisses with her eyelashes. "Are you quite, quite sure, William? I don't need to be married to love you."

"You're going to be, though." He ran his hands down her back, lingering over the swell of her hips. "Make no mistake about that, my Lady Hero. I will not lose you again."

"Then let's get married in the chapel at Bruton Manor. Alec and Marie Claire are already there. Marguerite can meet her new baby cousin, and Marcus can be your best man. What could be more perfect?" She moved sinuously above him, her hips lifting a little in invitation, sleepiness miraculously forgotten.

"Nothing," William agreed, his hands on her hips as he entered her slowly.

"And we shall make babies," Hero murmured, moving above him. "It's time Marguerite had other children to play with."

"I need to learn to be a father first," he demurred, his eyes holding hers as he watched for the moment when she drew close to her climax. He loved to see the sudden quickening light, the look almost of surprise that suffused her in that moment.

She shook her head. "I beg to differ, sir. I have seen you with your child, and you seem to know exactly how to be a father . . . Oh . . ." She bit her lip, a smile gathering in her eyes. "Oh, how I love you, William Ducasse."

"And how I love you, Hermione Fanshawe." He held her tightly as she fell upon him, and he yielded to his own climax a second later, with the same glorious knowledge that all, at last, was right with the world.

ABOUT THE AUTHOR

Jane Feather is the *New York Times* best-selling author of more than thirty sensual historical romances, including the Blackwater Bride series. She was born in Cairo, Egypt, and grew up in the south of England. She currently lives in Washington, DC, with her family. There are more than 10 million copies of her books in print.